"*The Blue Butterfly* is an unfiltered, first-person narrative told in glittering detail. It is the almost mythic story of a glowing, spirited woman who is captured and showered with riches beyond imagining - a butterfly in a gilded cage. In this very fast-paced book, which spares no detail in the telling, we see how dearly Marion Davies paid for her willing captivity."

—LAUREL DAVIS HUBER, author of the award-winning
The Velveteen Daughter

"Leslie Johansen Nack redeems the tragic legacy of Marion Davies, William Randolph Hearst's long-time lover, in her newest, *The Blue Butterfly*. Dripping with diamonds and gilded with grandeur, *The Blue Butterfly* takes readers from the bowels of the New York stage to the glittering life of Hollywood and its stars. Haunting and heartbreaking, *The Blue Butterfly* elicits the gut-punch that what we do for love colors our lives forever."

—ASHLEY E. SWEENEY, author of the award-winning
Answer Creek

PRAISE FOR *FOURTEEN: A DAUGHTER'S MEMOIR OF ADVENTURE, SAILING, AND SURVIVAL*

— ◯ —

2017 Independent Press Awards Winner in Memoir
2016 Beverly Hills Book Awards Winner in Memoir
2016 Indie Excellence Winner in Young Adult Non-Fiction
2016 Readers' Favorite Awards Bronze Winner in Non-fiction: Travel
2016 Next Gen Indie Awards Finalist in Memoirs (Overcoming Adversity/Tragedy/Challenges)

"A debut memoir reveals a turbulent adolescence. At first glance, the voyage of Bjorn Johansen and his three daughters from San Diego to the islands of Tahiti in 1975 . . . has all the makings of a standard adventure story. In keeping with the tone of the project as a whole, [the] ending, while somewhat abrupt, is powerful and inspiring. Perhaps the only quibble is that Nack leaves readers wanting more. An engaging account, gripping from start to finish, that should appeal to a wide audience, including sailing enthusiasts."

—*Kirkus Reviews*

"The raw and emotional debut novel by Leslie Johansen Nack has it all: mid-Pacific monster storms, emergencies at sea, a young female heroine, sex and drugs all while exploring the world on a 45-foot custom-built sailboat. All of this intrigue combines to tell the incredible true story of a young teenaged girl, as told by the author, her two sisters and their father, as they untangle the daily web of incredibly wondrous and equally appalling experiences while sailing from Oceanside, San Diego, to the Marquesas, Tuamotu and Society islands. Full of conflict and secrets, adventure and survival, this page-turner is as good as it gets and will be passed on to passionate sailors for decades to come."

—*Pacific Yachting Magazine*

"*Fourteen* is the riveting story of a girl and her sisters coming of age and struggling to survive staggering odds as her father pursues his dream of sailing his own boat to Tahiti. This book totally captures the intrigue and romance of arriving under sail in the South Pacific during the mid-'70s."

—John Neal, Offshore Cruising Companion and author of *Log of the Mahina*

"*Fourteen* is the poignant and gripping coming-of-age story of Leslie Johansen Nack, a smart, strong girl who sails to Tahiti with her two sisters and predatory father in 1975. With him as captain of their 45' boat, Nack's life depends upon him . . . until he falls ill. The skills and confidence Nack gains from sailing, combined with her indomitable will, help Nack fight back against her father's abuseÐand might even help her save his life. In candid, clear, even-handed prose, Leslie Johansen Nack's Fourteen is an important book, one that takes us on a lush journey to distant lands and through the complexities and resilience of the human spirit."

—JANNA CAWRSE ESAREY, author of *The Motion of the Ocean*

"*Fourteen* is a simply beautiful tale of wild bravery."

—SAN GABRIEL VALLEY TRIBUNE

"Nack's interest in sailing is not superficial. She has a respect for the ocean that her father teaches her; this is one of the reasons she is so close to him. But she knows she has much more to learn. She battles the standard teenage demons of boys and school, but her unconventional home life is a fascinating tale. Set against the background of life with a floating home, the teenage angst is not the focus of the story. [Fourteen] is not just a sailing story, nor is it a coming of age tale, but a splendid mix of the two."

—SAILING MAGAZINE

"As the story unfolds, you find yourself simultaneously holding your breath for the next episode of her dad's strange behavior, and cheering for Leslie's growing strength in dealing with it. She not only survives, she shows an amazing strength in dealing with situations that would overwhelm many adults, let alone fourteen-year-olds. I found the book gripping."

—CAROLYN SHEARLOCK, The Boat Galley.Com

"Despite a dysfunctional family life, 14-year-old Leslie Johansen learns to stand up to her father's abuse and becomes an accomplished sailor. This true adventure about sailing the South Pacific is an uplifting testament to the strength of a young teen."

—*THE ENSIGN*

The BLUE BUTTERFLY

The BLUE BUTTERFLY

A NOVEL OF
MARION DAVIES

LESLIE JOHANSEN NACK

SHE WRITES PRESS

Published 2022
Printed in the United States of America
Print ISBN: 978-1-64742-347-6
E-ISBN: 978-1-64742-348-3
Library of Congress Control Number: 2021923636

For information, address:
She Writes Press
1569 Solano Ave #546
Berkeley, CA 94707

Interior design by Tabitha Lahr

She Writes Press is a division of SparkPoint Studio, LLC.

To the bubbles in the champagne

CHAPTER 1

NEW YORK, 1907

Mama named me Marion Cecilia Douras, and I was the baby in the family of five children. By the time I was ten, I had to fend for myself. Mostly, I liked it that way. I was a tomboy, and being a troublemaker came easy to me.

Mama wasn't exactly neglectful. She just ran out of hugs by the time I was born—the fifth child in eleven years. She was tired and always preoccupied with my three older sisters and brother. Five-foot-two, with big bosoms and a stern voice, Rosemary Reilly Douras was discreet, mighty, and fierce, like a quiet thunderstorm. When she smiled, her eyebrows lifted, her mouth opened a little, and her face became soft and tender. When she smiled at me, which wasn't often, my whole world lit up.

Mama saw the bleak economic realities for women like us. Our opportunity to meet and marry wealthy, eligible men was in the theater, where the lines between the classes blurred. In the fantasy world filled with glitz and glamour, relationships between distinguished gentlemen and dancers were not openly acknowledged by high society, but they were prevalent. "It's a way to get your foot in the door to a better life," Mama always said. Some might say she encouraged us to be gold diggers, but I say she helped us navigate the world the best she knew how.

I hid in the shadows, sneaking in and out of rooms, watching my two oldest sisters Reine and Ethel dress and do their hair before heading off to jobs in the theater. My third older sister, Rose, who was just two years older than me, stuttered like I did, which created an unspoken bond between us. Rose loved to boss me around, and we were in constant competition over everything.

Of my three sisters, I was most like Ethel in personality. We were jokesters, kidders, and tricksters and strove to make people laugh, if not to outright shock them. We didn't look alike at all. I had curly blonde hair and big blue eyes while Ethel had kinky brown hair and brown eyes—opposites on the outside, but twins on the inside.

One time when I was eight, as a prank we hid in the pantry and sewed the meat of Reine's roast beef sandwich together with a needle and thread. I held the sandwich and Ethel pushed the needle and thread up and down a few times so the meat wouldn't pull apart when Reine bit into it. When we sat down to lunch, it was hard to keep a straight face as our dainty older sister, with her perfect chestnut hair and red lipstick, pulled and yanked the sandwich from her mouth. I snickered softly and the joke was up. Mama smacked my hand and gave Ethel a squinty-eyed scowl. Honestly, I hoped to grow up elegant like Reine, but funny like Ethel.

Our only brother, Charlie, drowned before I could form too many memories of him. I was four and he was eleven when they found his body in the swamp behind our grandparents' home in Florida. Mama never talked about what happened other than to say how it devastated Papa to lose his only son. In fact, Papa kind of slipped away from all of us after Charlie died, finding relief in drinking, gambling, and other women's arms. Mama never said anything bad about Papa, but I saw her avoid eye contact with him. She didn't have time to comfort him—she had four girls to raise in a society that favored wealthy men.

In the early 1900s, women from all walks of life were uniting in their fight to gain the vote, silent movies were the rage, Theodore Roosevelt was president, the Ford Motor Company ruled the world of automobiles, and the only way for women to ascend their station in life was to marry up. Mama considered it her full-time job to get us girls ready for the Vaudeville stage and as close as possible to all those rich gents who frequented the theater district. We all took singing and dancing lessons from the age of five. I went with Rose to tap class and excelled at backbends, walk overs, and the splits. Reine loved the Hesitation Waltz with its ballet-like features, while Ethel's passion was the foxtrot and the fast dances.

By the time Reine and Ethel were eighteen and sixteen years old, Mama knew she needed to get them closer to the work they were trained to do. This was how we came to live in the semi-posh neighborhood of Manhattan called Gramercy Park. I say *we* came to live, but really it was just Mama, Reine, and Ethel at first. Rose and I had to stay with Papa in Brooklyn during the week for elementary school and dance lessons.

Compared to the Victorian house in Brooklyn, Gramercy Park felt like we'd taken a giant leap up in the world. The houses were brick and brownstone rowhouses, upscale and fashionable as were the people walking their dogs and pushing their baby carriages.

I played basketball well enough to make the championship boys' team in Brooklyn. But an athletic tomboy wasn't valued at my house, so I vacillated between being a brash, outspoken romp at school in Brooklyn, and a prissy, elegant girl twirling and dancing in our Gramercy Park living room on the weekends, the kind of daughter I knew my mother wanted.

One weekend in Gramercy Park, I joined the Second Street Gang, a pack of seven boys who played in the park across the street from our house. I placed my hair in a cap, put on some old trousers and a baggy shirt, and marched across the street, asking to join them. The leader, an older boy named Butch, said I could join if I could make it through that evening's "fun."

Fearful of stuttering, I nodded and stared at the ground.

"First, we gather old fruits and vegetables from behind the stores and put them in bags," Butch said as he chewed a blade of grass.

John, another gang member, leaned toward me with a scowl and said, "After that, you follow our lead. Got it?"

I nodded again and followed the boys' lead as we snuck to the back of the store to steal our ammunition. I grabbed rotten peaches, mushy plums, and stinky heads of brown lettuce. We ran to Prospect Park, where all the rich people lived. Butch ran up the stairs and rang the doorbell. We stood shoulder-to-shoulder at the bottom of the stairs, and when the door opened we fired our stash of produce at the butler until he slammed the door shut. Laughing, we ran to hide in the alley. We did this twice more. I wasn't expecting it when Butch pushed me, so I stumbled back against the brick wall where I couldn't hide my giant smile.

"You're in," he said. "What's your name?"

"Marty," I said in a low voice, happy I hadn't stuttered *and* was part of the group.

At the fourth house, we got rid of the rest of our produce—apples and carrots—but the police pulled up, surprising us. "Run!" Butch yelled and we scattered like cockroaches in the light, but the cops caught me, Butch, and one other boy.

At the police station, after they hauled the boys down the hall, one of the cops asked me to take off my hat. I cowered in the bright lights, shaking as I pulled my newsboy cap into my lap, my blond hair tumbling to my shoulders.

"Where do you live, little girl?" he asked.

I gave him my address, and the policeman delivered me to Mama, who hauled me inside by my ear as she swatted my head.

He cleared his throat, waiting for a chance to speak. "Ma'am, I thought you should know that one of the houses bombarded with rotten fruit was Mr. William Randolph Hearst's house. His butler called to report the hooligans."

"Oh, I'm so sorry. I had no idea," Mama said, closing the door in embarrassment.

"You're a hooligan now?" Reine asked me as she sat on the couch, painting her nails. Reine was not somebody who'd join a gang, but I could tell she was pleased with me.

"We're so proud of you," said Ethel, looking up from her magazine to wink at me. She had a tomboy streak too.

"Stop encouraging her," Mama scolded. "We all need to keep a better eye on her."

Looking at me, she said, "Don't you dare smile, little girl. I am sending you back to Brooklyn first thing in the morning."

I lowered my head in defeat as Reine and Ethel snickered quietly. "Don't laugh," I yelled at my sisters for Mama's sake, but flashed a sly smile at them before marching upstairs. I missed dinner that night, but Ethel snuck me cookies and came to read and snuggle with me in bed. Watching the Second Street Gang play basketball from our living room window, I knew I'd never play with them again.

— ⟨⟨⟩⟩ —

Reine and Ethel's work on the stage earned enough money to pay the rent on our four-bedroom, two-bath house in Gramercy Park. They were the first to change our last name to Davies. They came up with the new last name when they saw a "Davies Real Estate" sign on the way home from the theater. Douras was too Irish of a name and was hindering them in getting jobs, while the last name of Davies was more European and acceptable.

Mama reminded Reine and Ethel constantly about their real purpose for working in the theater——which was to marry a rich patron. I tried not to roll my eyes while she preached about avoiding the traps of romantic love. Money was more important than love, she told us.

Reine, now twenty-one, was the first to make good on Mama's wishes when she married a newly rich, forty-five-year-old theater director named George Lederer and they immediately had two children, Charlie and Josephine. We all called Josephine "Pepi," because she was. After a few years of marriage, they moved to Chicago where George turned his money into an absolute fortune with a chain of movie theaters. That's when she invited all of us to move to Chicago to live with them in their palatial three-story, twenty-five room mansion on the lake.

I was thirteen and brought my tomboy toughness to Chicago, even though I was starting to get attention for my looks. The more attention I got, the easier it was to play the part—wearing fancy dresses, jewelry, and a little makeup. Ethel would compliment what she called my "angelic face and show-stopping eyes" whenever we were alone.

Rose's looks blossomed as well, but it seemed she veered away from the delicate features everyone admired. She felt slighted that I was getting all the attention and it was driving a wedge between us, but when we were getting along, we had plenty of fun. We stole the flowers from the vases in the entryway of George's mansion and sold them on the street for candy and movie tickets. If we couldn't raise enough money for the movies, we'd show up at one of his theaters and inform the cashier that we were the Lederer children and should be admitted for free.

During our second year in Chicago, I almost lost my best sister Ethel when she fell in love with a rich manufacturer. But after he asked his wife for a divorce and they fought, he had a heart attack and died. I know I shouldn't have been happy, but I was. Ethel was mine, and I didn't intend on sharing her with anybody.

— ◎ —

Reine had the freedom to work on stage, starring in some of the biggest plays in Chicago, because Mama watched Charlie and Pepi. One evening the whole family attended the premiere of her latest play. I got to watch her from the wings of the theater, standing just offstage with Mama, Ethel, and Rose. The split-second costume changes, and the men scurrying behind the curtains in a coordinated effort to raise the curtains and change the sets, captured my complete attention. At the end of the play, after Reine sang in the grand finale but right before the curtain came down, I ran onto the stage to face the audience. They clapped and laughed at my shenanigans, when one of the stagehands tried to catch me with his stage hook and missed. It was comedy and I was hooked on it. I bowed and curtsied as I ran around the stage, evading him until I was sure the crowd loved me.

The noise from the audience filled me up and made my insides glow. That feeling stayed with me and I looked forward to the day when I could be on stage in a production. Mama, of course, was less than pleased, and when they finally hauled me off stage, she grabbed me by the ear, forced me outside, and gave me a good spanking.

— ◎ —

Reine and Uncle George got divorced when I was sixteen, and we were all moved back to New York, where Ethel and Reine started their acting careers all over again. Even though George paid child support, twenty-seven-year-old Reine moved in with us, and we all helped with Charlie and Pepi.

CHAPTER 2

NEW YORK, 1914

My own stage career began with an introduction to a well-connected dancer. I was a tall and thin seventeen-year-old with barely a hint of curves. One evening, not long after settling back into our old neighborhood of Gramercy Park, I pushed the food around on my plate mindlessly. "Mama, please can I go to the theater to watch Reine tonight? She promised to introduce me to her friend who might be able to get me a part in a pony line."

"Me too, Mama. I want to go too," Rose, now nineteen, said as she stuffed a forkful of potatoes into her mouth. "I've got to get out of that dance hall job."

Rose still competed with me in every area of my life, and I had grown impatient with her jealousy.

"Yes, you both may go, after you eat."

I nibbled my food for a few minutes, but when Mama left the room, I grabbed my jacket and ran out the kitchen door. Rose followed close on my heels, whining for me to wait.

At the theater, Hank the doorman recognized us and waved us through. Still panting from the run from the subway, we found Reine in her dressing room, chatting with several other women who were changing into their costumes. They sat at mirrored tables lined up against the wall.

Reine introduced us to one of her friends and fellow dancers, Marie Glendinning. She had connections from years of starring in several first-rate productions. Standing to greet us was a statuesque woman with shining black curls piled high on her head. She smiled warmly at Rose and me and then slowly focused in on me, stepping forward to close the space between us. My flushed face, messy blonde hair, and sweaty body were scrutinized, and I shrank. Before she could say anything, I took a deep breath and launched into a tap routine from my after-school lessons. "You are stunning," she said. Her British accent made me wonder if she was related to the King of England. I stopped dancing.

"What about me?" Rose asked. "I can dance too. Watch." Rose danced the same routine I had danced.

"Very good," she said to Rose and turned back to me. "You're very pretty, Marion. It's nice to see you again after so long. You've grown up beautifully." She touched a curl on my shoulder. "You probably don't remember that we met when Reine just started in the theater years ago."

"I remember you," Rose interrupted, but Marie continued to look at me.

"No, I don't remember you, s-sorry," I said, stammering on the final word with a guilty smile.

"You're almost fairy-like, aren't you?" Marie said, continuing to examine me. She took my hands and raised them up slightly. "You're blossoming into a rare beauty, and I can see you're not finished yet. You're a world away from that ten-year-old brash tomboy. But I guess it's a natural transition, from awkward duckling to elegant swan."

I blushed and looked at Reine, who was adjusting her hair in the mirror as usual.

Marie let go of my hands. They were hot and sweaty, which embarrassed me. I rubbed them on my shirt.

"Can you meet me tomorrow at the Globe Theater at noon?"

"Sure, I can," I said quickly.

"I can too," Rose said, stepping closer to Marie.

"Okay, see you then," she said before slipping out the door.

Reine squeezed our arms lightly before she disappeared down the hall. I followed her to a side area of the theater. From that vantage point I could see the action onstage and yet be hidden from the audience. Rose stood behind me. "Let's go, Marion. Mama will be waiting."

"Shhhh! Let's just watch for a minute."

Several stagehands moved around us. "He's cute; look at him," Rose whispered in my ear.

"How can you care about boys now? Look at the stage, the lights, and the magnificent costumes." I melted into the lights, imaging myself dancing solo in front of a packed house. "Besides, Mama would kill you for dating a lowly stagehand."

— ◎ —

The following day at The Globe, Marie flung us out onto the stage, where we found ourselves singing and dancing for the director. He offered me the job as a pony girl in the Broadway production of *Chin Chin*. I squealed and shook from excitement even though a pony girl was the lowest position in the theater, given to inexperienced girls who entertained the audience by dancing in front of the curtain during set changes and intermission.

The director turned to Rose and said, "Maybe next time, Sweetheart," and disappeared down the hallway. Rose's face drooped and she skulked down the hallway toward the door.

"Oh, I'm sorry," I said, catching up to her and putting my arm around her shoulder.

She shrugged my arm off. "Why do you have to be so good at everything *and* so pretty? It isn't fair Marion." She pushed open a door that led onto the street, letting it slam behind her. I stared after her, stunned, my heart broken for her. I ran back to the stage to study the other dancers.

— ⓪ —

The next week I was placed in the second line of the pony girls. I'd heard that our director, Mr. Burnside, had a fair and honest reputation. When he glanced in my direction with his penetrating black eyes about six months into my new job, I stopped cold. Our eyes locked for a long moment before I looked away. "Come here, girl. I want to see those big blue eyes up close."

My curves had finally made a small appearance and I hoped that if things continued to grow in certain key areas, I was on my way to having a figure I could be proud of. I walked over and looked into his eyes.

"Oh my! You are innocence, pure and simple. How tall are you?" he asked.

"Five-foot-five," I whispered aware my toothpick knees were knocking together. He stepped back and looked at me. "You're skinny, that's for sure. How old are you?"

"Seventeen."

He lifted my chin up with his finger. "How long have you been dancing for me?"

"Six months." My heart beat so wildly I could barely hear my own answer.

A scuffle on the far side of the stage saved me. A stagehand called out for him and he ran off.

I stood in shock, when I heard a woman from behind me say, "Remember this day. Your life is about to change." I whirled around as she studied me for a few minutes. "You're like a blue butterfly with dew on its wings."

I didn't know what she meant, but later found out she was Frances Marion, screenwriter for Mary Pickford. She was correct about my life changing, because the very next evening I was promoted to the chorus line. Now in the front line, the audience could see me and I could clearly see them. We wore emerald satin one-piece body suits with matching shoes and a feathery hat. I learned to guzzle a few glasses of champagne before going out onstage to calm my nerves. It also made it easier for me to ignore the well-dressed men in the front row. I had been dating young men off and on, slyly keeping my romantic life from Mama. There was one older gentleman I had openly dated for the last several months, a fairly influential newspaperman named Paul Block. He liked me way more than I liked him, but it was fun to hang on his arm and go to the fancy parties. Paul attended the theater a few times a week and I'd see him in the audience admiring me.

My saving grace was meeting a girl my age named Pickles St. Clair, who took me under her wing. Taller and a bit heavier than me, she had straight brown hair with bangs cut sharply above her eyes. Working hard came easy, especially with Pickles educating me about all the important people in the audience and egging me on to try new dance steps. After eight weeks, we both left *Chin Chin* to dance in various productions over the next year until we reunited in *Stop! Look! Listen!* starring Eileen Percy. Irving Berlin wrote all the music and lyrics and it was a smash hit. Pickles and I were prominently featured in Eileen's extravagant number, "The Girl on the Magazine Cover."

CHAPTER 3

NEW YORK. 1916

"Did you see that man in the middle seat of the front row? The one with the long face, graying hair, and big smile?" Pickles asked.

I nodded, struggling to remember which man she was talking about.

"That's William Randolph Hearst, the richest man in the country. He owns fifteen newspapers and dines with President Wilson. He also owns the two middle front row seats—one for himself and one for his tall hat—and he's here most nights."

I remembered the name William Randolph Hearst because of the incident when I'd thrown rotten fruits and vegetables at his door, and also when Mama read us the newspaper announcement when he married his wife, a showgirl just like us. When I went onstage for the next night's performance of *Ziegfeld Follies*, I zeroed in on him and his hat right up front. I danced, repeating the same steps night after night, almost without thinking. Whenever I looked at him, he'd smile and his eyes lit up with warmth and kindness. I guessed him to be in his late forties but soon found out from the girls backstage that he was in his early fifties—the perfect marrying age, according to Mama.

— ◎ —

After a few weeks of flirting and eyeing him from stage, Pickles warned me to stay away from him. "He's a stage-door Johnny," she said, sitting down on the bench and taking off her lace-up toe shoes. "A wolf in sheep's clothing."

"I'm only looking at him because he's always looking at me."

"Aren't you dating Paul Block?" Pickles asked.

"I don't know. It's fizzling out."

In the big dressing room filled with mirrored makeup tables, we hurriedly changed our costumes.

"And why should I avoid Mr. Hearst?" I knew there were many reasons, but I enjoyed being provocative. I ripped off my sweaty black tights and tried to cram my foot into the leg of a flouncy pink leotard.

"How about the fact that he's married with lots of children?" Pickles shot me a stern look as we ran back down the hall for the grand finale. I shrugged.

Several days later, a dozen long-stemmed red roses showed up at the theater for me with a note that read,

"YOU WERE WONDERFUL. —WR"

"That's Hearst," Pickles observed, peering over my shoulder as I read the note.

"Oh yeah, so it is. William Randolph Hearst," I mumbled to myself.

A week after that, three dozen equally beautiful long-stemmed roses arrived—red, yellow, and white. This time the note read,

"I ADORE YOU. —WR"

When our eyes locked onstage during this time, he'd wink at me, smile, and tilt his head in a knowing sort of way. Intrigued by it all, I didn't know what to think of him. Other gifts arrived sporadically, including a diamond wristwatch in a small Tiffany box. The note read,

"YOU DESERVE IT. —WR"

Receiving lavish presents from Mr. Hearst left me expecting them at the end of the show. I didn't know what he was doing. Was he courting me? He was already married, so why was he sending me presents? I had to admit he intrigued me. The flowers arrived weekly for months. The other girls gawked at my gifts, especially the blue box from Tiffany.

Pickles gasped. "Who does he think he is?"

Despite her warnings, I couldn't take my mind off Mr. Hearst. I had to meet him. I'd lie in bed wondering if I would bump into him backstage, or if he'd be waiting for me outside the stage door after a show one night, or if I'd meet him at a fancy party while wearing a beautiful dress.

But that's not how it happened at all.

— ⊚ —

I finally exchanged words with him on a trip to Miami Beach with Mama visiting old James Deering, the farm equipment tycoon. My grandmother grew up with Mr. Deering, and I feared Mama had designs on one of us girls marrying him. His huge coral-and-white mansion, named Vizcaya, felt like a stuffy museum. I used every excuse to sneak out of it to visit my dear friend and fellow dancer Ella Widener, who was staying at a little hotel in Palm Beach. It was there we ran into Gene Buck, the lead songwriter for Flo Ziegfeld, at the pool one afternoon.

The sun shone brightly, and the pool was filled with swimmers. I had on my new pink bathing dress with ruffles and polka dot shorts. Mr. Buck swooped down in an empty chair at our table. "Nice to see you ladies here today," he said in a very hawkish manner. He had flirted with me a few times backstage and had even asked me out for a drink once, but I declined as sweetly as I could, making up some excuse about my Mama not being well. I didn't like the look of him. His self-assured, serious way looked like he would devour me. Plus, he had a "reputation," always showing up with a different girl on his arm, enjoying his power over them.

"Nice to see you here today, too, Mr. Buck," Ella said.

I faked a smile and looked away, well aware that he expected a lowly dancer like me to pay attention to him, even fawn after him as the other girls did.

"Let's go on a bike ride around the shoreline. The hotel has some loaner bikes just waiting for riders," Mr. Buck said.

"Come on, Ella," I said, thinking it might be fun as long as I wasn't alone with him.

She smiled lazily. "No, you two live wires go ahead. I'll be right here when you get back."

I made a sour face at Ella, realizing I couldn't politely get out of the bike ride, so I set off beside Mr. Buck. We'd just rounded the beach a half-mile from the hotel when he yelled, "Look there, the Hearst Caddy!"

I looked up to see a maroon limousine barreling down the road toward us. I don't know why the image of it shook me up so much, but I swerved and lost control of my bike, falling off and landing dramatically on the grass with my dress over my head.

The car pulled up right where I'd fallen, and I felt a man's presence. I knew it was Mr. Hearst. I yanked my dress down and our eyes met. We held each other's gaze for a second, and I saw a spark of recognition, then a flash of what looked like desperation. He almost smiled but instead put up a wall of distance between us and spoke formally.

"Are you hurt, young lady?"

Before I could answer, I glimpsed a woman sitting in the back of the limousine. I stiffened as I realized it was his wife, Millicent. She was thin, starched, and mannequin-like, wearing a large white hat with a veil. She leaned out the door and lifted the veil to take me in. Seeing the hardness in her stare, I felt embarrassed splayed out on the grass, disheveled and discombobulated. I had the distinct impression she was an empty shell of a woman.

"May I help you?" Mr. Hearst asked, darting his eyes back to catch Millicent's stare before offering me a hand.

Just then Mr. Buck arrived at my side.

I felt my face flush hot and I nodded absently, placing my hand in Mr. Hearst's big palm. He pulled me to my feet, and my mind raced in a thousand different directions as I tried to regain my composure.

When I looked at Mr. Hearst again, I could see his eyes held a world of pain. This was our first in-person meeting, and it seemed we had very little to say to one another.

Mr. Buck quickly filled the silence. "Hello, Hearst. I thought that was you in the Caddy." He then looked over to the car. "Good day, Mrs. Hearst."

Mr. Hearst smiled and mumbled, "Nice to see you, Buck."

I lowered my eyes and focused on my skinned knee, pulling my dress down again to cover my legs. I tried to stop blushing from embarrassment.

"We ought to have a doctor take a look at you," Mr. Hearst said.

"I'm not hurt. I don't need a doctor," I insisted.

I couldn't wait to get away from him—and her. I grabbed my bike and pedaled back toward the hotel while Mr. Buck hurried to catch up.

— ◯ —

Locked in my room back at Mr. Deering's house, I laid on the walnut four-poster bed and stared at the red velvet wallpaper and gold Grecian pillars. The large crystal chandelier refracted light balls onto the ornate walls. *Mr. Hearst probably lives like this*, I thought, walking into the bathroom and turning on the hot water to the tub. I added silky bubble bath and watched the water rise. Earlier I'd snickered at the gold claw-footed tub and been taken aback by the solid gold baby swan tub handles and faucet shaped as a mother swan. Whoever thought of this outrageous design had style, and I could get used to living like this.

As I lowered myself into the tub, I wondered about Mr. Hearst. The pain in his eyes was obvious, and it was clear to me that the pain came from *her*. He was married but not happily. He was definitely older, but not in a stuffy way like Mr. Deering. I felt attracted to his quiet, smooth, strong persona in a way I had never experienced before. His elegance and strength made me feel protected. But after today's encounter, I felt funny. Why was he sending me gifts and flowers? Maybe he sent stuff to lots of girls. Maybe I wasn't special. Anger rose in me at being made a fool, and I smacked the water. Who did he think he was to lead me on this way? I flicked the bubbles, sending them flying out of the tub. Just because he was rich didn't give him special rights. I was my own person. I decided. Money can't buy everything. I sunk back into the warm water and stared blankly at the wall—darn his yearning eyes. They told a different story. One of longing and kindness and sweetness.

— ⊙ —

I determined the next time I saw Mr. Hearst at the theater in New York, I'd find a way to tell him just what I thought of him and his wife. But once we got home from Florida he seemed to disappear— his two front-row seats sat empty night after night. I went to the late-night parties and dinners with the other girls in hopes of run-ning into him. Each night, I went home alone and wondered about him. I practiced the speech I planned to give him over and over.

A few weeks later, he showed up at the theater, watching me

from his regular seat. Our eyes met, and I looked away immediately. It didn't take long for the smoldering anger to bubble up again. After the show, I ran into the alley behind the theater looking for him and found him getting into his fancy limousine.

"Hey, Mr. Hearst!" I called out.

He stopped in his tracks and turned to smile at me. "Marion, it's nice to see you again. You were lovely tonight, as usual."

"No, you don't. You don't get to be nice to me tonight when you treated me like a stranger in Florida. I've been waiting to yell at you for weeks. Where have you been?"

"You've been waiting to yell at me? Well, aren't you just the little bear cat," he grinned.

"Where have you *been*?" I insisted, stomping my foot.

"I've been out of town managing my newspapers and working. What did you want to yell at me about?"

"Why do you send me flowers and gifts, leading me on, when you have a wife like her?"

He stepped closer, and I caught the scent of citrus and musk. "You're even more beautiful up close than you are onstage under all those lights."

His height was imposing, and I took a step back so I didn't have to look up so high.

He grinned. "What do you mean 'like her'?"

"Your wife is tight and stiff and unhappy and mean." I put my hands on my hips and stood statue still while I waited for an answer.

He laughed from deep inside. Not a condescending laugh, but a low, full chuckle that softened me a bit. He looked around, seeming to make sure nobody was within earshot.

"You're a good judge of character, you know that?"

"So why are you making passes at me when you have her? And why do you have her if you're so unhappy?"

He lowered his head and his face turned serious. His blue-gray eyes gently swirled and I almost fell into them.

"I can't help myself. You are a magnet. I love to see you dance. It brings me happiness." He brushed a curl from my shoulder and quickly withdrew his hand as if he had taken too much liberty.

I stared at him and then looked down at the ground, swishing the sole of my shoe against the concrete. The anger had disappeared. I wasn't ready for such silk and cream coming from him. Turning away, I ran back through the theater door without saying goodbye. My anger had betrayed me, and my heart had melted. Now what?

—⊙—

After that night, Mr. Hearst disappeared again, but the gifts began arriving with the very next performance. Each night I received a different bouquet of flowers—roses, daffodils, tulips, and carnations. I received boxes of candies in all shapes and sizes, and bottles upon bottles of perfume and champagne. I overheard some of the girls quietly call me a gold digger—even Pickles, which hurt. They were jealous, but how could I be a gold digger? *He* sent me flowers and candies; I wasn't chasing him. I had hidden the diamond Tiffany watch he gave me in my bag for months and had only shown it to Pickles when we were out of town for a show in Boston. She had marveled at it, turning it over in her hand and trying it on when we went out one night after the show. I wasn't willing to share it with anyone in my family yet.

When I brought the flowers and gifts home, Ethel and Reine smiled at me, patting my back and kissing my cheek as if I had anything to do with it. Rose, on the other hand, scowled whenever she saw my gifts on the kitchen table, refusing to look at me and leaving a silent divide between us.

One night, I grabbed a vase of blue irises I'd received from Mr. Hearst and headed upstairs to our shared bedroom. The door was closed but I knocked lightly anyway. "Go away!" she yelled like she did when we were kids.

"Come on, Rose. I have something for you." I opened the door just in time to see her putting away a small flask. "I brought you these beautiful irises."

She sniffled. "I don't want them. They're yours."

I put the vase on her bedside table and caught a whiff of whiskey in the air. "Why are you drinking up here by yourself?"

"Just leave me alone." She turned away.

"I hate this tension between us. What's wrong?"

"You wouldn't understand even if I tried to explain," and then added with disdain, "gorgeous and desirable Marion." She got up and left the room, leaving me staring at the swaying branches of the giant English Elm outside our bedroom window.

I wondered if Rose and I would ever be close again. It seemed our relationship was disintegrating right in front of my eyes. It wasn't my fault her appearance seemed to edge toward the handsome as we grew up. She forgot she had talent and beautiful skin and a wonderful smile, only focusing on comparing our looks.

Looking at myself in the mirror, turning my face to the side to see not only the differences between Rose and me but also what interested Mr. Hearst, I saw a touch of Reine's delicacy in my cheekbones and lips, and a hint of Ethel's bawdiness in my nose and mouth, but other than that, I just looked like me—a closet stutterer like Rose, and the youngest of the Douras girls.

— ◎ —

Mama questioned all the flowers and gifts, and I told her that Mr. Hearst had sent them and that we had not been properly introduced yet—which was the truth. "You should not be accepting tokens of affection from a married man. There is no legitimate future there."

I didn't know where things were going, since the last two times I had seen Mr. Hearst I made a complete fool out of myself. But from that moment on, I avoided Mama and all her questions, promising myself that the next time I saw Mr. Hearst I would talk to him without embarrassing myself.

My chance came the following week after Friday night's show, when he was waiting for me in the backstage hallway of the theater.

"Can we talk?" he whispered. He bent over like a gentleman bowing at court and kissed my cheek as he put a dozen white roses in my hands. His skin was smooth and soft, his lips full and flushed. The distinct smell of musk and citrus surrounded me.

"Sure," I said, closing my eyes and breathing in his scent.

"There's a note in the flowers," he whispered. I opened my eyes as he straightened up, smiled, then politely said for anyone who might have been listening, "Good evening, Miss Davies." He then left.

He walked down the narrow backstage hall, a head taller than all the people he passed. The theater door opened, slammed closed, and he was gone.

Taking the flowers into my dressing area, I found a small note tucked between the thorny stems. Looking around to make sure nobody was watching—already feeling the need to sneak and cover up—I plucked out the note, unfolding the slip of cream-colored paper low in my lap as a key fell out. I picked it up and examined it, reading the note: "10:30 p.m., tomorrow night, 2109 Broadway." His handwriting was refined, curly, yet masculine and strong with the "t" in "tomorrow" crossed deliberately. I could still feel his strength and power as it lingered in the scent of musk and citrus. I closed the note over the key and tucked them into my purse.

CHAPTER 4

I shared the note with Ethel when I got home. On her bed, with the door closed, we studied it while breathing in the white roses.

"He's got nice handwriting. And the paper is so thick and rich," she said.

I fiddled with the thin skeleton key, looking at Ethel, squinting my eyes, "What's happening?"

"You're in play, Marion. Maybe I should go with you."

"Nah, I can't bring my big sister. I have to go alone. And Mama can't know I'm going to meet him," I said without breaking eye contact with Ethel.

"Okay, but if you change your mind and want me to chaperone, let me know," she said as she nudged me from my trance-like state.

"Can I wear your mauve-colored chiffon dress?" I asked.

She rolled over on the bed until we were next to each other. "Of course, little dear." And then she kissed my cheek. A surge of adrenaline pumped through my body. I let out a huge sigh as I laid my head on Ethel's shoulder.

—⟨⟩—

The next evening, I arrived at the address by taxi. Other girls in the show rendezvoused with men this way but I had never. My mind raced at the possibilities—maybe he would rip my clothes off and devour me. Pickles had called him a "wolf in sheep's clothing." Still, I longed to meet him.

Taking a deep breath, I stepped out of the cab and looked up at the Beaux Arts building with its decorative flare and monumental eighteen-story grandeur. It was just like him, tall and imposing. The winter wind whipped down the street, and I pulled my scarf tighter against my neck. The shot of gin I'd downed right before leaving the house had spread out all over my body, filling me with warmth and courage. If he tried anything unseemly, I would fight like a longshoreman. Sniffing briskly, I summoned the strength borne of a bullied stutterer, the pain of which had hardened in me these past years. I walked up to the entrance and greeted the doorman with a nonchalant nod.

"Miss Davies to see Mr. Hearst," I attempted to say with some authority.

He motioned me inside. "Good evening, Miss Davies. Ned, there in the elevator, will take you to the eighteenth floor."

I rode the elevator in silence, studying my reflection in the shiny walls, happy with my curly hair and the glow on my cheeks. Soon I stood before 1814 and took a deep breath.

Hearst opened the door in response to my tentative knock. "Come in, Marion."

I noticed his voice was a bit high for such a large man. He wore black slacks, a white dress shirt, and a soft, fuzzy blue sweater. I took off my coat, trying to slow down my mind as it flitted from thought to thought—the room, the way he smelled like musk and citrus again, the music, my sweaty palms, his expectations, my expectations. Whenever I got nervous, I still stuttered—that old childhood bugaboo—so I braced myself and prayed for sureness.

The apartment was small and well furnished—nothing opulent or ostentatious like Deering's place in Florida. The walls were beige with dark wood crown molding around the ceiling, but nothing gold or velvet or stuffy. The sitting area had two leather club chairs and a brown leather sofa, a coffee table in between them, and a fireplace at one end. Mr. Hearst had already made a fire, and the heat felt inviting.

"Please sit down and warm yourself. Would you like a drink?"

"Thank you, Mr. Hearst," I said as I sat on the couch.

"You don't have to call me Mr. Hearst when we're alone. Call me WR or William."

I hesitated a moment and tried to lighten the mood. "Can I call you Bill?"

He turned around and saw that I was grinning. He chewed on his bottom lip. "I don't know if I like that one. Let me think about it."

WR sat in the chair closest to me, popped open a bottle of champagne, and poured us both a glass. The silky, smooth bubbles slid down my throat effortlessly. Scott Joplin's piano ragtime played softly on the radio. We chatted about the weather and the show I was in. My nerves disappeared quickly, and I could feel my whole body relax as it filled up with tiny champagne bubbles. A glowing feeling began in my belly and spread, soon loosening my muscles.

I told him more about my sisters, even though he already knew they danced in shows. Settling back on the couch, I felt comfortable telling him truths about my family—I didn't stutter.

"I miss Papa, but I've gotten used to not having him around. He and Mama settled into a truce of sorts, where he comes to the house and spends time with us girls without having to fight with her."

WR watched me intently, nodding when I described the truce. I told him a bit about how I'd always loved to dance. He refilled my champagne glass and reached over gently to catch a drip of champagne that hovered on the side of my mouth. It was the most sensual thing that had ever happened to me, making it hard to find my next thought.

He said, "You're a great talent. Audiences respond to you."

Suddenly shy, I scrunched my nose. "Like they responded in laughter the other night when I said my first line on stage?"

"Oh, don't worry about those silly people. They don't know anything," he said.

I sat back against the silky European shams and looked up to the ceiling.

"Why are you blushing?"

"Because I'm ridiculous sometimes. When the director asked me to wear that stunning blue tulle gown that fizzled and popped in the light, I just couldn't say no. I've never seen a dress so beautiful."

"Your blue eyes sparkled and matched it perfectly."

The blush crept up again in my neck. "It should have been easy. The director told me to descend the staircase and say, 'And I'm the Spirit of Spring.' At first, I declined even though that gorgeous gown called to me."

"You mean you almost didn't try the scene?" WR asked.

"That's right. It was opening night, remember? The house was packed."

"Yes, I recall it perfectly."

"When my musical cue came, I descended the stairs feeling proud I hadn't fallen, and then my brain froze as I looked at the audience. The lights were bright and hot, and when I opened my mouth, the only thing that came out was, "And I . . . I . . . I . . . I."

"I know, my dear."

"They laughed. They all laughed at me. All I could do was run."

"When you disappeared, I wanted to run after you and protect you." He slid over from the chair, sat next to me on the couch, and held my hand gently.

"Thank you, WR," I whispered.

He let out a low grumble as he sank back into the couch and said, "I'm under your spell, sweet Marion. Let's make movies together. It's time you graduated from the stage."

"You want me to make movies after that fiasco? I can't even speak properly."

He took my chin and tilted my head up. "You were more beautiful than any other woman in that playhouse. You shone under the lights, and the audience was enraptured. Forget the rest of it," he commanded and paused for a long moment. "Besides," he continued, "there's no talking in the movies."

I felt warm inside and glowed at him, not sure if it was the champagne or his presence. I excused myself to the bathroom where I leaned against the counter, taking deep breaths. The gold towel racks held cream-colored towels that felt like plush silk rugs. The evening was happening so fast. After checking my lipstick and powder, I returned to the living room where WR stood. He held his hand out for me to dance with him. The radio played Strauss's "The Blue Danube Waltz," and WR moved me around the small room with ease. When the song ended, I sat down beside him, reached up, and kissed his cheek. It was time for me to go. Ethel would be waiting.

As I stood up, I reached into my pocket and pulled out the key. "Thank you for a wonderful evening." I handed him the key.

"You keep it. This is your apartment now. Come here whenever you wish."

"What? I can't accept that," I said, taking a step backward.

"Keep the key and think about it." He helped me with my coat and opened the door. I pushed the key back into my pocket.

"Goodnight, WR."

"My driver's waiting to take you home. See you soon, I hope," he said before turning and stepping back inside.

As Mr. Hearst's limousine pulled away from the building, I leaned my head back against the leather seat and touched the key inside my pocket. My heart raced with the possibilities ahead of me. I saw WR's eyes as bright stars in the sky and reached into my purse for a cigarette. I'd been dying for one all night but didn't dare light up. Taking a long drag and feeling my whole body relax, I wondered what WR wanted from me. Maybe he really did just want to make me a movie star, but maybe he also wanted more of me. The thought intrigued me. Either way, I could live like this.

CHAPTER 5

After my show the following night, I hired a cab and went to the apartment alone to see if my key really worked. WR had not been at the performance.

The doorman opened the cab door and said, "Good evening, Miss Davies," like he was expecting me.

My heart beat hard as I crossed the lobby and entered the elevator. "Good evening, Ned." He smiled and pushed the button to the eighteenth floor. "Beautiful evening tonight. The moon is almost full."

"Yes, it's gorgeous," I managed to say, not believing I was riding the elevator without anybody questioning me.

The doors opened. "Have a nice night, Miss Davies," Ned said as he held the door for me.

"Thank you." I slid the key from my purse and put it into the lock. Once it clicked, I turned the handle and swung the door open. The apartment was empty and dark. I felt for the light switch, which turned on the chandelier.

Sitting on the couch, I lit up a cigarette and looked at the paintings I hadn't even noticed the previous night. A *Madonna and Child* hung on one wall, and a hunting scene from ancient times hung on the other. On the side table I saw a bare-breasted statue of a Greek goddess without any arms. How had I missed them last night? I wandered into the kitchen and turned the radio on. Jazz played softly.

All alone, I felt like I was trespassing. But WR had clearly said, "This is your apartment. Come here anytime." The fully stocked refrigerator held two bottles of champagne. My mood lightened immediately as I popped the cork and poured myself a glass, swaying to the music.

A copy of the latest issue of *Cosmopolitan* lay on the kitchen table. I flipped through the pages between sips of champagne, almost missing the knock at the door. I was startled but pleased to find WR standing there, having waited for me to answer rather than just barging in. Maybe this really was my apartment.

"Hello, may I help you?" I teased.

"Yes, I was looking for Miss Davies. I heard she lives here," he said as he entered and took off his suit jacket. I sashayed back to the kitchen and sat down at the table, expecting him to follow me.

WR entered the kitchen hesitantly. I could tell he was trying to gauge my mood, but when I grinned and made eyes at him, he sat down next to me. My hand lay on the table nonchalantly, and he covered it with his own large masculine one. *He does want more than to make me a movie star*, I thought.

"May I have a glass of champagne?" he asked, again treating me like the rightful owner of his apartment.

Rising quickly, I pulled my hand out from underneath his and filled a glass for him. Sitting down, I found myself magnetically drawn to him. I wanted to put my hand underneath his again and snuggle up to him for warmth and comfort. Instead, he took my hand, brought it up to his mouth, and kissed it. Then he downed his champagne before standing up and gently pulling my arm, indicating to follow him.

He walked ahead of me with his arm extended behind him, holding my hand. I followed as my head filled with a million doubts and wonders. Was I ready for this? He walked us past the bed and into the bathroom, where he turned the water on to fill the tub. He swooped me up in his arms and kissed my neck and face. I hung on tightly, allowing him to cover me in kisses. Warm, humid air filled the small room. He put me down gently on my feet and began unbuttoning my dress. The ivory buttons flipped in his fingers as he easily pushed them through the buttonholes, one by one, slowly revealing my slip. He pulled the dress over my shoulders, and it fell to the ground around my feet. His eyes held a promise and my heart slammed in my chest harder and faster as an ache rose up in my groin, my legs went weak.

"You are so beautiful," he said softly. Quickly unbuttoning his shirt, he let his trousers fall to the ground. His body was strong and smooth. I remained still as he removed my slip, unlaced my corset and brassiere, and—lifting me up so easily that I felt like a feather—gently deposited me into the warm bath water, where he soaped me up with a slow, methodical intensity. I felt uncharacteristically strong and calm and found my eyes seeking his. He was fully engaged in the admiration of my body, much as an artist or a sculptor would admire a fine piece of work. He lifted me again and placed me carefully on the bathmat, drying me as if I might break. Then he took my hand and led me to the bed where he lowered his mouth over mine. I'd like to say it was wild, pure passion from start to finish but that would be a lie. It felt more important than that, and I didn't want to disappoint. Even though this wasn't my first time with a man, I wasn't a seasoned expert either. I was falling for WR and felt his passion and earnestness like a luminous light around me. I allowed myself to be surrounded and consumed by the light as he expertly worshipped my body from top to bottom.

— ⊕ —

We met at the apartment quite frequently after that, as I got more comfortable with him. I moved a suitcase of my clothes into the empty drawers and closet, taking time to place each item carefully—a few dresses, undergarments, sleeping dress, housecoat, and slippers in addition to some bathroom necessities.

We couldn't go out together in public. Married men as powerful as he was did not date young starlets and remain in respectable businesses. WR could control what was published in his own newspapers, but he couldn't control the others.

He explained it one night, saying he was trying to extricate himself from his other "affairs."

I knew he meant his wife, but we didn't discuss her openly or his clutch of five sons aged eleven, eight, and seven, and twin baby boys. The brood was full at the Hearst house.

It was easy to forget the outside world as WR doted on me. His sweet, kind, and quirky personality made my life interesting. When I saw him at the theater, we slyly acknowledged each other. The gifts continued, and he showed up at the rare party I attended for the theater group. I felt his loving gazes from across the room as we smiled and winked at each other, like we had our own separate language. We were building a bubble around us.

Some nights, after he watched me in the show, we'd have a late dinner back at the apartment, where he always brought me some extravagant gift like diamond earrings, a musical jewelry box, or a jade pin for my hair. Our evenings were filled with laughter and charades and dancing. "Swing me around again," I'd say with my head thrown back. He'd pick me up and twirl us both in a circle until I got dizzy. "Put me down, put me down!" and we'd both fall down onto the couch, panting and laughing. Sliding his head into my lap and lacing his fingers through mine, this high-powered businessman who ran an empire turned into a silly, fun-loving man.

"Someday soon we'll travel together and play outside on the beach or in the mountains without a care in the world," he told me. "One day we'll have our freedom."

I was desperate to believe those words as truth. "My dreams are smaller, WR. I dream of dinner out, just the two of us over candlelight, or being able to arrive as a couple to a party where we know everyone and I'm able to be my affectionate self."

"Someday," he promised.

Until then I had to be patient.

— ⟨⟨⟩⟩ —

At the theater, I danced and kept all my commitments, but my focus was elsewhere. Pickles admired the dozen yellow roses I had received from WR. "You have disappeared from our aftershow parties, and I miss you."

I stood up to leave for the evening and kissed her cheek sheepishly saying, "I know, I'm sorry, I miss you too," and then smirking at her adding, "but not enough to change things right now."

Our secret love nest felt so big sometimes I believed I would burst. Our evenings together sometimes spilled into me occasionally spending the night. Waking up next to him, we'd entwine our bare legs as I lay on his chest, listening to stories of his privileged childhood when he was free and happy. We only allowed in things that brought us happiness and fun, like music and champagne. WR was like a man on vacation when we were at the apartment together—insistent on keeping away the realities of his other life.

— ⟨⟨⟩⟩ —

Ethel, my confidante, encouraged me along the relationship with WR.

Brushing my hair one evening, she said, "Listen to your heart; it will tell you if you must leave the relationship."

"How will it do that?" I said, looking at her reflection in the mirror.

"You'll have tugs of doubt and shards of anger bubble up when you're together."

I chose not to tell Ethel about the doubts I already had about him getting a divorce. Neither was I honest with Mama. In fact,

I straight-out lied when I told her that I was going out of town with the theater company for a long weekend, just so I could spend the entire time with WR at the apartment. She didn't say much except to remind me that I was supposed to be looking for *eligible* men. Maybe Ethel and Mama talked, I don't know. But avoiding the subject of WR allowed Mama to live in a paper-thin state of denial for a time.

In the past year, WR had given me my own car with a nice older driver named Norman. Now it was easier to rendezvous with him discreetly. He set up accounts for me at several department stores on Fifth Avenue: Lord and Taylor, Macy's, Bloomingdale's, and Saks Fifth Avenue. "Shop whenever you wish. Take your sisters. Enjoy yourself," he said one afternoon as we lay in bed snuggling.

I never knew where Norman stayed or lived or even parked the car, but whenever I needed him, he was outside the house or theater. When I'd wanted some time alone at the apartment, or to go for a drive through Central Park with Ethel for a confidential sister talk, Norman was outside waiting. Whenever I'd approach, he'd rush to open the door for me, bowing a bit and saying, "Good evening, Miss Davies. Where to tonight?" Oh, how I adored being treated as if there were a crown on my head.

One afternoon, Norman took Ethel and me to Fifth Avenue to shop for a dress for an outing to the racetrack WR was organizing.

At Saks, Ethel and I each tried on several dresses as the old-fashioned, snooty clerk watched us as if we were going to steal something. I guess we didn't yet exude richness and refinement.

"Do you have anything more modern?" I asked, politely holding up a dress my own mother would object to. A fiasco ensued when the clerk stood so close, I nearly fainted from her bad breath. I made eyes at Ethel as I turned around to see the hem of a pearl-studded dress accidentally catch on her garter, threatening to rip the dress and showing way too much leg.

The salesclerk gasped as Ethel pulled the dress down. A snicker escaped at the outrage of this ancient clerk. She lifted her nose up and said, "These are the finest dresses in the world, made from the richest materials, and so I'm sure I don't know what you are talking about."

We left Saks without buying a thing and headed to Lord and Taylor and then to Bloomingdale's. As we tried to learn the ways of refinement at each store we shopped at, it became an irresistible game. At Bloomingdale's, Ethel and I stood in front of a mirror admiring each other's dresses and then broke into a dance from our childhood, hopping and jumping in unison and sashaying back and forth. "Stop that right now," the salesclerk said. "That is no way for a lady to behave in public." We hooted and ran to change our clothes.

If we didn't buy something from Bloomingdale's, we might not get any dresses at all, so I straightened my face and gathered our choices in my arms. Mine was a flowing layered scoop neck white gossamer dress with a simple cotton voile underdress. Ethel picked a light blue embroidered afternoon dress at my insistence.

"We will take these two, and we need shoes to match if you please." The old biddy scrunched her nose at us, seeming to question how we would pay for all of it. I said kindly, "I believe you will find an account for me, my name is Marion Davies."

She rushed to her table and flipped through a box of cards until she pulled out the one with my name on it. Reading it slowly, she looked up. Suddenly a smile spread across her whole face. "Of course, anything you want. What size shoe do you each wear?"

Ethel winked at me and twirled me around in a circle. "You make a good rich woman, Miss Davies."

On the drive back to Mama's house drained from our long afternoon, I thought about the talk WR and I needed to have about his marriage. I wanted to stop hiding out all the time. I was falling for him, and we needed to make some decisions soon.

I bit the inside of my cheek as I said to Ethel, "It's time to talk to WR about . . . *her*."

Ethel nodded. "Yes, you need to talk about Millicent, that's true. But there's also Mama. I can't keep her at bay much longer."

I had two lives: my public life as a dancer on the stage with friends and my sisters, and my secret life with WR. Even though I was only nineteen, I knew it was time for me to have a heart-to-heart with WR.

— ⓪ —

The following day, I put on my new dress and Norman drove me to the apartment at the appointed time WR and I had agreed to meet.

Waiting for him to arrive, I poured myself a glass of champagne and lit a cigarette. WR arrived shortly after looking very dapper in his black suit, white shirt, and black tie, his white fedora in hand.

"Can we talk please?"

"Of course." He sat down next to me. "What's on your mind?"

I crushed out my cigarette in an almost-overflowing crystal ashtray and turned to face him. "I'm not sure what's happening between us," I started. "Don't get me wrong. I'm happy with everything, of course. I'm just wondering what it all means—the accounts at the stores, the driver, the clothes, the apartment."

"I hope you can tell I'm in love with you, Marion. I have never been this happy in my life—not ever. I can be myself with you. We laugh, we play, we are so well suited to each other. I love you and want to give you everything."

A wave of love came over me. "Oh, WR, I do love everything. I do! However, we can't hide in this apartment forever."

Before I could ask about Millicent, a knock at the door interrupted us. He said quietly, "I promise I'll make some changes. Right now let's be spontaneous. That's Carl and his date at the door. He's one of my editors who knows all about the horse races. We are going out today to have some fun and maybe make some money."

"Going out in public?" I asked, raising my eyebrows.

WR smiled and nodded. "Sort of," he said as he opened the door and welcomed his guests. Introductions were made as it became clear that his friends knew exactly who I was to him. Delores was about my age and very pretty in her pink-and-white checkered summer dress. Carl was jolly, and we all loaded into a new Pierce-Arrow limousine.

"Ladies first," WR said as he held open the door. Delores looked impressed as we both found our seats in the dark space where red velvet curtains gave us complete privacy. Rays of sunlight crept in through the edges, giving us just enough light to see each other.

Carl offered his flask of whiskey as we made the hour-long drive to the track, talking as if we'd known each other for years. Delores and I chatted amiably.

"Yes, I'm in the theater, but I've never starred in a show," I confessed. WR squeezed my leg at one point and kissed my cheek in front of Carl and Delores. Here we were, practically out in public I mused, happy as I'd ever been.

"What do you do, Delores?" I asked.

"I paint," she said, then I noticed her smudged fingernail edges. "I am having a private show in a few weeks. You should come," she added.

I leaned over and kissed WR grandly on the mouth. Happy, Dolores and I took several more long sips from Carl's flask, but WR refused any at all. As we neared the track, the men became consumed with the race paper.

I had never been to a horse track before, only to a dog track in Brooklyn with my father years earlier. Horse racing was quite a bit more luxurious in my humble first impression. Our private tour began as WR whisked us to the top of the box seats in his own private elevator. We had an all-encompassing view of the oval-shaped track, marked with a start and finish line. The horses were being warmed up in the area to the right of the track, and with our binoculars we could see the jockeys in their colorful pants and shirts. We spent the afternoon watching the horses, eating from the catered food WR brought in, and drinking from Carl's bottomless flask as discreetly as we could. We encountered nobody else the entire afternoon. As far as keeping us from public view, WR had thought of everything. I tried to convince myself we were making progress.

CHAPTER 6

Rose gave details to Papa and Mama about my relationship with
WR. I could have kicked her as she gossiped about me, but it
backfired on her as Papa seemed pleased that I was being wooed
by the most powerful newspaperman in the country. Each time
he visited, he peppered me with a thousand questions. "Does WR
have his own private secretary? How many cars does he have?"

When I didn't have an answer, he usually finished his inqui-
sition by saying, "He seems like quite a man to get to know."

The whole question of what exactly my relationship with
WR meant was being pushed to the next level. I knew I had to
introduce him to my family somehow, but my stomach soured
each time I thought about asking him to my humble family house
in Gramercy Park to eat plain food with my plain parents. I also
knew there would be no peace in my heart until my family met
him face-to-face.

Shortly after our foray to the racetrack, I just blurted it out
next time we were at the apartment. "You have to meet my parents. Come to dinner. They're all dying to meet you."

He sipped his hot tea carefully while studying me over the
cup. "Okay, set it up. I look forward to meeting Mama Rose
and Papa Ben."

"Don't forget my sisters, Ethel and Reine," I said, then reluctantly added Rose.

The following Tuesday, Papa made the trip from Brooklyn for the big dinner. He wore a work suit because he didn't own a dinner jacket or anything fancier. He looked exactly like himself: a hard-working, low-level lawyer. He sat quietly in the living room with a drink and a newspaper waiting for WR's arrival.

The smell of onions, garlic, and pot roast filled the house. I had spent two hours getting dressed, wearing a dark red skirt with a wide black belt and white blouse I'd bought on account at Saks recently. My hair was down with a hint of curl, the way WR liked it.

"Have you finished setting the table?" Mama asked from the kitchen.

"Yes, just finished. He should be here soon. It's nearly six."

Mama made me the most nervous when it came to WR, and then I worried about Rose's sharp tongue and unapologetically bad manners. Leading up to this day, Mama had complained to everyone within earshot that we were having a married man with five sons to dinner so he could court her youngest daughter. The absurdity of the evening wasn't lost on me, of course. She despised the whole charade, and I couldn't blame her. I despised it as well, wondering if having him to dinner could possibly change anything in my quest for a legitimate relationship.

As I stood in the dining room surveying my work setting the table, my stomach churned with nerves.

"The roast is resting," Mama announced, joining me in the dining room. I refolded a napkin and placed it on the plate.

"Mama, I know you don't approve, but the fact that WR is coming here tonight proves his intentions are honorable, otherwise why would he put himself through it?"

Mama only shrugged at me.

Ethel arrived in the room wearing the long yellow dress I had bought for her on one of our shopping sprees. It brought a glow to her face and looked perfect with the ribbon in her light brown hair.

"Looks nice," she said, eyeing the brightly colored napkins. "I'll make the drinks once he arrives. He's probably used to people making drinks for him." She winked at me.

"He makes his own drinks too," I said, watching her prepare the drink cart and wondering if I'd go on defending him this way all night long.

"Not when he's been summoned for dinner to be inspected by the parents," Rose commented from the stairs. She entered the dining room and immediately began fussing with one of the beads on her blue dress, the fringe sashaying as she walked.

"Very funny. He wasn't summoned," I said. "And I love the beads and fringe, by the way."

"Do you think he gets summoned often? Like maybe by the Queen or the President?" Mama asked.

"Are you serious? How should I know?" I murmured.

"Don't chew your nails, Marion." Rose said. "I'm sure Mrs. Hearst doesn't chew hers. It isn't ladylike."

I took my ragged fingernail out of my mouth. "Rose—stop! If you say anything unpleasant tonight, you can be certain I will kill you." I lit a cigarette and took a long drag.

"Girls, girls, girls," Mama said, looking at us across the dining room. She turned to Rose. "Keep your mouth shut tonight. It's not your place to publicly call out the folly of this evening's dinner. That task falls to me, and I plan on giving Mr. Hearst the benefit of the doubt for the next few hours." I felt like Mama had thrown me a life ring.

"I'll try . . ." Rose's voice trailed off as she spun around and headed to the living room with Papa.

"Where's Reine?" Ethel asked, clinking the glasses on the cart.

"Upstairs settling Charlie and Pepi. She'll be down presently," Rose answered.

The doorbell rang. I crushed out my newly lit cigarette and flew to the door. In the portico stood WR wearing a long black overcoat and a black Western Stetson hat. He carried an

umbrella and a bouquet of daisies and beamed when he saw
my face.

"Hello," I whispered, and planted a light kiss on his cheek.
I turned around immediately to make sure nobody saw.

"May I take your coat and hat?" I asked, nerves twisting in
my stomach.

"Why, sure, my lady," he said, handing them to me and
winking.

As I hung them up, I spotted my father approaching us.
"Papa Ben, this is William Randolph Hearst, or WR for short."

"Nice to meet you, Mr. Hearst," Papa declared, extending
his hand.

"Please call me WR, or William." They shook hands.

I saw Reine out of the corner of my eye standing at the
bottom of the stairs, elegant and beautiful, fussing with the
skirt of her sunset floral translucent dress. She looked lovingly
at Papa, who was paying excessive attention to WR.

Ethel served the drinks as I introduced my sisters to WR. While
they chatted, I drank heavily of my gin and tonic, trying not to
gulp but needing the liquor like a drowning man needs air. Mama
entered the room with a sour look on her face. I hoped she'd keep
her word and hold her tongue. I hated that she wasn't happy for
me, just as my career and love life were blossoming. "Mama, let me
introduce you to WR," I said, sweeping my hand in his direction.

"Nice to meet you, Mr. Hearst. I hope you're hungry. Dinner
is ready."

I cringed at her abruptness, but WR smiled kindly at Mama. "I'm
starving, Mrs. Douras." The hint of a smile appeared on her face.

We sat around the table and spoke of Broadway shows,
newspapers, politics, and the weather. Everyone participated in
the conversation except Mama, who hadn't said a word. Watching her across the table, I worried she was a dormant volcano.

Papa put on his best attorney face, serious and stern, sitting
back in his chair with a glow from the red wine, two fingers on

his chin, and said, "The sinking of the RMS *Lusitania* was a tragedy, wasn't it?" He was grasping at important subjects to discuss with WR, to show off his knowledge.

"Those Germans believed the ship was carrying war supplies. It was a tragedy to lose so many lives," WR responded.

Owning so many newspapers, WR could have flexed his knowledge on so many topics, but he didn't. He was humble, kind, gracious, and respectful. A surge of passion and happiness washed over me as I watched him discuss all the important topics of the day with Papa.

"Shall we have dessert and tea in the salon?" Ethel asked.

"Great idea," answered Papa, indicating with his hand for WR to follow him. I had never seen Papa play up to somebody quite so much, nor Mama ignore somebody so completely.

Mama gave us girls a pointed look, and we began gathering dishes and taking them to the kitchen as she followed WR and Papa into the salon. My stomach knotted up tighter. Would she speak? What would she finally say?

As I stacked the dishes in the sink, Ethel plated the pie, and Reine made the tea.

"Hurry up, let's bring the dessert now," I urged, seeing that the teapot was ready.

"Okay, okay, calm down," said Ethel. She grabbed me by the shoulders and shook me a little. "He's really wonderful."

I didn't realize I was holding my breath until I exhaled. "Boy, is this ever painful. He's really on display tonight, isn't he?"

Just then I heard WR say, "Yes, she'll be perfect for the job. I'll teach her everything."

"I'm sure she'll be fine under your supervision, Mr. Hearst," Papa agreed.

My chest expanded when WR declared, "I love Marion dearly and will take good care of her. I can promise you that."

By now we girls had frozen in place and were listening intently just outside the living room, like we did on Christmas morning.

"I'm sure you will, WR. You don't need my approval; however, I give it anyway," Papa declared magnanimously.

"Do you plan to marry her?" Mama almost demanded of him.

I thought I might faint, and I squeezed Rose's arm to keep myself steady.

"Yes, Ma'am, just as soon as I can get a divorce," WR said quickly.

"And how long will that take?" Mama pressed.

A small nervous laugh escaped WR. "I'm working on it now."

"I'm glad to hear it. We'll be anxious to hear any news as it becomes available."

I released my breath slowly, swallowing hard, and stared blankly ahead with my sisters' smiles in my peripheral vision. Ethel grabbed my arm. The wheels on the cart squeaked, and Mama cleared her throat and walked toward the doorway where we all stood at the ready.

"Would you like some apple pie and tea, Mr. Hearst?" Mama asked.

We filed into the room and sat on the long couch. I tried not to look at WR. My mouth went dry, and I began chewing my nail.

They ate pie, drank tea, and chit-chatted. I pushed the pie around on my plate, feeling the need for fresh air like never before. Papa and WR drank cognac and talked until WR left at ten o'clock.

"I'll talk to you tomorrow. Thank you for enduring that," I said, ushering him out and receiving the same small kiss he'd given me on his way in.

"Your family is wonderful," he whispered in my ear.

"Let's never do this again," I whispered back and took a deep breath after the door closed behind him. I looked at Papa, sitting on the couch with a drink in his hands.

"You sure have hooked a big one."

"Papa! Don't talk about him like that, he's not a fish, for goodness' sake."

He winked at me.

Mama peeked into the salon from the kitchen. "Just remember, you deserve to be the wife."

"Yes, Mama," I agreed dutifully.

"He's dreamy," murmured Ethel, sitting next to me and lighting a cigarette.

"So handsome and well-mannered," said Reine with a smile.

"I like him," Rose said with a smirk. "I don't even mind that he's got that high voice."

I knew this was the best compliment I could expect from Rose and felt grateful for it. But I felt especially grateful the night was over. Never again would I put myself through that kind of torture.

I took Ethel's cigarette from her hand and took a big drag.

"Now you girls get in here and help me clean up," Mama demanded.

"Can't we leave it for Netty in the morning?" I begged, longing to go upstairs and talk to my sisters privately.

"No, we aren't leaving this mess for her."

Groaning, we all headed for the kitchen, Ethel pushing the dessert cart and Reine pushing the drink cart. Rose put her arm around my shoulders and whispered, "I was dying to ask about his sons all night but didn't. How is that for restraint?"

Knowing she was teasing me, I bumped her hip and thanked her. Papa sank back into the couch with a satisfied smile. I couldn't remember the last time he looked so relaxed.

CHAPTER 7

The months shaped themselves into a routine that became two years of me living in denial of WR's marriage—blindly hoping he was still working on a divorce. I continued to dance for Flo Ziegfeld in the various *Follies* productions. Each day I rushed around tending to the public life I had carefully created in New York, rehearsing, performing, attending classes, celebrating with friends, and filling in the gaps with my family.

WR often left for long stretches, traveling to visit his newspapers or scheming with his political friends. None of that political stuff interested me in the least. Old men fighting over seats in government that would keep them fighting with other seats in government—no thank you!

His life away from me seemed to be growing and demanding more of his time. I was running out of patience, and it all came tumbling out one morning as we lay in bed.

"I'm leaving on an extended trip west. Will you be okay without me?" he asked.

I threw the covers back and got out of bed. "You're gone more than you're here," I said, stopping in front of the bathroom door.

He sat up in bed. "I'm sorry you feel neglected."

"It's more than being neglected, WR; it's my life here. I keep wondering when our life together will finally start. It's been two years since you told my parents you would get a divorce."

He looked out the window. "I know it's been a long time."

I walked to the window and saw blue sky and puffy white clouds. "Where is this relationship going?" I asked.

"I love you, Marion. I want to be with you."

"I need more than hiding out with you all the time." I left the apartment without another word.

— ⊚ —

I believed our relationship was fizzling out and tried not to dwell on it too much. If it ended, I would miss Norman, my accounts on Fifth Avenue, all the flowers and jewelry, and the apartment, but I wouldn't miss feeling like a stowaway in my own life.

Real success was happening for lots of girls on the stage, and rumors of film offers buzzed about for many of us. WR had promised me a film career but like his divorce, nothing had happened yet.

My friend and fellow dancer, Anita Loos, was having fantastic success on the stage, but also as a scriptwriter and that fascinated me. Connie Talmadge, another dancer friend was having great success in film. My career seemed to be stalled on the stage. I was performing in my fourth Broadway production in less than a year in the only kind of role I seemed to be offered—one that showed off my legs, my face, my hair—but not my talent.

I'd opened at the Fulton Theater in what had been billed as a "snappy revue" called *Words and Music*. I played a pretty geisha in the first half, and a beautiful French doll in the second. I had been dancing these type roles for years and could do them in my sleep.

That's exactly how my career felt: asleep. It was drab. I fancied myself a bit of a comedian and kept hoping somebody with decision power would see the funny in me. I staged a few mishaps for our director—pretending not to see a chair and tripping over it but gracefully recovering at the last minute. The stagehands laughed, but he didn't. I was dying to take a giant step up in the world.

For months, an idea for a movie script had been churning around in me. I had seen Mary Pickford's latest movie, *The Poor Little Rich Girl* at least a dozen times since it had come out. The story was simple enough, how hard could it be to write a script? I soon found out as I began writing one, with no experience at all. Ethel called it youthful exuberance. Reine called it stubbornness. I refused to tell WR, wanting to show him I didn't need him as much as he thought.

— ◎ —

Sitting at the dining room table in Gramercy Park, I wrote my script over the course of a few weeks. My movie featured a young girl kidnapped by gypsies and almost forced to marry, except she escapes by dressing as a man. Mama offered her suggestion of a title: *Runaway Romany*. It was perfect. After some edits and finishing touches, script in hand, I called everyone I knew who might be able to help. The funding came from my old beau, Paul Block. I was careful not to give Paul the wrong idea about my personal availability, but I figured it couldn't hurt to entice him just a little.

I played the lead role of Romany, and Reine's ex-husband, George Lederer, donated his time as director, as did a few other actors I knew from the stage.

Runaway Romany took less than three weeks to film, ran just under thirty minutes, and cost $23,000 to film at Pathé Studios in New York and the wilds of New Jersey. It was shown in several small New York theaters and bombed immediately and spectacularly. Paul refused to attend the premiere, wishing to distance himself professionally. George and I sat through opening night together and were aghast to see our movie through the eyes of the audience who failed to clap at the end, with some even leaving halfway through. The idea was good, but the execution—the direction, editing, and yes, even the acting—was dismal. Scriptwriting and moviemaking were harder than they looked. I was humbled. And to top off the bad news, Paul was circling around again for a reconciliation. Life was a mess.

—— ◎ ——

I should have known WR would hear about *Runaway Romany*. He'd been producing short films, serials, and newsreels for more than five years as an offshoot of his newspaper empire. A day after my movie was pulled from all theaters, I received his telegram and bouquet of roses. "I'm back. Can we talk?"

I met him at the apartment that night, part of me feeling proud that I'd been able to make a movie at all, but mostly feeling ashamed at how badly it turned out.

When I walked in, he was sitting at the table. "Darling." He got up, holding out his arms. "Please, let me hold you again. Come here."

Unable to resist his warmth for even five minutes, I folded myself into his arms for a long hug. I closed my eyes and breathed him in. The familiar citrus and musk enveloped me. He kissed me gently.

"There, that feels better," he said and kissed me again.

I made eggs and toast for myself while WR reviewed some paperwork. As I was tidying up the kitchen, he asked nonchalantly from the dining room, "How were the box office receipts on your movie?"

I crushed out my cigarette in the ashtray and shook my head, grinning.

"What movie?" I called out coquettishly from the kitchen.

"That little picture of yours, *Runaway Romany*. You know, I saw it."

I approached him at the dining room table. "You saw it? And now what—you want to make fun of 'my little picture'?"

The grin disappeared. "Oh, well, darling, I only meant I saw promise, and I know we can do much bigger and better together."

"You always want it bigger, don't you, WR?" I teased.

"I want to make you president of the new movie studio I'm creating," he announced, startling me.

"I'd rather be your wife."

He put his pen down and shook his head slightly. "I'm at an impasse with her. She won't budge; however, I have another idea." He got up and stood behind me, caressing my shoulders. "I need more time. Please don't leave me," he whispered into my neck.

"What idea?" I said, my bottom lip out.

"I think she's seeing somebody in Palm Beach. I'm having her followed by a detective."

I laid my head on his arm. My heart thawed as silence filled the room for a long moment. "Promise me it won't be much longer until we have our life together," I said.

"I promise."

WR returned to his seat. "Now, what do you say about coming to work for me?"

"I don't know anything about running a movie company. George and I patched *Runaway Romany* together with string and tape, and you saw the results."

"George, you, and Paul's money," he emphatically pointed out.

"It was all business. I needed to do this project on my own and be independent."

"I see. And do you feel better now?"

"I do."

"Promise me you won't use his money again—ever."

I paused for a moment, not wanting to agree to anything too quickly. "I promise," I finally said.

This time I stood up and massaged his shoulders. He brushed his face against my hand, taking it and leading me to the bedroom, where he made me believe I was the most important woman in the world.

Snuggling in bed after our lovemaking, I confessed to WR how we had run horribly over budget while making *Romany*, how Paul practically shut down production before we filmed the ending, and we only got half a butter sandwich each for lunch.

Pulling me closer into a bear hug, he said, "I'm secretly glad you ran over budget and cost Paul lots of money. Do I get to say that?"

"Yes," I giggled, "you get to say that." I paused and then added, "I guess."

"You guess?" he asked, moving his fingers up my ribs one bump at a time as I squirmed and giggled. "And it does feel like he was starving you. You've gotten thinner, I believe."

Pushing him away, I rolled over on my side to face him. "But that wasn't the worst of it," I continued. "I almost got arrested and thrown in jail!"

At this, WR pulled away and searched my eyes. I told him how the Yonkers police descended on us while we were filming *Romany's* big getaway scene on the railroad tracks out in the middle of nowhere New Jersey—and the police accused me of breaking the law by cross-dressing as a man even after I explained that I was in character, and that it was Romany, not me, who was dressed as a boy, and that she was only trying to escape her captors.

"My word, darling, how did you get out of it? Did Paul save you?" he asked, unable to keep the sarcasm from his voice.

Annoyed, I bristled, "I don't need men to save me. I can save myself." His eyes warmed and his face softened. With my nose in the air, I finished the story. "I got out of it by offering the officers free tickets to see the show, and they let me go."

WR paused a moment. "You think well on your feet, young lady—which is exactly why you'll make a great president of my new movie studio. I rented the old River Park Casino building on the waterfront in Harlem and am turning it into a movie studio to be called Cosmopolitan Pictures. I'll pay you a big salary."

I nodded my acceptance, kissing him all over his face. At twenty-one years old, I quit the stage where I was making $75 a week as a showgirl and began working as president—and first movie star—of Cosmopolitan Pictures. I made $500 a week.

CHAPTER 8

NEW YORK, 1918

A few months later, at home in Gramercy Park, wedding bells rang when Rose married George Van Cleve, a set manager in the theater district. Now two of my sisters had married a George. If Ethel could just find a George, we'd have a threesome. The wedding was small but respectable and held at our local church.

"You're a beautiful bride," I said, pinning a white rose in her hair before she walked down the aisle. We had found sisterly love again since the awkward family dinner starring WR. Our relationship felt like a warm sweater, and I snuggled into her.

She was never happier than when we all fussed over her. Since it was her big day, we lovingly obliged. Reine adjusted a fold in Rose's silk wedding dress, which had lace panels and a round neckline that clung to her figure just right. I reshaped a curl that hung too low as Ethel watched Rose beam in the mirror.

George Van Cleve was a kind, forty-two-year-old man who cared more for family than getting rich—a blessing in my eyes but not in Mama's. When Rose moved into George's less-than-fancy home a few miles away, Mama scowled but seemed resigned to the reality.

Done with being passed over on the stage, Rose quit acting and began to try for children. I hoped she'd married George for love, but like the murky waters of the sea, nothing was clear when it came to Rose. She had all her truths and treasures buried like a good pirate.

As she settled into her new married life, I began my employment at Cosmopolitan Pictures, working sixteen-hour days filming my first full-length feature called *Cecilia of the Pink Roses*, about a spunky Irish girl faced with the death of her mother. I was not just the movie's star, I was the producer and the president as well, giving WR the role of ringmaster, teaching me all aspects of the movie industry, and paying me for multiple positions. I was the circus worker trying to balance plates on my head while spinning them in opposite directions.

As ringmaster, WR knew the industry from top to bottom, with players like Adolph Zukor and his Paramount Studios located just across the river in Astoria, Long Island. Cecil B. De Mille and D.W. Griffith were filming all over New York, along with producers Thomas Ince and Samuel Goldwyn.

WR had gotten in on the ground floor of the industry in early 1905, first by producing short newsreels to promote his newspapers and then episodic film serials like *The Mysteries of Myra* and *The Exploits of Elaine*, which would run before feature-length pictures in movie houses. Cosmopolitan Pictures was the next step in WR's evolution as a ringmaster-studio owner-head of industry.

There wasn't a studio job at which WR didn't consider himself to be superb, including writing, directing, editing, and, most of all, advertising. Words like "masterpiece, stupendous, and colossal" were used to describe me and the production of *Cecilia of the Pink Roses*.

I was hesitant to bring it up, but the advertising of me and the movie was getting out of hand, so much so that even my mother had mentioned it. We sat in his studio office having tea during a break in filming.

"Mama called again today to say she saw the full-page ad for *Cecilia*. It's the fourth one she's seen in just the last few days. She says the photos of me seem to be getting bigger."

He glanced up at me. "We're getting close to finishing this picture, and I'm ramping up the publicity."

No kidding, I thought.

He continued, "I featured you heavily in the advertisements because you are the star and you are beautiful. I want the whole country to know it."

It stung how he promoted my beauty but never my talent. I took a final sip of my tea, "Believe me, everyone knows about this movie," I said, leaving his office feeling hurt and misunderstood.

"Good!" he called after me, oblivious to my concerns.

I burned with self-doubt. WR had such belief in me, but it seemed I was only a pretty picture to look at. I loved acting, but moving from the stage to movies required a major revision of my skills. The movie camera caught every little facial gesture, and I needed to learn to control the movements of my eyebrows and mouth. The art of saying my lines, fully aware that the audience couldn't hear me, took some practice. As in all silent movies, the written lines flashed on the screen in a frame all their own after I spoke them, so the trick was not to enunciate the words too much but rather to speak normally—and of course without stuttering.

The next afternoon during another break in filming, I headed to WR's office and overheard one of his newspaper men announce the arrival of a telegram from Millicent.

I stopped in the hallway and stood stone still, listening. WR said, "Read it."

Paper crinkled and a voice read, "Stop promoting that girl so much in your papers. You are making a fool of yourself, swooning over that child. Our friends are beginning to talk."

I tiptoed away before anyone caught me eavesdropping and avoided WR for the rest of the afternoon. How could he not see he was overdoing the publicity? I saw it. Ethel and Mama saw it. Millicent saw it too. I hated seeing eye-to-eye with her. I never wanted to be on her side. Never. But I had to admit she was right to chastise him.

WR joined me at the studio dining table a few hours later as I waited for my dinner to arrive. A full kitchen with a chef and server were employed on site so we would have no reason to leave the building during filming hours. Blowing smoke from my cigarette toward the door, I sipped my tea.

"I'm decorating the Rivoli for opening night," he boasted. "I want everything to be perfect and predict there won't be a dry eye in the house when the film ends."

The Rivoli Theater was in the Broadway district and the sister theater to the Rialto and Roxy. I couldn't imagine how WR was going to decorate it for the opening of my movie, since the Rivoli's interior looked like the Parthenon. But I was learning there was no dissuading WR when he got his heart and mind set on something. I tried not to feel overwhelmed by it all—wanting to be a serious actress and do a good job, while also pleasing WR.

I also wanted my dinner. "Your plans sound wonderful, but I'm so hungry I can barely speak. I need food." The workers were changing the set from a kitchen to a living room scene. I listened to them putting down carpeting, bringing in a sofa and two chairs, lighting the room like a home.

He plowed on. "I've hired a press agent to create some inter- est in you as an actress and of course in the movie. Her name is Rosy Shulsinger, and she's coming to meet you tomorrow."

"A press agent? Do we honestly need more press?"

"To be a legitimate actress, you need a press agent. Mary Pickford has two press agents," he said matter-of-factly.

I stared blankly at the men working, acutely aware that WR wanted my career to go exactly the way Mary Pickford's had gone, with worldwide fame and dozens of successful movies to her credit. I wanted that too—maybe, but WR seemed to need it immediately for reasons I surmised included proof of his success as a movie studio owner. At that moment, though, I didn't care about press agents, publicity, or premiere night. Not bothering to hide my short-temperedness, I whined, "My feet hurt and I have a headache. I need some food." I crushed out my cigarette and walked away from the table to take a breath, irritated at absolutely everything.

"Of course, darling," he said.

When I returned a few minutes later WR was gone, but pot roast, mashed potatoes, and carrots had finally arrived.

— ◯ —

We attended the premiere of *Cecilia of the Pink Roses* a few months later amid freezing temperatures in June, the likes of which hadn't been seen in decades, the papers said. Shaking from the cold wind whipping outside, I entered the Rivoli and found thousands of pink rosebuds attached to the wall around the movie screen with electric fans blowing the heavenly scent directly toward the audience. Men and women alike rushed to touch the roses before taking their seats, pointing and chatting about the spectacle. Wearing a pink chiffon dress with pink rosebuds in my swept-up hair, I smiled to myself at how big WR made everything. I really did love him and his impressively quirky ideas—and how he could turn them into reality. I squeezed his hand and he closed his palm around my fist, nesting it securely and warmly.

Earlier in the day he'd had pink rosebuds personally delivered to me. I now saw that the roses around the screen matched the rosebuds in my hair. As ringmaster he knew how to take people's breath away, mine included.

It was strange and uncomfortable to see myself up on the enormous screen. The movie was so much more professional than *Runaway Romany*. Still, I cringed and was fascinated in equal parts. At the movie's end, the audience didn't cry their eyes out in happiness as WR had predicted. Instead, they clapped hesitantly. I had learned from *Runaway Romany* that watching a movie with a live audience was very different than watching with the editors and director at the studio. I looked at WR to see if the lukewarm response disappointed him, but he seemed content. My beginner acting skills needed work, but I hadn't embarrassed myself too badly.

I took the audience's reaction as a fire under me to get to work, learning from Pickles and the theater girls to work hard every day. I vowed to do better, hoping to talk WR into some silly, rambunctious roles.

After the party that evening, as I removed the many pink rosebuds and brushed out my hair, I caught WR studying me in the mirror from the bed, taking a break from reading one of his papers.

"Thank you for a wonderful premiere tonight. The roses were just gorgeous. You wowed everybody. Can I just ask that you stop featuring me so prominently in your newspapers? It feels like you're trying to convince the audience I'm a good actress, when I'm not yet."

"Nonsense. You were beautiful, little Rosebud. I'm sorry you're uncomfortable with the publicity. I hope you'll get used to it."

"I don't think I will," I mumbled. But he didn't hear me.

"I own these newspapers, and I own the movie company, and I—"

"Don't you dare say you own me."

WR squinted at me, "Of course not, darling. I was going to say I can use my newspapers to promote my own movies if I want."

Feeling defeated, I lit a cigarette. "Speaking of owning things, did the detective find anything in Palm Beach?"

It had been another year since WR had said anything to me about his progress in getting a divorce. Avoidance of the subject seemed to be his permanent tactic.

He folded the newspaper that had been resting on his lap and drew in a long, deep, and exasperated breath. "No, he hasn't found anything. Millicent is as pure as ever. She's not an alcoholic, abusive to our children, or an adulterer. I can find no grounds to sue her for divorce."

"Indeed. *We're* the adulterers, WR."

"No, I won't say that. You're the person I should have always married, not her. We are meant to be together. I will never admit I'm an adulterer."

I asked softly, "What are we going to do?"

"She doesn't want the divorce because it would mean expulsion from high society. She would become an outcast. I fear she'll never agree." His voice dripped in sorrow.

I climbed into bed and turned out the light. WR snuggled in behind me and put his arms around me. "Please don't give up, Sweetheart. I'm not giving up. I have a few more new ideas about how to motivate her. Give me some more time."

"Call me Rosebud again," I said quietly.

"I love you, Rosebud," and he showed me.

— ⟨◯⟩ —

The following morning over coffee and toast, I read the reviews in the non-Hearst papers, which matched the tepid response the film had received from the audience. They wrote about the lavish theater decoration and all the roses. The actual movie, however, only got a small mention. As to my performance, they said I was "talentless, lacking in poise and grace while facing the camera." *Motion Picture News* blamed "over-direction" for the failure of the movie. Like a small child, part of me wanted to hide under the covers. But another part of me realistically assessed my efforts and thought, "Let's make another one."

One glowing review, by Louella Parsons of the non-Hearst paper the *New York Telegraph*, felt like the first daisy on a spring morning. I decided to invite her to lunch to see if her review was genuine, or if she had ulterior motives and was just looking for her own publicity. My press agent, Rosy, set up the lunch at the Bridge Cafe for the following week. It was agreed that neither of us would mention it to WR. I discovered Rosy to be a go-getter. I could tell we were going to work well together—that she was going to work for me, not just WR.

I arrived at the red brick building on the corner of Water and Dover Streets fifteen minutes late so I could make a bit of an entrance. I found Louella, looking fierce and sitting at a corner table furiously scribbling in a notebook. Her dark blue suit and white blouse were professional, and her plain shoulder-length brown hair was parted on the side. I recognized a Singapore Sling in front of her, a drink I had grown to love in the past year.

"Louella, it's nice to see you. Thank you for meeting me," I said sitting down, feeling the nerves in my stomach churning. I lit a cigarette and took a long drag.

"It's nice to meet you too. Boy, it's true what they say about your blue, blue eyes—they certainly are piercing."

"You're very kind." I put the cigarette out, took a roll from the basket, and buttered it.

The waiter arrived and offered us menus. I ordered a Singapore Sling.

"If you don't mind my asking, how long have you been making films?"

"Well, let me think," I said, stuttering on the final word and blushing. "It's been less than two years, I guess. Not much time at all."

"You are just adorable. I can't get over it. You're like a glowing crystal chandelier."

I tried not to blush deeper at her compliment. "Thank you for such a kind review of my movie. *Cecilia* was a fair movie, and my acting was less than fair, according to the newspapers, so I especially appreciated your kind words, if they're genuine." I took a bite of my roll.

"Of course my review was genuine. I'm trying to make a name for myself, too, darling. Don't be so down on yourself. You have no false illusions about your own talent even though Mr. Hearst and his newspapers promote you to a fault. Your performance was solid, and if I were you, I'd be proud. It's a great little picture," she said.

Getting an outsider's honest appraisal of my work gave me a small bit of courage to relax. Of course, the two Singapore Slings didn't hurt. Louella and I shared stories and gossip from the theater, realizing we knew many of the same people.

"Have you heard that Frances Marion was put under contract to Mary Pickford after the great success of *The Poor Little Rich Girl*? She's making $50,000 a year now. Unheard of!"

I wondered if WR had heard this news and made a mental note to ask him. We got on famously sharing small bits about our families, laughing along the way. Louella was funny, fearless, and unapologetic. After telling her of the day I met WR, she boldly said, "Gene Buck is a lecherous old man. I'm glad you steered clear of him."

Louella was a beacon in the newspaper industry for me, a woman I could form a professional friendship with. My career was being built one brick at a time, and I hoped Louella could be a critical piece. She gave me one more reason to forge ahead, and I held my head a little higher that day.

— ⓪ —

I soon learned that making four or five movies a year was the industry standard. With only a week of rest after the release of *Cecilia*, we began filming my next picture, *The Burden of Proof*. I opted to stay at the Gramercy Park house with Mama and my sisters. I wasn't specifically avoiding WR, although I didn't worry too much about how he felt, knowing he had so many things occupying his time. Instead, I reasoned with myself that I needed some family time. I especially missed Ethel and needed some shopping, walking, and talking time with her. Settling into the permanent life of a mistress, I needed guidance from my rock.

A telegram from WR arrived on the third day I was at home: "I miss you. Come home."

I called Norman to drive me to the apartment that afternoon, and I found WR working at the dining room table. "Rosebud, I've missed you. Why are you staying away?"

"I'm not staying away. I miss my sisters and Mama, not to mention Charlie and Pepi," I said as I made myself a cup of tea. "Please, don't take it personally."

"I do take it personally when I come to the apartment and you're never here."

He immediately began to tell me that he'd been looking for a large place for my family on the Upper West side. "I've been considering this for a while since I know how close you are to them, and I want Cosmopolitan's only movie star living in the luxury she deserves."

"So, it's a publicity thing?"

"Don't get upset. It's not all publicity—not completely, but it is important you live like the star you are, and I found a gorgeous building on Riverside Drive with seven bedrooms."

I suspected that in WR's eyes, living in Gramercy Park wasn't nearly star-like enough. "That's definitely big enough," I said, liking the idea of my entire family, including my little niece and nephew, living in a palatial estate. A quick flash in my mind saw Mama happily reading a newspaper in her lavishly ornate bed. I took my empty cup and saucer to the kitchen and stared out the window at the tops of all the buildings and the bright blue sky. This was an important step in our relationship, I could feel it. I tried not to get swept up in the luxury of it all. I returned to the living room. "Wait a minute, don't Millicent and your sons live on Riverside Drive?"

Ignoring my question, he opened his arms up beckoning me to him. "I want you to be happy, my dear."

I curled up in his lap, wrapping my arms around his neck. He cuddled and kissed me. "You haven't answered my question," I whispered into his neck.

"Yes, they live three long blocks up the street. Why does it matter? It's a nice neighborhood."

I leaned back and looked deeply into his lapis blue eyes. I could see my life straight ahead on a platinum path to stardom, fame, and wealth, but that path would be tainted, always, by Millicent, who stood like a statue in our lives. Still, how could I turn him down? He was offering to lift my family into super wealth. The butterflies in my stomach fluttered at the idea of being able to truly take care of Mama. *Publicity may not be so bad after all*, I thought. I cleared my throat. "It is *definitely* a nice neighborhood." If he didn't care that his wife and kids were so close, then why should I? "Can we still keep the apartment for you and me?" I whispered, kissing him all over his face.

"Absolutely, and I'm looking at a penthouse just for us near Central Park as well."

I kissed him deeply. "Thank you for everything."

CHAPTER 9

Mama, Ethel, Reine, Charlie, and Pepi, along with Rose and George—who were expecting again after a miscarriage—all moved with me to 331 Riverside Drive in the late summer of 1918. Mama insisted on our housekeeper Netty coming with us even though WR had hired a full staff to cook and clean. The five-story Renaissance-style building had high ceilings and marble floors. The red velvet drapes hung from ceiling to floor and gave the formal living room a stately feel that made Ethel ask, "Gawd, are we this fancy?"

We each got an allowance from WR to decorate our bedrooms. "When can we go shopping?" Rose asked standing in the hallway, looking at a row of bedroom doors. "I'm decorating one as a nursery," she said, allowing her hopes to soar. A marble fountain with two cupids was the centerpiece of the sitting room, just outside my bedroom. Mama's bedroom was the biggest, and WR had installed a cherry wood Renaissance queen canopy bed that looked like an actual queen slept there.

"Oh Marion, how can we ever get used to living like this?" Mama almost cried as she spoke. "You tell WR how grateful we are. How can we possibly accept this?"

The library was paneled in dark wood, and the shelves were filled with rare editions of bound leather books. WR had taken it upon himself to educate me on the classics.

A sense of pride and love grew inside me that WR was taking care of my family. He loved me and wanted my family to be comfortable. Me, the tomboy and youngest sister had delivered in a way Mama couldn't have possibly imagined.

I didn't mention Millicent's close proximity, although I secretly wondered whether she and Mama would run into each other strolling through Riverside Park—not that Millicent would recognize my plain-looking Mama. Some self-satisfied feeling grew in me at them sharing the same outdoor space.

A few months after we moved in, WR bought Papa a four-room apartment next door in the twin Renaissance building. Papa told his friends in Brooklyn it was an office allowing him to be closer to his family, but everybody knew he was living there too. His pride wouldn't let him acknowledge the ostentatious gift.

The lifting of my entire family into super wealth had been achieved. A twinge of something twisted ever so slightly in my stomach, making it the first inkling I had of trading myself for my family's well-being.

— ⟲ —

During the last days of filming *The Belle of New York,* I stood at the window in our shared apartment overlooking the Manhattan skyline, searching the distant horizon in vain for WR. He had been gone for an eon, it felt. My thoughts cast inward as my hand rubbed my belly at the beginning of yet another day alone. The puffy white clouds were painted with the morning light when a wave of nausea begin to build, at first small and then increasingly larger until my mouth watered and I raced for the bathroom where I heaved what felt like everything I'd eaten in the past week. This went on for days.

I hid out at the apartment now, away from the watchful eye of Mama, Ethel, and especially Rose, who had lost yet another pregnancy and was preparing to try yet again for a child. The hope she possessed boggled my mind.

Panic about my condition overcame me at times. I sent for Sophie, the midwife our family had used since Mama began having babies thirty years earlier. She arrived at the apartment promptly, her trademark unruly gray hair refusing to stay in a bun at the base of her neck.

"You must not say anything to Mama or my sisters about this. Promise me now," I pleaded.

She closed her eyes for a long blink and nodded. A short time later she confirmed my fears. "You're pregnant, due late spring/ early summer." The words slid into me like a knife.

Shock was my first emotion. We were always so careful. I had recently begun using a new contraceptive method from the Netherlands called a diaphragm. It obviously failed. My second emotion was pure panic at what WR would say. My heart beat alternately between hope that he'd be happy and despair that he'd be angry.

I took time to think, walking alone through the wind-whipped commercial streets of New York on a day that felt very cold for late fall, matching the way I felt inside. I wrapped a scarf around my neck and shuffled my feet down the street, staring ahead in a trance-like state until the smell of freshly brewed coffee floated out of a nearby restaurant and startled me to the unfamiliar neighborhood I had wandered into. The smell nearly gagged me, and the bile came up my throat, when normally coffee would have tempted me. I made it back to the apartment, crawled into the darkened bedroom and hid out under the covers, wishing to escape. The fact of this baby grew larger every day. I loved WR. I knew that much. This baby was confirmation of our love; however, I wanted to be his wife, not his pregnant mistress hidden away from respectable life. I wished life were simpler and that picking a wedding date was my only concern. I laid out my options like stones on a path ahead of me.

Having a baby out of wedlock as an unmarried woman would be the end of my life with WR, my career, and everything we had built together. There would be no mystery about the fact that WR was the father, given the rumors already swirling around us for the past few years. Having the baby would force high-society folks to actually acknowledge our sinful relationship instead of politely looking the other way, and I would lose everything—ostracized from decent society.

Powerful men sometimes got away with philandering, but never women. WR had told me how the world treated famous architect Frank Lloyd Wright after he left his wife and family for another woman.

"Frank and Mamah Borthwick Cheney fell in love, left their spouses and children behind, and escaped to Europe for a year. When they returned to Chicago, they were pariahs—and Frank couldn't find design work for years."

My mind swirled with the additional fact of a baby. There would be no way WR would abandon his entire life, his newspaper empire, Millicent and the boys, and run away with me to Europe to have this baby.

Our choices were few: adoption or abortion. Abortion was illegal and would be a heartbreaking choice. Money would give me access to safer alternatives. Sophie was a discreet resource, and I kept the fact of the pregnancy between her and myself while I pondered my choices and continued to work.

I ran Cosmopolitan Pictures via telegrams with WR while he was visiting his aging mother, Phoebe, in San Francisco, and his family property in San Simeon, California, for more than two months. Communicating via telegram meant I would ask WR questions, then he would decide what to do, send me a telegram with instructions, and I would implement the plan. He was gone so long this time, we were able to film the end of *The Belle of*

New York and begin filming *Getting Mary Married*—an ironic title considering my real-life situation. Joking with WR in my telegrams, I called the film *Getting Marion Married*, although he never acknowledged my nudges. The daily runs were sent to him via courier, no matter where he was, for review and approval.

At the studio, we still laughed and had fun filming, though we certainly weren't as focused or dedicated as WR would have wished us to be. But he was gone, and I was alone facing it all by myself.

I was able to forget my pregnancy in the afternoons while we worked. Fun was what I needed, darn it. My handsome costar Norman Kerry, who played my love interest in *Getting Mary Married*, enjoyed a practical joke as much as I did, and we tried to one-up each other regularly. During one specific three-day period, we were wild and silly. I'd emerge on cue from the side door with one of my teeth blackened so that in closeups my smile would shock, or he would arrive on set dressed as a woman. This fun only confirmed that my real joy in life was comedy. I wished WR would let me play to the audience for laughs instead of casting me in such serious parts.

The downside of all the games we played while WR was out of town was the cost. Arriving late each day due my morning sickness, taking longer lunches and breaks that may have included a drink or two, and staging our practical jokes meant the director, cast, and crew of designers, costume, and hair people sat around while we had our fun dancing and playing music. This burned up WR's money. I knew WR's business associates reported on our behavior, but he looked the other way and let us have our fun.

As the days ticked on, I became anxious to be near him again and confront our difficult choices. He'd been gone more than two months, and my morning sickness raged on. A telegram arrived one morning informing me of his imminent arrival that evening, so I decided to go shopping for a new dress. Cutting out of the movie studio early, I headed to Lord and Taylor. A surge of anger at WR for making me wait for him so long overcame me, and I bought seven dresses.

That evening I ordered champagne for the occasion, making sure all my dresses hung prominently around the living room. I waited hours as the champagne warmed, going over how I would tell him about the baby. I went to bed at midnight exhausted and dejected.

Sometime in the early hours, he crawled into bed and pulled me close, nestling into my neck. Shrugging him off with a whimper, I scooted closer to the edge and he eventually rolled over and fell asleep. I listened to his breathing for a time and then fell asleep myself, despondent and hurt yet desperate for him.

I woke to an empty bed the next morning and found him in the kitchen having coffee. "Are you redecorating the living room with dresses, or do you have something to tell me?"

"I went overboard yesterday, I know, but I'm mad at you for leaving me alone so long. I swear I almost bought the entire women's department at Lord and Taylor just to punish you."

He put his coffee down and lifted my chin up. His eyes were soft. "Tell me what's going on."

The smell of the coffee gagged me and I ran from the table. He called after me. "Marion, are you okay?"

There was no gentle way to break the news. When I emerged from the bathroom, I blurted out, "I'm pregnant."

"Oh love." He hugged me close, caressing my hair as I laid my head on his chest. He kissed the top of my head and whispered, "What shall we do, my sweetheart?"

"I want to keep it," I said, and crawled up on his lap, wrapping my arms around his neck, burrowing in.

"I don't know how we could do that," he whispered, stroking my hair.

"Can't you fix it? You fix everything else in our lives. Get the divorce now before I'm too far along, and we can get married."

I sat up in his lap and saw him staring into space, looking pale and as if he might also throw up. "I want to keep it as well love, but . . ." His voice trailed off as he turned his head away from me.

A heaviness hung between us. I twisted my fingers and stared at the wall. "You have five sons. Maybe we could have a daughter," I said.

He stared like he was a thousand miles away. He needed to think. He needed time. "I'm going for a walk," I announced. I got off his lap, grabbed my coat, and left the apartment. The cold wind whipped between the buildings. I pulled down my hat and tucked my scarf around my neck. WR's response to the pregnancy was expected. He was a serious man of business, and although I truly believed he loved me, I knew he couldn't give up everything for this baby.

When I returned, he was reading. I sat on the arm of his chair and put my hand on his shoulder. "I'm so very sad. I know we can't keep the baby. I wanted to believe you could miraculously work it out."

"I wish there were some miracle I could perform, I really do," he said.

— ⟁ —

I slept for two days, unable to leave the bed, eat, or even pull back the drapes. WR made my excuses at the studio, saying I had the flu.

On my next visit home, I confided my problem to my best sister Ethel and dear sweet Rose, who was pregnant yet again.

"WR and I have talked," I explained after breaking the big news, "and I'll have to decide what to do soon."

We figured Rose was about four weeks further along than me, and the fact that we wouldn't be sharing our pregnancies and child-rearing was heartbreaking for me. I wanted nothing more than to share this baby with my sisters.

Rose lit a cigarette, handed it to me, then lit one for herself. "My heart breaks for you. What will you do?"

"I'll get Sophie to help me no matter what I decide."

"Sophie's a jewel. Will you tell Mama?" Ethel asked. Always steady, loving, and supportive, it seemed that nothing could rock her. I marveled at her reaction—no shock—just practical problem-solving and love.

"I haven't decided yet. My first reaction is no. I don't want to upset her when there's nothing I can do to keep the baby."

We sat in silence for a while longer as we smoked, considering it all. Rose looked content and put her hand over mine. Ethel added hers on top in a show of solidarity. Outside the kitchen window were bare branches, and the sky was a gray shade of winter. There was no time to waste, a decision had to be made in the next week.

— ⓪ —

George called a few days later. "Come quickly, Rose is having difficulties." I arrived less than an hour later to find Mama, Reine, and Ethel with Rose as she lay in bed with severe cramps. I rushed to her side and gave her a kiss, taking her hand in mine. Sophie placed warm rags on her forehead.

"I'm losing it . . . again," she sniffled. "I've been bleeding for the past twenty hours, and there's nothing Sophie can do."

I hung my head and kissed my sister's hand. This would be her third miscarriage.

After the procedure was finished two hours later, Rose lay dozing when I brought her tea. Pulling the chair closer to the bed, I slept fitfully through the night and climbed into bed with her in the early morning hours.

I left for work on the assurance that Mama would call if Rose got worse. That afternoon an idea struck me, and I rushed back to the house and burst into Rose's room.

"What is it, Marion? Please tell me what has happened," Rose said, looking pale. Closing my eyes tightly, I took a depth breath and blurted it out fast. "What if we never tell anybody you had a miscarriage, and instead you and I go away, I have this baby, and you adopt it and raise it as your own?"

Rose was quiet, so I grabbed her hand. "WR would pay for everything."

"Of course he'll pay," she said quietly. She had a small but genuine half-smile on her face, and she cocked her head to the side and lit a cigarette. "I don't know. Maybe it could work."

"I haven't even asked WR yet. I'm sure he'd support whatever I wanted," I said. "It's better than adopting the baby out to strangers, or worse, having an abortion."

"You're right about that. I can't imagine either of those things," Rose said.

"We won't ever be able to tell anybody the truth. I will always be Aunt Marion."

"Except the family, right?"

"Yes, except the family."

"I'll talk to George tonight. You talk to WR," Rose said, straightening herself.

I took her hand and gazed at her for a long moment, overwhelmed with so many emotions—happiness and gratitude, fear and longing. A tear welled up, and I turned away from her.

"What is it?" she asked, taking my hand.

"Oh nothing, just me being sappy and grateful to be on the same side again and maybe finding a solution we can both live with." I turned her hand over in my lap, twisting her wedding ring and wondering if we were moving too fast. "You *can* live with this, right? Do you need some time to think before we ask the men?"

"Absolutely not. I don't need any more time. It feels right to me." Then she added, "I, too, am grateful to have you solidly back in my heart, sweet Marion. I love you, sister."

"I love you too, Rose." The tears welled up again, and I let them come. I curled up with her, and she rubbed my back. We huddled together like we were young girls again, both crying and hanging on to each other. I cried for the loss of motherhood and marriage and for the hard choices we were both making.

After the crying had stopped and we lay quiet for a while, Rose sniffled and wiped her nose, asking, "Do we want a girl or a boy?"

"A girl," I whispered, hugging her close.

It had been a long time since I overflowed with hope and excitement for the future. Coming from the near depths of despair at my choices with this pregnancy made the ascent even sweeter. Not only did I have a solution for my predicament, but Rose had a solution for hers as well.

— Ⓧ —

At the apartment that night, I shared my idea with WR, who looked skeptical.

"Please! It's the perfect solution for us—and for Rose." I beamed at him. "She'll adopt our baby, and we'll be the best aunt and uncle we can be."

"Will you be able to let Rose be the mother? Will you be able to distance yourself from the baby in that way?" he asked.

"I believe I can," I said, then repeated myself with more force.

"The world will find out. There's already so much gossip about us. And when they do, what will happen?" WR asked as he caressed my arm.

"We'll deny it. We'll deny it until our death. They won't be able to prove it."

"And your family? Do you really think they can keep quiet?"

"I know they can. Their hearts are broken for the three miscarriages Rose and George have had. They would be devastated if I adopted this baby out to strangers. And they're so grateful for everything you've done for them that they would never betray me . . . or you."

"If you're certain, then okay," he said, rubbing his forehead.

I kissed him, holding his face in my hands and looking deeply into his eyes. "I'm certain. You won't regret this, I promise."

CHAPTER 10

PARIS, 1919

George, Rose, and I left for Paris in early spring when I was a little more than five months pregnant. We sailed incognito aboard a French ocean liner under the name Van Cleve just to be safe. WR picked the French ship because it was currently sailing back and forth between New York and Le Havre, France, ferrying American troops home after the war. "You'll be aboard a mostly empty ship going back to France, and nobody will bother you," WR had said, and he was right.

First-class passage meant two well-appointed cabins connected by a stately living room and library. The butler and maid took care of all my housekeeping and culinary needs. The first few nights aboard the ship, I smoked too much, crawled into bed, and cried myself to sleep. I missed WR so much my chest ached. I had never been to Europe before and knew we'd be gone until at least July. It would be an eternity before I would be home again.

About halfway through our nine-day trip, the seasickness ended and I began to feel stronger. WR had fresh flowers delivered to my bedside table every day at sea. I marveled at the lilies, roses, and tulips but burst into tears the third day at the thought of him arranging the daily deliveries before we left New York. Pregnancy had made me a sap, and I loved him dearly. I found a bag of books WR had sent with me for possible movie stories we might produce together, including *Howards End* by E. M. Forster, *The Restless Sex* by Robert W. Chambers, and the heartwarming tale of *Lad: A Dog* by Albert Payson Terhune.

When I was finally feeling well enough to eat in the dining room one evening, Rose, George, and I enjoyed steak, shrimp, and clam chowder. As I swallowed a bite of bread, I felt a swishing and tugging in my belly. I grabbed my stomach in reflex and gasped for air. "He wants out already," I said as I put my fork down and pushed back against my chair.

"Nonsense! He just loves the rocking of the ship and is keeping time," Rose said as she smiled at George.

"Yes, I suppose you're right," I grinned, making myself imagine the baby in their arms as they cooed over him. I denied myself any sentimentality about the baby, trying to be strong and do as I had promised everyone, knowing it was good for me to see this baby as Rose's before he was outside of my womb.

This trip was a honeymoon of sorts for Rose and George. They stole away to dance after dinner, played cards with the few other passengers in the game room, and attended services in the chapel a few evenings a week. I was happy to let them have their time together as I read my books in bed, walked the decks, and wrote long letters to WR and my family.

After our long ocean crossing and another long day traveling from Le Havre to Paris by train, we checked into Le Meurice, a hotel WR had arranged. The weather was spectacular, warm and bright with blooming trees and flowers everywhere. A few days after we arrived, we were met by Alice Head, one of WR's London business associates who took us to see two apartments. Alice was warm and friendly with a round face and figure and a dozen or so years older than me. Rose and I debated the choice of apartments while sitting at a sidewalk café, watching crowds rush past.

"I like the neo-Gothic building in the Latin Quarter. It's on a quiet dead-end street across from a busy square, and close enough to the hospital, don't you think?" I said to Alice as I sipped my tea.

"Yes, I believe the hospital is only four kilometers away," she nodded. "Good choice."

WR had obviously informed Alice of our intentions and predicament and probably threatened her silence in the matter. I was grateful not to have to discuss the intimacies.

"It'll be perfect for watching the horse chestnut and linden trees swaying in the breeze, and entertaining to watch the Sorbonne students in the plaza," Rose added, looking at George for confirmation.

We were settled in comfort, luxury, and tranquility within a week of arriving in Paris. We unpacked, and I rearranged my books and papers on the living room desk.

A few days later, George returned to New York, leaving Rose and me to find a routine. Three weeks into our stay, word came by telegram from WR that his mother had died. I read part of the obituary enclosed in the telegram to Rose: "At seventy-six years old, Phoebe Apperson Hearst died of complications of the flu."

"That's terrible," Rose said, taking a puff of her cigarette. "The pandemic has spread over the entire country, and it's tragic. What else does it say?"

"Not much. It gives the details of the funeral in San Francisco. WR says he hopes to visit me soon."

"Is WR's father still living?"

"No. George Hearst was much older than Phoebe, maybe forty years older. He died decades ago." I lit a cigarette and stared out the window.

"Tell me a little more about his family."

I tried to remember what WR had told me. "I know WR is an only child and heir to the silver fortune amassed by his father in 1860s California. His mom and dad both came from a small farming town in Missouri. It doesn't seem possible when you look at him."

"Farmers? No. I would have guessed European aristocracy or something," Rose said, her eyes lighting up.

"I know his mother was a teacher, and when WR was ten she took him on a year-long tour of Europe where they visited castles, museums, and various cultural centers to learn about history firsthand."

"Wow, that's impressive. I wish Mama would have taken us on a European tour."

We sat in silence while Rose read her magazine, and I watched the students in the square across the street dodge the rain that had begun to fall. I knew from his letters that WR had been on the West Coast organizing the architectural plans at his family property in San Simeon. I also knew how grateful he must have been to be near his mother when she passed. I took a sip of my tea. I would never meet her nor have a mother-in-law I could share my child with. In fact, as far as anyone in the world was concerned, I would never have a child at all. Oh, how I wished things were different.

At twenty-two, I wished for all the things that weren't possible: to be WR's wife and to raise our child together; laugh and hear stories of his youth from his mother; and be a family together. A pang rose in me at the choices I felt forced to make.

Since arriving in Paris, I had a glimpse into what my life might be like living here. Why not have the baby and raise it alone in a gilded life WR set up for me? After all, wouldn't he be with Millicent and their five sons in San Francisco burying the great Phoebe Apperson Hearst, sharing memories and family time? Wouldn't I always be off to the side of WR's life, alone and away from his real family like I was now?

I looked at Rose sipping her tea, grateful for my sister and her willingness to step into the motherhood she deserved. Trying not to feel denied and shaking off the self-pitying thoughts, I sent my condolences to WR.

— ◎ —

Nearing my eighth month, after we had just returned from another doctor's appointment and a long walk along the Seine, a sharp knock at the door startled us. Exhausted with swollen ankles, I shot Rose a look. "Can you get it, please?"

She opened the door to a wall of yellow, red, white, and purple roses.

"Oh my," she said.

WR pushed his face through the opening between the roses. "I'm looking for Rosebud and Rose," he said. The cart of flowers came through the door with force, driven by the doorman. WR's toothy grin covered his entire face. He tipped the doorman and closed the door behind him. My heart filled with love and my eyes blurred at the sight of him in his long traveling jacket and hat. His eyes sparkled and I waddled over to him, crying, "WR, you're here!"

He bent over and let me kiss his face. "Here, take these and I can give you a proper hug." He held two boxes wrapped in gold paper, one with a white ribbon and one with a pink ribbon. He handed them to Rose and scooped me up gently, planting kisses all over my face. "How is my sweetheart, my little Rosebud? You are beautiful—glowing like a candle."

"Oh, I'm fine. Fat and swollen and ready for this baby to come out." I was positively gushing at the surprise of him being there. "I was beginning to wonder if you would make it before the birth."

WR simply couldn't be in Paris at the time of the birth to keep him clear of any possible scandal. We had agreed back in New York it wasn't safe. I accepted the conditions WR had laid out with the logistics of this birth and knew he was taking good care of me. Sneaking to see me this close to the birth was a gamble, but I knew he was careful. We couldn't forget the price we'd both pay if this story ever made the papers.

WR kissed Rose on each cheek in the French custom, and she blushed when he pulled a single purple rose out and handed it to her. "Thank you for taking such good care of our girl. How are you, dear?"

"I'm fine. Have some tea with us. I'll order a special dinner," Rose said, adding, "My condolences for your mother."

"Thank you." WR sat down next to me and took my hand. "Do you have any idea how long it takes to travel from California to Paris? More than twelve days!" He brushed my cheek lovingly with the back of his hand.

"But you stopped in New York and London for a few days of business, right?"

"Yes, my dear. I have to take care of things as I pass through town," he said.

"Well, thank you, my darling, for enduring such hardship. It's delightful to see you." I gave him a kiss. "Did you bring each of us a gift?" I asked, eyeing the boxes. He coaxed me into his lap, and I wrapped my arms around his neck. "I don't seem to fit as well as I did before," I said, adjusting myself.

"Nonsense, you fit perfectly. Open them, yes. Let's celebrate!"

"You first," I said to Rose.

She opened her box with the pink ribbon and pulled out a gold Tiffany cocktail watch encrusted with diamonds. The light sparkled off the gemstones as she held it up. She gasped like a child on Christmas morning, fitting it to her wrist. "Thank you so much. It's absolutely beautiful," she choked out. He nodded.

"You next," she said to me.

Inside my blue Tiffany box, I found the most exquisite solid gold olive leaf and pearl tassel necklace.

"Pull it out," WR instructed. "It's long." I lifted it out and saw that the gold chain was covered in mini pearls with a tassel at the bottom and a dozen short strands of baby pearls splashing out.

I put it over my neck. "Exquisite," I said as I held the tassel. "Thank you, my sweetheart." I kissed him and looked over at Rose, who looked as enchanted as I felt.

•—⟨⟨⟩⟩—•

The week flew by like a streak of light. WR had to work a few hours each day editing stories for his newspapers and such. We spent late mornings in bed eating and reading, talking very little about my pregnancy, only reviewing our agreement on the adoption to Rose and George. The baby was business to WR now—a series of decisions that needed to be made discreetly. He was being strong for both of us, and I tried to join him in this thinking.

WR gave Rose and me a tour of the Louvre until my feet throbbed; he nearly had to carry me to the car. We found alone time in the afternoons to walk near Notre Dame Cathedral and the Seine. Enjoying the breeze off the water and the bright pink canopy of cherry blossom trees made me believe in magic and wishes and dreams that come true. I tucked an arm through WR's and leaned in toward him as we walked. He squeezed my arm and talked about life back in New York, telling me that even in my absence both my movie premieres in March and April were stupendous. "Rosy handled the events masterfully. And, I have news about your next movie. I've hired Frances Marion to write the script for *The Cinema Murder*."

"She's supposed to be very good."

"I've also hired her to write the script for *The Restless Sex*. Did you get a chance to read the book?"

We stood in the courtyard in front of Notre Dame Cathedral, staring up at the ugly, menacing gargoyles. I shook a little from their fierceness. WR moved us along. "Yes, the book was excellent. I'm so glad Frances is working with us now. I can't wait to focus on my work again."

On his last night in Paris, WR insisted on taking us out to a fancy dinner at the world famous Pavillon Ledoyen, an eighteenth-century restaurant located on the Champs-Élysées. I imagined he knew how much it would impress Rose, especially.

"Are we having a history lesson with our dinner tonight?" I teased.

"I'm afraid so. I must tell you that Napoleon ate there, and many more heroes of the past."

"I don't care about them. Tell me they have duck or lamb and I'll go," I said.

"Boy, do they have duck. Their duck is world class."

— ⦾ —

Later that evening, he escorted Rose and me from the limousine to the two-story restaurant with its massive windows and ornate ceiling. We each wore the jewelry WR had given us, and I caught WR's eyes sparkle in pride to show us off. Our table was in a corner on the first floor near one of the arched windows with a view of the lighted gardens. My big belly was impossible to disguise, even under the scrumptious powder blue dress I'd bought for the occasion. My eyes darted around the room as we approached our table to see if people were staring at us.

"God, I'm huge, aren't I!" I said, catching my reflection in the window. "I shouldn't be in public. It's scandalous."

"No, sister, not here in Paris. It's nothing. Look, there's another pregnant woman over there at that table."

"She's barely showing," I insisted, feeling exposed and wrong in coming out so late in my pregnancy to such a fine restaurant.

A tuxedoed man sitting by himself a few tables away seemed to be scanning the room but stopped when his eyes landed on our table. "See, that man is staring at us—at me and my belly." My eyes darted from Rose to WR to the man.

"Maybe he recognizes WR."

I challenged her with my eyes, answering forcefully, "He doesn't. He's scandalized that I'm in public like this."

Rose looked down, averting my eyes.

"Why are you so nervous, darling? He's only staring because you're so beautiful, absolutely shining in this light—your blue eyes matching your goddess dress."

I shook my head, disbelieving his flowery words.

"I think he's looking for somebody," Rose whispered.

Discreetly assessing the room, WR leaned toward me. "Rose is right. He's looking for somebody. Don't worry, darling."

"Okay, if you're sure," I said, trying not to look at the man and instead concentrating on the menu.

When the waiter arrived and took our order, the man left and I realized they were right. Nobody cared! WR and I were out in public, and I was nearly ready to burst with this baby—and nobody cared. "You know, this is the first restaurant we've eaten at in public, WR. Do you realize that?"

He stroked my arm. "Yes, it is."

I saw what a legitimate life would look like in Paris if I were to live here full time. The Parisians were progressive and accepting, unlike Americans who were stuffy and uptight.

— ◎ —

The next morning, we said our tearful goodbyes at the front door of our apartment. "Come home to me soon," WR said. "I'll keep the bed warm for you, darling Rosebud." He kissed me on the tip of my nose, smiled, and closed the door behind him. I knew he was headed for London to meet with Alice and his staff there, then back to New York.

Rose insisted on a walk that day in the gardens near the apartment. It was late May and we strolled arm in arm, admiring the cherry blossoms all around us.

"We are just weeks away from the birth. I am ready for this

baby to be yours now," I said as we walked. "I know it's a boy—I can feel it. WR has five boys, after all."

I told Rose what I hoped would happen—that I would deliver him and she would immediately take him as her own. I wouldn't breastfeed. I needed to release him to her right away to make a clean break and become his aunt, and for Rose to become his mother.

She squeezed my arm as we walked. "Whatever you wish," she said quietly. "Have you thought of names?"

"I don't know . . . maybe George. It's a name that appears on your side and on WR's side as well. What do you think?"

She nodded her agreement. "What if it's a girl?"

"It's not a girl. I know. I can feel it."

—◯—

Ten days later, I checked into the hospital with heavy contractions. Rose was not allowed to stay with me during the birth, and I burst into tears as they wheeled me away. I couldn't wait for it to be over. Later I wouldn't be able to recall much about the birth at all, only that I was sedated. When I woke up a nun placed the eight-pound, fifteen-ounce healthy baby girl in my arms and left the room.

"Hi, you little surprise of a girl. You were supposed to be a boy." I stroked the rolls on her arm that escaped the tight swaddle. Tucking her arm back inside the warmth of the blanket, I whispered, "Your daddy would be proud to have a daughter. I am so proud to be your mother." She was like a perfect loaf of bread just out of the oven, doughy and soft. Tears ran down my cheeks and my heart filled up with a new love I had never experienced before. Clearing my throat, I gave the speech I had been practicing.

"Rose will be your mother, but I won't be far and neither will your daddy. We will love you and watch you grow." I pulled her close to my chest, kissing her bald head.

The door opened and Rose peeked in. "Come in," I said, over-come by emotion welling up and swallowing hard to choke back a cry.

"How are you feeling? Did everything go okay?" she asked, leaning over to examine the baby who lay asleep in my arms. "She's so beautiful, Marion . . . scrumptious. Look at her tiny nose and fat cheeks."

Tears rolled down my cheeks. I wanted WR to be there to hold her and kiss her.

"And she's a girl," Rose said.

"Isn't that the best? She's our girl—healthy and so beautiful." We locked teary eyes for a moment. "Do you like the name Patricia?" I whispered. "I've always loved Patricia. It's so feminine."

"Yes, I love it, and it suits her perfectly."

"Patricia Van Cleve," I said in the steadiest voice I could muster, "meet your mother." And I gave my sister her daughter as she breathed in her scent.

CHAPTER 11

Three weeks later, we arrived quietly back in New York Harbor late in the evening. During our ocean voyage, Rose took to motherhood like an angel to the heavens. I stopped myself from helping or saying anything. I accepted Patricia as Rose's, and I could feel myself letting her go as I stepped into the background. WR had sent the script for *The Cinema Murder*, and I focused my attention on learning my part.

As we disembarked, I saw my car and Norman waiting for us. As previously agreed, WR didn't come to meet us. He waited for me at our apartment.

"Meet Rose's daughter, Patricia," I said to Norman as we loaded into the car. "Isn't she beautiful?" Her big blue eyes and long, thin face peeked out from the swaddling blanket.

It was the first time I'd introduced Patricia as Rose's daughter, and each time after that it got easier. We drove to Mama's house to drop off Rose and the baby. No introductions were necessary as George rushed to Rose and kissed her face, nearly squeezing the baby between them. Mama rushed to Rose's side. "Let the grandmother through." George traced a finger down Patricia's cheek then stepped back to share her. They all surrounded her, Aunt Ethel clapping and jumping up and down as they enveloped Rose and Patricia in a family circle that made my heart swell.

"Where's Reine, Charlie, and Pepi?" I asked, suddenly realizing they were missing.

"They moved to a house of their own on Long Island while you were away," Papa said.

"They'll be here tomorrow after school to welcome you all home," Mama added.

It was expected that Reine would find her own house and life. Rose, George, and Patricia would be next, I assumed. The family was growing and moving into their own worlds. I backed away to watch them. Rose held Patricia and soaked in the attention with George coaxing her to the couch to sit down. I left them in their bliss. I needed to find my WR.

— ⏀ —

When I arrived at the apartment, he was working as usual at the dining room table. I rushed to curl into his arms, and we moved to sit on the couch by the fire. The cold evening wind belied the late June calendar. I told him every detail I could remember about Patricia and the birth. He listened intently, stroking my arm and cheek and hair—not able to take his hands off me. It felt good to be home. "She's all tucked in with my family. They are quite the picture of love and warmth. I couldn't be happier for Patricia," and then added quickly, "and Rose." He caressed me and kissed me and loved me with new passion that night.

WR met Patricia the next evening when I insisted he come to the house with me. We found everyone in the library. Rose held Patricia as nine-year-old Pepi goggled at her and Reine watched. Charlie had his nose in a book, completely engrossed. Mama and Papa sat in matching leather chairs. Mama was knitting something pink.

"Hi everyone," I said, heading for the couch.

"Nice to see you all again," WR said, following me and eyeing Patricia as he entered the room.

Rose stood up with Patricia in her arms.

WR looked drawn to Rose and the baby. "She's beautiful," he cooed.

"Come on everyone, out to the kitchen where Grandma has some cake. Let's leave WR and Marion to visit with Patricia," Rose said.

"No, please stay, everyone," WR said. "I've come to be part of the family and meet your daughter, Rose and George."

The air tightened up immediately, and Rose shot me a questioning look. WR was never going to acknowledge Patricia as his own, even here with my family in private.

"Yes everyone, stay," I felt obligated to say, unhappy that WR's presence had brought a seriousness to the air.

"I'm getting cake," Charlie said, putting his book down. Mama followed him out of the room.

"May I hold her?" WR asked, sitting down in the leather chair Mama had just vacated.

Rose handed him Patricia wrapped in her soft pink blanket. "She's such a good baby. She barely ever cries," she said.

He expertly cuddled her in the crook of his arm, supporting her head while she slept peacefully. Enraptured with her face, WR gazed at Patricia. He untucked her hand from a fold in the blanket and held it, looking at the tiny fingernails and completely oblivious to the staring crowd. Father and daughter had finally met, and I could feel my eyes filling up with water. I held the picture of them together in my mind, not wanting it to ever end.

The ticktock of the grandfather clock filled the silence as I noticed Rose looking at George, avoiding eye contact with either of us. I looked at Reine and Ethel standing against the bookcase across the room. I couldn't think of anything funny to say. My eyes pleaded with Ethel to break the heavy silence, but she merely shrugged.

"Would you like some tea, WR?" Papa asked. "Or maybe a drink?"

He looked up at Papa, the trance between him and Patricia broken. "No thank you, I have to go soon," WR said, handing Patricia back to Rose. "It was a pleasure seeing you all." He nodded to everyone. "Thank you for sharing Patricia with me. I look forward to watching her grow." He headed for the door. I followed him into the hallway.

"Where are you going so fast?"

He looked at me with an arched eyebrow. "I have work," he said unapologetically as we walked to the back door where his driver waited in the alley.

"You didn't spend much time with her."

"Marion, Sweetheart, let's not make this more difficult than it already is. You wanted this arrangement. You need to respect my position. This is what I'm capable of now."

"Okay," I said and hung my head. He lifted my face and kissed my mouth. "Come home when you're finished here. I'll be waiting." Then he turned and left.

I admonished myself for rushing the transition with Patricia. I wanted it to be perfect and for us to be one big, happy family. Heading back to the library, I entered and said, "Okay family, what the hell was that?"

— ⓪ —

Life settled into new routines for all of us. WR traveled and tended to his empire and political aspirations, and I worked with Nigel Barrie on *The Cinema Murder*, a film about a young stage actress who thinks she witnessed a murder. I kept away from Patricia for weeks on end, needing some space from the stabbing pangs of letting her go. I owed it to Rose and George to give them time as a family. They were like a gorgeous sunrise—a love bubble of bliss. It broke my heart for my own life.

At the studio, I found my rhythm again, working sixteen-hour days and avoiding going home to the empty apartment. The hole inside from missing Patricia nearly swallowed me. My answer was to have Norman take me by the theater district each night to drink and play with my friends. It was harmless fun and a way to fill that hole. Men sought me out for a drink or a laugh at various parties and bars, and I enjoyed the attention. But somebody began reporting my whereabouts to WR because a pair of well-dressed suited men started showing up around me, watching. They were solemn and conspicuous but just out of reach. Nobody knew who they were or what they were doing. Whenever I caught their eye, they looked away.

I sent the studio errand boy to the telegraph office with a message for WR: "Are you having me followed?" The answer was delivered a few hours later: "It's only to keep you safe, my dear."

The Volstead Act had just passed into law October 1919, outlawing the purchase of "intoxicating liquors," making it only somewhat harder to find a place to drink and dance. Prohibition created an underground network of speakeasies that operated in the shadows, run by ruthless gangs who controlled the distribution of illegal alcohol. But Prohibition wasn't going to stop me from showing WR who was the boss of my life.

My anger flared at WR trying to control me. How dare he! I wasn't married to him. He didn't own me. I decided to show him who he was dealing with. I rounded up some girlfriends for a much-needed girls' night out. Eleanor Boardman got into my car, teasing, "I was wondering when you were going to have us out in your personal limousine to paint the town."

"I guess today's your lucky day. Scooch over Ellie, you're taking up too much room," I laughed, passing her the flask. We stuffed in Connie Talmadge and Pickles as well, who was now retired from the stage and a married woman. The air was light with fun and games.

We began at the apartment, raiding the liquor cabinet and dancing with the music too loud. "So how is it living with the rich newspaperman?" Pickles asked as she poured another round of drinks.

"Fabulous! Just fabulous, can't you see?"

I pushed the hurt down with a long draw on my whiskey. "How's married life?" I asked but didn't wait for the reply. Jazz blared while Connie and Ellie swung each other around the room. "Come on you guys, let's get out of here." I grabbed my coat and purse and opened the front door. The ladies followed me down to the car.

"I know a place and have the password," Ellie said, reciting the address to Norman.

"I love it. Take us, Norman," I called as I threw my head back against the seat and raised my flask.

After a short drive, we walked down a darkened alley arm-in-arm. Ellie led us past a metal gate, down twenty steps to a subterranean entrance, before rushing us through a long tunnel and knocking on the unmarked door of The Back Room speak-easy. She gave the secret word, and the door opened blasting our faces with warmth and the smell of bourbon and cigarette smoke. The room was huge and dimly lit by table lamps and several chandeliers. Jazz played as young people danced. Two huge Renaissance sofas with red velvet cushions, a long wooden bar with stools, and velvet-covered walls invited us in, but the series of large modern paintings on every wall made me stop.

The paintings included a nude woman sitting by a stream in the forest, a bare-breasted woman lounging on her side in the bedroom, a naked woman reading a paper in the park, and then my favorite—a woman singing in a bathtub.

"Do you know these artists?" Pickles asked.

"Sure. I love art. These were done by Hoen, Biberstein, and Alten." Ellie shrugged. "I may have come here before. Who knows?" she said, giving us a sly grin.

My skin tingled at the danger of it all: the shadowed room, the need for a password, the hulking man at the door, the paintings. We ordered the house specialty, scotch and milk, which arrived in teacups to be inconspicuous in case the police arrived unannounced.

Within minutes, Ellie wandered off with somebody she knew, and Connie went to the powder room with Pickles. As soon as I was alone, a table of young handsome men waved to me.

"Hello, Miss Davies. Is that you, from the movies?" the blond one asked me.

I took my cigarette and teacup and joined them. "Good evening boys, how are you doing tonight?"

"Miss Davies, let's do the Charleston," one of them said as he grabbed my hand and pulled me to the dance floor, where I spent most of the night. I drank a few-too-many scotch and milks that night, and we climbed the stairs out of the club at three in the morning.

— ⬭ —

WR always said he loved my inner rebel, but that came to an abrupt halt when I rebelled against him and his spies. As predicted, somebody reported that I was "entertaining men." Maybe it was Norman, maybe the doorman at the speakeasy, or maybe those nondescript suited men who appeared at the corner table later in the evening. Who knew? WR seemed to know everybody.

But the telegram said it all: "Behave yourself." My head still banged after sleeping all of five hours, so ignoring WR was easy. I slept the day away, missing my call at the studio and hoping my absence and non-reply would bring WR home to argue with me in person.

It worked.

Late that evening, he returned from who knew where— maybe it was California or just as close as Riverside Drive where he stayed with Millicent and the boys. That thought reignited my anger. He found me in bed reading.

"Hello, my darling."

"No 'my darlings' tonight WR. You can't leave me for months and spy on me when you're gone!" I yelled. "I'm not your good wife Millie. You don't own me." Sarcasm dripped from my mouth like acid.

"It's only been one month, and I'm sorry." He reached out to touch my arm. I moved away.

"I don't like it when you entertain men," he said.

"So my little plan worked. Your spies sent word that I was having fun. Fun is not illegal, WR! Do you know that I work all day and then come here to the apartment alone? I can't be at the house with my family because it's too hard with Patricia now. I love her so much—and she's not mine. I can't be here either because I'm always alone. So all I do is work and have some fun with my friends, and you have the gall to spy on me!"

"Sweetheart, calm down, please," he whispered.

"I should spy on *you*," I hissed. "You probably have another mistress in California. Maybe that's why you're always gone." I picked up the crystal figurine on my nightstand and turned it over in my hand. Impulsively, I threw it at him and watched as it collided with the marble floor. I wanted WR to see how much he made me suffer, but even as the cherub shattered into a hundred pieces, I knew I was being impetuous.

WR stepped back, ignoring the shattered glass. "I don't have a California mistress. I'm building a magnum opus project in San Simeon."

Tears spilled over. "Why do you talk to me that way? I don't know what 'magnum opus' means!" I glared.

"It means the most important work of one's life." His voice warmed.

"And what is that?"

"I'm building a great big project on my family's property."

I ran to the bathroom and slammed the door shut. When I emerged, WR was sitting in the overstuffed chair in the bedroom with his head in his hands. "I'm going out," I said, rushing past him.

"Where are you going?" He followed me to the door. "Don't go darling, please." I slammed the door.

I stayed with Connie, hiding out from absolutely everyone in my life.

He didn't know where I was staying so he couldn't bother me with telegrams, flowers, and letters, which I began to miss after a few days. I found the silence between us unbearable. I telegrammed him: "Let's not fight. I'm coming home."

This was the beginning of a dynamic between WR and me which would play itself out over the next few years. It seemed anything I did out in public was reported to WR by his huge network, which included private detectives he hired. His extended trips for business or with Millicent and his boys left me without any legitimacy in the world. I was William Randolph Hearst's girlfriend, and I had everything a girl could ever dream of—except for an authentic life.

CHAPTER 12

SPRING 1920

Driving home to our new apartment overlooking Central Park months later, I marveled at what my tantrums produced. WR had surprised me with this penthouse after our fight, and I was in the process of decorating it. I still worked long hours filming *The Restless Sex* at Cosmopolitan Pictures. As we drove home, WR put his papers down and leaned over toward me. "What do you think about filming your next movie in Hollywood?"

"Really?" I said with a rush of excitement followed by a wave of fear through my body. *Was I ready for Hollywood?* I wondered.

"I've got a possible deal with Zukor at Paramount. Let's go out West and look around a bit, okay?" He took my hand and kissed it.

"It's where all the serious stars are making movies, isn't it— Pickford and Fairbanks?" I mumbled and then added, "Connie and her sister Norma both just left for Hollywood."

"Yes, let's go and look. We can take Rose, the baby, and your mother if you'd like— at least for the first part of the trip before you begin filming."

I smiled and laid my head on his shoulder. He knew taking the baby was the best idea he could have suggested. I was proud of myself for giving Rose and Patricia bonding time, but I nearly squealed at the thought of spending whole days with Patricia on a trip. "She's crawling now, WR." He leaned over and kissed my cheek.

We couldn't travel openly with WR, so he went first and a week later the Douras women, minus Reine, followed. We arrived at the Hollywood Hotel exhausted from our train journey from New York. Patricia was not only crawling but teething as well. We all took turns helping Rose, who was desperate at times. At the hotel, I took the penthouse suite, while Mama, Ethel, Rose, and baby Patricia shared a three-bedroom suite one floor below.

I slept ten luxurious hours in a feather bed and woke to several bouquets of flowers from WR and a telegram reading, "See you in a few hours."

While having coffee and a late breakfast with my family, WR blew into the suite, commanding the space as he usually did.

"Darling, it's so nice to see you." I walked over to him.

"You are a vision indeed!" He bent over and pecked me on the lips, taking my hand as we stood admiring the rolling hills outside the bay window.

"Can this really be February? It's so warm and sunny. California is absolutely lovely," I said.

"I see you all made the trip without incident," WR said as he spotted Patricia crawling on the floor, his face softening noticeably.

"Yes, the journey delighted all the senses. We have such a beautiful country. I so enjoyed watching the mountains and plains go by," Mama said, spreading jam on her toast.

Patricia had found a chair and was trying to pull herself up as WR towered over her.

"Boy, is she ever happy this morning," Ethel said.

WR picked up Patricia like a man who had five children and held her over his head, smiling his toothy grin at her. She continued to coo and smile at him.

"Another tooth broke through last night. She's a princess again," Rose sighed.

"She's always a princess, so beautiful," WR said, looking to put her down, "and so big."

At the sight of WR and Patricia, I rushed to wrap my arms around them briefly then gave Patricia back to Rose.

— ⓪ —

WR took me to downtown Los Angeles and to his newspaper the *Los Angeles Examiner* for a tour. As we drove, I watched the bustling streets mobbed with people in dark overcoats and hats. Men scurried along, cutting in front of cable cars, while women walked two-by-two in their long black skirts and jackets. The *Examiner* building was a point of pride for WR, as most of his properties were.

"I bought the land in 1913 and had a talented young architect named Julia Morgan design the structure to match the California Franciscan Missions with their arches and low red clay roofs. It opened in 1914," he boasted.

We parked in front. "It's very nice," I said, trying to be interested in a building.

We walked through the entire operation, and I met the men who ran the paper for WR. Standing in a large room filled with desks and working reporters, WR commanded their attention.

"Gentlemen, let me introduce my friend Marion Davies."

Most of them weren't subtle enough to hide their stares, shooting each other glances when they thought I wasn't looking. We all smiled and exchanged pleasantries, but a heavy feeling set in like I wasn't privy to the joke.

Walking back to the car, I confronted WR. "You surprised me by introducing me to those gawking men. Do they all know Millie?"

As WR studied my face, I could tell he was trying to gauge my mood. "She's visited the paper a few times in the last year when she came to see the progress at San Simeon."

We got into the car, and I slammed the door hard. "The house you're building there, it's for her then?"

"No, I'm not building it for her. I'm building it for myself, on land that's been in my family for more than sixty years. Camp Hill is a cherished place where I spent time with my father as a boy."

I shook my head, lit a cigarette, and opened the window a crack. "Does she even know about me? About us? Do you two talk about me?"

WR's head snapped around. I had never asked such a direct question before. I met his gaze straight on. His eyes shifted to the street behind me as he bit his lip and considered his words carefully. "We don't talk about you by name."

"Really?"

"She accuses me of overly promoting you in the papers."

"At least we agree on that."

"I haven't told her I'm in love with you, although I'm sure she's aware by now."

I was not sorry to let Millicent twist with this knowledge. It had been nearly five years since we'd started this crazy relationship, so of course she knew about me. I was so tired of striving and stretching to fit in a corner of WR's life, living in the shadows. The adversaries were now identified, and Millicent knew I was here to stay. Lines had been drawn and I felt battle-ready.

"I still intend on winning you," I professed, and the grin on his face told me he enjoyed hearing that.

We drove in silence until I asked him to tell me more about San Simeon.

"I hired Julia to design some houses so that my sons and I don't have to sleep in tents. I'm not getting any younger, you know."

Grinning at the notion of old Millicent sleeping in a tent, I secretly hoped she'd been tortured by the experience. She was fifteen years older than me, and probably not a tomboy who loved to camp.

WR continued, "We've been working on the architectural style for months and have just finished the drawings for three small guest houses and one large grand house."

After a short pause, he said, "Let's have lunch with an old boyhood friend of mine, Orrin Peck. You'll like him. I've enlisted his landscaping talents up at San Simeon. He can tell you about that."

"When do I get to see the progress at San Simeon?" I asked.

"Soon, darling. I promise to take you up the coast soon."

If there's one thing WR knew how to do well, it was to placate me with his promises. I settled in, having grown used to waiting for things.

The following day, WR and Orrin went up the coast to San Simeon after a telegram arrived from his architect with an emergency decision she needed help making.

"Will everything be okay?" I asked as WR threw on his jacket and headed for the door.

"It's just a special delivery of some rare marble and stone at the dock. It'll be fine. I need to get up there to coordinate. I'll be in touch once I get settled in a day or so."

"This young architect hasn't stolen your heart, has she?" I asked.

"Julia? Not a chance. You'll meet her soon." He winked at me.

"What are we supposed to do with ourselves while you're gone?" I asked, standing at the doorway.

"Rosy has the contacts and will help you. Take in the coast, do a tour of Hollywood. I'll have a car ready for you this afternoon," WR said as he stepped into the elevator and waved goodbye.

An invitation soon arrived for all of us. Eileen Percy, with whom I'd danced for Ziegfeld, was having a garden party for her mother's eightieth birthday on Sunday. Eileen and her husband Harry Ruby had moved out to Los Angeles for her to star in a Douglas Fairbanks movie.

— ⓒ —

After shopping for dresses and garden hats, we arrived at the somewhat modest two-story Craftsman in Beverly Hills and knocked on the heavy oak door. A housekeeper in a black and white uniform answered.

"Welcome," she said. "Follow me please."

We followed her through the living room and out the French doors to see the sloping green hills of the backyard. The rectangular pool sparkled in the sunlight and was surrounded by tables filled with people under umbrellas. Women strolled in the distance carrying parasols. Three well-dressed men stood together in the distance, looking oddly out of place. I tried not to stare at them or wonder about WR's spies. On a deck chair sat an older woman I assumed was Eileen's mother.

"Marion! It's so good to see you in California." Eileen kissed and hugged me. She wore a pale yellow dress with darker yellow crochet accents and a wide-brimmed white hat.

"It's so nice to see you too." I introduced Mama, Ethel, and Rose. The four-piece jazz band played under a tree. Ellie waved from a table on the deck. I blew her a kiss.

Eileen introduced us to her mother, and I handed her the wrapped gift and introduced my family.

Eileen pulled me away as Mama and Ethel spoke with Mrs. Percy. "I have to introduce you to Douglas Fairbanks and Mary Pickford." I gazed out at the crowd of people wondering if I might be able to spot them. "And you also have to meet Charlie Chaplin, who is a flirtatious bugger, so watch out."

She locked arms with mine as we walked to a table. I recognized all of them right away of course: Mary with her angelic curls and Doug sitting next to her. They looked to be in the middle of a serious discussion. I also saw Rudolph Valentino and my old screen buddy Norman Kerry toasting and laughing. Eileen made introductions all around the table as silence descended. I felt their eyes on me like spears and wondered if they knew something about me.

"Sit down and join us," Charlie said, pulling out the empty chair next to him. His face was as bright as a jewel with a big smile and warm beckoning eyes. I had seen him in movies as the Little Tramp and assumed he looked the same in real life. But without the bowler hat, bushy eyebrows, and tiny moustache under his nose, he looked completely different—handsome and confident, with a definite magnetism. My body buzzed ever so slightly. I had never experienced a physical reaction like this before. I kept my voice calm. "Thank you, but I can't. My family is here. It was very nice to meet you all. I hope to see you on the movie sets."

"Are you filming something?" Doug asked.

"Yes, WR is making arrangements."

"Oh right, Mr. William Randolph Hearst, newspaper tycoon," Charlie said very slowly, almost challenging me.

So, they did know who I was. I nodded.

"How much older is Hearst than you?" Charlie questioned.

"Stop that," Mary said. "I apologize, Marion. Forgive Charlie, he doesn't have any manners."

Eileen grabbed my arm and pulled me away. "You see what I mean about Charlie," Eileen whispered in my ear.

"He's adorable, even if he is impertinent." I resisted turning around for one more delicious look.

Together again with Mama and my sisters, we found a table and I watched Charlie across the lawn, silently answering his question: *over three decades, Mr. Chaplin.*

CHAPTER 13

The next morning, I awoke to a knock on the door. I quickly slipped on my robe and checked through the peephole: It was WR in his black overcoat holding a bouquet of red roses. I threw open the door and embraced him. "Why are you knocking? Come in, you silly. I missed you."

"Good morning, Sweetheart." At this I leapt into his muscled arms. "Oh okay, careful now," he laughed and carried me into the suite. "I've come to invite you away for a few days." He put me down on my bare feet.

"It's cold on the marble floor!" I cried out, running back to the warmth of my bed. "Come and get warm with me," I beckoned, throwing back the covers. He smiled slyly while undressing. "Where are we going?"

"Family vacation is over, my darling. It's time to begin work on *Buried Treasure* with Norman next week." He nuzzled me in bed.

I whispered, "You sure know how to romance a girl, don't you? Where are we going?"

He softly outlined my belly button with his finger—around and around as I squirmed.

"I'm whisking you away on a special romance-filled trip—just me and you."

I kissed him deeply. He held me like a baby bird and made love to me as if I were porcelain.

The rest of the day, WR refused to divulge any details about our upcoming romantic getaway except to say we were going north. I thought maybe he was taking me to visit his family property in San Simeon. Either way, it was time for my family to go home. I said my goodbyes and put them all on a train back to New York the following morning.

We headed north in a Rolls Royce Silver Ghost Tourer. WR drove us one hundred and fifty miles up the coast to Santa Maria, a quaint little town north of Santa Barbara, to the new English country-style hotel aptly named The Santa Maria Inn. As we unloaded from the car, I tried not to pout. "We're not going to your family property in San Simeon? Aren't we rather close?"

"Oh Sweetheart, no, we can't go there. It's just men working, and tents and camp food cooked on the fire. There are no accommodations yet."

"But you will take me soon? I am anxious to see it," I said, tucking my bottom lip back in.

We checked into a private suite and spent four love-filled days dining on simple but delicious pot roast, pork chops, and shepherd's pie at the hotel restaurant and walking among the fields of swaying yellow grass.

"I fall more in love with you every day, and I can't imagine my life without you," WR murmured one evening while we sat side-by-side in white rocking chairs on the wraparound porch.

"I don't remember what my life was like before you. Let's be together forever," I said, holding his hand.

"Don't worry, my dear, I will never let anything hurt you."

I stared off into the distance at the orange-and-yellow sky and put my cigarette out. *What an odd response,* I thought. My stomach soured like a lemon. "Hurt me? Do you mean Millicent can ruin all of this and take you away at any moment?"

"No, she won't. We are closer to reaching a compromise every day. Please don't worry about her."

"Okay, I won't," I said, forcing myself to keep the goodness between us going. "You know, this long weekend feels like a honeymoon of sorts. You haven't worked the whole time we've been here except to check your messages a few times," I said.

"This is one honeymoon. We will have many more in the years to come, I promise."

As I watched the orange sky become more brilliant behind the treetops, I justified WR's love for me. "Love isn't always created at the altar. It doesn't always need a wedding ring," I said.

"You are my little Rosebud." He took my hand and kissed the back of it.

The four days ended too quickly, but I could tell WR was restless to get back to his empire. We drove south on Highway 101 with the top down through the morning heat back to Hollywood. "Are you ready to start working, my dear?" WR asked as he looked over at me fidgeting with the scarf around my hair as the wind blew.

"Yes, I'm ready. Did I tell you I saw Norman at Eileen's garden party? It'll be great to work with him again."

"Yes, I heard you girls were quite the hit."

I looked at him.

"Stay calm. I only heard you met all the heavy hitters."

"You heard from your spies? The well-dressed men?"

"I don't have spies. Stop that right now," he said, narrowing his eyes at me.

"Oh yes you do. You don't call them spies—but I do."

He stared straight ahead and didn't answer me. I tried a different tack. "And how were my mother, sisters, and I a 'hit'?"

"I only meant that Norman said he saw you and everybody whispered about who you all were."

"Oh really? Is that what he said?" I lit a cigarette and stared out the window at the vast Pacific Ocean. WR stared straight ahead, focusing on the two-lane road that hugged the coastline. I dropped it, not wanting to ruin the end of our first honeymoon. But the hurts were building inside: of not seeing San Simeon, the spies following me, and especially of Millicent still being his wife.

— ⦿ —

WR returned to San Simeon two days later, and I met Norman at the studio to begin filming.

"Nice to see you, sweetness," he said, then kissed my cheek. His dark hair was ruffled, and he smelled of the ocean—clean and bright. We stood in the Paramount offices, waiting for George Baker, our director.

"Hollywood sure agrees with you. Better than dirty old New York?" I asked, overtly eyeing him up and down. His sky-blue knit shirt clung to his well-defined chest.

"I love it here. Weather is beautiful all the time. You can't beat it." An office door opened, and George waved us in. "Come on in, you two; let's talk about the film."

Buried Treasure would be my tenth picture allowing me to show off my acting talents by taking on two lead female characters in a story about reincarnation. I felt confident in the acting skills I had acquired in New York, but being in Hollywood with the big stars made me question myself all over again.

The filming was set to take place at Paramount Studios in LA, but first we would film all the ship sequences aboard a chartered yacht as we traveled to Catalina Island for the beach and cave scenes. Catalina felt like a faraway land where blue sky and azure ocean joined at the horizon like magic, instead of an island just twenty-six miles off the coast of California.

Two weeks into filming in such close quarters, I found myself playing with the idea of seducing chiseled, young, and alluring

Norman. It was a game that kept me occupied during our long breaks in filming until one day when it became real.

Electricity bolted through me during a scene when our hands touched unexpectedly. He pulled his hand away and then searched my eyes for confirmation of the zing. When I looked away, he put his hand on my back to lead our characters through the scene. I then searched his eyes, and this time he avoided eye contact with me. Was I imagining this? Had my daydreams come to life?

On our third attempt at a deck-side kissing scene, I tried very hard to ignore the magnetism between us. During the kiss, I forced myself to think about my brother and how sad my father was when he died. My body pulsed for Norman, but my mind was filled with sadness. The kiss was uninspired.

"Let's film that again," George said. "The two of you are timid and cold with each other today. What's going on? Let's get this done and get back to LA. Action!"

This time Norman grabbed me hard and kissed my lips with real feeling. Thoughts of my brother abruptly fell away. We embraced like real lovers, and the kiss went even deeper.

"Cut!" George yelled. "That was it, you two," he said and walked off.

With the scene over, Norman left without a word. My mouth hung open just for a moment at the electricity flowing through me as I watched him stroll down the deck after George.

CHAPTER 14

Back at my suite at the Hollywood Hotel, I didn't have long to wait before WR phoned. "I've missed you so much. How was filming?"

"Just fine. I'm exhausted from the travel and a little seasick from the boat ride. I miss you too. When can we get together?"

"Darling, I have some bad news. Millicent is insisting on bringing the boys up to San Simeon. I haven't seen them in months, and she's on her way now. There's nothing I can do."

"What do you mean there's nothing you can do, WR? Tell her no. Tell her to stay away," I cried.

"I can't, Sweetheart. I promise it'll be quick. I'll be in touch in a few days."

My hand shook as I placed the receiver back on the hook. An ache throbbed in my stomach, and I poured a gin and tonic. I needed to hit something, throw something, let out my anger. Why does she get to go to San Simeon, and not me? Aren't I the one he loves? Walking onto my balcony, I let out a scream that made pedestrians below look up. I stepped back into my suite and closed the door.

WR would pay. I would make him pay. I could ruin his reputation by quitting the film. My disappearance would embarrass him and ruin his time with his family. That would show him.

I took a deep breath. It would hurt my reputation too—maybe more than his. Being "on loan" to Paramount Studios from Cosmopolitan Pictures, meant this movie was my introduction to the power players in Hollywood filmmaking. I couldn't run. I needed to stay and finish the job. If things didn't work out with WR, I'd need my work. After two more gins on an empty stomach, I resolved to do what was best for me and thought about Norman's arms and chest as I fell asleep.

I awoke the next morning to the phone ringing. "Good morning," Rosy said. "The car will be here in one hour. Should I send up some breakfast?"

"Just coffee and toast, please."

I got out of bed clutching my pounding head, my stomach roiling from the gin. While showering, I imagined WR laughing with Millicent at something cute one of the boys did. The hurt turned to anger at them sharing an intimate parental moment as I slept alone in a hotel. How dare he.

After toast and coffee, my stomach felt infinitely better. By eight-thirty, I was at Paramount Studios in my dressing room, staring at myself in the mirror and fixing my resolve to leave WR. I hung my head in defeat, knowing how difficult it would be to extricate myself and my family from him. A knock on my dressing room door brought me back to reality.

"Ready, Miss Davies?"

"Yes, five minutes," I said, continuing to stare at myself in the mirror. I poured myself an orange juice and eyed the vodka on the drink cart in the corner. It was only 9 a.m., but I needed a splash. I then stood in front of the mirror to try on a smile—I needed to act my way through the day. My smile looked fake, but after guzzling another orange juice and vodka, a natural smile came easier and I felt my bones loosen up. Grabbing the black wig for my dual role as Lucía, I put it on and marched onto the set, ready for my ethereal reincarnation close-up.

— ◎ —

After four grueling hours of doing my scenes, I was taking a late liquid lunch in my dressing room when Norman opened the door looking tanned and clean. His black hair was slicked back, and his thin black shirt showed the muscles I fell asleep dreaming about.

"Come have a drink with me. I'm celebrating the end of this picture."

He squinted at me and cocked his head to the side. "It's a bit premature, don't you think? I'm not done shooting yet, and you still have one more scene to do."

"Have a drink with me now." My speech was slurred as I raised my glass high in the air and crushed out a cigarette in the overflowing ashtray.

"What are we drinking?" he asked, closing the door behind him.

"I don't know. Everything's over there. I'm drinking gin," then added, "now." I patted the seat next to me on the sofa.

"Now?" he said.

"Yes, now," I answered impatiently. "This morning I drank vodka, and now I'm drinking gin. Okay?" I asked with a challenge in my voice.

"Okay, Sweetheart," he said.

"Was there something in that kiss we shared the other day, or was it just me?" I asked.

He looked at me sideways with a small grin as he put ice into his glass.

"You know, more heat or something?"

"You mean the one on the deck?" he asked.

"Yes, that's the one. Hurry up, make the drink," I demanded.

"What's the hurry?" He sat down next to me, and the smell of the ocean enveloped me.

"You smell good," I said, rubbing my hand up and down his leg.

"Thanks, but what about the big guy?"

"He smells like musk." I laughed a little too loud. "And right now I hate the smell of musk. Make me another drink," I ordered as I lit a cigarette.

"Haven't you had enough?"

"Nope. Never enough."

"What happened?" he asked.

"I don't want to talk about it." I hung my head.

"Let me catch up with you at least." He downed his drink in three gulps.

"There's no time to catch up."

I wanted to see his tanned chest, feel his fresh skin on mine, and for us to dive deep into each other. I began unbuttoning his shirt one button at a time, searching his face for affection. He fumbled with the buttons on my blouse and pulled me close. We slid down on the sofa and into each other's arms. His kiss was warm and welcoming as we found our bodies fitting together nicely. I ran my hands down his strong back, helping him push his pants down as he slid my skirt up. We were moving and melting with every thrust, me nuzzling into his neck which smelled of the beach and sunshine. We climaxed and the fog of sleep descended so heavily on me I couldn't fight it.

A knock on the door interrupted my light after-sex doze on Norman's chest. "Miss Davies, you have a delivery," a stage boy said.

Norman shook me gently. "Princess, get up."

"Bah! The delivery's only flowers, or a present from him. I don't want that. I want this," I pouted, as I snuggled deeper into Norman's side.

"We must get up and get ready. We each have one more scene to shoot," Norman insisted, pulling away from me.

"Will there be more kissing?" I smiled at him with my eyes closed.

"Nope, no more kissing on set today. Maybe we can see each other this evening."

"Maybe," I said as the door closed and Norman left.

Fifteen minutes later, I opened my dressing room door to see a five-piece string orchestra. The violin player stood up and asked, "Marion Davies?"

"Yes. Who are you?" I walked toward them.

"We're the Marion Davies Orchestra." They began playing "The Blue Danube Waltz," the song WR and I had danced to the very first evening I went to his apartment. My knees felt weak. How could he do this to me? I sucked in a deep breath and held it. A young boy handed me an envelope. The note inside read:

"TO THE LOVE OF MY LIFE. HOPE THEY'RE PLAYING OUR SONG. — WR"

I felt nauseous and lightheaded and couldn't imagine how I could face WR. I nodded at the musicians and returned to my dressing room, which still smelled of liquor and Norman. I sat on the couch slumped in shame.

I finished my final scene that afternoon and without a word to WR or Norman, skulked away to New York. Drinking myself into near oblivion each of the five days the train pushed across the country, I arrived at Mama's house beaten and bruised inside.

A telegram waited for me from WR: "Where did you go? I came to the hotel, but you had checked out."

I couldn't answer. A few days later, I received ten dozen red roses and a note:

"The Bungalow is on the bum,
The studio is stupid.
For life is slow unless there's some
Companionship with Cupid.

Mars is all right to strive and fight
And from our foes to screen us
But there are times when thoughts and rhymes
Turn longingly to Venus.

So while I write with much delight
Of armies and of navies
The sweetest thing of which I sing
The Muse to whom my soul I fling
The Idol to whose feet I cling
Is lovely Marion Davies."

— ⓪ —

I met WR at the penthouse the following day. He was at the table working when I arrived. "Did you get my poem? I wrote it myself, for you."

I nodded and he came to me and kissed my neck.

"I hate the hold she has on you. It's stronger than the hold I have on you."

"No it isn't, my darling. I swear it."

But I knew differently. My affair with Norman helped me see the way I needed to take care of myself. However unconventional it was, I needed to find my own way to deal with being rejected and shoved aside. I could share part of my life with WR and still have my own life.

Pieces of the puzzle I had struggled with for years finally came into view. The last piece was inserted when WR abandoned me to be with Millicent and the boys, and I ended up in the arms of Norman. I could see the life I would always have, as second choice, even if WR continually promised me I was his first choice.

I saw the whole picture and began to deal with it.

CHAPTER 15

NEW YORK HARBOR, OCTOBER 1921

The weather was unpredictable in New York City. One week it was cold, the next balmy again—almost exactly like my relationship with WR these past fifteen months. Finally accepting my fate in this gilded relationship, I let go of the dream of marriage and a traditional life. I went out more when WR was gone, enjoying time with girlfriends and a very few choice men on the sly. If I was WR's second choice, I would make myself first choice and do what I liked. And I liked an occasional man.

Duping WR's spies wasn't so easy, but I found my ways. One time I arrived at an underground bar as a blonde and, thanks to a theater friend bringing me a wig, left as a brunette. Most times I did what I wanted, ignoring WR's spies because I would love to have that fight if he ever confronted me. He couldn't demand my fidelity when his was in question. The men were never anything serious, just fun and games I felt I deserved.

WR was spending considerable time in California, including the entire month of June with Millicent and the boys at San Simeon. Whether she knew it or not, The Black Widow—as I had taken to calling her—seemed to be winning. Privately, I imagined us dueling and ruminated on how I could get back at her by stealing him away.

It was sweltering the early October night WR returned to New York. Out drinking with a few girlfriends after work, I was startled to see him standing against the wall of the Landmark Tavern speakeasy, looking very out of place at such an establishment, watching me drink and laugh with Louella and Connie. I wore a blue chiffon dress with fluttering sleeves. Despite the heat, he wore a navy overcoat with his gray fedora hat and stared at me over his glasses with a half-smile, half-scowl.

"Girls," I said, meeting his eyes, "my baby grand has returned. I have to go. Call me tomorrow." I walked to WR without breaking eye contact. "Aren't you hot in that thing?" I asked, pulling at the lapels of his coat.

He bent down and scooped me up in his arms, kissing me deeply in public for the first time. "Well, well, well," I breathed. We made our way to his limousine.

"When did you get in?"

"Just now." He kissed my neck and cheeks as he settled in next to me.

"How's the Black Widow?" I asked as he continued kissing my bosom and neck. It was hard to hold onto my feelings of neglect and spite when he was in such an affectionate mood.

He said to his driver, "To the *Oneida*."

"What's the *Oneida*?" He shook his head, refusing to answer, holding my hand and gazing at my face with childish expectation. "Where are we going?"

"Just be patient, my darling."

We got out of the limo and stood near the docks in New York Harbor. Staring at a very large yacht, WR's hand slid around my waist and he whispered in my ear. "There she is, *our* ship, the *Oneida*." Of course I zeroed in on his emphasis of the word "our."

"Really? Our ship?" I exclaimed.

"Follow me, I'll show her to you."

My tour began on the observation deck where I could see the captain and his officers poring over a chart. He dashed me through the formal dining room with its long table covered in white linen. "What's the rush?" I asked, but he whisked me along, pushing us through the galley and the stately library, and then stopping altogether, an expectant look on his face as he opened a set of mahogany doors to reveal the movie theater.

"I had this built just for you," he said, swinging his arms wide.

"Oh my," I said, flabbergasted, eyeing the large screen and about thirty red velvet cushioned seats, half on either side of the aisle.

Before I even had a chance to take in its splendor, he was calling me on to the next thing. "We'll be back here later," he said. "Now I have the most important thing to show you. Follow me." He grabbed my hand as I continued to marvel at the movie theater. My heart fluttering at the lavishness of it all, we climbed down a staircase to a long hallway with doors on either side. "These are the ten guest cabins." He opened the door to one cabin and said, "Go in and look, they're newly decorated."

I went inside and found a plush mini-suite with a large bed, dressing table, closet, and sitting area. "WR, these are gorgeous." He stood in the doorway, gloating at me. I ran to him and threw my arms around his neck and kissed him deeply.

"Come now, my dear, and see where *we* stay." He led me to the end of the hallway, and we climbed up the stairs again to the stern of the boat. He opened another mahogany door. "Welcome to our cabin, my dear." I stepped inside and found a two-bedroom suite with an adjoining sitting room. WR's room had mahogany desk furnishings, dark red damask hangings, and notably soft bedding accessories on a custom-built mahogany bed just for WR's six-foot-three-inch frame. My room, done in white ivory and gilt, had a canopy bed with a lacy curtain and a gold inlayed bathtub. The porthole had a dark velvet curtain pulled over to keep out the light. A brass nautical clock hanging on the wall rang out chimes. My breath caught at the magnificence of it all.

"I've been remodeling her for months now." He was like a peacock with its plume extended, and while I loved the splendor of it all, it made me realize just how little I knew of WR's life away from me.

WR reached into his jacket pocket, pulling out a diamond necklace. "Try it on darling. There are twenty-five one-carat stones."

"Oh my, WR. You have outdone yourself." I took a seat on the small sofa near the fireplace and lifted my hair so he could clasp the string of twinkling rocks around my neck.

I turned to face him. "Darling," he said, "I'm not sure about much these days except that I love you, and I'm trying to show you. May I kiss you?"

"Oh, now you ask. And when we're in public, you just grab me?" I teased. He bent down, caressed my cheek, and kissed me fervently.

"Darling, I don't remember you being quite so ferocious. Has something happened I should know about?"

"Only that I miss you terribly, and I'm going to show you in every way just how much."

Pulling me to my feet, he unbuttoned my dress, which landed in a heap. Sliding my slip off my shoulder, he unlaced my corset and all of it fell to the floor with a swish. Standing back his eyes drank in my naked body like a desert traveler. I was pleased to still have such an effect on him. I felt strong, confident, and happy.

"You are so gorgeous, Marion. The necklace sparkles just like your eyes." He picked me up, took me to bed, and we made mad, passionate love like we hadn't in a long time. Laying sweaty on top of the covers, catching his breath, he murmured, "I have another surprise for you."

"More than the necklace? More than the ship?" I whispered incredulously.

"Yes, more, always more for you my darling."

I sighed and closed my eyes, feeling my body smolder like an ember.

—⟐—

We slept on the ship, waking to eggs benedict delivered to me in bed as WR, already up and dressed, explained that we were hosting some family and friends that day on the ship, where he would screen my latest movie, *Enchantment*.

"We're watching my movie tonight?" I sat up straighter in bed. "Who did you invite?"

"I thought you'd enjoy having Mama and Ethel. You have just enough time to go back to the penthouse and grab some clothes for another overnight stay, then you and Norman will swing by and pick them up, and return here late this afternoon," he told me.

"Who else is coming?" I asked hesitantly.

"Just a few people from the studio, my darling. They deserve this treat. They've all worked so hard for us."

"Of course, WR. Of course!" I hid the disappointment I felt at not getting a chance to weigh in on who else we might invite, like my girlfriends here in the city, but WR didn't know them, so I understood. I peeked out the porthole and saw Norman on the dock waiting for me. I got dressed quickly and bid WR farewell. "I'll see you this afternoon—and thank you for such a wonderful evening of surprises," I said as I closed the door to our suite softly behind me.

When I got back to the ship later that afternoon with Mama and Ethel, we found the group in the movie theater waiting for us. There was Josef Urban, the most highly sought-after set decorator in New York who had built the most extravagant set to date for my current movie, along with his daughter, Gretl, an up-and-coming costume designer. Two other men from the studio were producer William LeBaron, built tall and thin like WR, and screenwriter Luther Reed.

My movie was a modern take on Shakespeare's *Taming of the Shrew*, and while the crowd enjoyed it, I craved a drink to relax. On an excuse for the bathroom, I ran to our suite to take a few shots of bourbon I had hidden in my bag. WR discouraged my drinking and had mostly committed himself to sobriety while the laws of prohibition dominated the land, except for the rare glass of champagne. Alcohol had become a sticking point between us.

I snuck back into the theater just in time to hear everyone applaud as the movie ended, with WR clapping the loudest and giving me a scowl for being gone so long. "Dinner is served," he announced to everyone. "Please follow me." Mama and Ethel had wide eyes and big smiles on their faces as we followed WR.

We found our seats, and the formally dressed dining-room waiters brought in rack of lamb, red potatoes, and asparagus with cream sauce. The room was lit with a chandelier and candles. WR, looking particularly austere in his crisp white shirt, gray tie, and long, dark dinner jacket, clinked his empty champagne glass.

"Are we getting some champagne?" I asked, staring at his empty glass. The waiter entered just in time and filled everyone's glass.

"Wasn't that Marion's best film yet?" WR asked, holding up his glass.

I tried not to gulp my champagne. "Darling, don't put them on the spot like that."

"Oh nonsense. These are your most loyal fans, and because of that I have a proposition for you all. I wish to invite you to extend our trip around the harbor and go to Mexico for a few weeks. Care to join Marion and me as we visit my three ranches?" He put his glass down on the table.

The whole escapade now became clear to me. He'd planned this series of surprises around needing to see some properties he had inherited in Mexico. And he wanted to do that with me, not

Millicent. It was my turn to be spoiled and pampered. I raised my glass to WR. The rest of the table looked pleased, if not a little stunned. The adventurous twinkle in WR's eye reminded me of Santa doling out presents. He raised his glass again to me. "Well, young lady, are you ready for an adventure?"

I stood up and kissed him boldly. The whole room erupted in applause.

"I guess it's settled then. Off we go to Mexico."

CHAPTER 16

NEW ORLEANS, OCTOBER 1921

I could feel the ship moving faster, rising up and down on the waves heading out to sea toward Florida. WR was nothing if not impetuously passionate about his travel plans, living out of a suitcase himself most of the time and expecting we could easily do the same.

"I know an overnight bag has its limitations, but I hope you can survive until New Orleans, where I will sponsor you all in a shopping trip for the items you need." Nods from everyone seated at the dinner table settled it. I winked at Gretl, knowing that shopping was an art for her.

"Tell us about the ship," Luther said. Lifting his chin and sitting up straighter, WR explained that the *Oneida* was 205 feet long, ran on two boilers and a steam engine, and her top speed was thirteen knots. She had a four-thousand-mile range and could sleep twenty-five comfortably.

As we sailed south past Palm Beach, where WR's precious Black Widow lived in the cold months, I privately waved to Millicent from the deck, secure in my knowledge that I was winning this round.

Steaming into the warm waters of the Gulf of Mexico, WR and I sat in the library, where the chairs were positioned in front of a big window so we could watch the sun set. Putting down the two movie scripts I was studying, I said, "This is just divine, WR. I love traveling by private yacht. It's nothing like the ship Rose and I took to France."

He smiled and patted my knee. "I'm glad you're enjoying yourself."

The oranges, yellows, and reds of the autumn sun cast their colors over the clouds. I picked up the script entitled *The Bride's Play* and began reading.

"How are you coming on those scripts?" he asked. We both knew I had six weeks to prepare. Our trip would end in California where the filming would commence almost immediately.

"It's so exciting! Is it true that the outside scenes will be filmed at Point Lobos on the Monterey Peninsula?"

"Yes, it is. I picked that spot because Mary Pickford filmed a gorgeous scene for her movie *The Love Light* there."

"Oh, that was a gorgeous scene. On a cliff near the edge of the ocean?"

"Yes, that's the one. And after you're done filming, I guess it will be time for you to see my special project in San Simeon."

Feeling light and silly and in need of a laugh, I got up and slid back and forth across the floor, swinging my arms, singing, "Finally!" to which WR laughed and grabbed my hand, pulling me onto his lap and kissing me passionately.

— ⓪ —

Snuggling in WR's bed on our eighth night at sea, I noticed the motion of the boat had ceased and that it was light outside. "I believe we've stopped, WR," I mumbled, laying in the crook of his arm.

"Yes, darling, we docked at 3."

"3 a.m.?" I said too loud, and his eyes flew open at the sound of my voice, only to close again slowly. "That's mighty early.

Were you up at that time?" I asked, climbing up on his body, sitting high and stretching to push back the curtains so that I could look out the porthole. He put his cold hands on my bare skin and I shuddered.

"Yes, I was working. I went to the bridge to confer with the captain on where we should dock."

"Did we get a good spot?"

"Of course. You can walk right off the boat and hail a cab."

"Oh, I can't wait. I'm starving. Let's get dressed and give New Orleans some hell," I said and rolled off the bed.

Breakfast was served in the dining room. Mr. Reed, Mr. LeBaron, and Mr. Urban were at one end of the table, discussing lighting or set design or some such technical thing that serious men like to discuss. "Boys, we're on vacation," I said as I passed them. They politely nodded as I took a seat at the opposite end of the table with Ethel, Mama, and Gretl.

"Are you ready to do some shopping and sightseeing today?" I asked as I picked up an envelope with my name on it and eyeing the other envelopes beside each plate at the table. Mama, Ethel, and Gretl all watched me intently as I found hundreds of crisp dollar bills inside. "My, my, my, WR has outdone himself again," I said, flipping through the bills. "I never know what he is up to next. It's quite exciting, isn't it?" Gretl put on her fur collar wrap coat, looking very pleased. Mama and Ethel looked almost embarrassed as they stuffed the envelopes into their purses.

"WR assures me we can walk right off the boat and hail a cab. Shall we?" I urged my female cohorts.

Ethel said brightly, "Yes, let's go!"

Our two days were filled with so much activity, we barely had time to unload our packages, dress again, and leave for the evening festivities which included jazz in the French Quarter. WR kept us happy and busy all at once. Gretl seemed particularly moved after our second day shopping, sitting in the ship's main cabin with our packages around our feet. "The skirts, blouses, scarves, and boots are just fabulous, but my favorite are the knickers. I mean, why should men only wear slacks?" she said defiantly. I really liked Gretl.

"Are we ready for our second night on the town? Dinner out and then somebody named Jelly Roll Morton?" I said, gathering my packages. "See you all on the gangway. WR says we're pulling out as soon as we get back to the ship tonight."

— ⓪ —

Later that evening, up front at the best table in the bar, I was raring to go. "Let's have some swanky fun, ladies," I crooned, pulling out my flask and splashing some bourbon into each of our teacups. I had seen Mr. LeBaron do the same thing to the men's cups a few minutes earlier. Of course, WR put his hand over his, needing to remain a teetotaler. He was a fuddy-duddy sometimes. He had a silly side, but he would never show it in public.

"I hope to be dancing the Turkey Trot before too long. I'm ready to show New Orleans how we do things in New York," Gretl said, her face shining bright.

"Show me the Turkey Trot right now," I said to Gretl, checking around to make sure nobody was watching us. She stood and moved back and forth while flapping her arms up and down quickly. "Okay, stop," I said, pulling her arm to sit down again. I checked the bar for oglers, and only saw WR's eyes lit up with joy.

"Please warn me when you do that again so I can move to a different table," Mama said, and we all burst out laughing.

Having WR on a trip like this for days and days left me overflowing with love and kindness for him. I fell asleep to the thought that everything was possible, and anything might happen. Living in a world where every day was about my comfort and pleasure gave me dreams indeed. New Orleans embraced us like a warm hug, showing us her sophisticated French side and sexy Spanish side.

The *Oneida* pulled out at 2 a.m. after our raucous evening. We slept long and hard.

— ◯ —

The next morning, Gretl and Ethel sat sipping their coffee when I dragged myself to the table to find the gift WR had left us on the breakfast table: a hand-cranked portable Victrola phonograph with records from Sidney Bechet and our new favorite, Jelly Roll Morton. "WR is so thoughtful and generous, isn't he?" Gretl gushed. Feeling a jolt of silliness, I took Ethel's hand and pulled her to her feet. Willing to indulge me in some fun, she let me spin her around once on the deck as my heart swelled. This trip had made me happier than I had been in a long, long time.

Chapter 17

Mexico, November 1921

We left the *Oneida* and traveled to San Antonio by public passenger train, then crossed the border into Mexico in a caravan of taxis. Next was an elegant private train with an enormous coalfired engine that pulled eight cars. Rolling along on the railroad tracks didn't feel so different from sliding along the waves on the yacht. It was constant motion.

WR wanted separate bedrooms aboard the train since they were relatively small and he needed to work at night without bothering me, but I insisted on sleeping with him anyway. My "pauper room," as I took to calling it to rib WR, was more than adequate, consisting of a quaint little bed against a wall with a hanging closet and a simple dresser and chair. WR's room, or the "king's room," as I dubbed it, was half the length of one train car with a large sitting area, a king-sized bed, and sizeable worktable for WR to spread out his papers. Colorful, Mexican-style area rugs covered the floor, and several lamps gave the room a warm yellow glow.

On our first night aboard the train, I woke up in WR's bed and found him working at the table. "Come to bed, WR; I can already see first light," I purred. He murmured something unintelligible, and I turned away from the light.

When I awoke to bright sunshine, WR was gone. The train had stopped, and out the window I saw the desert floor with cactus and small brush. I dressed quickly, anxious to find everyone else.

Mr. Urban, Mama, Ethel, and Gretl were in the living room car looking out the window at a group of women with carts. WR was talking to them and buying their food. "Where did they come from?" I asked.

"We don't know. There is no village close by," Mr. Urban said. "At least not one we can see."

Herds of cattle were visible in the distance, and beyond that there appeared to be green mountains.

"Good morning, Princess," Gretl said, teasing.

I scrunched my face at her and danced a little jig. "*Olé!*" A sudden jerk of the train had me grabbing the chair mid-step as we began to roll forward.

I joined Gretl in the matching overstuffed green velvet club chair. A book lay open on her lap. Out the window the countryside looked more like the bottom of an evaporated ocean than anything inhabitable by man. The door to the compartment flew open and WR blew inside with a burst of warm desert air.

"Tamales, avocadoes, *pico de gallo*, papaya, guava, and strawberries," he sang out. "I've been shopping for everyone, looking for local culinary treasures. Mexican women are excellent cooks. I've sampled all the food and it's delicious. Follow me to the dining car to taste what I found."

Walking through the car, my stomach churned at the wafting scent of corn and chicken, with a whiff of cilantro. A few too many drinks with Gretl the night before left me feeling queasy, but hungry. We had stashed a few bottles of bourbon in our luggage in New Orleans like a couple of daring girls.

"How many of you have had tamales before?" WR asked, beaming with pride and clearly relishing playing tour guide and host. Gretl and I shook our heads. Mama and Ethel leaned forward to get a better look.

WR continued, "They're made from a dough of masa corn, which is wrapped around cooked chicken, beef, or pork, and then wrapped in a corn husk and steamed. They're delicious plain, or you can put *pico de gallo* salsa on them." He pulled a corn husk out of the basket and opened it up to reveal the tamale on the inside. WR cut the chicken tamale into several bite-size pieces and offered it to us. Soon enough we were all feasting on the foreign delicacy, enjoying our culinary experiences.

— ⓪ —

Our train pulled into the small village of Chihuahua late that afternoon, where we were greeted by a dozen men wearing Mexican palm cowboy hats and big spurs on their boots. We had arrived at the crown jewel of WR's three Mexican properties: the one-million-six-hundred-thousand-acre Babicora Ranch.

He indicated that we should all stay on the train until he made initial contact. I looked out the window and watched him greet the ranch hands. Anxiously awaiting our next adventure, we could see in the distance a bustling marketplace where locals sold fruits, vegetables, and pottery on small wooden carts. Past the market were modest adobe houses with dirt yards.

It was decided that WR and Mr. Urban would follow the cattle men in the morning to the ranch for inspection. Mr. LeBaron and Mr. Reed would stay with the women on the train. "I am also leaving two local cowboys, called *vaqueros*, for security. They're related to the men who work for me at the ranch," WR explained. "I'll set up a tour of the town for you all before I leave."

Gretl and I didn't want to stay on the train. "Can't Gretl and I go with you? We want to ride horses and see the property." But WR refused us, saying he didn't know what to expect and wanted to focus on the business of the ranch.

WR and Mr. Urban left early the next morning, hoping to return before sunset. We toured the town, played cards, and read late into the evening. They arrived back at the train very late. WR was busy saying goodbye to the men when I went into his room to retrieve a pair of earrings I had left there. As I walked past the worktable, I saw a telegram from Millicent. I rarely snooped around WR's papers but couldn't stop myself from reading: "William, the advertising for *Enchantment* is excessive for that young girl you see. The film hasn't even opened yet. Please revise it. Love, Millicent."

I threw my head back smiling, reading over the words "that young girl you see." *Ha, that's right, you old biddy*, I thought. *You know my name, so use it,* I dared her in my mind. The Black Widow was making her next move, trying to ruin my publicity.

I opened a folder containing telegrams from Joseph Moore, WR's editor in New York. It seemed they had been going back and forth regarding my publicity since New Orleans. One from Joseph read, "Millicent insists all advertising be distinctly on picture and not on the star." This one had arrived just after we left New York.

WR had responded from Chihuahua the day before: "I cannot do that. The picture may fail if we don't have coordinated advertising around the country." Another telegram to Millicent read: "Advertising the movie and the star is necessary to comply with Paramount's requirements and give the picture any chance of success."

A smile crept across my face. I closed the file and left the room, giggling to myself.

— ⦾ —

We finished our time in Mexico by traveling south to Mexico City so WR could pay homage to newly elected President Alvaro Obregon and thank him for his country's warm hospitality. We met the *Oneida* in Heroica, Veracruz and sailed for three days the one thousand miles across the Gulf of Mexico back to Galveston.

WR and I parted with the group, settling in for the two-day trip to LA in separate cars, having to travel as though we weren't a couple now that we were back in the States on public transportation. WR was anxious to get to San Simeon to meet with Julia Morgan on critical design issues for his ranch house, and I was ready to get to Paramount Studios and begin filming *The Bride's Play*.

CHAPTER 18

1922

The Bride's Play finished filming in Monterey. True to his word, WR sent a black limousine to pick me up for the ninety-mile trip south to San Simeon. I was excited to be done filming and looked forward to seeing WR for a few days—my knight, my man, my benefactor—after a month apart. Driving took half a day as we hugged the craggy coast of California whipsawing back and forth down Highway 1.

"We're getting close, Miss Davies, look at the elephant seals on the beach," Stan said.

Out the window, thousands of them crowded the beach vying for the best position. "Look at that," I said, seeing the pier WR had talked about, extending far into San Simeon Bay where ships docked.

"That's the pier WR built," Stan said. "The longshoremen unload building supplies from the ships that arrive from San Francisco, place them onto trucks, and drive them five miles up the hill to the construction site."

I looked up the hill as we turned, getting stuck behind one of those very same delivery trucks spewing black smoke and chugging slowly uphill with a load of lumber and what looked like Spanish stones. Ahead I saw an upscale Venetian-style tent and WR's lanky body sitting beneath a shaded structure.

As we approached I yelled, "Stop!" Practically jumping out of the moving vehicle, I ran toward WR. I wore the riding knickers, white blouse, and boots I had purchased in New Orleans, hoping for a ride on one of WR's Morgan horses. The day was spectacular with a blue sky and a view of the Pacific Ocean—so clear that it almost made me believe I could see Hawaii off in the distance.

"Darling," WR said, smiling and walking toward me. "You are a sight for my eyes," he said, brushing a curl from my shoulder. "How was your trip?" He eyed my clothing approvingly and kissed my cheek.

"Fantastic! I'm so excited to finally see your 'magnum opus'—isn't that what you call it?"

"Yes, it is." He squeezed my hand, turning to a petite woman nearby. "Marion Davies, this is Julia Morgan, my very talented architect."

Not quite five feet tall, she wore a long black skirt, white blouse with a black bow tie around her neck, and an extremely tall black bowler hat that must have added six inches to her height and nearly swallowed her head. Who knew what color hair she had underneath it. I bent sideways just a smidge to see her round glasses and dainty face under the wide brim.

"Miss Morgan, it's a true pleasure to meet you. WR goes on and on about your talent. I see you have quite a project going here."

"Miss Davies, it's a pleasure to meet you as well. Welcome to Camp Hill," she said, waving her arm around to encompass the hillside.

"It's a large construction site, isn't it?" I asked, spinning around. "And you can't beat the view."

She lifted her eyebrows as she studied the view next to me. "You need a tour to truly appreciate the scale of what we're attempting here," Julia said.

"That's where I come in." WR grabbed my hand and we bid Julia farewell, WR promising to catch up with her soon. "This is La Cuesta Encantada," he told me as he led me through the grounds. "It means 'Enchanted Hill' in Spanish." He pointed to a few dirt lots that had been cleared and prepared, where buildings would someday stand. On the other side of the hill from where we stood, I glimpsed what looked like a small city for the construction workers: humble tents for the hundred men tasked with making WR's dream come true.

After an hour of more of the same, WR turned to me and said, "I'm sorry I can't offer you accommodations here. Stan will drive you back to Los Angeles tonight, and I will come very soon."

"I can't stay with you?" I asked, squeezing his hand. "Just for one night?"

"I'm sorry, my dear, but I cannot do that." Then more quietly he added, "Millicent and the boys have been here several times and stayed with me in the tents. I'm afraid Julia might quit and the men revolt. Please understand. I will see you back in LA."

I shot him my nastiest look and quickly walked to the car, having spent less than two hours there. I slammed the door shut, leaving WR watching me as he waved like nothing had happened, which only made me madder. Stan raced back to the car and started the engine. Tears streamed down my face, a lump in my throat making it hard to swallow. "Los Angeles, Stan, please," I choked out.

I would always be second. Always.

— ⓪ —

Arriving back in LA late that night more than a little drunk from the bourbon I had stashed in my bag, sniffling, with swollen eyes and a quivering lip, I checked into the hotel and went straight to bed. There was no way to just leave for New York the next morning like I wanted, my work always dictated my schedule. I had another week of shooting to do on my next film called

Beauty's Worth. We'd shoot all the outdoor scenes here in the hills around Paramount Studios and the interiors back in New York after the new year.

Telegrams arrived from WR promising his arrival in two days, only to be canceled by another telegram explaining that problems persisted with the construction. I filmed my outdoor shots and left for New York alone five days later.

I drank myself into a blackout every night aboard the train, reminiscing about Mexico and feeling like I would never be that happy again. I had a small accident on the train with an overfilled ashtray, but the smoldering mess was extinguished quickly by the porter.

Once home, my family nursed my broken heart with the cheer of a warm Christmas Eve, sitting around the fire drinking apple cider.

"Marion! Merry Christmas! We're so glad you made it home in time," Ethel said.

"Thanks. I'm glad to be here too."

Reine, Charlie, and Pepi were there, and Rose informed me that Patricia was asleep and I could see her first thing in the morning.

"Where's WR?" Reine asked.

Quietly shaking my head and with my lips quivering at the mention of his name, I poured myself a drink, settling in to watch the fire crackle.

"What's wrong, my dear?" Mama asked, snuggled in next to me. "Where is WR?"

The lump in my throat returned. "San Simeon."

"Is he joining us later?"

"Probably not." Tears fell, and I laid my head on her shoulder and folded my knees underneath me, letting her comfort me.

My only happiness came the next morning, watching pudgy Patricia, two-and-a-half years old, open her presents on Christmas morning and dance to the radio.

"Dance with me, Mama," she giggled as she twirled, making her dress fly up.

Rose, who looked more haggard and unkempt than I'd seen her, didn't hear her. George read the newspaper on the sofa, also oblivious to Patricia's pleas. Her curly blonde hair, lapis blue eyes, and long straight nose harkened after me and WR. I tried to forget my past decisions, feeling a tidal wave of pain descending on me.

"I'll dance with you, darling," I said. Patricia squealed as I grabbed her little hands, spinning her around and twirling with her on my hip as she lay her head back, giggling. Stopping to catch my breath, I heard, "Again!" and happily obliged.

— ⟨ ☉ ⟩ —

A few days after Christmas I picked up the newspaper to find a picture of WR and Millicent, sitting across from President and Mrs. Harding while they enjoyed a meal. I had been staring at the picture for a few long minutes when Ethel walked in.

"What are you up to today?" she asked, pouring herself a cup of coffee. I pushed the newspaper toward her. "Oh God," she said.

"Now I know why I haven't heard much from him," I said, realizing WR's political dreams of running for governor of New York had taken a front seat in his life. How could he be governor on top of everything else he did? God, I hated politics.

I had an overwhelming feeling of alienation from WR. He was here on the East Coast and hadn't even let me know he'd arrived. Was he at the Riverside Drive home a few blocks away with Millicent and his sons? He hadn't telegrammed or sent me flowers. No word from him at all. There was empty space all around me.

"I'm sorry, sister. Are you okay?"

"I don't know. If he wins as governor, then my life with him is over." I looked back at the picture of the Black Widow smiling like she'd won. Damn her.

I changed the subject. "Tell me what's wrong with Rose. She looks terrible and she barely acknowledges Patricia."

Ethel confided that Rose's marriage to George seemed to be unraveling, and Rose stayed out later and later, coming home drunk and sleeping all day. It worried me for Patricia, but Ethel assured me that she and Mama took good care of her.

"She says 'frog' whenever I read her *The Adventures of Danny Meadow Mouse*. It's so funny. She won't say 'mouse,' but she yells 'frog' on every page she sees him," Ethel said, squeezing my hand.

I let that bit of news sink in and warm my heart.

— ◎ —

Burying myself in the only thing that brought me any pleasure besides Patricia, I worked sixteen-hour days the first couple of weeks of January, finishing the movie I had started in LA before the holidays—the interior shots for *Beauty's Worth*. I then started ice skating lessons for a winter carnival scene in my next film, *The Young Diana*.

The damn Marion Davies Orchestra, the five-piece band given to me by WR as a present the previous year in California, were camped out at Cosmopolitan Pictures incessantly playing their happy music. They felt like a prick in the eye.

My workday was packed. WR had scheduled three movies to be filmed back-to-back during the first six months of the year. Maybe he knew he needed to keep me busy while he ran for governor. I worked and drank with my girlfriends, trying unsuccessfully to forget him.

We began filming *The Young Diana* in mid-January, but the new French director was fired by WR after only a week without any explanation.

We all shifted our focus to the next film in line, *When Knighthood Was in Flower*. It was the biggest costumed spectacle we'd ever done, featuring me as a lady of means and manners, Mary Tudor, sister of Henry VIII, who falls in love with a guardsman

far beneath her class. The script only fed my growing disappointment with WR, because I had teased him in a playful, fun way
for a light-hearted comedy.

"But comedies don't garner the same respect as dramas do,"
WR would say dismissively.

I disagreed with him but had yet to find the nerve to make
my case passionately. Josef Urban was building the sets, and my
dear Gretl was designing the elaborate costumes.

"I cannot tell you how many bolts of silk I will need for the
wardrobes, hundreds maybe, along with taffeta and cashmere,
but WR has assured me he will spare no expense in making them
grand," Gretl had told me when I saw her at the studio.

Many of us at Cosmopolitan Pictures were working on both
movies at the same time, filming or on standby with *The Young
Diana* while studying, building, and preparing for *Knighthood*
in our off time. I put my ice-skating lessons on hold until a new
director could be found for *Diana* and started fencing lessons
for *Knighthood*. Life was more than full.

— ⟲ —

A few days before the January 22 premiere of *The Bride's
Play*, WR finally came home to me at the penthouse late one
evening without any warning. I would have blocked the door
with furniture if he'd given me advance notice of his arrival.
I was dozing on the couch when the lock clicked. My heart
jumped a little as he ambled toward me, bending over to kiss me.
"Hello, Sweetheart."

Ignoring him, I picked up the script I had been reading and
stared at it. He sat down next to me and tried to hand me a few
pages of paper. "I have a belated birthday gift for you. Will you
look at me?"

I raised my eyes, but not my face.

"Oh, I can see how mad you are," he said. "Is there nothing
I can say or do to make it up to you?"

I lowered my eyes but the words in front of me were a blur.

"You cut your hair!" WR said, only just noticing. "When did you do that? It's gorgeous!" He touched a curl hanging near my ear.

"Are you really going to act like nothing's happened and we can talk about my hairstyle, for God's sake?"

"I'm sorry," he said. "I don't know how to break the ice with you. It's been so long since we were cozy together."

"Why are you here, WR? Why did you come over now?" He didn't answer.

On January 3, I had spent my twenty-fifth birthday alone. At the time I'd thought my anger at being forgotten by WR at Christmas, then at New Year's, and then again on my birthday would burn me up inside. I had sent no fewer than a dozen telegrams to him over the past month, but I'd only received a few business-type responses. His real life seemed to exist behind a thick wall that I couldn't penetrate.

He tried to hand me the papers again. I didn't move but indicated with my eyes the stack of newspapers on the coffee table. "You've been busy lately."

WR's run for governor of New York, his publishing empire, and movie business were featured in several articles, but it was mostly his run for governor that burned me.

Ignoring my comment, he tried a third time to hand me the papers. "These are the titles to two office buildings in Manhattan that I've put in your name. One, I am publicly renaming The Marion Davies Building. The others are the titles for your mama's house and your papa's apartment on Riverside Drive. I was hoping you could give them the titles for me."

"You could have delivered them yourself if you had stopped by at Christmas or been at my birthday party."

"Darling, I am sorry I missed your birthday. I really am. Can you ever forgive me?"

"And Christmas. And New Year's too," I said. A lump grew in my throat. I took a deep breath.

"Come here, my precious girl. Come here and let me hold you."

I threw the papers at him and yelled, "You abandoned me—again!"

He scooped me into his arms, carried me to his favorite chair, and sat down with me curled like a cat on his lap. "How can I make it up to you? My life is out of control, and I am so sorry, my dear. The last thing in the world I want to do is hurt you. I love you."

"How is your life out of control?" I whimpered.

"For some reason I believed I could win the governorship of New York."

"You didn't even tell me you were going to run."

He said nothing.

"Who will be your first lady?" My hurt began boiling over into anger. "You can't take a mistress to the Governor's Mansion." I climbed out of his lap. "Have you decided to end it with me and pursue your precious politics?"

He looked up with daring, pleading eyes. "Darling, darling, darling, please stop this nonsense. I could never leave you." He grabbed my hand, but I pulled it away.

"When you win, it will be Millicent moving into the Governor's Mansion with you, and I will stay here—hiding out? Is that the plan, *darling*?" I laid on the sarcasm.

"I hadn't thought that far ahead."

I shook with humiliation. Every moment of my life was a lie. "It's no life at all waiting for someone to come home. I think I'm done." I picked up my purse and left.

— ⟨Ⓞ⟩ —

The Bride's Play opened two days later at the Rialto Theater with heavy publicity from WR's papers. I had returned to Mama's house to live, where flowers arrived every day, along with a pearl necklace and several poems from WR. I could feel my defenses melting but I shored them up again like a dam that needed constant reinforcements. I would not cave so easily. Damn him anyway. Why did our relationship have to be like this?

At the premiere, WR offered me a seat in the theater with a wave of his hand. I smiled and politely said, "Thank you." We sat next to each other, rubbing elbows and smiling like everything was fine, but I still wasn't speaking to him. It felt good to make him suffer.

"Do you like the song the orchestra is playing?" he whispered to me as the lights went down.

"Yes, it's nice," I said.

"George wrote it for you."

"I'll be sure to thank him," I said, as I realized what WR was saying. He'd gotten George Spink, who played the butler in the movie, to write the song. I listened to it for a few minutes. It was a waltz—our favorite dance. My heart warmed a little, but I kept my stoic face on, and as soon as the movie was over, Norman drove me to Mama's house. I fell asleep replaying the song in my head.

I couldn't forgive WR until the race for governor was over. He could make his play for power in the political world, but it might cost him me. I would not be hidden away while Millicent lived in the Governor's Mansion. I could not stomach that.

The next morning, I sat next to Ethel reading the reviews from the movie premiere. I watched as hungover and disheveled Rose patted down her hair and primped herself. Patricia played on the floor with her dolls.

Pouring a cup of tea, Ethel broke the silence. "Listen to this: 'Miss Davies, in a variety of moods, did excellent work.'"

"Bravo, sister," Rose said a little too loud and happy, trying desperately to bridge the gap between us.

"Thanks. Can I have a cigarette?" I asked, eyeing her pack. She slid them to me, her eyes darting up in guilt as I lit one.

I hadn't done any looking into Rose's life, not really wanting to see the truth. All I really cared about was knowing that Mama and Ethel loved Patricia and took care of her. Rose was giving up on the dream of marriage and motherhood, and what could I do about that? We all make our choices.

"Mama, Mama, hold my doll," Patricia said, handing the doll to a bored-looking Rose.

"I'll hold her." I reached my hands out to Patricia, but she put the doll in Rose's lap, ignoring me. Why did I expect Patricia to favor me? She barely knew me. If one more person rejected me, I might run away and never come back. I grabbed my teacup and left the room.

— ◎ —

Fencing lessons continued four hours a day for *Knighthood*. I threw myself into the physical challenge, which caused me to suffer spasms in my lower back. A massage therapist and a chiropractor worked on me after every training session, and I grew stronger as the weeks passed. Josef built the magnificent British monarchy sets. Gretl worked with a dozen seamstresses to accomplish all the costumes in time for the start of filming.

All winter as the snow swirled and the wind whipped, I held the cold front between WR and me strong, even as I received love notes and flowers from him. Life was only business as we traded telegrams about filming and set design.

Bob Vignola became available, and we began filming *The Young Diana*, putting *Knighthood* on hold for a month. I saw WR at the studio during all this commotion but stayed away from him, at first to protect myself, then to punish him. I blocked him in every possible way until he left me alone, finally seeming to accept that I needed time to myself. He continued to pursue the governorship of New York, so we lived in a state of limbo for months until he arrived at Mama's home in mid-May with four bouquets of lilies.

"I need to talk to you. Can we go to the penthouse, please?"

I got my things. We didn't speak for the short ride, awkwardly staring out the window.

"I'll make tea," I said once we arrived. WR was uncharacteristically quiet. After putting the teapot on the fire, I turned and stared him down. "Let's have it. What's going on?"

"Slow down. Let's visit for a minute. It's been so long since we've been alone." His voice was lilt and sweet.

"I can't. Just tell me what's going on."

"Okay. I have some bad news. Something that will make you hate me more than you already do." He fidgeted in his seat.

"You haven't even won the governorship yet, so I can't hate you more—yet."

"I set sail tomorrow morning with Millicent and the boys for a family trip to Europe that Millicent is insisting on." His voice was raw.

My stomach soured so fast I feared I might heave. I turned off the whistling teapot and threw a teacup at WR's head. "Damn you!" I screamed.

The cup missed his head and he jumped up. "Marion! Stop that!" His face was like a wound.

"So you're ending it with me now? You've decided politics and *Milly* are your ticket to happiness?"

"No, no, nothing like that." He had gone pale as a stone, but reached for me. I recoiled. "I'm not ending it. I could never do that. It's been excruciating without you these past months. I love you. But I have to go with her on this trip. She's threatening to expose us. She's furious with me. Please, darling." His eyes were soft and pleading as if he were on bended knee.

"Threatening to expose us?" I lit a cigarette and blew the smoke directly at him.

"She's insisting on equal time with me after our Mexico trip."

"Equal time? Is she crazy?" I picked up a saucer and threatened to throw it.

"Don't," he said, backing up to the doorway.

"Why not? I hope I hurt you. You constantly hurt me!" I yelled.

"Sweetheart . . ."

I put the saucer on the counter. "No 'Sweetheart' for you. Just go. I don't want to see you again," I said, fighting back tears as I followed him to the living room. Grabbing a heavy crystal ashtray full of cigarette butts, I threw it at him as he approached the front door. It crashed against the wall, shattering and spilling its vile load down.

"Marion! Stop this now," he said, opening the door.

"Out, you bastard! Get out!" I yelled.

The door closed and tears poured out. I ran to the bedroom, climbing under the covers and cried myself to sleep.

When I woke in the middle of the night, the ball of hurt expanded as I relived the entire scene over again, tossing and turning until first light.

Picking up the paper from the stoop the next morning, the caption nearly crushed me: "William Randolph Hearst Family Off on European Adventure." They stood together in front of the *Aquitania*, Millicent looking self-satisfied and stoic in her dark suit, an almost imperceptible smile at the corners of her mouth, and WR next to her looking like his skin was a size too small. The three eldest boys, George, Bill Jr., and John, were dressed in suits like upstanding young men. I figured the seven-year-old twins must be staying home.

I sat on the kitchen floor and sobbed. She must have insisted on the publicity picture as another way to get back at me. Touché, m'lady.

I found a bottle of vodka and drank myself to sleep, longing for how things used to be.

CHAPTER 19

D ays disappeared. I woke up hacking, having smoked every cigarette I owned before passing out. My head pounded, and I clutched my empty stomach from the self-imposed fast and four-day isolation. The anger had melted into nostalgia and longing. I hobbled into the kitchen, poured myself a glass of water, made some toast, and cried again for how much I missed WR.

A few hours later, a telegram arrived: "I miss you. I love you so much. Life just isn't worth living without you. Please take the next liner to England, and we will be together again. My heart aches in loneliness. Love, WR."

"Love, WR," I whispered to myself, clutching the telegram to my chest. He couldn't live without me. Yes, to London. He would sneak away from *her*, and we would have time together after all. I packed hastily and phoned the studio telling them I would be on hiatus for a few weeks. I'm sure they were happy for a vacation.

Next, I phoned Ethel and shared my detailed plan. "What if he can't get away? What if you go all that way and don't see him?" she implored.

"He has publications and employees in London, and business to attend to there. He can always get away." I crushed my cigarette out with force.

"Okay, sis, good luck and take care. I'm here if you need me," she said and hung up.

Arriving in London a week later, I had spent my time aboard primping and fussing over every inch of myself, making myself ready for a reunion that would be reminisced about for years to come. I was taken by limousine to a luxury hotel suite in the theater district of London, where WR had arranged for a sweet gray-haired man named James McPeake, the publisher of WR's British *Good Housekeeping* magazine, to take me to dinner.

"WR will be here tomorrow. He sends his best wishes," James told me when he introduced himself.

I was grateful for the dinner plans and the distraction, but I counted down the hours until I could be with WR.

The next morning I opened the newspaper to see a picture of WR and Millicent standing next to Prime Minister Lloyd George, dressed like they were leaving for the opera. The caption read: "American publishing tycoon, William Randolph Hearst, and his wife dine at 10 Downing Street."

I rolled over, clutching my chest. Tears fell on my pillow, and my chin quivered as I tried to stuff all the pain back down. What a fool I was, always hoping things would change.

I didn't get out of bed until 2 p.m. when a knock at the door brought Mr. McPeake back. I had just poured myself a vodka.

"Good afternoon, Miss Davies," he said, biting his lower lip. "I am sorry to say Mr. Hearst has been delayed. One of his guests, a Mr. Guy Barham who accompanied him from New York, was stricken with abdominal problems late last night and rushed to the hospital."

"Oh my," I said absently. "Which hospital?"

"I'm not sure. I can find out if you wish."

"No, it's fine. Thank you."

"I am sorry, Miss Davies. Mr. Hearst is quite upset."

"Thank you." I closed the door and looked out my window at Piccadilly Circus. My fresh vodka sat in the windowsill, and I took a big gulp.

Three hours later, another knock on the door brought a delivery boy wearing a square cap on his head and a matching blue striped vest. "Telegram for Miss Davies," he said.

I swapped a small tip for my telegram, which read: "Mr. Barham into surgery two hours ago. Not successful. He passed away from complications. Hoping to get away soon and will come to see you. I am so sorry, Sweetheart."

I did feel sorry for Mr. Barham, but the world seemed to be conspiring against our reunion.

I mixed another drink. The more vodka I drank, the more acutely I felt my broken heart. Maybe I needed surgery to remove it. *How could I hide away in this hotel in London and wait for him . . . always waiting?* Although he was only a few miles away, he may as well have been on the moon. I ordered some much-needed food and tried to eat.

Finally, at 9 p.m., a third knock brought WR himself to my door. His cheeks were sunken, his chest smaller somehow, his normally bright eyes had dark circles under them and were empty of light on his ashen face. My anger evaporated.

"Oh, darling," he said, "it's so good to see you." He slunk into the room, distracted and tentative. I rushed to him and wrapped my arms around him and burst into tears.

Holding each other, we walked to the chairs and sat down. "Sweetheart," I said, "you look terrible. Have you been awake through the entire ordeal with Mr. Barham? You look so tired."

"Yes. The hospital, the doctors, the panic, the emergency surgery, Mrs. Barham, the news that Mr. Barham died in surgery, and the entire experience has shaken me deeply."

I crawled up into his lap and lay my head on his chest, wrapping my arms around him, nuzzling into his musk and citrus scent.

He felt broken and beaten, and I only wanted to heal him, love him back to health, and make him believe in happiness again.

Softly he spoke. "I don't have much time. I'm sorry. Please pack your things. We leave in the morning on the *Olympic* to go back to New York. I have booked you a room."

I sat up and looked at his face. "We're going back?"

"Yes, we're going back. I will escort Mrs. Barham with the body of her husband. They were my guests. I can't just ship them back alone."

"What about . . ." I hesitated, not wanting to say her name.

"Millicent and George will continue on with the European tour. George is eighteen now and wants to see the famous sights. William and John are younger, not impressed with history yet, and wish to return to New York with me." His voice shook just a little.

Was it heartless of me to admit my happiness at stealing him back and maybe even getting to watch his sons from afar?

I caressed his face and hugged him again. He continued softly, barely audible. "I hate hospitals. They're for the old, the sick, the dying, and I don't want any part of that. Please don't ever ask me to go to a hospital."

"Is that why you didn't stay for Patricia's birth?" But as soon as I uttered the words, I instantly regretted them.

"The hospital had little to do with it then. There were many reasons I didn't stay for her birth." I waited for him to finish, hoping to hear the truth of it. He continued, "It was wrong to share the moment of her birth with you since we weren't going to be her parents."

The memory changed the mood. He attempted to stand up, but I was still curled up in his lap like a mouse not wanting to move.

"I'm sorry, never mind. What's the plan for tomorrow?"

"I'll send a car for you at 6 a.m. and meet you on the ship once we've set sail."

"Come to bed with me and sleep for a few hours," I said, brushing away a strand of silver hair.

He looked at me with loving yet dull eyes and just a hint of a smile. "I'm heartbroken at how this has turned out for you. I never meant for you to come all this way to sit and wait."

"I know, I know. But it's over now and we're going home."

"Yes, we are going home." We moved to the bed and lay down, holding each other close. His eyes immediately closed as exhaustion took over. I lay still as stone watching him breathe in and out, tears rolling down my face, overcome by my desire to protect and love him.

— ⟨⟨⟩⟩ —

I embarked on the *Olympic* the next morning and found my suite. A few hours later, WR stood at my door not looking any better than he had the night before.

"Don't speak," I commanded. "Just come in here and be with me."

He must have been completely undone by the experience of his friend's death. He didn't make love to me as he normally did after a long absence. In fact, he was incapable of being intimate with me. He stared at the ceiling for a while and then slept like a child. I wondered how, at fifty-nine-years-old, he would recover after facing his own mortality and perhaps realizing for the first time that he wasn't as invincible as he imagined.

Over the next several days, he recovered with sleep and food and much doting from me. I liked taking care of him. He needed me now in ways that were new. We finally made love and found some of our old rhythm. He became more carefree with me in public and less concerned with appearances. We strolled the deck together, ate openly in the dining room, and didn't avoid public places like we usually did.

"We're not hiding anymore," he told me one afternoon as we sat having tea in the restaurant. "I'm done sneaking around, hiding my happiness and love for you from the world. Let the chips fall where they may."

Proof of his newfound freedom in the world came only thirty minutes later when his teenage sons Bill Jr. and John entered the restaurant and took a seat at our table. Introductions were made with WR introducing me as a "special friend." Pleased as ever, and maybe just a bit nervous to finally meet two of his boys, I inadvertently fumbled my response, "I-I-I-I'm so pleased to meet you boys." They smiled politely at me.

WR ordered ice cream sundaes for the boys. John stared and generally seemed infatuated with me, admiring me openly before finally saying, "You look like a daisy," which made me blush. That day I wore a white dress covered in yellow daisies. From then on, all WR's boys would call me Daisy. I couldn't have been happier.

CHAPTER 20

Upon our return to New York, WR and I regained our equilibrium and life resumed as normal. He adored me with presents and affection, and I let him, watching him bloom back into the man I had always known. I picked up filming *When Knighthood Was in Flower*, while WR worked in his office at Cosmopolitan Pictures. While shooting the final scenes for *Knighthood*, I noticed my five-piece band was playing a song I didn't recognize next to the sound stage. A moment later, WR grabbed the script off my lap in a playful gesture.

"Can you hear the new song?" he asked. "I commissioned Victor Herbert to write it just for you. I call it 'The Marion Davies March.'"

I was stunned. Reaching up and wrapping my arms around his neck, I kissed him deeply. When I opened my eyes, several of the crew were looking. I buried my face in his chest.

"Oh, who cares? These people work for me. They know we love each other." He took my arm, and we began waltzing to the song as the whole crew watched.

"You really are braver since we returned from London, aren't you?" I said.

I loved that he needed me even though he had everything in the world. I was good for him—my laughter, my youth, my pranks, and even some of my naivete and inexperience.

I needed him, too, for his sureness about my acting, his insistence on how beautiful I was, and his belief in my intelligence. I'm not sure how he knew I could be a savvy businesswoman, but he did. Late at night when the house was quiet and we lay side by side in bed breathing in and out, I knew we were a perfect match.

— ◯ —

My fourteen films up to this point were referred to as "program pictures," meaning they were made quickly and on a relatively small budget. I'd learned the craft of acting through trial and error making them; there were no schools or mentors to call for help. The critical reviews were my schooling. With WR's publicity of me, there was an aura of purchased fame that hung around my neck, calling into question my legitimacy as an actress and making it harder to succeed and be taken seriously.

On September 14, 1922, the day *Knighthood* was released, everything changed. This film was in a different category. Theaters were sold out eight weeks in advance. The success was genuine and not a product of WR's publicity hoopla. I had matured into my career. With this movie, I *was* Mary Tudor. I embodied her and knew her inside and out.

Of course, it didn't hurt that no cost had been spared in the set production—using three New York area movie studios at the same time. Mr. Urban had outdone himself with an "unlimited budget," as WR put it. He built the largest indoor set anyone had ever seen, with thirty-two buildings replicating two city blocks in old Paris, a Gothic cathedral, part of London's Billingsgate district, and the Tower of London.

"I know the public will pay premium prices for costumed spectaculars with true-to-life sets, which bring history to life," he'd declared, and nobody challenged him. The sets were decorated with WR's own private collection of antiques. Three thousand extras were employed for the crowd scenes.

WR lavishly remodeled the Criterion Theater for opening night, adding ornate loges patterned after the royal boxes seen at the jousting tournament in the film. On the corner of 47th Street and Broadway he built a billboard and put my face on it so huge that *Variety* magazine commented on its size—over three stories high.

The morning after the premiere, a stack of newspapers with reviews worth reading out loud to WR sat on the kitchen table at the penthouse. I slid my hand on top of his and quietly read from *Variety*: "'While this is a fine picture for all concerned, it is a finer one for Marion Davies, for *When Knighthood Was in Flower* implants this handsome girl right among the leading players, those who can act—something mighty few beautiful women of the screen ever accomplish. . . .'"

I got up from the table and twirled around the kitchen, letting my nightgown billow out around me.

WR smiled as he watched me. Grabbing a paper from the stack, he read from *Exhibitor's Trade Review*: "'Marion Davies gives a performance . . . that is not only the best thing she has ever done, but one of the finest performances ever given by any actress.'"

I screamed, throwing my head back and twirling again. "Finest performance ever given by any actress!" I yelled, jumping up and down. "Stop! Can this really be happening?" I asked, coming to a standstill in the middle of the kitchen.

"Yes, my darling, it's really happening. Pinch yourself because I'm going to pinch you in just a minute." He smiled slyly and picked up another paper. "This is my favorite review right here. It's the one that mentions the scene where you're praying to Mary near the stained-glass window." He cleared his throat for effect and held the paper out like he was reading a proclamation: "'And Marion Davies in an attitude of prayer is one of the finest moments we have seen in the cinema.'"

"You old men. What is it about a young girl praying at a stained-glass window anyway?" I said, suppressing a giggle.

"It's virginal, I suppose," WR said, bemused.

After reading a couple of more glowing reviews aloud, I looked up and saw WR admiring me and enjoying my childlike wonder at all the love I felt from the critics. It was glorious, and I was so grateful to WR for guiding my career to this pinnacle point.

He took my hand and we went to the bedroom, where we tried to be intimate but were unsuccessful. Since London, WR's virility had waned. I tried to be positive, admitting that the large age gap between us was sure to have this kind of outcome, at least some of the time.

Knighthood ran for months for the outlandish ticket price of $2.00 for the better seats and opened to general release nation-wide in February 1923. *Camera* magazine reported that six weeks after release, not a single empty seat could be found at any performance, and a thousand a day were being turned away. Special booths were set up in theater lobbies and department stores to sell *Knighthood* souvenir books, enlarged stills printed in sepia, and portraits of me in full costume. WR loved all these marketing gimmicks. It became a pet project of his to design trinkets and treasures for each of my movies from then on.

My comedic moments in the film were well received, even though WR was convinced that the regal quality of the character Mary Tudor was what the public most loved. We had to agree to disagree, since I always pressed to do more comedy.

"Anybody can take a pie in the face. Not just anybody can move my emotions," he would say.

To which I'd reply, "If you're going to make me do drama all the time, with heavy costumes from ages past, you can't forbid the kissing."

To which WR would reply, "Absolutely no kissing."

— ◎ —

162 THE BLUE BUTTERFLY

The only pushback we received for *Knighthood* was directed
at WR and his bragging of the regal sets. It came from my dear
friend Louella who wrote, "Marion Davies is a good actress, a
beauty, and a comedy-starring bet. Why talk about how much
was spent on the lovely costumes and the production costs?"

As I sat on the sofa reading him her review, he said, "Invite
Louella to dinner next week at Delmonico's. Let's talk to her."

The following Wednesday, we sat at a table for three—
me, WR, and Louella. I waited for WR to bring up the review,
but he filled the evening with pleasantries. We sipped our gin
fizzes, and when our steaks arrived, Louella said, "I'm sorry you
didn't get the nomination for governor. You must be terribly
disappointed."

I blurted, "Really, WR? You lost the nomination? When
did this happen?"

"Oh, just yesterday. Don't worry, darling. I'm through with
politics." He cut his steak and avoided my surprised look. I was
happy for myself but wondered how WR felt now that a dream
of his had died.

We finished the rest of the meal in silence. I avoided WR and
concentrated on my food. When the bill was paid, WR stood up,
extending his hand to me as we prepared to leave. He looked
at Louella and said, "I read your review of Marion's movie. It
was good. Write more things like that. And then come to work
for me."

Louella had an almost imperceptible smile at the corners
of her mouth. Within weeks she'd negotiated an outlandishly
lucrative contract for herself and began writing for WR within
the year.

CHAPTER 21

HOLLYWOOD, 1924

Without WR's political campaigns weighing down our relationship, hovering over us like an impending storm, I found myself
carefree and happy with professional capital to spend on the
heels of *Knighthood*'s success. WR made good use of that capital
and negotiated a place for me with Louis B. Mayer and MGM.
Within a few months, I and my entire family were living in
Hollywood, minus Papa, who stayed back in Brooklyn.

WR purchased a white two-story Mediterranean-style house
for me with a red tile roof, five bedrooms, and six baths at 1700
Lexington Road in a posh Beverly Hills neighborhood. I lived
there with Mama, Ethel, Rose, and Patricia. Rose's marriage
to George was over, and he'd opted to stay back in New York.
The house was put into Mama's name to keep the New York
press and Millicent off our trail. Reine, Pepi, and Charlie rented
a small house of their own a few miles away on Bedford Drive.

The house was located on more than an acre, had a circular
driveway, step-down wood paneled living room, fireplace, and
beautifully detailed plaster ceiling. There were windowed double
doors opening to a large portico with a pool and tree-trimmed

garden. WR immediately made plans to add a grand salon for dancing, as well as a library and tennis courts.

Not long after settling into the house, Rose cornered me in the kitchen. She had jumped at the chance to move to Hollywood. She had straightened up her life and drinking and was participating in the care of Patricia again, according to Mama and Ethel.

We stood near the kitchen table as I was building a small sandwich. "Sister, can I ask you something?"

"Sure." I bit into a finger sandwich.

"I'd like to make a movie—star in it myself. Do you think you could help me get started?"

I stared at her, not sure what to say.

"I want to make my own movies," she pressed on, "and if I had an investor, then maybe I could hire a good director and a male star." She took a drag on her cigarette.

"I could find you a part in a movie already being made," I offered, thinking that a much better path forward than what she was suggesting, which was far too ambitious.

"I don't want that. I want my own thing," Rose said defiantly, picking at her sandwich and avoiding my looks.

"You don't know anything about making a movie."

"Why can't you let me have my own thing? Why do you have to control everything? I'm just asking for an investment, say $10,000, to make my own movie." She leaned forward, challenging me.

"Damn, Rose, that's a lot of money."

"For me, yes. But for you, it's nothing," she said. "Look at this house." She waved her arms around.

I felt a pinch in my gut. "What about Patricia? She's due to start kindergarten this year."

"What about her? Mama loves tending her, and she'll support me in making this film."

In the garden, the grass sparkled after being watered. "It feels extravagant and reckless," I said. "I'd like to see you get some experience acting in somebody else's film. It's more complicated than it looks."

"You're always raining on my parade. Ten thousand dollars is nothing to you. Just give it to me and I'll show you what I can do."

"How is that possible? I am *not* raining on your parade!"

She left the room in a huff, slamming the kitchen door on her way to the garden.

I bit into a pickle and watched her stomp to the chairs by the pool. She had no respect for WR's money. She also had no respect for a hard day's work, which she hadn't performed since before Patricia was born. WR's money ran like a faucet in her life. It made me cringe inside to think of it, but I didn't want a prolonged fight with Rose.

When I talked the matter over with Mama that night, she came to Rose's defense. "She needs a project, something to focus on instead of drinking. She's very unhappy now that her marriage is over."

I caved in and reluctantly gave Rose the money, hoping for the best but bracing for the worst, like a fearful ride on a roller coaster.

—— ⊚ ——

My contract with MGM was finalized. I was to be paid $10,000 per week, with MGM paying 60 percent and WR paying 40 percent, but WR would receive 30 percent of the profits on all my films. I would work forty weeks a year. Cosmopolitan Pictures also paid me a flat salary of $100,000 a year to produce. With all the money details negotiated, I began filming *Zander the Great* on the Universal Pictures lot each morning because MGM didn't have a big enough sound stage yet. *Zander* had me playing a pigtailed orphan trying to find the father of baby Zander, whose mother had died. Written by the highly esteemed Frances Marion, I starred with Harrison Ford and Hedda Hopper, and that's where I met Charlie Chaplin for the second time.

I was filming a nerve-wracking scene with a full-maned lion whose cage I had to enter for a pretend kiss. In actuality, I would be kissing a glass partition, and movie magic would later remove the glass. The lion was supposed to roar his love for me, and then the scene would end. George Hill, the director, said it would be easy and that the lion didn't have any teeth.

My knees trembled, and I squeezed my hands together. "Do I really have to go in, George?"

"The script calls for the scene, Marion. The glass partition between you and the lion will protect you."

"Action!" George yelled.

Without another word, I marched into the cage, but before I could get to the center, the lion let out a terrible roar, shook his mane, and showed his great pointy teeth. I turned and ran out yelling, "Help!" I hid behind George's chair, and everybody laughed.

"You said the lion didn't have any teeth!"

"Whoops! Guess we picked the wrong lion," George said, turning away from me with a smirk on his face. Minor practical jokes were standard fare on the set. My reputation as a practical joker was known, but this felt more devious than normal.

"Very funny, George. Even behind glass he's pretty scary." I wanted to be the willing actress on the set and laugh it off, but I was terrified.

"I'm sorry!" George yelled after me. "Maybe we went too far."

Heading for my dressing room to have a few minutes to myself, I saw Charlie talking to George. I instantly adored him again, with his penetrating ocean-blue eyes and boyish qualities. George yelled to me across the sound stage, "Change out of your dress, Marion, and give it to the costume director."

"Why?" I asked.

"Charlie's going to do the scene for you," he said.

Studying Charlie for a moment, I shook my head and smiled. He acknowledged me by raising his eyebrows twice. I handed over the dress, and a few minutes later Charlie emerged wearing it and a blonde wig. Truly, he was a gorgeous girl, the same height as me at five-foot-five inches. I sat by the makeup man enthralled, nervous, and scared for him all at the same time.

They filmed him from behind as he walked into the cage. The lion stood on his perch when Charlie entered the cage. Nothing happened. Charlie leaned forward and kissed the glass partition. The lion then roared, showing his big ugly teeth and I flinched, leaning backward in my chair. Charlie was still as could be, then turned around and left the cage with nerves of steel.

"Cut! Good, Charlie! Can you do it one more time?" George asked.

I flew out of my seat, "Don't make him do it again. Once is enough."

Charlie smiled at me. "Don't worry."

George yelled, "Action!" and Charlie did the whole thing again.

When it was all over, Charlie left the set without a word to me. He was flanked by a man I would come to know as Kono Toriachi, his valet and personal secretary.

I yelled, "Thank you, Mr. Chaplin!" He didn't turn around but held up his hand as if to wave goodbye, and he skipped a little with his feet like he always did in the movies. He was indeed the tramp.

— ⓪ —

When I got off work later that day, Charlie was waiting for me outside the studio door. His face lit up as he watched me walk toward his silver Rolls Royce. I tried to hide my happiness, but a smile snuck out. I had spent the afternoon thinking about him and was pleased to see him. He leaned over and pushed the door open. "Want a ride home?"

"Sure," I said, knowing my life was about to change. The electricity I felt at the garden party years ago crackled to life around me. I could hear Eileen's voice in my head from the first time I had met Charlie. "Watch out," she'd warned.

WR was in San Simeon hosting Millicent and the boys and wouldn't be back for weeks. The ongoing push/pull for WR's time continued. I was alternately in love and angry at him, depending on how much time he spent with me. At least now I had Hollywood to distract me—or better yet, Charlie.

"Hop in, let's go," he said. We sped away, leaving WR's spies and the Universal lot in our dust. The top was down on his convertible, and my hair blew in the breeze. Charlie took my hand, brought it to his mouth, and kissed my open palm, all without taking his eyes off the road. "Do you have time to go to the beach?"

My hand was about to start shaking from excitement, so I pulled it away. I tried to act normal, like driving to the beach with the famous Charlie Chaplin was perfectly normal. "Do you do that to all the girls?"

"Only the pretty ones." He paused then asked again, "Well, do you have time for the beach, you little blue butterfly?"

"Where did you hear that name?"

"Some article about you, and it came to mind immediately when you got in the car, which means it was an accurate description." He had a sly grin on his face and after a pause said, "Well?"

"Yes, okay, sure. Let's go to the beach."

He smiled big and bold, never taking his eyes off the road. We traveled in silence for a few minutes, and I tried to regain my composure.

"Th-th-thanks for helping me today with the lion," I stumbled as I mentally admonished myself, but he didn't seem to notice.

"I love lions," he told me. "I have two of my own but they're toothless."

I laughed. "Why couldn't I have had a toothless lion today instead of that beast with the huge fangs?"

He took my hand again and threaded his fingers through mine. "The truth is they're old lions, and the studio saved them from certain death."

"How noble of them." I stared out the window as we drove on Santa Monica Boulevard, the fields flying by. I unlaced my hand from his and lit a cigarette, and we drove in silence for a while. He was eight years older than me at thirty-four, but he didn't look a day over twenty-five; and he moved like a tiger, his muscles rippling on his arms and chest.

"Here we are, princess, Santa Monica beach." The sun hung just above the horizon on a clear evening. The ocean smelled fishy and felt damp on my face as we walked to the water's edge. Charlie took out a flask, took a long draw, and without looking handed it to me. His whole manner unnerved me. I watched him in fascination.

"Thank you." I took the flask and drank, feeling the warm liquid spread over my body. We sat on the sand and watched the oranges and reds fill up the sky as the waves rolled under the pier. "Tell me a secret, sweet Marion."

I stared out at the sparkling ocean trying to hide my ever-present smile. "A secret? I don't have any secrets."

He stood and grabbed my hands, pulling me to my feet and placing his hands on my hips. Standing face-to-face with him, I tried not to stare at his soft, sensual lips. Without anywhere to hide, I looked past him to a sandpiper chasing the receding water. When I looked back, he was studying me so closely that a slight gasp escaped me.

"Race you to the water," he said and took off. A flock of seagulls took flight and the sandpipers scurried away at his sudden movement.

I didn't run but walked behind him, needing to catch my breath. Burying my toes in the sand, I quickly got wet up to my ankles with a swoosh of an incoming wave. I shivered. Charlie held his pant legs up and jumped from side to side on each foot, smiling.

I waved him away. He swooped in and planted a big kiss on my cheek while slipping his arm around my waist. Then he was gone, racing back to our spot on the dry sand before I knew what had happened.

I tingled all over. "What's *your* secret, Charlie Chaplin?" I stood in front of him.

He gave me a big toothy smile but didn't say a word. Instead he put his hands out so I could pull him up to standing, and we walked back to the car in the gathering darkness.

— ◎ —

The summer of 1924 unfolded in extraordinary fashion as my new life took shape in sunny California. An excitement built inside me at all the possibilities. Not only did I have secret bursts of passion for Charlie, but I also had the freedom to go anywhere I wanted. WR spent the summer six hours up the coast in San Simeon.

I worked all day filming *Zander*, letting George and WR hash out the scenes via telegram while I escaped to the adjoining studio where my best girlfriend Connie Talmadge was filming her own movie. We snuck into each other's dressing rooms on set, having lunch together and catching up. Other girlfriends from my Ziegfeld days had also made the move to California, including Dorothy Mackaill, Marie Glendinning, Eileen Percy, and Anita Loos, and we gathered for pool parties at each other's houses. Louella even showed her face occasionally for a girls' night but was mostly kept busy working for WR. The girls all encouraged me to declare myself my own person, now that I was away from WR body and soul.

"Grab the world by the tail, Marion. Your arrival in Hollywood has caused quite a stir. Have some fun with it," Connie said. I wasn't ready to dump WR, but I *did* intend to enjoy a bit of the single life. I didn't say anything to the girls about Charlie, feeling like a schoolgirl with a secret crush.

Charlie picked me up on days when his schedule allowed, and we drove to Venice Beach and up to Mulholland Drive for the view late at night. We talked about my movies mostly and my love of comedy, and I began to let my personality out as I felt more relaxed around him. We always drank from his flask; sometimes he even had a bottle in the trunk. I teased him and poked silly fun at things. We discussed our love of travel, and he told a few heartbreaking stories of his childhood in London. Our friendship was real and solid; we were two magnets drawn to each other.

One evening we drove south, down to the harbor in San Pedro. We had dinner at a quiet little restaurant in anonymous bliss, and on our walk back to the car, I felt silly and tried to imitate the Tramp. I used my umbrella as a cane, walking with my feet turned out, bouncing just a little.

"Very good," Charlie said. "It'd be better if you had the hat and baggy pants." He took the umbrella and did the Tramp walk.

"Show off," I teased.

— ⦿ —

The following day Charlie waited for me again.

"People are going to start talking," I said as I slid into his Rolls Royce, waving to WR's spies standing at the soundstage door. I wrapped my scarf tightly around my head and neck.

"Let them talk," he said and sped off, barely allowing me to close the door before taking a turn so sharply that I had to hold on.

"In a huff today, are we?" I asked.

"I've got heavy things on my mind. Never mind."

We drove in silence until we reached a house—his house, I assumed.

"Come in for a drink," he commanded and slammed the car door, heading down a long portico without bothering to see if I agreed. I had never been inside his Beachwood Canyon house before. I got out and followed him through the front door. Kono nodded as he passed me on his way out the door.

"Good evening, Miss Davies."

I nodded to him as the door shut. "Charlie!" I yelled. But he was nowhere to be seen. I stopped walking and took in the beauty of his Moorish-style house. In the entryway, the dome over my head reflected Mediterranean blue mosaic tiles. "Your house is fantastic!" I called out. "I love the stained-glass windows."

"Do you, now?" he said in a quiet voice from behind me. I jumped. He snuggled up to me from behind and slid his hands around my waist. He kissed my neck softly. "I'm so glad you love my house. I intend to hold you captive here for the next several hours."

"So, what? You weren't really upset?"

"Poppycock, I am mad about work, but now I'm here with you at my house."

A rush of adrenaline left me frozen for a moment. Still standing behind me, he removed my jacket, letting it fall to the ground. "Charlie, I'm not sure this is such a good idea."

"Oh, it's a good idea alright. I've been planning this ever since I stood in for you in that lion's cage." His hands settled on my hips, and he caressed me up and down. The heat rose in me. He removed my hair clip, letting my hair tumble to my shoulders. I was warm pudding, wiggling like I would melt right there. He took my hand, leading me upstairs. He stopped in front of a carved wooden door, backing himself up to it and pulling me close.

"Once we go in here, life will never be the same again."

"You sure think highly of yourself, don't you?" My sarcasm flowed so easily.

His serious face caught me, and WR flashed across my mind, disappearing as quickly as he came. I looked into Charlie's azure-blue eyes, melting all the way to my bones and giving in. He led me to a four-poster bed, where he took my face in his hands and kissed me softly. I kissed him back, unable to contain the flood of emotion. The kiss became harder as he fumbled with the buttons on my dress. His hand fell down my thigh, and he slid my dress up, slipping his finger between my garter belt and my leg. His hand went up and I closed my eyes. I pulled my dress over my head as he lifted me up and put me down on the bed as gently as if I were a feather. I opened my eyes and watched him take off his shirt and unbuckle his pants, letting them fall to the floor. He climbed onto the bed. "This is my secret, sweet Marion: I am hopelessly in love with you. Now let me show you." His voice was gentle in my ear, sweet as summer rain. I drifted away with him, shutting out the world completely.

CHAPTER 22

I loved WR with all my heart and soul, there was no denying it, but his long absences and decreasing ability to be intimate left a hole in my life. I justified my liaisons with Charlie as fulfilling my physical needs. But there were further justifications—like my no longer tolerating being owned and ordered around while WR entertained his wife and sons. Being treated like a mistress was the worst part of being a mistress.

I fought my heart and head as they each had something to say about sex with Charlie. My head told me to stay away from him, but my heart needed his wild, artistic inspiration and mad lovemaking. We were like teenagers, unable to go more than a few hours without seeing each other.

A few days after that first visit to Charlie's house—having made love in his garden, his bathtub, his car, and on the beach late one night—we had our first hot, sweaty sex in his office at Charlie Chaplin Studios, which was more like a home than an office. We lay on our backs, naked in bed, panting as we stared up at the dark wooden beams on the ceiling. I was on a long lunch break, thinking about how wonderful it was to be Charlie Chaplin's bed slave. Outside it was quiet with only distant voices audible between breaths.

"M-M-Marion, my dewy blue butterfly. Get me that bottle of whiskey over there."

"You get it yourself. I can't walk."

"I was that good?" he said smugly, then added, "I'm parched. I'll give you a thousand dollars if you get the bottle."

A bead of sweat rolled off my forehead. "You were adequate, and I'll give you two thousand dollars to get it *and* my pack of cigarettes."

"I'm thirsty and dying here. I need that bottle, and no smoking in bed." His hand reached out toward the bottle, fingers scratching the air.

I rolled off the bed using gravity to land on my feet. Swigging a mouthful of whiskey, a chill came over me and I shivered. Charlie stared at me from the bed. "You are a beautiful sight, my dear Marion, now come here."

I stared back at him, proud to be so desired. I grabbed the whiskey bottle and two glasses.

"Open your mouth," I commanded, and he did. Holding the bottle high, I drizzled the whiskey slowly into him. "There, that should make you happy for a minute, Mr. Parched Man." Charlie swallowed hard and tried to grab the bottle.

Using my most authoritative voice, I said, "Be still. Do not move an inch." I placed the heavy highball glasses on the soft part of his stomach. I poured the whiskey into one glass, then the next, raising the bottle high as I poured, causing the whiskey to splash onto his torso.

From his clenched mouth, he said, "Darling. Sweetheart. Hurry, I can't hold my breath for long."

"Shallow breathing, that's what's required here," I said. "Steady, Mr. Chaplin." I lowered my mouth and licked up a splash of whiskey from his belly with a flick of my tongue. Finally, he grabbed both glasses and lifted them off his stomach, holding them high above his head, breathing deeply.

"Put them back," I commanded. "Right now." My lips were pursed playfully. He deliberately knocked the glasses above my bare breast in a toast so that the whiskey sloshed out and ran down my nipple. The challenge in his eyes was fierce, his chin jutting up. I gave him a stern look. He put the glasses back on his stomach. Drops of whiskey ran down my body.

"Oh, the hell with it," I said, drizzling whiskey all over his chest.

"That's it!" Charlie yelled, grabbing the glasses and sitting up. He chugged the liquid in both glasses and placed them down on the mattress. I took a long draw from the bottle and climbed up to straddle him.

"You're covered in whiskey, my dear," I said, holding the bottle.

"Don't waste it; it's our last bottle."

"Waste it? I would never." I took another long swig of the amber liquid and smacked my lips. Running a finger around Charlie's lips and down to his belly button, I poured more whiskey onto his stomach. He grabbed the bottle from me and pulled me down on the bed, straddling me and pinning my arms next to my body. Whiskey soaked the sheets.

"Where's my thousand dollars?"

"I'm going to give you a thousand dollars, my dear. Don't you worry." He gulped from the bottle and put it down on the floor. We made hot, heavy love again and fell straight to sleep.

— ⓪ —

I knew WR would appear back in town at any moment. A feeling of dread hung over my heart. How could I be so happy, so fulfilled in this secret life with Charlie? I knew it couldn't continue. I needed to get back to reality, but like a good dream, I didn't want it to end. At the studio one day late in July I received a present from WR with a specific message—The Al Jolson record "I Gave Her That" about an ungrateful lover. I wish I could have pushed WR away for just a bit longer, but it wasn't possible. It was time to wake up.

It happened late one evening when Charlie was in my dressing room, picking me up for dinner. We heard three knocks on my door followed by a pause and two more knocks. It stopped me cold. "WR's on the lot," I said, looking at Charlie, who jumped up from the couch in a motion that belied his years. We had come up with a code to warn us of WR's arrival and shared it with Vera Burnett, my movie double. When the security guards called the set to announce WR's arrival at the front gate, Vera would let me know, giving me a few minutes to prepare. Charlie quickly departed my dressing room through the back door.

Looking at myself in the mirror, I straightened my clothes and fluffed my hair, catching the reflection of the Al Jolson record behind me. Back on the set, I stood by George when WR's car pulled up. He unfolded himself out of the car, walking toward me with a big smile. "Hello, my dear," he said, brushing the back of his hand against my cheek.

I smiled. "Hello, dear." I kissed his cheek as he bent down. "George. How's it going today?"

"Just fine, Mr. Hearst. We're making great progress. Did you see the daily runs from yesterday?"

"Yes, I did. They're wonderful."

He turned to me. "I missed you desperately. Are you done for the day?"

"Yes, buy me some dinner. I'm starving."

At Musso and Frank's, we ordered pot pies and afterward went to his suite at the Ambassador Hotel. The phone was ringing when we entered, and WR answered it. I stared out the window at the Hollywood hills, considering my new life and friends. WR hung up the phone and sat down next to me. "Reports have you spending lots of time with Charlie Chaplin."

"Reports from whom? Your spies?"

"Marion, please don't start. They keep an eye on you because I worry."

"Don't *you* start. You spy on me like I'm a criminal. And don't question my friendships. Charlie is a friend. He's a mentor for my comedy, so talented that I'm just hoping some of it rubs off on me by proximity."

"I think he's a genius too. Can we invite him for dinner or something?"

I tried my hardest to answer nonchalantly, "sure," but my heart raced. WR said he had work to finish and that I should go to bed. When I woke in the morning, I could tell he had slept next to me because the sheets were mussed, but he was nowhere to be seen. I stretched my hand across the sheets to see if they were warm. "WR?" I yelled toward the living room. No answer. On the table, I found a note. "Gone downtown to see my guys at the *Examiner*. See you this evening."

Previously, I would have been devastated at being treated like an afterthought, but now I shrugged it off, yearning to get back to my dream life with Charlie. Never had I been so happy, so fulfilled, so in love. I was euphoric with Charlie and yet possessed with guilt and dread when I looked at WR. It must have been how WR felt when he met me and was cheating on Millicent. I dressed and headed for the studio, getting a telegram later that day saying WR was returning to San Simeon immediately on some urgent news from Julia. I breathed a huge sigh of relief. It seemed we both had our passions these days and they weren't each other. WR was in love with the building of his castle. It was his mistress in many ways.

— ⟨①⟩ —

With WR gone again, spending copious amounts of time with Charlie was my only priority, even to the exclusion of my family and girlfriends. I couldn't wait to get back to the dream. Our intimate, romantic time together at his house was a refuge from everything. After several days of not seeing him, I ached inside for him. The only thing that kept me from him was work. I was still filming *Zander* because WR kept rewriting all the scenes from San Simeon. Nothing pleased him. He was full of spit and vinegar, firing George and hiring another director. I stayed out of the negotiations, leaving the details to WR. Even the scene where Charlie stood in for me with the lion was cut from the movie.

One afternoon, I headed over to Charlie's house for a rendezvous. We stood in the kitchen separated by the black-and-white Italian marble counter. I swirled the crystal glass of whiskey he put in front of me, lifting it to toast him. "Thank you. What have you been doing these past few days?"

"Working," he said, staring down the front of my dress. He raised his eyebrows twice and wore a tantalizing smile on his face.

"With Lita?" I asked. Lita Grey was starring in his latest picture, *The Gold Rush*, and I'd heard rumors about their affair.

The smile disappeared. "What's your point?" He sliced tomatoes and brie on a cutting board.

"I don't know, I heard you two were an item. Are you?" He placed a slice of tomato on top of a thick slice of brie and slid the cutting board to me.

"We are not an 'item,' as you say. She lives with her parents." He stared at me, offering nothing more.

I took the piece of cheese and tomato. "Her parents? How old is she?" I said self-righteously, but he fired back immediately.

"Don't *you* live with your mother? Besides, how old is Hearst?" He popped cheese and tomato in his mouth.

"Okay, okay, let's stay out of each other's lives, why don't we?" I said, leveling my gaze at him.

Of course, Charlie and I had no official arrangement for our mad passion, so I guess it was just my innocence that had me secretly hoping I was enough for him. I pushed the thought away. The combination of his eyebrows raised and his mouth curling around whatever words spilled out drove me wild. His ease of moving like a tiger in the bushes left me feeling like his sumptuous prey. My stomach flip-flopped whenever I saw him. We fit together in so many ways, like sand and the ocean or whiskey and ice.

"Where's Kono?" I whispered.

"Gone," he said and came around to my side of the counter, pushing himself up against me, sliding my dress up my thigh. "You're jealous of Lita?" he crooned. I took a long drink of my whiskey, trying to bury my real feelings. He kissed my neck, sliding his hands over my body and unbuttoning my dress, pulling the ribbon, opening my camisole so that I shivered.

"Maybe, maybe not," I said, pressing as close to his warm body as I could, like a lizard on noonday rocks. Lifting me up on the counter, he unbuttoned his pants and slid out of them. I whimpered in pleasure.

When we were finished, he carried me naked to the backyard hammock and put me in it before running back into the house for a blanket. "Scooch over," he said climbing in next to me, swinging the hammock back and forth until I giggled. "Don't flip us."

Curling with the blanket over us, wrapping our arms around each other, we fit together perfectly. "Don't worry about Lita," he whispered, kissing my shoulder, moaning low and snuggling into my breasts while he closed his eyes. "She's got nothing on you."

I lay quiet, gazing at a hibiscus plant with hundreds of pink blooms, praying for more times like this. We swung in silence until the evening brought cooler winds.

"I need some dinner. How about Montmartre Café?" he asked, putting his pants on. I found my dress and underclothes in the kitchen.

"It's Saturday night, though. Should I call ahead?" I asked.

"Nah, let's just go. We'll get a table in the back, in the dark." His eyebrows shot up twice.

Café Montmartre was a two-story nightclub and restaurant, the new hot spot in town on Hollywood Boulevard and Highland Avenue drawing all sorts of famous and want-to-be-famous people. Decorated as an Italian Renaissance palazzo, it had imported carpets and Romanesque chandeliers. Settled in a secluded half-circle booth with our drinks, I lit a cigarette. "There's nothing like a drink and cigarette," I said, staring at the smoke wafting across the table, "except whiskey and sex." Isham Jones's "It Had to Be You" played while Charlie studied the menu. Glasses clinked, people talked, smoke filled the ceiling. I snuggled up next to Charlie in the dark booth and whispered in his ear, "Lucky for us, they had a booth we could hide in. It's packed in here. We probably should have stayed home."

"Never are we going to hide away. Besides we're Charlie Chaplin and the lovely, sweet Marion Davies, and they will always hold a table for us to dine."

Charlie commanded respect, and I loved watching him. "Order for us both. I don't want to look at the menu tonight," I said, staring at the crowds pushing their way to the bar and swaying on the small dance floor.

"Let's dance," he said and pulled me out of the booth. The song was slow, and Charlie pulled me close with his mouth on my neck. I closed my eyes and drifted with George Gershwin's "Somebody Loves Me." When the song ended, we returned to the booth. "I'm getting the full treatment tonight—dinner and dancing." I kissed his cheek.

As we slid closely together, Charlie put a hand on my thigh under the table. His fingers reached down between my legs. I adjusted, giving him full access.

"Good evening, Mr. Chaplin. Are you ready to order?" the waiter asked.

His fingers pressed down harder in that moment and a shot of adrenaline coursed through me as I struggled to maintain my composure.

"Yes, I will have the pork chops, applesauce, and mashed potatoes," he said, maintaining total composure. "Miss Davies will have a bowl of your clam chowder with sourdough bread."

I sucked in a mouthful of air quickly and tried to pull his hand away from my crotch, but he pushed down harder and I let out a slight gasp. His mouth was tense, his eyes focused intently on the tablecloth in front of him. "Charlie," I whispered. He moved more of my dress to the side and put his whole hand between my legs. "I'm going to slide under this table in a minute," I said. "Please . . . stop."

He rubbed his finger up and down until my head fell back against the booth and I glowed inside. Finally, he removed his hand and I let my forehead rest on his shoulder. I closed my eyes and heard a man's voice, loud and close, "Good evening, Charlie. Out for a late dinner, I see."

I sat up and faced forward. "Miss Davies." The man nodded in my direction. I smiled and nodded back.

"Nice to see you, Ned," Charlie said, all but ignoring the man. He leaned over and kissed my cheek just as a flash of light illuminated the booth. Ned peered out from behind his camera with an awkward grin and quickly walked away.

The flash woke me up—to the newspaper that would surely hold that picture the following day, to the riotous objections I would endure from WR, to the distance I would have to keep from Charlie now that this had happened. I felt sick with the thought of it all rushing to me after such an intimate, dangerously sexy moment with Charlie. The roller coaster was in full tilt. "Let's go," I said, grabbing my purse and sliding out of the booth.

"No, let's not. Let's eat and then go," Charlie said calmly, patting the seat beside him. "The damage has been done. We'll deal with it tomorrow."

I reluctantly joined him, only picking at my food. I knew two things clearly. One, I would stay with WR no matter what—I couldn't imagine my "real" life without him, his status, or his money. And two, my jealousy about Lita now felt ridiculous. Charlie and I would never end up together as a couple. He was a player who enjoyed very young women, and this wasn't "real" life. I was practically an old hag to him at twenty-seven. This time with Charlie was a bit of fun. Nothing more. And it felt like the jig was up.

CHAPTER 23

NOVEMBER 16. 1924

At home by the pool the next morning, having breakfast with Mama and Ethel, I nearly choked on my toast when I read the headline aloud, "Cozy as Two Bears, Charlie and Marion Go Everywhere Together." I showed the paper to Ethel and Mama.

"Seems like things are getting out of hand," Ethel said as Mama looked to the distance shaking her head.

I breathed deeply, feeling betrayed they weren't on my side. The article detailed our dinner and dancing at the Café Montmartre. *Good ole Ned,* I thought. I wondered why the picture hadn't been included. The phone rang before I had time to finish reading.

"Have you seen this morning's paper?" WR insisted.

Mama and Ethel took their cups and breakfast plates and returned to the house, giving me privacy.

"Yes, and it's nothing really," I lied, taking a drink of my coffee, and lighting a cigarette.

"In that case, invite Charlie for a weekend cruise on the *Oneida.* Let's go to Catalina and San Diego. I want to talk to him. I'm a huge fan." He paused, then added, "I've invited Thomas Ince. I've got business with him, and we haven't been on the boat for a while."

I knew Thomas Ince was a prominent producer and screen-writer with whom WR was trying to work out a deal.

"Let's not invite Charlie," I countered. "I'll invite Louella and maybe Mama and Ethel. Gretl maybe? Connie and Marie?"

"Sure, anybody, but do invite Charlie, or I will. I need to talk to him," he demanded.

"About what?"

"Business and life, you know, the regular subjects," and then he added, "I miss you, Rosebud. Please make time for me."

My heart softened just a little when he used my pet name. "What time is your train due in?" I asked as my insides puckered.

"Three o'clock this afternoon."

"See you this evening, love. I'll make the invitations." I hung up.

As I stared at the blue sky over the pool and the oak trees on the green rolling hill beyond, I wondered how many men had been in a position to choose lovers? And how many women by contrast? I raged against the double standard.

— ⓪ —

That afternoon, I entered my dressing room for a costume change and found Charlie splayed out on my sofa. "Who let you in?" I asked, feeling a bit irritated. His arms were outstretched in a "come here" attitude. "Did you see the article in the paper this morning?" I chided. "WR is on his way back from San Simeon and he's angry." Ignoring me, he continued with his "come hither" gesture. "I'm due on set in ten minutes for a retake."

"Ten minutes is a long time."

"Don't be silly. Besides, I have bad news for you," I said.

"Well, I have good news for you. Me first," he said. I stared at him, waiting. "Did you notice there was no picture in the paper?"

"Yes," I said, unsure where he was going with this.

"Kono and I found Ned after you went home last night and had a little talk with him. Voilà—no picture." He swept his arms out.

"That's fantastic. But the article still ran and I'm in hot water and now so are you."

"What? Why?"

"WR's insisting you join us for a few days on the *Oneida*. He's courting Thomas Ince to produce and write movies for me, and he needs a few days alone with him in a relaxed atmosphere."

"Why in the world does he want me to go?"

"To talk to you." We stared at each other for a long moment. I added, "Don't you see? He suspects us and so this is a little game to him—setting us up on the *Oneida* to see how we behave."

"Lita's father called me this morning. He saw the article and wanted to know what's going on with you and me."

"Why would Lita's father call you? How old is she really?"

He lowered his head to his chest. "Sixteen."

"Oh Jesus, Charlie! Is she pregnant?"

"Three months," he confessed, a little too easily.

I quickly added up the months we'd been sleeping together and realized they overlapped. My heart sunk. "Will you marry her?"

"I must. Her father is forcing me to."

"Didn't you learn anything from your last child-bride fiasco?" I barbed at him.

Everyone knew that four years earlier he'd married an under-age girl who was supposedly pregnant: Mildred Harris. Sadly, though, young Mildred lost the pregnancy, then got pregnant again and lost the child three days after giving birth. Charlie was devastated it was reported, and they divorced shortly thereafter. He'd never mentioned anything about this. It was common knowledge as all the lurid details had ended up in the newspaper.

Charlie sighed like a defeated man, "I don't want to talk about it." His shoulders were hunched over. It wasn't the defensive reaction I was hoping for.

I wanted to fight, but quickly realized I had no claim to make. It was none of my business. I shook my head in disbelief.

CHAPTER 24

WR arrived that afternoon and checked into his usual suite at the Ambassador Hotel. I didn't want to provoke him in any way, just wanted to smooth things over. I was exhausted and hungry after a long day's work when I arrived at the hotel after dark and found WR working at the dining room table.

"Hello, Sweetheart," he said distractedly, looking at a pile of papers in front of him.

I kissed him. "Hi darling. I'm going to order dinner. Have you eaten?" I asked. He didn't answer. "WR, have you eaten?" I said a little louder.

"Yes, I ate. I've got an emergency in New York and need to work all night. I'm so sorry, Rosebud. Can we talk later, on the boat for our big weekend away?"

I kissed him again. "Of course, darling. I'm exhausted anyway. Good night."

The next morning WR headed for San Pedro harbor where the *Oneida* was docked. I had convinced Charlie to accept WR's invitation, making him promise to be on his best behavior. We needed a believable front for WR and now with my knowledge of Lita, I'd be pulling back from Charlie anyway. It would make the trip that much easier to pull off. Charlie and Louella dropped by the set of *Zander* to pick me up after a half-day of work, and we all headed for San Pedro. Charlie and Louella were old friends from their early acting days in Chicago and thankfully talked for the entire drive.

We boarded the boat, and the porter showed Charlie and Louella to their suites. The weather was calm and clear, the seas flat.

"I have an article to finish before we leave the dock," Louella said.

"Okay, see you at dinner then." I said. "Don't work too hard."

Charlie turned to both of us and said, "I'm not working at all. I'll explore the yacht." And with that he disappeared.

In my suite, my chambermaid Penny unpacked my clothes while I secured my jewelry in the safe. There was a knock on the door, and I knew it would be Charlie. "Thank you, Penny. You can come back later and finish." When she opened the door, Charlie moved aside so she could pass. As soon as he entered, he closed and locked the door behind him.

"What do you think you're doing?"

He stood back against the door with his arms stretched out, and his head hung low in a dejected, funny way, like he was hanging on a hook. "Take me, dear Marion. We're going to have a bang-up few days sneaking around in a game of cat and mouse."

"No, Charlie," I said, pulling a bottle of whiskey from my vanity and pouring two drinks. He unbuttoned his shirt and pulled the fabric apart so that I could see his chest. He had a hold over me, but I reminded myself of Lita and her condition. Taking a swig, I held out his glass. "Not going to happen. Control yourself. You should have brought Lita with you."

Charlie made a sour face at me.

"Chug this drink and go," I said.

"If you promise never to mention Lita again," he said, picking up his glass.

I took the last mouthful of my drink.

"Don't deny me this weekend, sweet Marion. I will find you. We will be together." He ran his hand down the front of my dress caressing my breast, swished back the last of his drink, and left.

Heat rose through my body as I watched him go—my body screaming for him to come back. I considered the weekend before me, then set off to find WR. He was in his shipboard office on the phone, standing by his desk and looking out the porthole at the limousines filled with guests arriving on the dock. I stood beside him and saw Ethel and Reine get out of a car and look around at the bright afternoon. Reine had on a blue skirt and white blouse with a nautical scarf. Ethel wore a green floral dress that hung to her ankles.

"You have to run it just like I wrote it," WR said to the person on the phone. I wrapped myself around his torso and lay my head on his chest for a long minute. Then, pulling away, I headed for the door and pointed at the porthole, trying not to interrupt his call. He smiled and waved.

Screenwriter Elinor Glyn arrived, wearing a mink stole. She exited her limousine just as Tom Ince and a young woman, not his wife Nell, departed another. Walking up the gangway, I said, "Tom, it's good to see you again. Welcome aboard."

WR had finished his call and came up behind me. "Welcome, Tom."

"Thank you, Mr. Hearst and Miss Davies. Let me introduce my friend Margaret Livingston."

"Welcome aboard the *Oneida*," WR said, spreading his hand out on my lower back. I knew he wasn't happy to have Tom's mistress aboard.

"Thank you, Mr. Hearst," Margaret said.

"And look who else is arriving," I said. "The good Dr. Goodman."

"Do we really need a doctor aboard?" Margaret asked as we watched him get out of his limousine.

"He's not here as a physician; he's a damn good screen-writer," WR said. "Shall we get you settled in your cabins?" He emphasized the plural of cabins for Tom's benefit. "Take your time getting settled," he said graciously. "Dinner will be at 7:00 p.m. The single women are on this deck, the single men one deck below. The porters will show you the way. I hope you both will be comfortable in your cabins."

I saw Tom and Margaret share a look at the fact of separate cabins.

"Of course, WR, as you wish," Tom agreed.

That's right Tom, whatever WR wishes, I thought with a little indignation.

Nobody was allowed to break the rules of decency. Even I had my own cabin separate from WR. Appearances were every-thing to him, even though the double standard of me being his mistress would never cross his mind. To him, we were different. He always said that I should have been his wife all along, and he really believed that.

— ⓪ —

I entered the dining room arm-in-arm with my two sisters, positioning us close to WR and Charlie, who stood in a corner chit-chatting. I dreaded the talk WR would have with Charlie and studied him. He looked very relaxed. The long dining table was set for twelve with fine china and crystal water glasses on a white tablecloth. The chandelier hung directly over the middle of the table and created sparkling ambience with reflection of the table candles.

"You three are gorgeous, have I told you that lately?" WR said, looking calm with his warm, friendly eyes.

Tom and Margaret entered the dining room arm-in-arm until they saw WR look away, obviously disapproving. Tom met my eyes, and I shook my head and frowned. I knew how to play my role.

I'm not sure how I would have felt in Margaret's shoes to see this double standard in play. Surely I would judge a woman like me as the height of hypocrisy. But Margaret and I moved in different circles. She read our glances correctly and separated herself from Tom as the rest of the guests filed in, including WR's personal assistant, Joseph Willicombe, known affectionately as "the colonel."

Charlie snuck a wink at me. My heart leapt at the daring and I immediately looked away. The rest of the party mingled and chatted around us.

"Shall we sit for dinner?" WR asked loudly enough for everyone to hear, and we all took our seats. WR and I sat opposite each other mid-table, at his insistence. Charlie was placed at one end, Tom at the other. The waiters brought in the food one course at a time— lobster cocktail, garden salad, roasted turkey, potatoes, and green beans.

Our conversation was polite, if not strained as we sipped our water—me, Charlie, Reine, and Ethel eyeing each other and looking for wine or champagne. But none was forthcoming. During the main course, our guest of honor, Tom, stood and raised his water glass, saying, "I was hoping to give a toast to my son for his birthday."

I took the opportunity to chide WR. "Aren't you going to break out the champagne or maybe some wine for our guests?" Eyes darted all over the place, nobody wanting to outright agree with me.

WR squirmed under the pressure as Elinor said, "Well, don't make a toast to your dear son with water. It's bad luck."

Raising his hand slightly, WR sent the maître d' to the kitchen for a bottle of champagne.

"Ah, so you were holding out on us." I stared at WR who ignored me.

When the bubbly liquid filled everyone's glass, Tom toasted his son, who was at boarding school back east. A collective sigh of relief was palpable as everyone sipped their champagne quickly, perhaps feeling a bit like prisoners instead of weekend partiers.

No more alcohol would be served publicly on the trip. I had several bottles of whiskey in my suite, and I'm sure Reine had a bottle or two for herself. Of course, we would never let WR know of our derelictions. He had lost all patience for alcohol and the messes that surrounded people who illegally drank under Prohibition. I wanted to stand by him on this publicly, but privately I needed a drink.

After dinner, negotiations continued between WR and Tom as they stood on deck under the stars. Standing behind them, out of the wind, I was enjoying a cigarette and admiring the sparkling path of the moon on the quiet seas when Margaret said, "It's a beautiful evening, isn't it?"

"Yes, it's gorgeous." I paused before asking, "How long have you been with Tom?"

"A few months. Has my presence here offended you or Mr. Hearst? We assumed that because you and Mr. Hearst weren't married, it would be okay if Tom and I had some time together."

"It's fine with me, but WR knows Nell very well and that makes it complicated," I said and waited for a dramatic pause. "It is *his* yacht."

"Yes, of course. We will be discreet," she assured me.

As soon as she turned to leave, an arm wrapped around my waist and a warm velvet kiss made me shiver. "Charlie," I whispered desperately, my legs going weak. "Meet me in Gretl's room. It's the third door down from my room. Gretl's busy in the library, playing chess with her mother."

He ran his hand across my back. "Be there in five minutes," he whispered before softly biting my ear.

My body quivered, and I closed my eyes. I could not stay away—he was like velvet cream—completely irresistible.

CHAPTER 25

The ship chugged along the moonlit night, the seas flat and calm. I snuck into Gretl's darkened room where I found Charlie in a chair cupping a drink in both hands, his eyes serious and full lips opened slightly. Closing the door and staring into his eyes, I pulled my dress over my head and let it fall to the ground. I slid the straps of my pink silk camisole off my shoulders, and it too fell to the ground. My knees shook ever so slightly at the thought of Charlie's hands on my skin.

Standing up, he let his pants drop while he finished unbuttoning his shirt. I slid into his nakedness and tasted his whiskey mouth, wrapping my legs around him as he held me. The blood rushed in my ears like a train bearing down on me as I moaned for Charlie to go faster just as I heard a voice from far away say, "Oh, excuse me. I'm sorry."

Charlie whispered in my ear, "That was Gretl."

"Oh my God, oh my God," I whispered, and yet neither of us stopped moving for a moment until I snapped back to reality, pulled away, and frantically put my dress on without undergarments. "Oh, Jesus, Charlie! This is bad. This is very bad!"

Charlie dressed and we made our way out of Gretl's suite to mine, a few doors down, making sure to lock the door behind us. Panting like children who'd been caught stealing candy, we threw ourselves down on my bed laughing. Suddenly, we heard a woman's voice calling, "Help!"

"Somebody's in trouble," he said.

"Quickly, you have to get out of here." I could hardly believe all the chaos unfolding within a matter of minutes. "Go now. Wait, let me check the hallway."

I opened the door and peeked outside. All was clear, so I waved my hand and silently scooted Charlie out of my suite. He ran the opposite direction from where the cries for help were coming.

Rushing down the hall, I nearly ran into Margaret as she opened the door and stepped into the hallway. "Margaret? Is everything okay?" Moaning and retching sounds were coming from behind her. "It's Thomas; he's very sick. The whiskey didn't sit well with him."

What whiskey? I wondered. "Let me get the doctor."

I ran to WR's room and entered after a rapid knock.

He was angry when he saw me. "Where have you been, Marion? I went to your suite fifteen minutes ago and it was empty. Where have you been?"

"I'm right here. But hurry. Tom is sick. We need to find Dan."

WR frowned as the words sunk in. "Okay, let's go."

As we hurried down the hallway, WR said, "Tom excused himself thirty minutes ago, complaining of pains."

Less than five minutes later, Dr. Dan Goodman was examining Tom, saying it seemed he had a stomach blockage and that we must get him to a hospital immediately. WR arranged it so that The *Oneida* steamed at top speed to San Diego Harbor, two hours away.

— ⟨O⟩ —

We arrived in San Diego after midnight where we were met by a Scripps Memorial Hospital ambulance. Tom was barely conscious when they took him by stretcher. Dr. Goodman went with him in the ambulance, saying he wasn't ruling out food poisoning. Margaret paced back and forth on deck, twisting her hair to one side, and chewing the inside of her cheek. She knew they would call Nell and that she'd need to fade into the background.

Thomas Ince died enroute to the hospital. We got the news from Dan himself, who returned to the *Oneida* less than an hour after he'd left. Our long weekend turned out to be less than a day-long trip.

Kono arrived in San Diego with the car to collect Charlie and drive him back to LA. As WR and I stood waving to him from the deck, I asked, "Did you ever get a chance to talk to him?" WR shook his head and with a deflated voice said, "I'll talk to him later, I suppose." I grabbed his hand and held it tight. The rest of our somber party traveled back to LA via the *Oneida*.

The news hit the world like a blast of heat with the press bearing down on us with a million questions, making up answers if they couldn't get them out of the guests. One headline read that Thomas died at a wild sex party at WR's ranch in San Simeon. Another claimed that WR had shot Thomas aboard the *Oneida* in a jealous rage over Charlie's and my affair. A third claimed that Thomas had been fatally poisoned with tainted liquor illegally served on *Oneida*.

Although none of these rumors were true, WR suffered the indignity of the scrutiny for all of them. It was the price of being the most famous publisher in the world. Rumors persisted that WR had gotten away with murder and that he could manipulate news coverage, which left him in a cloud of suspicion.

— ◎ —

We arrived at the ranch-style estate on Benedict Canyon Road to pay our respects to Nell and console her the best we could. Sitting on the baroque sofa, surrounded with Spanish renaissance furniture, WR explained that he would not attend the funeral because of the scrutiny and publicity.

"I understand, WR. They're after you something fierce," she sympathized. "You should take care of yourself."

I watched WR's pale and withdrawn face as he struggled with his obligations to Nell.

"Thomas has had stomach problems for years," Nell assured him. "His ulcers were very bad at times, completely debilitating him and putting him in the hospital. Was he drinking on the boat?"

WR relayed the story of the toast to their son and looked her square in the eyes before adding, "When I offered the champagne, I had no idea he was sick."

"Of course you didn't," she said, patting his knee. "Nobody knew. And I have no doubt he was drinking whiskey later in the evening, not champagne. He'd been feeling better lately, talking like he was cured. He hadn't had a flare-up in months." She walked to the window, staring out the sheer curtains to the green sloping tennis lawn court. "Do you think he drank to impress Margaret?"

I raised my eyebrows and shot WR a sideways look. With a pained expression, WR whispered, "I don't know."

A knock on the door interrupted our time. "It's my sister and mother," Nell said, walking to the door.

"It's time for us to go," WR announced. "Know that I'm here for anything you might need." We kissed Nell's cheek and bid her goodbye.

In the limousine on our way to the Lexington house, the air was thick with silence and sadness. I held WR's hand. Staring out the window, he pushed himself back against the seat looking like he wanted to disappear. All I could think of was how WR would continue to endure a public scandal that involved him and me and other various rumors. It was our fourth public humiliation in the past few years. First was the death of Guy Barham in London, second was a party I attended at Reine's Long Island home where a neighbor wife had shot her husband. Then there was the Jimmy Fallon trial, where Mr. Fallon had alleged in court that I had given birth to WR's twins while on our trip to Mexico. And now this. Millicent would undoubtedly scold him. I could see her skinny finger wagging in the air as she lectured about morality and decorum.

WR broke the silence. "Can you ask Charlie or somebody else to attend the funeral with you?"

"Are you leaving for The Ranch?"

"Yes, in the next few hours." Pain and grief clouded his face.

"Maybe I should come with you." I squeezed his hand, hoping he'd look at me, unable to read him. I knew he felt bad for Nell, but he probably also felt guilty for allowing Margaret onboard.

In a trance-like state he continued to stare out the window. "No matter how hard I try, everything seems to turn into a public mess. It's deflating and tiresome and this time so very sad. It was supposed to be a party."

"I know, darling, but this wasn't your fault any more than Guy's death was your fault in London."

He nodded slightly as we pulled up to the house. "We're here," he said and straightened up. "Sorry for just dropping you, but I really do need to get up to The Ranch immediately. I'll call you soon, darling. I love you." He picked up my hand and kissed it.

I kissed him goodbye. "I love you too. Please let me come up when the funeral is over and things have calmed down."

"Fine, Sweetheart. I look forward to it," he said solemnly and drove away.

CHAPTER 26

SAN SIMEON, DECEMBER 1924

Ten days later, I joined WR in San Simeon where I found him light on his feet, happily working with Julia on the construction of the big house Casa Grande, editing his newspapers, and living a quiet life. The smaller guest houses were now finished, and he'd moved into Casa del Mar, the house facing the ocean. I had only been to The Ranch a few times but felt strongly it was becoming our bubble—a vast ultra-private space where we read, slept, played cards, did puzzles, and walked together, enjoying the sweeping views. Our time together cemented again my quiet, strong love for WR.

We prepared for Christmas. I insisted on three Christmas trees of varying sizes, poinsettias everywhere, silver bells hanging over the entryway to the Assembly Room, and red, green, and gold balls with cranberry garland, which we strung ourselves in front of the fire at night. Without having discussed Christmas plans, I just assumed our time together would continue.

"Can we stay like this forever?" I stared dreamily into the fire.

"If forever is two more days, yes," WR said hesitantly while stringing popcorn.

"Meaning what exactly?" My voice snapped back from the dreamy fog.

"The boys are coming to spend Christmas here," he said. "I haven't seen them in months. I didn't know when to tell you. I'm sorry, Sweetheart."

"Just the boys? Or is the Black Widow coming too?"

He nodded sheepishly.

"I get to spend Christmas and New Year's alone *again*." One might think I'd be used to this treatment from WR by now, but I was not. I left him and headed outside to visit with my new favorite marble statue, The Three Graces, recently installed in the main fountain outside Casa Grande. The replica of Antonio Canova's statue showed the sister goddesses/daughters of Zeus—Splendor, Joy, and Abundance, looking adoringly at each other. It was the best quiet place to sit and stare off at the ocean where puffy clouds hung on the horizon. Reaching for one of my hidden bottles of bourbon near the bench, under a bush, I drank and quaked with indignation.

I headed to my room and turned on the radio. Jelly Roll Morton's "Hesitation Blues" played and I laughed out loud at the irony. On my fourth glass of bourbon, noting that WR hadn't come looking for me, I packed my bags. Finally, he knocked on the open door and I turned up the radio, yelling, "Get out of my way before I throw something at you!"

"Darling, I'm sorry. Please forgive me. I promise to make it up to you."

I fired two small pillows at him with all my force. "Ahhhhhh, go away!"

He stared at me. I slammed the door in his face.

When I opened the door an hour later, WR was sitting in a chair in the hallway. He held Helen, his dachshund. They both had puppy eyes.

"I'm ready to go. Please let the driver know." I pulled my bag down the hallway. WR picked it up for me and followed.

"You don't have to leave now. Please stay the night."

"Why should I?"

WR lowered his head. I hoped the Black Widow would ask him who had decorated the house and that he'd tell her the truth.

I slammed the door of the limousine, resolving to be with Charlie whenever I could. His marriage to Lita a month earlier in Mexico left him with less free time, but I knew he'd find time for me. Our love was a refuge and still burned bright and strong.

For most of the holiday season, I would do my usual routine of drinking too much, staying in bed for days on end, calling my girlfriends and going out, and, of course, spending time with my family, including lovely little Patricia, who was now five-and-a-half and growing up so fast.

CHAPTER 27

JANUARY 24, 1925

Back at work on a Saturday with my favorite director George Hill, I was now filming *Lights of Old Broadway* with rising star, Conrad Nagel. It was the story of twin girls separated at birth. One is raised in a wealthy Fifth Avenue home, the other in the slums of New York City. I was playing both parts and looked forward to the script's comedic moments. After half a day of shooting, we were let go for the day.

At home that afternoon, I received a telegram from WR that read, "I love you and miss you terribly. I have a surprise for you. Please be ready at 4:00 p.m. and make sure to be dressed in a gown." It had been almost three weeks since I'd heard from him, and fifteen minutes after receiving the telegram, three dozen light-pink roses arrived. They were lovely, but it was getting harder and harder to ignore the pain I felt inside.

Being with WR was like being on a ship far from land on a voyage to some imagined exotic destination that was our perfect life together, and no matter how awful the journey got, there was no way to get off the ship. The ship was either in good weather or bad weather, it didn't matter. I took comfort that I would always be on the ship with him. We were tied together, and I knew he would never leave me, just as I would never leave him. We had made some survivor pact and we'd never abandon the ship. In many ways, it was his job to shower me with love and gifts and promises, and it was my job to accept the fact of his other life with Millicent and the boys.

Lying on my bed clutching the telegram, looking out the window at the swaying oak tree, I yelled, "Ethel, come here. I need your help."

"Don't yell for me," she said, standing in the doorway, holding her book. "We aren't young girls anymore."

"Funny. I was just thinking about the old place in New York, when you used to help me pick out what to wear."

"What do you need?" she asked.

"WR's surprising me, probably for my birthday because he feels bad for dumping me again. I must wear a gown. He won't tell me anything more."

"Well, you have that beautiful white crinoline antebellum gown. It's way in the back of your closet. I don't believe you've ever worn it."

"Oh yes, let me try it on." I ran to my closet and found the dress. "It exudes pureness and wholesomeness." I held it up high. "Perfect," I giggled.

"I don't know how you do it. You live under a lucky star."

I rolled my eyes at her and began dressing. "Yeah, if the lucky star had a black hole in it for WR to stuff his promises, flowers, and jewels."

She adjusted the dress on me, and for a second I glimpsed her life void of adornments or a lover and felt instantly guilty. I kissed her on the cheek, and she startled at me with a quizzical look. "Thanks, sister, I love you," I said and spun in front of the mirror.

— ◍ —

WR arrived later that day, coming inside and waiting for me in the foyer like a proper suitor. As I descended the stairs all in white, my hair swept up in a swirl dotted with pearl clips, he whistled low and smiled. "I do declare, Marion, you take my breath away every time I see you." He held out his large, soft hand, and I put mine inside. Bowing down, he kissed my hand in a grand gesture that melted my heart. It never got old to be adored like a princess. Mama and Ethel watched from the foyer, smiling at the spectacle.

Stan drove us in WR's limousine to Santa Monica beach, pulling over by an empty lot. "Happy Birthday, Sweetheart. Do you see this concrete foundation?"

"Yes," I said, wondering where he was heading with this.

"Pretty soon you'll see a three-story beach house here—all for you. It'll have a ballroom, a pool, tennis courts, and of course many bedrooms. You will live like a queen," he said. His sparkling eyes beamed at me. "And you'll be able to sit on the porch and watch the waves crash ashore."

"WR, I'm beyond words. How could you plan all this and not even hint about it?"

"I've been planning to surprise you for a while. Julia even came down from San Simeon to give us her expertise on the construction of the pool and the guest houses."

"There are guest houses? Oh, WR." I leaned over and kissed him. "And you are so bad for sending me away at Christmas. You break my heart, you know?"

"I'm sorry, Darling. I hope you love your new beach house. It will be the envy of every person who sees it."

I stared at the blue ocean and the whitewater breaking on the sand. My heart clutched as I wondered which emotion would win out when we reached the end of this wild ride—hurt or joy. At the moment it was joy.

WR kissed my hand as he glanced at his watch.

"Why am I so dressed up, anyway? Where are we going?" I asked.

"We have to make a stop, and then you'll find out."

As we pulled away from the beach heading south on Highway 1, WR pointed to a large white Mediterranean-style house and said my boss at MGM, Louis B. Mayer, lived there.

"Are you really fading into the background now that Cosmopolitan Pictures merged with MGM?" I asked as the house disappeared behind us.

He explained that he wasn't fading anywhere in my life and then went on to describe Mr. Mayer. "He's only about five-foot-six-inches tall and he's twenty-one years younger than me, but we won't talk about age and height anymore."

I laughed. WR was proud of his height at six feet, three inches, but not his age. He was now sixty-two and I knew he was feeling it. I suppose sizing Mr. Mayer up in real numbers was a way for WR to assert some authority over the most powerful man in Hollywood.

The gift of the beach house and the anticipation of the next surprise felt like butterflies in my stomach. We stopped at the Beverly Hills Hotel, where I waited ten minutes in the limousine. When WR returned, he carried a dozen red roses and a gift box. He was dressed as Henry VIII, complete with a puffy-sleeved velvet waistcoat, dark blue tights, and a matching flat velvet cap with a feather in it.

I couldn't stop myself from laughing. "Mr. Hearst, you look sumptuous in those tights," I said as he got into the limousine. "I had no idea your legs were so attractive."

"No laughing. We are pretending tonight. You are the queen, and I am the king."

"I don't want to be your Anne Boleyn. Can I be Catherine of Aragon instead?"

"You can be anybody you want tonight."

Shaking off the silly for a moment, I said, "This isn't like you, WR. What's going on?"

"Just wait a bit longer." He handed the roses and the box to me.

Inside the box were diamond earrings the size of my pinky fingernail. My breath caught as the light flickered through the stones. I put them on just as the limousine pulled up to the Ambassador Hotel. WR guided me through the ornate lobby to the grand ballroom, where hotel guests stared at us in our costumes.

"Isn't that William Randolph Hearst?" a voice asked from across the room. "And the movie star Marion Davies?"

WR opened the door to a packed room of guests milling around. The sounds of jazz in the distance, chatting, laughing, and frivolity filled my ears. There must have been three hundred people there, all dressed in costume. The waiters buzzed around the room wearing knee-length satin knickers, black shoes with silver buckles, and white wigs like members of the French court. The great hall's crystal chandeliers cast spotlights on the diamonds and sequined gowns. Most people held champagne glasses. The buffet tables stretched the length of two walls and held flaming dishes like crêpes suzette and cherries jubilee as well as cheese, fruit, roast beef, shrimp, and lobster. The tables themselves were decorated with plants of every kind: ferns, miniature palm trees, mint leaves, and vases filled with roses in every color. Dozens of round guest tables draped with white tablecloths filled the middle of the room, adorned with glittering centerpieces of baskets in both matching and contrasting hues.

WR squeezed my hand. I stood in shock at the spectacle. "Let me get you a glass of champagne while we say hello to everyone."

As we walked across the ballroom, people stepped aside to greet me. "Happy Birthday, Marion." I nodded as I took it all in. I was secretly astonished when I saw Rudy Valentino dressed as a sheik and Natcha Rambova as his Arabian dancing girl. John Barrymore was dressed as Hamlet. Lillian Gish and her sister Dorothy revived their French Revolution roles from *Orphans of the Storm*. Joan Crawford was decked out as a gypsy, and Norman Kerry was Peter Pan. I couldn't miss petite Mary Pickford standing next to her husband, Douglas Fairbanks. Both were dressed as circus performers, and there was Charlie as Napoleon, perfect for his height and attitude, with his pregnant teen wife, Lita, as Josephine. Her pale blue velvet gown had sparkling diamonds embroidered on the very low-cut bodice showing her ample bosom. The long, deep folds of the skirt hung in a way to mostly conceal her pregnancy, but I knew she was seven months pregnant under there. She wore a velvet wrap, matching blue gloves, and a gem-encrusted tiara.

"You did all this?" I asked WR.

"Well, I had some help from Louella, Ethel, and Reine. They are the force behind all this magic."

As if on cue, someone behind me placed their hands over my eyes, and I heard Reine's giggle, which was high and light. "Are you responsible for this?" I asked once she removed her hands from my eyes. Ethel stood before me dressed as a ballerina with pigtails and pink ribbons in her hair.

"Adorable," I said, kissing her cheek. "You were good this afternoon, not letting on a thing." She nodded and handed me a full glass of champagne. I drank in gulps so that I was finished too soon and in want of another.

Reine was dressed in a black three-piece suit with a matching fedora hat like the kind WR usually wore, her hair stuffed up underneath it. "Handsome, sister," I said, and added, "Where's Mama and Rose?"

"Mama's with Patricia. You know her, she hates crowds," Reine said.

"And Rose is too busy with her film. It opens in a week, you know, and she's frantically finishing up the editing," Ethel said. I nodded my understanding, pushing aside my irritation at this expensive potential fiasco of hers.

From my side, I caught a glimpse of a cowboy hat and Louella's face mostly hidden underneath. "Well, howdy, Cowgirl," I said as I ran my gaze up and down her figure. She wore a black button-up shirt and black pants, with a white scarf tied around her neck. A holster with two guns and extra bullets hung low on her hips. "Howdy, little lady," she said, bowing to me.

I reached my arms out in an attempt to encircle all three of them. They closed in toward me. "Ladies, thank you. I never suspected a thing. This is just spectacular."

When I turned around, WR had disappeared.

"Let's get you something good to drink," Reine said as she pulled out a flask from her jacket pocket and passed it around the circle. I took a long draw and felt the warmth fill me up. A short distance away I saw Charlie standing next to Lita with sad eyes and a "come here" look that I knew all too well.

"Ladies, will you please excuse me? It seems I'm needed."

I walked over to introduce myself and gave him a kiss on the cheek. Lita looked so mature and beautiful, glowing with pink cheeks and red lipstick. "Oh you don't need to introduce yourself to me," she said with bright eyes. "Everyone knows who you are." I smiled at her.

"I need to talk to you," Charlie said, almost disregarding Lita.

"Charlie, don't be rude," Lita said. "It's an honor to be here tonight, Miss Davies. I just love your earrings. They make your whole face sparkle."

"Aren't you the sweetest. Thank you for noticing them."

"Nobody can miss them. They're huge," she said, lingering on "huge." "And your gown is simply perfect on you. I can see why you're a movie star."

Charlie grimaced. "Can we talk *now*?" he snapped.

"Okay, fine." I said, trying to hide my irritation at his rudeness.

"Not here," he said, looking around the room.

"Will you be gone long?" Lita asked.

"No," he said curtly.

"Lead the way," I said. Charlie took my hand and began to gently tug me. "Goodbye for now, Lita," I said, trying to keep things from being too awkward. "I hope to see you soon." I kept looking at her as Charlie whisked me into the crowd. Her smile disappeared in my last glimpse of her.

"In here," Charlie said, opening a door that led to the backroom where the waiters staged the food on trays. He took my hand firmly and led the way. We walked to a smaller room and into a closet, where he pulled the door closed behind him. "Charlie, this is a closet. What are we doing here?"

When he leaned forward to kiss me, I pushed him back gently. "Not here. I can't do this tonight, only feet away from our better halves. Besides, look at this dress. It's a Victorian nightmare."

"What do you have on underneath it?" he said, attempting to lift up the heavy hooped petticoat.

"Charlie! Stop!" He pulled back, startled. In a quieter voice I said, "We can get together next week when things have calmed down." I reached for the doorknob. "Okay, Napoleon?"

He wrapped his arms around my waist, looking desperate. "I need you now."

"Charlie, please don't. I have to go. WR . . ." I let my sentence die midway through and left. Walking across the service area, Charlie ran to catch up, and I thought to ask about WR before we returned to the ballroom. "Hey, did WR ever talk to you about us?"

He offered his flask, and I took a long swig. "Yes, he called from San Simeon a few days ago to thank me for being such a dear friend and comedy mentor, blah, blah, blah. He also not so subtly reminded me of how precious you are to him and for me to focus on my life."

I handed the flask back to him. "Really?" My eyebrows rose.

"Yes, it seems he really does love you—just like me." He threw his head back and drained the rest of the flask, then rubbed his hand down my arm while leaning in for a kiss.

I pushed him away, grateful there were no service staff present. "You will ruin everything with this tantrum you're having now. Leave me the hell alone tonight." I adjusted my gown.

"He's been through a lot with Ince's death," I said, not that I owed Charlie an explanation. "I don't want to hurt him anymore than he already is."

Turning away, I fluffed my hair and opened the double doors to the ballroom and saw Lita standing near the buffet with John Barrymore. They each had plates in their hands, and John was pontificating about something. I rushed away to find WR in the crowd.

I passed men I recognized from the MGM and Universal film crew. I smiled, saying hello as I passed and heard "Happy Birthday" in return. "Hey Joe, how is your son doing?" I asked as I passed Joe from the maintenance crew.

"Oh, much better, Miss Davies. Thanks for asking."

I waved to Conrad Nagel and the woman he was with, finally catching up with WR in deep discussion with Louis B. Mayer. They were standing in the middle of the party so close to each other you would have thought they were swapping secrets. I slid in next to WR and put my arm through his. "Are you two discussing business at my party?"

"I'm trying to tell Mr. Hearst here that there's money in the movies," Mr. Mayer said, winking at me.

"Yes, I know—mine!" WR grinned, pointing to LB, who let out a laugh.

"Well just remember Mr. Mayer, this is a party," I said, leaning in and hugging WR's arm.

"I know we haven't properly met since you started working at MGM, but please, call me LB."

I nodded, "LB it is."

LB said, "We can't hear a thing in here. Can you indulge us for a few minutes if we step outside the room? Afterward, I promise to properly enjoy your birthday party."

"Of course," I said.

"My seventeen-year-old daughter, Irene, begged for days to accompany me to this party. She's sitting right there," he said, nodding toward a young woman in a Raggedy Ann doll costume. She looked over our way and smiled.

"Would it be too much to ask you to say hello to her?"

"Not at all. I'd be happy to," I said as I walked toward her. "Cute costume," I offered, sitting down.

"You're Marion Davies," she said with a wide-eyed expression.

I nodded. "So you came to the party with your dad and he's abandoned you?"

"I'm used to it. He's always talking business with somebody. I came to see all the stars."

"And are you getting your wish?"

"Yes, I am. I saw Charlie Chaplin a little bit ago. That was exciting." I nodded, enjoying her childlike wonder. "Would you like something to drink?" I asked. "I'm going to get some champagne."

Gretl slid in next to me with a full flute of champagne. "Here, I brought you this. Am I interrupting? I've been trying to catch you all night."

I raised my glass in thanks to her. "You're not interrupting. It's good to see you, my dear." I introduced the two girls, and we chatted about the food.

An hour or so later, I rounded the front of the room and saw my ensemble, the Marion Davies Orchestra, performing near a small dance floor. I waved and smiled as they played on, grabbing another glass of champagne from the bar as I strolled right into a crowd of actors.

"Happy Birthday, Marion," Mary Pickford said, looking adorable in her trapeze black, pink, and white striped leotard. Her hair was pulled into a small bun.

"Thank you. When are we going to lunch to plan our attack on this outrageous notion of adding sound to movies?"

"It is ludicrous, for sure. How about next week? Doug is going on location to film in the desert for a few days."

The buzz all over Hollywood was the addition of sound to

movies. Nobody could believe it, especially the actors. After making movies a certain way for our whole career, everything was about to change. "Perfect, let's do it," I said as Charlie sauntered up to us.

"Charlie, how are you? What do you think of the talkies?" Mary asked. I nodded at him as if I hadn't seen or talked to him yet this evening.

Charlie's face looked pained. "It's an abomination and can't possibly last."

The evening continued this way for hours. Making my way through the huge crowd as I looked for WR, Ethel, and Reine, I bumped into guests and had short bursts of conversation. I drank more glasses of champagne than I should have, and a headache set in shortly after the birthday cake was wheeled out and everyone sang. WR and I danced to our favorite song, "The Blue Danube Waltz," and afterward we retired upstairs to WR's suite. Tipsy and feeling warm and fuzzy, I was carried over the threshold by WR.

"Ah, what an amazing birthday. Thank you, Sweetheart, for everything."

He put me down on the bed and pulled down the six-hoop petticoat. My heart filled with love and tenderness as my dress deflated and fell to my body. "Oh, thank you. Can you unlace the back, please?" He unlaced me, tossed my dress over the vanity chair in a sweeping motion, and turned back to me.

"How did you enjoy your Hollywood coming-out party?" he asked.

"Is that what it was? I enjoyed myself tremendously. Thank you for everything."

He placed a hand on either side of my face and with tiny kisses caressed my body all the way down to my ankles. We made love like the old days, with tenderness and a slow rhythm. In the morning we snuggled, and I found my favorite spot near his shoulder and chest, nestling in like a duckling.

"What does LB say about sound coming to the movies?" I asked.

"It's inevitable, my darling. You must start preparing for the transition." I buried my face in the blanket and WR stroked my head gently. "You'll be fine," he said.

Anxiety built inside at the thought of speaking on camera, having to perfect the art of movie conversation without stuttering. It felt like a tidal wave was headed toward me in slow motion. I shook my head, willing all these thoughts away. "When will the beach house be finished?"

"In about a year," WR said.

"That long?"

"Let's order coffee and breakfast. I'm starving," WR said. "I have work to do."

"Don't work today. Let's go back to Santa Maria for a second honeymoon."

"I think of those days so often when we're apart, but I'm afraid I've worn them out."

"Good. Let's go and make new memories and disappear for a few days just like the old days when we were just visiting LA and our homes were in New York."

"Soon. We'll go soon," he said, picking up the phone to order breakfast.

CHAPTER 28

A few days after my big party, Rose's film, *The Mad Marriage*, premiered. Agreeing to go to the premiere as a family, Ethel, Reine, Mama, and I waited for more than two hours for Rose to come home and get us. We smoked cigarettes, made small talk, and read magazines until we finally gave up, changed into our pajamas and robes, and got comfortable.

"Do we know where she is?" I asked.

"Not a clue. I haven't seen her in days," Mama said. Reine and Ethel shook their heads too.

Rose never did come home that night, so the next day I made some calls and found out that her movie starring Harrison Ford— my friend and costar in several recent movies—had only opened in two lower-wrung B theaters in Hollywood and nowhere else. I'm sure she was too embarrassed to say anything. Her answer was to run away, I guessed. It was probably what I would have done in her place.

A week or so later Mama relayed that Rose had rushed into the house and packed a bag, saying she was headed to San Francisco with a friend. "What friend?" I pressed, but Mama didn't know. She only knew the friend was a man. I shook my head in disgust when I thought about how willing she was to abandon Patricia and give all responsibility for her parenting to Mama and Ethel. I wished I had time to devote to Patricia. I promised myself to be a bigger part of her life.

— ◎ —

My work schedule never let up and neither did my clandestine rendezvous with Charlie at his studio office. I took my dinners with him most nights, staying late in the evening after our mad lovemaking. I'd leave the house early and come home late, not even seeing Mama, Ethel, or Patricia regularly. Later I would regret being so disconnected from the events in my family's life, especially after learning of the deep troubles that plagued Rose. Asleep in my bed at the Lexington house, the phone woke me at 3:00 a.m.

"Hello?" I murmured into the receiver.

"Marion, it's me." Rose's voice was slurred. "Please come and get me. I'm at this horrible place, and I don't have any money."

"Rose? Where are you? Are you back from San Francisco?" I asked, shaking the sleep from my brain.

"Yes, come and get me now!" she demanded.

"Give me the address." I scratched the address on a piece of paper and got dressed. On my way downstairs, I saw Mama standing at the end of the hallway. "Was that Rose on the phone?"

"Yes," I said. "I'm going to get her now."

"Hang on. I'm coming with you," Ethel said, emerging at the top of the stairs wearing a coat over her pajamas.

"We have to talk when you get back," Mama said.

Ethel and I drove to Westchester, a farming community south of Beverly Hills, passing fields of lima beans, wheat, and barley lit up by the moonlight. "What's going on with Rose?" I took Ethel's cigarette from her and drew on it as we drove in the dark.

"When she got back from San Francisco, we only saw her intermittently. I thought you knew she was back. She's been disappearing for days at a time. She met a carpenter on the MGM lot recently, and when that fell apart, she started seeing a boxer."

"I didn't know she was back. Why didn't you tell me all this before?" I could feel her eyes on me as I drove. She didn't say anything. "What?" I said, irritated at the silence.

"Because you've been otherwise engaged ever since we arrived in LA," she said with a defiant tone. "Mama's worried sick every night that she doesn't come home."

"Jesus! If Mama's worried sick, you need to tell me. Don't ever hold back information again, okay?"

Out of the corner of my eye, I saw her nod. She was right, though. I had been spending less and less time with Mama, my sisters, and Patricia, leaving myself out of the loop on family matters as a result. Work was distracting, and then there was Charlie.

"I guess I should tell you the whole truth before we pick her up," Ethel began.

"The whole truth?" I was incredulous.

"Patricia is gone. George took her a few times for long weekends . . . he took her two weeks ago, and they haven't been back." I raced through my memories to the last time I saw Patricia playing in the pool or in the living room with her dolls. "We thought it would be good for Patricia to spend time with her father, but he didn't tell us he wasn't bringing her back. We didn't want to panic at the time, but now we think she's really gone."

"What does Rose say about it?"

"When she's sober, she whines and cries and complains, but she doesn't take care of her. She can't. She's always high on cocaine or drunk."

"She's taking cocaine?" I shook my head. We drove in silence for twenty minutes while my mind tumbled through the facts. My baby was missing, and nobody told me. My sister's a drug addict and nobody told me. What was happening with my family?

"Turn here. The house is down here," Ethel said.

"You've been here before?"

"Yes, twice," she said. "Slow down. On the right side, there's a driveway. And there she is, sitting by the side of the road."

"What? Our sister is sitting by the side of the road in the middle of the night?"

"Stop!"

I slammed on the brakes, and we got out of the car. Rose clutched her purse in a hunched over position. "Rose, we're here," Ethel said. Rose lifted her head and I saw bleary eyes. Grabbing under her arms, we loaded her into the back seat. She lay down, dirty, drunk, and stinking like a bar.

"You're welcome, Rose," I bristled, getting back behind the wheel. She looked homeless and nothing like the sister I knew. We drove back in silence. Once we took her to her room, we stripped off her clothes. Bruises covered her legs and arms. The sun was coming up just as we put her to bed.

In the hallway, I said to Ethel, "We can talk later tonight. I'll be home by dinner. Let Mama know." I went to my bedroom. Ethel followed me and stood in the doorway as I quickly changed my clothes. "And let Rose know too. We all need to talk."

The day before me was a big one. Luckily, I was only an uncredited player, doing a favor for my new movie studio. The movie was *Ben Hur: A Tale of the Christ*, starring Ramon Navarro. An all-hands-on-deck call had been put out for extras for the chariot scene being filmed at Thomas Ince's Culver Studios. I would be joining many of the people from my birthday party, including Pickford and Fairbanks, John and Lionel Barrymore, Dorothy and Lillian Gish, Samuel Goldwyn, Sid Grauman, Carole Lombard, and Joan Crawford. We would spend the whole day perfecting the shot. By the time I got back home, I was exhausted.

I found Mama reading and my sisters in the library, listening to jazz on the radio while doing needlepoint. Rose sat alone, sulking in a corner.

"Hi, everyone. How was your day?" I asked, reaching for a cheerful tone in my voice.

"We're all fine, Marion. Let's just get through this," Rose said without looking at me.

"Let's start with Patricia. Where are they—she and George?" I asked.

"I don't know. Maybe they went back to Minnesota to visit George's family," Rose responded.

"I understand they've been gone weeks. Shouldn't we be worried?"

"I don't think so." She pulled a piece of yarn from her sweater until it got longer and longer. Silence filled the room. I looked at Ethel and Mama and raised my eyebrows, hoping they would begin.

"We're worried about you, Rose. What kind of trouble are you getting into?" Ethel asked.

"I'm not getting into trouble. Tony is nice."

"How nice is Tony to let you sit by the side of the road at 3:00 a.m.?" I asked.

"Don't judge me. I'm doing the best I can."

The doorbell rang, stopping our conversation.

"Are we expecting somebody?" I asked. Nobody answered.

Ruby, our cook and general helper, came into the library and said quietly, "There is a Mr. Tony here to see you, Marion."

Rose jumped up and ran to the entryway. I followed with Mama and Ethel trailing after me.

"Tony, what are you doing here?" Rose asked.

"I'm here to do business with your famous sister," he said, stepping away from Rose.

"What do you mean? Get out of here right now!" Rose yelled. Mama and Ethel dragged Rose by the arms out of the room. Reine followed with squinted eyes and pursed lips, leaving me to talk to the infamous Tony.

"Okay, here we are. What do you want?" I asked.

"I need money. I'm in trouble and I can't go home. A thousand dollars ought to do it."

"You are brazen. I'll give you that."

"Yeah, well . . ."

"Will a thousand dollars keep you away from Rose permanently?"

Tony considered my offer for a moment as he slid his foot back and forth on the white marble floor. "I don't know . . ." he said as his voice trailed off.

"Come with me." I marched to my office. Sitting down at my desk, I pulled out a checkbook.

"I can't take a check. I need cash—now!" I put the checkbook away, opened a larger drawer at the bottom of my desk, and pulled out an envelope. I knew it had three thousand dollars in it as petty cash. I held it out to him, saying, "Promise me you'll leave Rose alone forever. This is a one-time payment."

Extending his hand, he said, "I promise."

I nodded and motioned for him to follow me back to the front door. Once I had seen him out, I closed the door and locked it.

As soon as I got back to the library, Mama and my sisters had a stricken look on their faces.

"Where's Rose?" I looked around the library.

"She ran out after you sent us away," Reine said.

"My God, what are we going to do?" Mama rubbed her forehead.

Taking a deep breath and feeling like I could tame this storm, I answered with authority. "We're going to hire security here at the house, get WR to help us find Patricia, and get Rose the help she needs."

CHAPTER 29

AUGUST 1925

"Listen to this idea, Sweetheart," WR said as Stan drove us to see the progress being made on my beach house in Santa Monica. "If readers of the *New York American* clip three coupons and pay nineteen cents, they can purchase a silver-plated spoon, embossed with the picture and signature of their favorite MGM star."

"It's genius. It'll be your next big marketing tool," I said.

The car bumped along as WR looked out the window, lost in thought. He enjoyed inventing marketing contests, having just completed one where the winner came to Hollywood and filmed a scene from a movie with me.

"Darling, can we consider our friends for a moment? Everyone is begging for an invitation up to San Simeon to see the spectacular castle you're building," I said. "Surely, we have accommodations enough to invite some friends for a long weekend?"

"Please don't call it a castle. It's 'The Ranch,'" he said curtly. "And yes, that'll be fine."

"Excellent. Mary has been subtly fishing for an invitation."

"Who else will you invite?" WR asked.

"How about Mary and Doug, Charlie and Lita, LB and Margaret, and maybe Greta and Jack?"

"I have a mind to invite a physicist I met in New York, a fascinating fellow," WR trailed off lost in thought. "I'll make the preparations and send out invitations after we attend Charlie's *The Gold Rush* premiere."

True to his word, formal invitations with tickets to his private train car were sent the first week in August. The letter gave details of the journey and the house rules:

Guests should arrive at the Glendale train station at 7:00 p.m. on Thursday, August 21, 1925. Cocktails will be served along with dinner as the train makes its way north. Guests will spend the night in private sleeping compartments until arrival in San Luis Obispo at 3:00 a.m., when the train will be sidetracked to allow guests to sleep until 7:00 a.m. Breakfast will be served. Limousines will drive the guests the forty-five miles north to San Simeon. Upon arrival, present this letter as your credentials to the armed sentries, and you will be granted access to the five-mile road that leads to La Cuesta Encantada. Once at The Ranch, Marion and I will greet you, welcoming you to our home. Guests will be taken to private suites with the help of servants to get you settled. No private valets will be allowed. No room service is offered. Breakfast is between 9:00 a.m. and noon in the Refectory. Lunch is at 2:30 p.m. Cocktails at 7:30 p.m. in the Assembly Room, and dinner will be served in the Refectory at 8:15 p.m. No private liquor should be transported to my home. No exceptions.

Yours, William Randolph Hearst

— ⟨O⟩ —

The date and time of our first Hollywood party at The Ranch
came quickly. WR and I arrived two days before our guests
to prepare and settle in. Separate sleeping areas for unmarried
couples were prepared; WR had plans to strictly enforce them. For
this particular group, only Greta Garbo and John (Jack) Gilbert
would have to spend their nights apart, or risk sneaking into
one another's rooms late at night—with immediate expulsion if
they were caught. (Of course, none of this applied to us. We had
a private apartment on the third floor, with separate bedrooms
connected with a parlor. Nobody would ever be allowed in our
private, shared space.) WR did not want any scandal or gossip in
LA about his weekend parties. He insisted everyone be respectful,
to the point that it felt like he was our parent. But I understood,
remembering that the public accusations of wild sex and drug
parties when Thomas Ince died nearly killed him.

Some rules were broken, but only by me. I transported my
own liquor to my bedroom, hiding bottles in the toilet tank—and
in other various bathrooms around The Ranch where I knew WR
wouldn't think to look. I believe he did know but chose to look
the other way to keep the peace.

Once at The Ranch, even the most learned person was
always impressed with WR's collection of art, paintings, and
statues around the main house, three guest houses, and considerable grounds.

We received four limousines on the appointed day. WR and
I stood arm-in-arm at the top of the stairs to receive our guests.
The day was hot, dry, and clear. The ocean sparkled in the distance under the bright sun. Each of our ten guests gasped and
gaped at WR's magnum opus, indeed a castle.

"Will you look at that view," Mary said, climbing the thirty
steps up to the main courtyard where WR and I waited.

"It's spectacular. Nobody could describe it accurately," LB
said, patting WR on the back when he arrived at the top. Lita
grabbed Charlie's hand for balance as they climbed the stairs,

and Charlie helped her in a sweet way. I honestly hoped things were going well for them. The Nobel Prize–winning physicist Dr. Millikan and his wife, Greta, were the only non-Hollywood guests, and I made a special effort to include them.

"Thank you for coming to see us," I welcomed them. "We hope the journey wasn't too grueling."

Garbo and Gilbert arrived on the terrace last, having stopped to inspect a statue of Venus near the bottom of the stairs.

Once the valets and chambermaids checked everyone into their rooms and unpacked their bags, we gathered around the giant fountain in front of Casa Grande for a planned tour. It was my pleasure to shock and amaze our guests, and I had practiced my speech. I cleared my throat and said, "We are beginning the tour through the main doors of the largest house called Casa Grande, here." I indicated the double doors that led into the Assembly Room. After opening the doors, I pointed to the exquisite tile on the floor and said, "This floor was acquired after an excavation at Pompeii, where it had been buried under ash since AD 79." Dr. Millikan and his wife, Garbo and Gilbert, Mary and Doug, and Lita all looked down. Not Charlie, who winked at me slyly. With dramatic effect, I continued, "People have died on this floor." They stopped walking and stepped gingerly, as if the dead bodies were still on the tiles. It was great fun. WR took over the tour after that, and I slipped away to prepare for cocktails and dinner.

At 7:30 p.m. sharp everyone except WR gathered for cocktails in the Assembly Room, where we were each allowed two drinks and no more. Garbo sidled up to me and whispered in her thick accent, "I beat Jack at a quick game of tennis." Her face was a bit sunburned and she glowed. Gilbert clearly surmised what she was telling me and objected loudly enough for the entire party to hear.

"You did not beat me at tennis, my dear Greta. You won one game, and I won two." Garbo rolled her eyes and turned her back on Gilbert, and we all burst out laughing.

At exactly 8:15 p.m., WR appeared through a secret door and ushered us into the Refectory, named by Julia Morgan after a monastery dining hall. The room had high windows, dark wood paneled walls, colorful banners from Siena hanging high above our heads, a thirty-foot French tapestry on the wall, a five-foot-tall fireplace, and a long mahogany table adorned with four-foot-high silver candlesticks. Except for the ketchup and mustard bottles and paper napkins WR insisted were more sanitary than cloth, it felt like a medieval castle.

Always obsessed with where the guests sat, WR liked to move people around the table like chess pieces. He occupied the middle of the long dining table, with me directly across from him. Lita and Charlie took their place next to WR, while Dr. and Mrs. Millikan were seated on either side of me. LB and Margaret next to them, Garbo and Jack sat next to Lita and Charlie. Mary and Doug were next to them.

Waiters brought out lamb chops, potatoes, shrimp, crab, rice, vegetables, cheese, fruit, and later a chocolate raspberry tart for dessert.

WR clinked a spoon against his glass and the room fell silent. Looking at Doug, WR asked if he embraced sound being added to movies.

"Yes and no," Fairbanks answered. "It's a complicated subject, but I do believe we all need to modernize. If we don't, we will be left behind."

Dr. Millikan leaned forward and asked, "Mr. Chaplin, what do you think? Will your comedy work with the advent of sound?"

Charlie shook his head violently but didn't say anything.

Undaunted, Dr. Millikan tried again. "Certainly there's risk in every undertaking of progress. You're the finest comedian in the movies, but your filmmaking is still a growing art, isn't it?"

Charlie's face looked pained. I knew he hated this subject. "I will never add sound to my movies. Not ever," he said vehemently.

Dr. Millikan looked dejected, but I jumped in to soften the blow of Charlie's rudeness.

"What Charlie meant was that we're all nervous about the addition of sound, and some of us haven't yet accepted it." I swept my eyes around the table and found Charlie's astonished eyes. It wasn't my custom to speak for a guest, but I took this liberty with Charlie this once. My job as hostess was to keep the conversation civil.

"If anybody cares to know what I think," LB broke in authoritatively, "I'll tell you that sound is coming like it or not. Almost every actor is frantically seeking to rid themselves of Bronx, Brooklyn, and European accents, and hiring speech coaches to help them."

I looked at Greta with her thick Swedish accent. "Is this true for you?" I asked.

"Ya, I am vorking vith a coach," she admitted.

I nodded slightly, wishing like hell to remain blissfully ignorant of the coming dread in my life. I needed to hire a coach to help me stop stuttering, and to rid of me of my Brooklyn roots, but not tonight. Tonight, I would keep my head in the sand.

After dinner, WR moved us to the theater where we watched my upcoming movie, *Lights of Old Broadway*. At its conclusion, Mrs. Millikan said as we stood, "You were just charming, Miss Davies." To which Mary added, "Romantic comedy dramas are your best, dear friend." Lita agreed, saying she just loved it. They applauded and complimented my performance. Admiration was a gift that overflowed in my life.

WR thanked everyone and excused himself. "Good night all, it's my bedtime." I alone knew that he was going up to his study to work all night long and sleep only from the early-morning hours until around 10:00 a.m.

The rest of the party moved back into the Assembly Room, where we played cards, danced, and surreptitiously drank champagne I found in the wine cellar. After midnight we migrated outside to stroll around the esplanade that surrounded Casa Grande and to admire the moon and night sky in the gardens. Melancholy settled over us as the moon covered us in peace and serenity. Charlie picked up the conversation from dinner, only this time in a defeated and subdued tone. "Naturally, I'm worried about talking pictures, but not for my sake," he said to no one in particular. "What worries me is that sound will become the art and steal the thunder."

"You're pessimistic, Charlie," Jack Gilbert said, wrapping his arm around Greta. "Talkies can be the boost movies need."

"Sure I'm pessimistic that art will be dead, because we must all have our imaginations."

Nobody took up the thread from there. Instead, we strolled in silence, letting those words wash over us as the night sky beckoned us to find sleep.

— ⟨ ⟩ —

The next morning, I found Lita sunbathing at the outdoor Temple Garden pool.

"We've never really had a chance to chat, have we?" I sat down next to her.

"No, I guess we haven't," she said in a meek voice. I wrestled with my feelings about Lita. One minute I felt sorry she was swept up in this scandal, being a mere child as she was. The next minute my thoughts were more sinister wondering if she was astute enough to realize the truth about Charlie and me. I reasoned it was to my benefit to get to know her.

Across the small pool, Garbo and Gilbert huddled together under a big umbrella. Wearing her perpetual scowling face, Greta pushed Jack away as she said, "I von the horse race, you dummy." Mary and Doug splashed playfully in the shallow end, hugging and kissing intermittently. Pulling a metal canister and paper cup from my beach bag, I poured myself a drink, glancing around cautiously.

"Champagne. It's mother's milk to me. You won't squeal on me, will you?"

Lita shook her head like a scared little girl, big eyes searching my face.

"Well, speaking of mother's milk, you're a mother now, aren't you?"

"Yes, Charlie Jr. was born in May."

"We never really got a chance to talk at the party earlier this year. You were adorable as Josephine. You looked terrific. I was jealous of you, do you know that? I thought I was the belle of the ball, and then you came along and stole my thunder."

"That's nice of you to say, Miss Davies. Actually I—"

I cut her off. "Please, call me Marion."

I dug back into my bag and pulled out a pack of cigarettes, offering her one. She shook her head but I lit one.

"I meet so many stuffed shirts that it's a pleasure to come across somebody who's home folk, like me. Not that I mind all the dodos." I chuckled and took a drink of champagne. "WR's the biggest dodo there is, and I'm head over heels about him. And your fella, he's sort of a dodo, too, and I'm crazy about him too."

When Lita's face startled, I said, "All I mean by that is that he's a hell of a great friend, and I'd hate not knowing him." I glanced around the pool to avoid Lita's eye. I continued, "No, I shouldn't call your fella a dodo. You're in love with him, I can see that."

"You're right. I love him, and he can be pretty formal when he sets his mind to it," she said.

"Can he ever! When you least expect it, he can fool you suddenly and have one amazing sense of humor about himself, wouldn't you say?"

"Yes," she said hesitantly, then quickly added, "Actually no,

I've never noticed the 'funniest man in the world' having a sense of humor about himself."

Trying to put her at ease about my relationship with Charlie was backfiring. Shifting the focus, I jerked my chin at the sad-eyed Garbo and Gilbert. "Did you ever see two more beautiful faces and two sadder-looking people? Jack's a great guy—all man with everything going for him, except the Swede. He's been at my house twice in the past month and both times flung himself down and burst into tears because she won't marry him."

I could tell I was overwhelming the poor girl and she had no idea how to respond to what I was telling her. I looked up to see WR heading toward us, but then he suddenly stopped and moved an imitation rock to the side to retrieve a phone. I quickly tucked my champagne back into my beach bag. He spoke into the phone briskly and then put it back behind the rock.

"Do you see that? He has those phones hidden everywhere," I said, nodding my head toward WR. He arrived at our side.

"Lita, nice to see you enjoying the pool. I hope you have everything you need. The boys will bring anything you ask for."

Turning to me, he asked, "Can we speak about this evening's menu?"

Winking at Lita, I said, "I'll see you at dinner tonight. Come see me anytime you need to talk, okay? My door is always open."

After a second day of partaking in horseback riding, hiking, tennis, and swimming, we repeated cocktails, dinner, and this time saw Charlie's movie, *The Tramp*. Dr. Millikan gushed as he held his wife's hand, "It's the best movie I have ever seen, and I think you're right about not needing sound in your movies. Bravo!" The rest of the group clapped and congratulated Charlie. I watched from afar as Lita soaked in the admiration for her husband, knowing Charlie hated being the center of such adoring fans.

Afterwards we played card games and danced late into the night. The weekend ended Sunday morning after breakfast.

Everyone loaded back into their limousines, but not before pro-fusely thanking WR for his wonderful hospitality. As the last limousine disappeared down the hill, WR said, "Well darling, that was fun."

"Yes, it was," I agreed, "and everyone behaved." He put his arm around me as we walked back to Casa Grande.

"What do you think about adding a zoo to the property?" he asked as he opened the door to the Assembly Room for me.

"A zoo!" I said, half-listening through my exhaustion.

Weekends like these helped me to feel I'd indeed arrived as mistress of San Simeon, and I held my position with glee. We would invite every worthy and not-so-worthy person in Holly-wood, along with a worldwide group of the rich and powerful. Winston Churchill, Charles Lindberg, Amelia Earhart, Calvin Coolidge, and Howard Hughes, along with regarded journal-ists and literary figures, world renowned sports figures, and famous artists too countless to name. They would all stay with us, absorbing the glory, history, and riches The Ranch had to offer. With Millicent finally gone from our lives, I was able to step into my rightful place next to WR.

CHAPTER 30

SEPTEMBER 1925, MGM LOT

At work in the newly built stages on the MGM lot, I spent more of my days than I cared to in the hideous community dressing room, a wooden two-story building for all the actors. I had never shared such a small space with so many people. The men occupied the first floor, the women the second. A big sign magically appeared one day at the bottom of the stairs: "No Men Allowed Upstairs." Not even the assistant directors would come up the stairs to get us. They'd just yell, "Hey Marion! You're wanted on the set."

There were six shared dressing rooms on each floor, three on either side of the hallway with a shared bathroom at one end of the hall. At the other end was an executive dressing room with a private bathroom. It was all mine, because WR had negotiated it for me. This caused a bit of jealousy from the other girls, but I didn't care. In the shared dressing rooms were Norma Shearer, Lillian Gish, Greta Garbo, Joan Crawford, and Sally O'Neill.

I was filming *Beverly of Graustark,* in which I played dual roles of an American student traveling in Europe who gets talked into masquerading as her long-lost cousin Prince Oscar. I decided on this film on the advice of Norma Talmadge, who had just finished a remake of *Graustark*.

Things were going well on set at first, but shortly after we began filming, I returned to my dressing room to find all my things moved to one of the smaller shared rooms. Livid, I yelled, "Who moved my things?"

Lulu, the dressing maid, peeked her head out of Greta's room and said, "Oh boy! There's going to be a fight."

"Lulu, who did this?" I asked.

"Miss Gish," she said, quietly backing away.

Greta emerged from her room in a robe, curlers in her hair, and in her heavy accent that made everything sound harsh, said, "Lillian arrived a short time ago. She said she's on loan from Universal to film *La Bohème* here on our lot and believes she vas assigned dat room in her contract."

"Well, this won't do. Who does she think she is? Did you tell her the room was mine?"

Nobody responded. I hauled Lillian's belongings to another dressing room, moved mine back into the executive suite, and slammed and locked the door. I sat at the makeup table trying to control my heavy breathing while waiting for Lillian to return. I didn't have long to wait when a loud knock startled me.

"Marion, open this door immediately. You're in my room."

"Who is it?" I asked, sugar dripping from my voice.

"You know perfectly well who this is. Get out here now," Lillian demanded.

I opened the door, holding a cigarette high with my pinky in the air. Her squinted eyes drilled holes into my skin, and a flush crept up her neck as she pushed past me in fury.

"What are you doing? Where are my things?" She swept around the room examining my possessions. "This is my room. Mr. Mayer said I could have the executive suite with the in-room bathroom," Lillian whined.

"Well, LB is wrong. This room is mine and only mine. It

was written into *my* contract so get out!" I yelled, pointing to the hallway.

Lulu, Greta, and Norma were all standing in the hallway watching. Lillian left, and I slammed the door behind her. Any time I left the suite after that, I locked the door behind me.

That night at dinner, I slunk into a chair and stared at the salad in front of me, picking up a carrot and chewing on it. WR looked at me with an all-knowing face. "I had a call from LB about the dressing room," he said. "What happened?"

"I have no idea why Lillian is trying to muscle in on my room. I swear she's jealous of me."

"Well, don't you worry about anything. I will build you a worthy dressing room."

"Oh, WR, you're too good to me," I sang as I happily bounced over to him and kissed his cheek.

— ⓪ —

A handful of months later I had my new dressing room, mere steps from the stage separated by a lawn where I took up some acrobatics. Before arriving on set, I'd do somersaults and cartwheels with the studio workers' kids. WR and I called my dressing room a bungalow, but it looked more like a two-story Mediterranean-style villa. It had fourteen rooms with two big bedrooms for me and WR on the top floor and four other guest bedrooms. The bottom floor had an office for WR, a library, living room, and a banquet-sized dining room. A full staff was hired, including my own dressing maid. The Marion Davies Orchestra were brought back to play on the wraparound porch during the weekdays. The entire house was decorated with antiques from WR's Bronx warehouses. Tapestries from Spain, white marble floors from Italy, and large Renaissance paintings hung from the walls. It wasn't long before the bungalow's first floor served as the heartbeat of MGM Studios, where visiting bigwigs and dignitaries were schmoozed.

Of course, news of my bungalow ricocheted around Holly-wood, causing quite a stir among my fellow actors. Satisfaction oozed out of every pore, and I hoped Lillian would be happy in her little room at the end of the hall.

— ◎ —

Six months after I christened my bungalow on the MGM lot, my Santa Monica Ocean House was ready. The newspapers said it cost more than three million dollars to build, which did not surprise me with WR at the helm. Move-in weekend was upon us; WR called before leaving The Ranch. "I'm on my way down, Darling," he said. "Has the furniture arrived yet?"

Hesitantly I said, "No," wondering what antiques he had decided to bring this time from his warehouses back in New York. Our interior decorating tastes were vastly different. I liked a more modern flair, but I would never tell him. He loved to spoil me with riches from the past.

Mama and Ethel would continue to live at the Lexington house. Ethel was taking care of Mama after a small heart attack. Papa was still working full time in Brooklyn. I hadn't seen him in over a year and missed him dearly, frequently begging him to join us all in California to no avail.

Patricia was still missing eighteen months later, even though WR had hired a private detective to find her. Whenever I'd ask about it, WR got flustered and said he was working on it. The only thing that gave me comfort was knowing George was a loving and conscientious father.

Reine, Charlie, and Pepi continued to live in their own house in Bel Air on a monthly stipend from me, like the rest of my family. Reine had a full-time job parenting sixteen-year-old Pepi, now a wild and unruly teenager who'd recently hosted an alcohol-fueled sex party in Mama's pool. I loved Pepi to death but could barely watch as Reine tried to reel her in. Charlie was twenty years old now and making a name for himself as a screenwriter.

After she came back from San Francisco, I bought Rose a home in Studio City, far enough away from Mama and Ethel to give us all peace from her unpredictable life. She showed up occasionally at the studio, ostensibly looking for work, but those conversations always ended in me giving her money, so she'd go away. Her monthly stipend never seemed to last.

When I moved into Ocean House, I only took my clothing and new bulldog, Buddy. WR provided everything else with his trainload full of decorations. Outrageous and colossal, Ocean House dwarfed all others along Highway 1 in Santa Monica. It was a WR and Julia Morgan design all the way, with regal construction and decoration. Situated on "The Gold Coast" with other actors and actresses on beach-front lots, Ocean House had 110 rooms, 37 fireplaces, and 55 bathrooms.

The dining room was from Burton Hall in Ireland, the banquet room originally the sitting room of the Duchess of Northumberland, and the ballroom a seventeenth-century Venetian palazzo. There was even a fifteenth-century tavern from Surrey, England, inside the house. Outside were several guest houses, servants' cottages, gardens, tennis courts, hundreds of lockers for guests' belongings, volleyball nets, and a great saltwater pool.

At our inaugural party, we invited all our friends from MGM, United Artists, and Warner Brothers, including all the set workers and designers and their families. Some called it the Versailles of Hollywood, they were so impressed with my new home. We barbecued several sides of beef, played beach games, and walked down to the pier. The children were the most fun to watch. They played in the pool and jumped the waves on the sand. I caught myself daydreaming about Patricia with her long blonde hair blowing in the wind while running across the pool deck, screaming, "Watch me swim! Watch me jump!" My heart ached to see her again. Would she remember me when we finally found her?

— ⟨Ⓞ⟩ —

The Sunday following the party, WR returned to his beloved Ranch and I finally found a solitary moment. I sat sipping champagne on the balcony overlooking the ocean when my butler, Thomas, came looking for me.

"Mrs. Lita Grey Chaplin is at the front door, quite distressed and demanding to see you immediately."

"Demanding?" I said, chugging the rest of my champagne. "Bring her to the library and bring us some coffee, would you? Thank you, Thomas."

I made my way to the library where Lita, sobbing, soon burst through the door. "Oh Miss Davies! Thank you for seeing me. I'm so upset."

"Lita, Lita, what is the problem? Please sit down."

She sat next to me. "I'm sure you've heard Charlie and I are splitting up."

"I have," I said. Newspapers were covering the divorce closely as papers were filed and made public throughout the proceedings.

"Well, we can't finalize the divorce because Charlie won't settle with me. I gave him two sons. All I want is a trust fund for each of them and for me. He should support me. He can't just use me and toss me aside."

I nodded but stayed quiet.

"I can tell the press about his . . . his unusual appetites in the bedroom."

My mind raced. *Was this child threatening me?* Thomas brought in a coffee tray, setting it down on the table between us. I poured the coffee as Lita continued in a matter-of-fact way.

"I know about you and Charlie. He confirmed it after your big party a few years ago when I was still pregnant with Charlie Jr."

"Lita," I said in a harsh tone. "Tread carefully. You've been through so much. Let me talk to Charlie and see what I can do."

She continued without looking at me. "Mr. Hearst has been wonderful to me, and I would hate to hurt him in any way. But I will tell the papers about you and Charlie if he doesn't give me what I want."

"Stop this right now. Do not threaten me, young lady." I stood up. "I will help you but take great care." I raised my finger in warning and bit my tongue.

She rubbed her eyes. "I need this settled," she said. "My father's having anxiety attacks every day. I am his only daughter, you know. This has been very hard on both my parents."

My heart thawed ever so slightly. The girl was in over her head, and she was the mother of Charlie's two children. What a bastard he was to leave her flailing like this. I was furious with Charlie that I had to be in the middle of their domestic affair.

"I will talk to Charlie, but I am not promising anything." I stood up, leading the way to the door. I wanted her out of my house. She followed me to the double staircase at the front of the house.

"You're not the only one he sleeps with, you know," she continued. "His appetite is astronomical. I know of at least four other women."

"So why come to me and not them?"

"Because I like you and Mr. Hearst. I can tell you have a good heart, and that you love Mr. Hearst." With that, she rushed down the steps and left.

I couldn't help feeling that her misguided affection toward me was in part due to her naivete. Back in my bedroom, I drank two quick shots of bourbon, lit a cigarette, and called Charlie. Kono answered and said Charlie was filming, but he would call me back before the end of the day.

"It's urgent, Kono."

"I'll let him know, Miss Davies."

At 6:00 p.m., after many more shots and too many cigarettes, I called Charlie again. He came to the phone, impatient and curt.

"What, Marion? What's the emergency?"

I relayed my conversation with Lita, trying not to slur, but hearing the words slide into each other. "Do you know what WR would do if this became public? Do you have any idea what could topple?"

He didn't say a word.

I challenged him. "What do you need the money for? You have more money than you'll ever need."

"Okay, I will take care of it. How long have you been drinking, darling? You're slurring your words."

"Don't you dare chastise me about my drinking. And don't you dare yell at Lita about coming here to talk to me. She's a child, Charlie. She was a child when you got her pregnant. Just settle and be done with it. Do you hear me?"

"Consider it done," he said and hung up.

The next morning Lita called and thanked me profusely on behalf of her parents and children. Shortly after that call, the newspapers reported the largest divorce settlement in US history—a $100,000 trust fund for each boy and $625,000 for Lita—pocket change for Charlie.

CHAPTER 31

OCTOBER 1927

Everywhere I looked, posters and billboards screamed, "See Al Jolson in *The Jazz Singer*." The age of sound had arrived, and hordes of people flocked to see the latest innovation in film. It was as if Charles Lindberg's record-breaking 3500-mile solo flight across the Atlantic five months earlier hadn't been enough excitement. The world was changing faster than I could grasp it, and at thirty years old I felt afraid of being left behind.

WR and I had visited New York in May, along with many of our Hollywood friends, to welcome the young, handsome Lindberg back from Paris. As he arrived in New York harbor aboard the *USS Memphis,* four million people lined the streets to catch a glimpse of the American hero. I'm not sure how I managed to lure twenty-five-year-old Lindy away from socialite Gloria Vanderbilt's Fifth Avenue gold-plated welcome party to our raging Hollywood fest of young people on the twenty-sixth floor of the Warwick Hotel, but I did. Arriving by police car to a mobbed lobby and street, he was whisked upstairs to my party where he stood stiff and straight like a military man while meeting Carole Lombard, Harry Crocker, and other stage friends. He was slender with clear blue eyes and tousled blonde hair and would have appeared severe in nature if not for his warm smile. It wasn't surprising to me that he was a teetotaler like WR, so there was no need for me to do my usual dance of slyly finding more alcohol for our guest of honor that day. He finally relaxed enough to play the guitar and sing, and I could certainly see why the whole country was in love with him.

— ⊚ —

A few months later, I persuaded Lindy to make his way out to California to join us in my bungalow on the MGM lot to meet LB Mayer, Irving Thalberg, and some of his favorite performers, Mary Pickford, and Norma Talmadge. The press crowded into the parlor, where we indulged them with a few pictures before I dismissed them. Hoagy Carmichael played on the phonograph and we all danced. Mary had a charming effect on men—after all she was the most famous movie star in the world. She was used to people fawning over her, but Lindy seemed immune to her. Using all the grace she could muster, she tried to find something to talk to him about.

"I understand you don't drink or smoke, so what do you do for fun?" she asked him.

Lindy responded matter-of-factly, "I do smoke and dance a little," then turned his gaze back to me. Mary rolled her eyes behind his back, frustrated. When we finally stopped dancing, we sat for tea, and I placed Lindy between Mary and me. He sat ramrod straight and stared directly ahead. Mary passed me a note behind his back: "He won't talk." To which I scribbled back, "Talk about airplanes."

By the time the party was over, Mary and I were exhausted from worrying about whether Lindy was having fun or not. As we met in the kitchen for another swig from my flask, she grabbed my hands with pleading eyes. "I'm done here. It's obvious he prefers you to all of us. Thanks for a wonderful afternoon. I'm going home."

That night, he stayed at my Ocean House where WR offered him a half-million dollars for the right to film his life story, but he quickly declined. He seemed completely unmoved by all of Hollywood.

We went back to the studio the next day so he could watch me film a scene in my latest movie, *The Fair Coed*. Then he was whisked away to San Simeon to visit The Ranch with WR as his personal guide.

When Lindy finally left California, I mourned his absence because it meant facing the fact of sound in the movies.

We started taking all our guests on the "grand tour" to my MGM bungalow, Ocean House, and WR's Ranch at San Simeon.

— ⓒ —

With fall upon us, we sat in the movie theater watching Jolson sing, dance, and speak effortlessly in *The Jazz Singer*. Darkness surrounded me in more ways than one. My throat tightened at the thought of having to speak on film. Leaning over to WR, I mumbled, "I'm ruined. I'm wrecked."

He put his arm around me. "You can do this."

At home that evening on the sofa at Ocean House, I curled up as small as I could make myself and whispered, "I can't do it, WR. I'll freeze and stutter, and the whole crew will lose patience with me and laugh."

"Nobody's asking you to sing," WR said stroking my arm. "Let's get you a speech coach immediately."

"No, WR. I'm not doing it. Let's just move to Europe."

"Darling, you can do this. Sit up and look me in the eye. I'm hiring a speech coach immediately and we will beat this thing."

I began working with a coach immediately. After two weeks of practice reading lines to each other, he pronounced me cured of my stuttering and Brooklyn accent, saying, "Your voice is of fine quality, slightly lower than contralto, which is a perfect timbre for talking pictures."

I had no idea what he meant but nodded my affirmation. I thought my voice was a bit low—a "whiskey voice" some called it—but I planned on winning the audience over with my humor anyway.

WR laughed, kissing my cheek. "See, you can do this sound test. The script came this morning by messenger. Time to start learning your lines."

I had a mild panic attack and ran up to my bedroom, locking myself in the bathroom and drawing a bath. I retrieved my bottle of vodka from the toilet tank where it was kept appropriately chilled and poured a full glass before sinking into the hot bubbly water.

Eyes glazed over from the vodka an hour later, I found a bit of courage and retrieved the script from my dressing table where WR had left it for me. The dialogue was horrible. Was I really supposed to say, "Do you think it's nice to be in a river with a caterpillar?"

I had an idea. I called Irving, telling him I was ready for my test.

"An old friend of yours, George K. Arthur from *Lights of Old Broadway*, is ready to read lines with you. Remember him?"

Of course, I remembered sweet and supportive George. He was funny and kind and the perfect person to do a screen test with me.

Thirty minutes later, I was in the car on my way to the lot. I had to ask my driver to pull over twice to dry heave from my nerves, and from my hangover if I was being honest with myself.

I arrived on the sound stage and found George in the back waiting. Bravado, like the kind men get on a sinking ship, overcame me. "Hey, George, let's ditch this stupid dialogue and make up our own."

"I've memorized these lines. What will I say when it's my turn to talk?"

"Just follow me," I said.

"I don't know," he said, wringing his hands.

I pulled out my thermos of champagne and poured us each a small glass. "Let's have a drink before we go on. I know I need some liquid courage."

We drank back a glass before being called to the stage where Norma Shearer's brother, Doug, was the sound engineer in charge. I breathed a heavy sigh of relief as my old friend Doug showed us where to sit.

I whispered to George, "We're at a dinner party. Just talk to me." My mouth was very dry.

The camera had a big mirror in front of it so we could watch ourselves act and talk. I hated it and avoided looking at it.

"Okay, begin whenever you're ready," Doug said.

"Aren't these delicious Brooklyn oysters?" I began, pretending like I was using a fork on the oyster.

"Oh, I don't like oysters. You can have them all," George said.

"What about shrimp? Do you like them?"

"Oh yes, my favorite is shrimp scampi."

Soon our sound test was over. It was easier than I thought, and I didn't stutter once. I had done it! I was so proud of myself.

Reine and Ethel were at Ocean House with WR when I got back. "Tell us how it went," Ethel prodded me immediately.

"It was nothing," I lied. "George and I made up some lines, imagining we were at a dinner party where oysters were being served."

"That's it? You talked about oysters?" Reine asked.

"Yep, that's it. We just talked regular. It was easy."

WR beamed at me from across the room.

Irving Thalberg called a few hours later and congratulated me on a successful sound test, saying they were drawing up my new contract immediately. WR and I danced in the ballroom to "The Blue Danube Waltz." I was happier than I had been in years. We didn't need to move to Europe—what a relief!

— ⓪ —

Ocean House continued to be the talk of the town. People often showed up uninvited, bringing friends and relatives to play tennis, jump the waves, or sit by the pool with a cocktail. Spontaneous parties popped up frequently: after-tennis parties, pool parties, dinner parties, movie parties. The fan magazines featured story after story about my jewelry, the number of servants we had, and the outrageous number of bathrooms.

With WR back in New York for Christmas with his boys, I invited Charlie over to help me with a few scenes I was working on for my upcoming film, *The Patsy*. I played a young woman in love with her older sister's boyfriend. This was a comedy, and I didn't want to make any mistakes.

"Do you even attend your own parties?" Charlie asked as he blew into my room without knocking.

"Not lately. I'm too busy."

Several parties were in full swing. The music blared, and forty people were dancing and drinking directly below us. We were in my suite upstairs, near the window where we could barely see the ocean and flock of seagulls huddled together on the sand through the thick fog.

"Do you feel like warming up some comedy downstairs in front of all those drunk people?" Charlie offered.

"What are you thinking?" I squinted my eyes at him, considering the proposition.

Charlie and I had been performing impromptu at cocktail parties for years. It all began one evening at San Simeon in an attempt to make WR laugh. Charlie pushed me slightly, and I fell over exaggeratedly, but he grabbed my hand in time to yank me back upright. I bumped into him, and he fell over a nearby chair, flipping and landing on his bum with his legs spread out. WR laughed hysterically, and I knew we were onto something. Our "shows" hit a high point when Winston Churchill stayed at Ocean House and Charlie and I performed a burlesque on Shakespeare for him. Mr. Churchill laughed so hard his belly shook. From then on, whenever Charlie was present, we extemporaneously entertained the guests.

On this day, though, Charlie had an idea. "Let's tango," he said with a sly grin on his face, grabbing my hand, twirling and dipping me low.

"You're in a mood today, aren't you?" I said.

He pulled my arm, and we ran downstairs to the party. I wore a pair of dark trousers and a pink blouse. Pants had become my most favorite clothing item. I was barefoot with my hair in a bun. Charlie grabbed a long trench coat as we made our way to the dance floor. He offered me one arm of the coat he'd already shoved one of his arms into, and I slipped in next to him. Pinned up next to each other, we walked around the room, smiling and bumping into guests who burst out laughing. He pulled his arm out of the coat and twirled me around, wrapping me with the sleeve, then releasing me, hurling the coat into the crowd with force.

He then took off his dark blue wool suit coat, lobbing it into the audience as well. Someone caught it with a cheer. He loosened his tie and flung that into the crowd with abandon. Then he began to undo his belt, looking around slyly, but I rushed to him and helped him buckle it, eyes darting around the room in exaggerated embarrassment. The crowd lapped it up. He took my hand off his belt, and we began to tango around the dance floor. I'd learned to tango from Errol Flynn the year before, and Charlie and I had practiced on occasion ever since. People moved back and let us have the entire floor, laughing and cheering us on. He dipped me, scooped me, and twirled me as he fell down, got up, and raced after me while I flung myself across the dance floor. Charlie was in exceptional form, limber and strong, and I merely followed, remaining loose and pliable. When the song ended, the crowd burst into applause. Charlie bowed, then pushed me into a bow, which made them laugh harder. I curtsied, and we ran off the dance floor and back upstairs to my suite, where we collapsed onto my bed, breathing heavily.

We couldn't help but ravage each other, Charlie placing a passionate kiss on my mouth while he held my face, and me fumbling with his belt to get his pants off quickly. We fit together in so many ways. He devoured me and I devoured him right back. Afterward, I sat exhausted on a wicker chair, wearing only a flimsy white slip, the strap of which kept falling off my shoulder. I drew slowly on my cigarette. Charlie wore just his briefs, and although it was January, we were hot from all the activity. I could feel the pounding of the bass on the floor below.

"Do your scene. Let me see it," Charlie said as he lay on the couch, cupping his glass of bourbon with two hands and taking a small sip.

"I'm exhausted. Can't I just rest a minute?"

"I have to run in a minute. I want to see it," he said.

On cue, I looked up as my character, the lovesick teenager who wants to dance with her sister's boyfriend, and made my fingers begin a tango on the tablecloth reminiscent of Charlie's dinner roll dance in *The Gold Rush*.

"Do you think they're going to know you helped me?" I asked, breaking character with a giggle.

"Shhhh! Keep going. Do the next one."

The next scene was meant to be a pantomime of various famous people. Moving quickly, I ran over to an imaginary wall and pretended to see mounted pictures of movie stars. Readying myself to look like Mae Murray, with pouting bee-stung lips, I twirled around, grabbing a shawl, and draping it over my head in imitation of my worst pal, Lillian Gish, a sad plea on my face. Lastly, I twirled again, grabbed a knife sitting on my dressing room table expressly for this purpose, and put it between my teeth before turning to face Charlie as the scowling vamp, Pola Negri.

Charlie clapped. "Very good. The knife will be a hit."

"I'm finished rehearsing," I announced. "Pour me another drink." I fell into my wicker chair. "What scene are we working on for you?"

"No scenes for me today. I want to relive your moment with Albert," Charlie said, grinning like a cat. "What was it you said again? Please say it so I can have a good laugh before I go."

We had attended a studio party earlier in the week in which Albert Einstein had been the guest of honor.

"All I said to him was, 'Why don't you get your hair cut?'"

He laughed and rolled onto the ground in typical Charlie fashion. "You are just a peach, you know that? Nobody but you would have the nerve to say that to the premier physicist in the world."

"Well, he does need a haircut," I insisted, swigging back the rest of my drink. Then came a knock on the door. "Come in!" I called.

"Miss Davies, it's Ethel on the phone," my maid said.

I picked it up. "Hello, Ethel. Are you coming to dinner later?"

"Marion, it's Mama. She's very sick." I froze, feeling like I'd been knocked back by a fierce blast of wind.

Charlie drove me to the house on Lexington where we found Ethel and Reine hovering over Mama in bed. "Where's Rose?" I mumbled. The drapes had been drawn and it was dark except for the lamp on the bedside table. Charlie and Pepi stood against the wall, watching quietly.

Reine answered, "Rose is in Europe now. She's been gone a few weeks."

"What happened to Mama?" I asked.

"She came upstairs for a nap. When I came up to check on her, she was gone," Ethel said.

I clung to Ethel in tears. Reine, Charlie, and Pepi joined in a group hug. "She was only fifty-six years old!" I cried.

Pierce Bros Mortuary took care of all the details. WR rushed back from New York, bringing my father and his second eldest son, twenty-year-old Bill Jr. The hard lines between Millicent and me had blurred of late with WR's five sons being occasionally included in our life. They were older and could make their own decisions, and it seemed Millicent began accepting that I was here to stay, as I accepted that she was never going away. Bill Jr. wanting to be present and carry Mama's casket meant the world to me.

It was a salve to my pain to see Papa. Before the funeral I sat with him in the parlor and cried. He said he was disappointed in Rose and Patricia's absence. I didn't have the heart to relay the difficult details of Rose's life, or that Patricia was living with her father permanently somewhere in the Midwest, so I didn't say a word. He hugged and tried to comfort me, but I was racked with guilt about Mama.

"I think Mama felt irrelevant in her last years," I cried. "She was all alone and didn't like Los Angeles much. The only thing she liked was us girls."

"Your Mama was proud of you, Marion. And don't forget that you achieved her greatest dream: financial success."

It was true, I had achieved financial success. Mama was the one who taught me good work ethics, and I did earn my own money. Maybe my legacy would be to prove that a woman could have both love and money.

"I miss her so much. Do you think she was happy?" I asked, knowing that I sounded like a lost little girl. He hadn't seen Mama in years, so he didn't know what to say to that. He just stroked my hand. I wrestled with enormous regret for not spending more time with Mama and leaving her with Ethel most of the time.

The next morning, Papa rode with me and WR in a white limousine, while my three sisters arrived by separate limousine. We all wore black dresses and veils. Mama's casket was carved mahogany and partially covered with a blanket of white gardenias accented by white orchids. It was carried by the men who loved and cared for me: WR, Charlie, Bill Jr., and my nephew Charlie. We laid her to rest at Hollywood Memorial Park, where I had purchased a white marble mausoleum by the pond intended to be the final resting place for my entire family. It gave me some comfort to know that we would be together in this mausoleum in the years to come.

CHAPTER 32

SPRING 1928

Getting back to work was the best idea for my mental health. Mama's death and my newly surfaced guilt over whether she was happy in California ate away at me. I sought out Connie and Ellie, along with some fellow actresses who had been to San Simeon multiple times and whose friendship consoled me during this time of grief. But when I learned that I had to share a sound stage with Greta Garbo, sparks flew.

My relationship with her had devolved as we had gotten to know each other over the past few years. It wasn't that anything huge happened, she was just a shrew, that's all—always in a bad mood with a scowl on her face. Honestly, I think she was a tortured soul because she needed to work but just wanted to live quietly with her girlfriend. To please the studio, she had to date men who invariably got the wrong idea about her attentions. She was constantly fighting them off, and it put her in a bad mood.

Her undeniable beauty and flawless bone structure played perfectly to the camera. She was tall and thin and moved like a gazelle on set. She also had an aura of aloofness and mystery. Men either threw themselves at her feet or ran the other way.

It was the same for some women who were drawn to her like a magnet. It was rumored she used her androgynous looks to hide in plain sight, eating out and attending events not as the Greta Garbo we all knew, but dressed as a man, anonymously blending into the crowd with whatever girl she might have on her arm.

My biggest run-in with her was over her double standard at the studio. She was overly private about anybody watching her work, yet felt entitled to watch the rest of us at MGM work on our movies.

On my first day back on set after burying Mama, I brought Pepi. I had promised Reine I'd give her a small part as a flapper in *The Cardboard Lover* to distract her from the wildlife she continued living. She was eighteen now and I was trying to do my part as her aunt to straighten her out. Walking her across the MGM lot to the dreary old wooden dressing room I had escaped, I decided on visiting my costar Jetta Goudal.

"Come with me to say hi to Jetta," I told Pepi, who followed me like a puppy. I was hoping to make some connection with Jetta as she seemed to despise me for no obvious reason—refusing to talk to me away from the set, insisting on speaking French and acting like she didn't speak English.

We stood in the doorway of her dressing room and I caught Jetta's eye in the mirror. "Jetta, I'd like you to meet my niece, Pepi," I said, brushing Pepi's long brown hair away from her shoulder. Jetta smiled in the mirror and nodded to Pepi but continued fixing her hair in the mirror without saying a word.

"Nice to meet you," Pepi said.

Suddenly we heard Greta's loud voice complain in her thick Swedish accent, "How can dey expect us to vork in dis heat?"

It was over ninety degrees and only ten o'clock in the morning. Even with the windows open upstairs, there was no relief. Greta's door was across the hall and cracked open. I saw her pacing back and forth.

"Does she complain like that a lot?" I asked Jetta, who ignored me.

"I can't vork today. It's too damn hot," Greta said again very loud.

I knocked on her door lightly. "Hello, Greta?" Pepi stood behind me.

She opened the door, looking startled, then glanced up and down the hallway like she was expecting somebody.

"Do you think it's hot today?" she asked. Her hair was pulled back and greased against her head, and she had no makeup on. She looked like a man.

"Yes, I do. It's a furnace in this building," I agreed. "Please meet my niece Pepi," I said. She eyed Pepi up and down and turned away.

"It's silly for people to vork in his heat. Come in and feel how hot it is in dis room—and not even a toilet."

"There is no breeze at all today," I said, trying to be kind. Pepi stood in the doorway. "You can use my bathroom over at the bungalow."

"No. I have my own." She pointed to a pot in the corner of her room.

"Oh my! That's horrible. Why don't you use the bathroom at the end of the hall?"

"There's a good reason to use the pot here—I can dump it on the director's head for making me vork today. How about dat?" She didn't laugh. Her expression was serious. An involuntary laugh escaped Pepi's mouth.

I wanted to laugh but I wasn't sure if she was kidding or not. "You wouldn't do that, would you?"

"I vouldn't, eh? Between the director making me vork in dis heat and my leading man, Jack, always a bit salacious, I am being tortured to death making dis movie."

"Aren't you and Jack Gilbert an item?" I said.

"He vishes." Greta walked me to the doorway.

"Come to my bungalow for lunch today. I'll have the chef prepare salads for us," I said as she practically pushed me into the hallway.

Moping with a long face, she said, "I cannot. I've been a naughty boy today."

Confused, I shook my head.

A dark smile came over her face and she said, "Come and see me sometime on the set," and shut the door in my face.

We left the building but not before Pepi said, "I like Greta—the way she looks, her forceful attitude—it's all wonderful."

I huffed my exasperation because I never knew how to take Greta's odd comments. Later that afternoon, I saw her standing behind my director, watching me work. After thirty minutes, she left as quietly as she arrived.

I asked Pop Leonard, my director, if I could step away from the set for a moment. "I want to watch Greta work."

"Not sure you'll be able to. She always has a closed set."

"She invited me." I walked onto her set and found her in the middle of a love scene. She yelled, "Dere's a stranger-r-r on dis set! Ged-out, whoever you are!"

"Miss Garbo doesn't want anybody on her set," her director said in a voice ten times more calm and polite than Greta's shrieking.

I objected. "She spent time on *my* set today, so I've come to repay the compliment."

Greta brushed past me. "Vhy don't you go back to *your* set?"

"I'm trying to take you up on your offer to visit."

"I came to your set to see Jetta Goudal, not you," she boldly declared.

"You came to see Jetta?" I balked. "Do you speak French?"

She cupped her hand to her ear and proceeded to make me feel like a child being scolded. "I hear them calling you to your set. You're vasting my time. Get out of here before I have you kicked off my set."

"Well, that goes both ways. Don't you ever come onto my set again," I said, stomping away.

The gall! The audacity! She was the worst person I knew next to Jetta—and Lillian Gish who stole my dressing room. These women loved to come party with us at Ocean House and The Ranch, acting like my friend in public and at parties, but absolutely hated to work with me! I promised myself never to invite either of them to San Simeon again.

— ⓪ —

It was an unusually hot day for April, with the sun shining brightly and the pelicans flying low to the water when I skipped out to the front porch at Ocean House to see WR. "Guess what? Guess what? *Variety* magazine has ranked MGM actors according to box office sales."

WR sat in a chaise lounge with a stack of papers on his lap. "What does it say?"

I stood in front of him, holding out the magazine like a court document. "The first three on the list are poopy men, so we'll skip those. Number four: Greta Garbo." I made a sour face and pursed my lips. "Number five: Norma Shearer, and drum roll please. Number six: Marion Davies." I bowed and tossed the magazine onto WR's lap, twirled, and did a curtsy.

"Very nice! I'm so proud of you! I knew you had talent, young lady."

"The best part of the list is still to come." I took back the magazine. "Guess who's rated number nine?"

"I have no idea."

"Guess!"

"Joan Crawford."

"No. Joan's listed as a featured player and not as an MGM star."

"Okay. Who then?"

"Lillian Gish." I made a sour face and stuck out my tongue.

"Marion don't do that. It isn't nice. You should get along with these women."

"It's not as easy as it seems. I do try to get along with them—just not Garbo or Gish. They can haul it out of here."

WR shook his head and picked up the magazine, looking over the entire list.

Grabbing the small blanket WR had on his legs, I wrapped it around my head and pursed my lips like Lillian, saying, "I am only number nine." I twirled around, dropping the blanket. "I'm the meanest Svede on the planet."

WR gave a belly laugh. "I do love your impressions."

I sat down in the chaise and stared out toward the sea. The day was cloudy and the ocean still. Number six was fine for now, but I wanted to be number one.

— ⬯ —

My new movie, *Show People*, was my fourth film in 1928. Exhaustion hung around the edges of my life, but I kept pushing myself, riding the wave of good publicity and positive reviews. My director, King Vidor, was well-respected and sought after. He set an ambitious thirty-day shooting schedule, which was lightning fast, even considering that most of my movies were filmed in sixty to seventy days. *Show People* was a look at Hollywood through the eyes of an aspiring actress from Georgia named Peggy Pepper. Some say it was a spoof on the career of Gloria Swanson, and who am I to deny that? Ms. Swanson's real-life snobbishness and pomposity in dealing with her fans was pretty tough to swallow, so I discreetly used this opportunity to portray a slightly malicious version of her in the movie, hoping nobody would notice.

As I was studying my lines one day in my bungalow, Charlie burst in and sat down next to me. "Hey there, darling. What are you studying?"

"My lines," I said, holding up the script.

"I think if this movie is about Hollywood, we should both make an appearance as ourselves in it."

I considered the idea. "Has anybody ever done that in a movie? It's brilliant."

"Charlie Chaplin could stumble upon you as Peggy Pepper, and you could be so obsessed with adjusting yourself and your appearance that you could miss meeting the one-and-only Charlie Chaplin. Your father could point me out as I leave the scene."

"Adorable."

"And while you're filming a scene as Peggy Pepper, the real Marion Davies could arrive by limousine to the set of her new movie that's a short distance away from your set. Peggy could stop and ask, 'Who is that?' to which her costar would reply, 'The movie star Marion Davies.'"

"Don't you think that's over the top and a little self-serving?"

"Not a chance. *Show People* is a look at Hollywood itself and its inner workings. It'll be genius on several levels. We get to poke fun at ourselves and our fame."

I thought about it for a minute. Hell, what did I care, it was going to improve my picture immensely to have the great Charlie Chaplin in it. "I'll talk to King about it."

Charlie kissed my cheek and left as quickly as he had arrived. I sat back on the couch, loving his idea more each minute. Charlie was my comedy mentor and muse, always so generous with his talents. In my afternoon call with WR, I shared the idea and he loved it.

"You could even include a brief scene where King himself makes an appearance in the film. Why stop at just you and Charlie?"

"Great idea!"

WR continued, "I'm making another change." He proceeded to tell me that I would not be taking a pie in the face as the script called for. "I'm afraid for your dignity, my Darling," he said in all seriousness.

"WR, it's fine. It's a comedy," I insisted. But he insisted the pie be switched for seltzer water in my face.

In the end, we didn't add just the three personalities, we added King's wife and my dear friend, Ellie Boardman, Douglas Fairbanks, Jack Gilbert, George K Arthur, Elinor Glyn, Harry Crocker, Norma Talmadge, Mae Murray, and Louella Parsons. They all had walk-on parts, along with many others. But Charlie and I had the biggest roles with Peggy Pepper. My movie double, Vera Burnett, played me during my scenes as Peggy.

The movie was a smash hit. We filmed in twenty-seven days, and the reviews were stupendous. Soon after the late October premiere, Charlie and I were in bed at his newly designed "California Gothic" home off Benedict Canyon one afternoon. I was snuggled into him when I began giggling uncontrollably. He demanded to know what was so funny.

"You. You are so funny. You changed my film and made it brilliant, and I adore you for it. Thank you." He kissed me and chuckled to himself, laying back on the bed with a self-satisfied look on his face.

— ⓪ —

Two months later, sitting by the pool under the umbrella at Ocean House, WR and I drank our coffee and read the morning paper. I was wrapped in a blanket with my legs tucked up underneath me, and WR had a scarf around his neck to keep him warm. The December day was crisp and clear with a hint of coming winter, California-style of course.

"What's new with Rose?" WR asked.

"She's been living quietly in her Studio City house—or at least the police haven't called me of late. She continues to make bad choices when it comes to men, alcohol, and drugs, as does Pepi."

He looked up from his papers at me, shaking his head slightly.

I continued. "For Rose in the last month, I paid off a gambler and a sailor to make them go away quietly. She's barely able to take care of herself, I'm not sure she'll be able to take care of Patricia when we do find her."

"Thank goodness she's with her father, even though he's hiding from us." WR stared at the cobalt-colored saltwater shimmering in the pool.

"What's the update on finding Patricia anyway?" I asked as I did regularly, but this time I was done being patient and kind about it. "Surely it doesn't take all this time to find one little girl. I mean shit WR, I've been waiting four-and-a-half years now! What can the problem possibly be?"

WR put his pencil down and looked out to the sea. "I can see you're upset. Let me tell you that George knows we're after him. Every time my detective locates him and hires a lawyer to file custody papers, George finds out and runs. He's moved from relative to relative in Minnesota, New York, and Maryland. I'm not sure our best course is to take custody away from him."

I searched WR's eyes, wanting to unload my anger and suspicions that he wasn't doing all he could, but I held back. "Maybe not," I said.

Scratching his chin with a faraway look in his eyes he said, "Let me change tactics. I'll offer him a good paying job at the paper and see if we can't entice him to move back to LA of his own free will."

"Thank you," I said, and walked to the ocean's edge. I was tired of waiting and wondering if WR was doing all he could. He obviously wasn't. Maybe he wanted her to stay away? Surely the most powerful man in publishing could bring her back to me. As the water lapped at my ankles, I saw Patricia as a toddler with her fuzzy blanket and stuffed animal. I missed her crooked little smile so much it ached inside me.

There wasn't anything to do but hope WR could strike a deal with George.

CHAPTER 33

AUGUST 1929

On a rare Douras family weekend at San Simeon, WR and I sat upstairs in the third-floor Gothic study, working and alternately watching the sun sparkle on the ocean. WR studied a stack of architectural drawings while I studied a script. Ethel, Reine, and Rose were downstairs in the game room playing cards. Rose had sworn off men for the time being, recovering from a particularly rough encounter with a longshoreman which necessitated an arm cast.

A telegram was delivered to WR, and I went back to staring mindlessly at the ocean.

"Darling, I have some good news. George drove a hard bargain, but we've agreed on terms and he's bringing our girl back to us. They arrive in San Luis Obispo on the 8:00 a.m. train tomorrow morning."

"Oh, thank God! What did it take to entice him?" I asked hesitantly.

"An editorial job at the paper that pays $24,000 a year!" WR said.

"Well, it's only money, right? Isn't that what you say?"

"Absolutely! It's only money and I want my Rosebud to have everything her heart desires," he said, beckoning me to him with open arms.

I went to him and kissed him deeply then ran down the narrow spiral staircase to the Assembly Room, bursting in and shouting, "Patricia's coming home tomorrow!"

Excited conversation flew around the great hall. "I hope she recognizes us," Ethel said.

"She's ten years old now," I said. "That's a big difference from five. What if she doesn't recognize us?"

"She will," Reine insisted. "I'll bet she's smart as a whip."

"I can't wait to hug her," I said, sinking into a big chair. "Five years is a long time when you're that young."

"Too bad Mama isn't here. She'd have loved to see Patricia again," Ethel chimed in.

Everyone but Rose imagined the reunion. Across the room, she had a worried look on her face. Sitting down next to her, I asked, "Are you okay?"

"I guess." She avoided eye contact. "I'm nervous, okay? I haven't seen either of them in a long time."

— ⓪ —

The next morning, we did our best to stand out of the blazing sun on the train platform in San Luis Obispo. WR, Ethel, Reine, Rose, and I watched the passengers exit the train, recognizing Patricia immediately when she disembarked with George. She had traces of WR's face, with his long, thin nose and wide forehead. As if reading my mind, Rose whispered, "She's so tall, and she looks like WR."

"She really does," Ethel said. I glanced at WR, wondering if he saw it as well but his face gave nothing away.

Wishing for Rose to take the lead and step forward, we instead watched her shrink from the responsibility. I moved toward Patricia. "We've missed you. Welcome home, Sweetheart." I scooped her into my arms and kissed her cheek. I pulled back to get a look at her happy and cautious face, shooting a glance to her father as he stood to the side.

George and WR acknowledged each other. Rose finally approached Patricia and wrapped her arms around her. "Mama," she said softly. I wrapped my arms around Rose, and we all enveloped Patricia in a big hug.

— ⓪ —

Back at The Ranch, Reine and Ethel fussed over Patricia, getting her juice and eggs, and offering to go swimming with her in the elegant and whimsical indoor Roman pool, where the stars were painted with gold inlay on the bottom of the pool and the fish swam on the ceiling. "Maybe you'll be brave enough to jump off the diving board with me? Reine's a scaredy-cat," Ethel said.

"It's pretty high," Reine defended herself.

Patricia's long legs followed my sisters around the dining room as she looked with wonder at the tapestries on the wall and the multitudes of colorful flags hanging over our heads. Her face may have looked like WR's, but her skinny legs and azure eyes were all mine. Rose sat across from us with a scowl on her face, next to George, who shifted in his chair and looked like he was searching for an exit. Standing up from the table, I said to Rose, "Let's go for a walk, shall we?"

I locked my arm through hers, and we walked through the garden, taking in the dazzling Pacific Ocean. "Let's be honest about this, shall we?"

"Yes, let's," she said. "I've never felt like her mother. You provided everything for her. She's really yours."

"Stop that, Rose. *You* are her mother. She hugged *you* and called *you* mama."

"I can't provide for her. I can't raise her. I don't want to raise her," Rose said.

"You *can* provide for her with me standing silently behind you. I will make sure you have everything you need."

"I don't live much of a family life, and I don't really want one."

"Damn you, Rose. You have to rally and forget the men and the partying and be Patricia's mother again. How can you give up so easily on our girl?"

"I'm not mother material."

"That is not true so stop saying it. Remember back in New York? It was your big dream."

"New York was a long time ago, Marion. I was a different Rose back then."

She was so right—a different Rose entirely. We both made choices years ago we were still having to live with. She laid her head on my shoulder, almost collapsing into me and I wondered what had become of her. I wanted to be Patricia's mother but that wasn't possible without abandoning my promise to WR to always keep her a secret. We sat on a stone bench and stared out at the sweeping view, huddled together in silence.

— ◎ —

The next morning, Rose, George, and Patricia left for Studio City, barely saying a word before disappearing. I found a note with a few scrawled words about a reconciliation and one last attempt at family life with Patricia. But a week later, George called my bungalow on the MGM lot.

"Can I bring her to you? Rose is a mess, and Patricia doesn't belong here."

"Take her to the Lexington house. Ethel will dote on Patricia until we can figure things out." My movie was wrapping up in the next few weeks and I asked George to give me some time.

I knew Ocean House was also no place for a child with the crowds and parties. I called Rose that evening, but there was no answer. The next day I found her asleep in her bed, still wearing a sequined dress from the night before. Her lipstick was smeared, and her eye makeup smudged. I gently reminded her that she had a daughter living in the house, but she just rolled over and

260 THE BLUE BUTTERFLY

grunted. "I told you this wasn't going to work. I'm not a mother, and I don't want to be a wife, so just leave me alone."

"Rose . . ." my voice trailed off.

"Jesus, Marion, leave me the hell alone, okay? He's divorcing me. Are you happy now?"

I drove directly to Ocean House, where I called George and invited him over for a visit. After a heart-to-heart talk in which WR offered him an even more lucrative position at his LA newspaper, it was agreed that Patricia could stay at the Lexington house with Ethel and start school there, visiting her father on some weekends. I breathed a sigh of relief for the moment.

CHAPTER 34

JUNE 1930

Driving with Patricia to Ocean House on a rare Friday night visit, I asked her if she'd like to come up to The Ranch when school let out for a long summer visit. I was heading up the next day to be with WR and wished Patricia would join me.

She shook her whole body. "Yes, yes, I would love it. School's out next week."

A week flew by and Ethel brought her up. We took turns doting on her. She loved the elephants and the tigers in WR's zoo, and loved to horseback ride, play tennis, and swim in both the newly redesigned Neptune pool during the day and the Roman pool at night.

She had settled into her new life in LA nicely in the past year, living with Ethel and attending elementary school, and visiting Rose and George as each parent desired. The whole arrangement was working beautifully.

Sitting by the big Neptune pool drinking our lemonades and reading, I noticed Patricia was unusually sullen. The day was gorgeous and hot, and we jumped in the water frequently to cool ourselves.

"What's wrong with my mother?" Patricia asked unexpectedly. I knew this question had arisen from Rose having missed several visits with her. I explained as best I could. "She has a sort of sickness," I said.

"Is that what makes her drink and take all those pills?" she asked.

I nodded, desperately wanting to change the subject. "Come on, last one in the water has to get us more lemonade!" I yelled as I stood up. She beat me, of course, making a huge splash as she landed in the water.

— ⓪ —

Two weeks into the visit, a telegram arrived addressed to Patricia from George, telling her to pack her things—that she was going back to Minnesota.

"No! I don't want to go. I want to stay here with you!" she cried.

George was due to arrive at The Ranch the following morning to get Patricia and I panicked, sending Ethel and Patricia out on a horseback ride after breakfast so that WR and I could talk to George alone. It was a crazy idea to try to hide her by sending her out into the hills, but it was the only thing I could think of.

George arrived in his car and we ushered him into the Assembly Room to talk. "What's changed in our arrangement? Why can't Patricia stay here for the summer and live with Ethel?" I asked.

George handed WR the Final Decree of Divorce from the courts, pointing at the sentence that deemed Rose an unfit parent with no parental rights due to her drinking and unexplained absences. WR read the document out loud as I shook my head, feeling like I was underwater and couldn't breathe.

George paced back and forth. "I just can't take you Hollywood types any longer. I want her back with my family in the Midwest."

He told us he'd found Rose half-naked with a man when he'd last arrived to pick Patricia up for a visit. "I want *my* daughter.

She *is* my daughter, isn't she?" he said with a piercing look on his face, bringing me back to the day I'd handed her over to them.

"Of course, she's legally your daughter, but now that Rose has faltered as her mother, I want to be more involved, and so does Ethel. She needs motherly love," I said. I walked to the table and lit a cigarette to calm my nerves, looking to the hills. I desperately needed a drink. I continued, "My father's moving to California soon, and he'll live at the house with Ethel and Patricia too. Don't you want her to know her grandfather?"

"Yes, I do, but I have family for her as well back in Minnesota."

"But isn't it reasonable that she stays here in California, close to me and WR—her birth parents and benefactors? Don't we get a vote?"

He sucked in a deep breath and nodded slightly, looking a bit defeated and overwhelmed. I could tell I was getting somewhere in my argument. I said, "We're not trying to exclude you. If you want to live with her in LA, we can talk about that. We just want her to stay here."

Ethel and Patricia appeared in the doorway holding hands, staring us down with sorrowful faces. Patricia said, "I don't want to go. I want to stay here with Aunt Ethel and Aunt Marion."

George nodded, giving in. Patricia ran to her father and kissed him. "Thank you, Papa."

This arrangement with George would be the closest WR and I would ever come to being a family with Patricia. Papa finally did move west a few months later, retiring at age seventy-six, living with Ethel and Patricia, the best doting females he could have asked for. I rejoiced that most of my family was together again.

—⊚—

I worked daily on filming *The Bachelor Father* about the feisty daughter of an English gentlemen. I had some comedic moments in the film, one where I was to slip on a carpet after entering the room. The carpet wasn't sliding properly, so every time I fell, I

264 THE BLUE BUTTERFLY

got another bruise. It happened to be the same day WR brought General Douglas MacArthur by the studio to see me film a scene. From the moment they walked onto the set, the cast and crew became tongue-tied, freezing like ninnies at the very sight of the General. Unfazed, I just wanted to finish the scene.

We pushed ahead and finally got the correct friction between the rug and the floor, and I even managed not to wince on my way down. The General laughed on cue but WR scowled at the silliness of it all. After lunch and more laughs, the General returned to his more serious life in politics.

We had plans to head off to Europe for an extended romp but not before Patricia came for a visit to say goodbye. She sat in an overstuffed chair in my bedroom at Ocean House, the chair absolutely swallowing her. As always, she was reading, this time one of *The Milly-Molly-Mandy Stories* when a tidal wave of maternal love washed over me. I watched her fiddling with her hair, adjusting herself and the pillow she clutched as she took a sip of her tea—completely unaware I was watching her. I fell deeper in love with her every day we spent together. Not only was she a kind, sweet, and considerate eleven-year-old, but she was also without vanity or narcissism. Rose was gone from her life and I yearned to tell her the truth about our relationship.

"Patricia, darling," I said quietly.

"Hmm," she said without looking up at me.

"I want to tell you something. I know you're ready to hear it. You're a mature, compassionate, and discreet young lady, and so, before we speak honestly, I must secure a promise from you to never reveal to anyone the secret that I'm going to share with you."

"Aunt Marion, what is it?" she asked, placing the book in her lap.

"I'm talking about the fact that I'm your mother, and WR is your father." She stared at me for a long time, considering my words, but had little to no reaction. It didn't seem to shock her at all.

"Did you already know that?" I asked, astonished.

She nodded. "Mama was mumbling one night after she drank a lot. We were alone, and I shook her and asked, 'Who's my mother?' She said very clearly, 'Marion. Marion is your mother.' Then she fell asleep. The next morning, she didn't say anything and neither did I."

"Oh Sweetheart! When did this happen?" I rushed to her and gathered her in my arms.

"When I first came back."

"Why didn't you ever ask me about it?"

"I don't know, I figured it was a secret. I can keep a secret." I kissed and hugged her and talked about why it was important not to ever mention it again. But I wanted her to know I loved her deeply and would always be there for her even if I couldn't be with her every day. She nodded and said she loved me as well, promising to keep the secret forever. She said it without any drama, then picked up her book and resumed reading like we had just discussed the weather.

I stared out the window at the crashing waves, a wondering pride glowing in me, marveling at how mature my daughter was and how grateful I was to be her mother.

Chapter 35

March 1933

The worst depression in our nation's history had been raging for more than three years. I continued making movies, hoping to make people happy with an escape from the bitterness of the world. I looked beyond helping my own family and sought out ways to quietly help in the community. One of my projects was building a Children's Clinic where needy children could be treated for free. At the studio, I anonymously paid medical bills for the crew, and family expenses when a movie technician or set worker was injured or laid off.

The depression had not hit WR and the Hearst Corporation yet. They were insulated from the downturn through his vast holdings in various sectors of the economy, not just the stock market. While other newspapers folded, none of the Hearst papers were lost. WR funded breadlines for the poor in New York, Chicago, and Los Angeles. He was an optimist about the future and continued acquiring properties and newspapers, not to mention spending vast amounts on continuing to build The Ranch and acquiring warehouses full of antiques. I would learn later that WR was in the habit of spending to the very limit and borrowing beyond that.

On a trip east to visit his papers, WR checked himself into the Cleveland Clinic for three weeks for a delicate throat operation. He didn't tell me about the surgery ahead of time. I only found out later that Millicent and his sons were with him, which very nearly broke my spirit. How could he just leave me out altogether? When I questioned him on the phone after he checked out of the hospital, I could hear the regret in his voice, and yet his response was woefully inadequate, offering me some pathetic excuse about my having too many commitments to drop everything and be by his side for weeks. He was right, of course, but I still would have wanted the choice. It dug in me a little that Millicent was comforting him even though we had found a sort of peace of late (her domain New York and mine California).

She was aware, as was I, of WR's struggle with getting older. He searched the fringes of medicine for new discoveries that would prolong his life and keep him healthy. He yearned for the proverbial fountain of youth. Our annual visits to Europe always included the world-famous German spa in Bad Nauheim, known to heal its visitors of whatever ailed them. We took "the cure," for an entire week, which seemed like good old common sense to me, but WR insisted it was "cutting edge." The treatments included vitamin mixtures that tasted horrible, colonics, massages, hot mineral baths, and lots of sleep.

WR's more eccentric exploration of health remedies included following the research of a certain Dr. Serge Voronoff, who claimed to rejuvenate the elderly by transplanting monkey glands into the human body. WR dispatched one of his favorite editors, Walter Howey, to find out more about the Chicago man who had the procedure, but the outcome proved inconclusive. New scientific procedures and contraptions became his obsession. As one friend put it, "It's an unwritten law never to mention death in his presence." I knew this to be true from as far back as the death of Mr. Barham in London.

— ⟨⟩ —

My never-ending duties as mistress of San Simeon had me hosting the grizzled and acidic literary lion, Irish playwright George Bernard Shaw, after WR returned to the west coast in the spring of 1933. Mr. Shaw had spent years writing articles and editorials for WR and his newspapers even after he received the Nobel Prize for Literature in 1925. WR had made multiple invitations, and Mr. Shaw finally accepted.

WR was ecstatic. It was our joint intention to wrestle Mr. Shaw's play *Pygmalion* away from him so MGM could produce it and I could star as Eliza Doolittle. Special preparations and invitations to the heavy hitters in Hollywood were made for Mr. and Mrs. Shaw's "grand tour" of the Hearst and Davies properties. They included LB and his wife Margaret, Irving Thalberg and Norma Shearer, brothers Jack and Harry Warner, Frances Marion, Eileen Percy, the King Vidors, William Haines, and my dear friend, Marie Glendinning.

On the appointed day, Mr. and Mrs. Shaw climbed the courtyard stairs where WR and I met our guests. Taking in the view, the Neptune Pool, and all the statues, he said to WR, "No doubt, this is the way God would have built the place if he had your money."

I laughed and WR smiled, unsure if Mr. Shaw was impressed or not. It was impossible to tell.

At dinner together on the first night in the Refectory, the tension ran so high I found it difficult to relax, laugh, and lead our party to gaiety. I very badly wanted Mr. Shaw to like us so he would sell us the rights to produce his play, but warming up to him looked to be a herculean feat, evidenced by the fact that he was surrounded by Hollywood stars and power brokers and seemed utterly unimpressed. He was most assuredly a wise, discerning seventy-seven-year-old teetotaler like WR, seven years his junior. As we gathered in the Assembly Room for drinks, our new rule of one cocktail apiece before dinner (due to a few guests consistently over imbibing in the past year) left me parched and in need of a quick exit to find some of my hidden stash before we sat for dinner. I slipped to the back bathroom in the kitchen, where I had a bottle hidden for emergencies, and took a few swigs so I could relax.

WR slipped in from his hidden door behind the carved walnut choir pews just as I returned to the room. "Dinner everyone," he announced as the bell rang.

Mr. Shaw sat to my right. His reputation for being grumpy and sarcastic made me glad of the lubrication I had swigged so I could verbally spar with him. Charlotte Shaw sat next to WR. She was a quiet, demure woman whose eyes darted around the opulent room. I could be sure WR's wealth intimidated most everyone, but nobody showed it more than Mrs. Shaw.

I practically ignored the rest of our guests in service to Mr. and Mrs. Shaw. Everyone in attendance had been to The Ranch several times and knew the routine. They found their seats on either side of us at the long dining room table without any help. I hadn't had a chance to talk personally to Mr. Shaw yet and took this opportunity to break the ice.

"May I call you George?"

"I prefer Bernard," he said. Scraggly hairs, like down from a baby duck, stuck out from his face. I had the urge to touch his beard but refrained. Charlie would be so proud when I told him.

"Really? How come nobody calls you that?"

"Because they don't listen to me when I say things," he quipped.

"Okay, well, I will listen to you, Bernard. It's a pleasure having you and Charlotte here with us at WR's magnum opus," I said, smiling slightly at WR and eyeing Charlotte who was paying intense attention to our conversation from across the table, looking like she was almost shaking from nerves.

"It's a pleasure to be your guest. May I call you Marion?" Bernard asked.

"Yes, you may, especially since that's my name." I raised my eyebrows twice at him in jest.

The water glasses were filled, and Bernard took a roll and buttered it immediately. Thinking it was our salad, Charlotte took the white orchid near her gold-rimmed saucer and ate it. I gulped hard, realizing just then how terrified she really was. I hoped it wasn't poisonous.

Oblivious to his wife's distress, Bernard said, "Oh, you're a cheeky one, aren't you?"

Witty banter was my goal and I responded, "Yes, I have two cheeks, and I use them quite frequently." The guests within earshot chuckled and William Haines said, "I can attest to that," and everyone laughed again. I could feel the tension in the room dissipate. I winked at William and saw WR beam at me.

Bernard smiled as he pulled at his white beard and pressed his moustache away from his mouth with his thumb and index finger, seeming to take stock of me.

I continued, "I have two great heroes as far as writing is concerned," I said, leaning a little toward Bernard.

Leaning a little toward me, he said, "Oh really. Who are they?"

"You and Mr. Shakespeare," I said, and took a drink of my water, grateful I had those shots of whiskey coursing through my veins.

A plate of rare roast beef was placed directly in front of Mr. Shaw, and I saw him gulp hard. WR had warned us he was a vegetarian, and yet somehow the waiter hadn't gotten the message. WR was absorbed in a moment with Charlotte and missed Bernard's expression.

The trick to witty banter is to keep the ball going like in a tennis match, but with the faux pas happening in the dinner service, I could barely keep up.

"Why mention me in the same breath as Shakespeare?" he asked, leaning away from the beef and toward me.

I caught WR's gaze and directed his eyes to the platter, and within seconds, he removed the plate and passed it to Franny Marion, who was seated next to him. I was conducting two conversations now and it was draining me quickly. I wished WR or anybody else at the table would jump into the conversation, but the entire party just watched and listened to Mr. Shaw and me.

"Well, *Androcles and the Lion*," I said, striving to impress him that I'd read his play, which I'd only done the previous day on the trip up to San Simeon.

"Did you read it?" Bernard asked, squinting as he watched Franny cut into her beef.

"Yes," I nodded, leaning forward, trying to draw his eyes away from the platter.

He scowled and said teasingly, "I didn't think you had the intelligence."

I exaggeratedly sat back in my chair and stared at him, hoping he was joking and testing me. I knew he supported women's suffrage from his articles WR had published, so I gave him the benefit of the doubt.

"I have the intelligence to read it. I just don't have the intelligence to understand what it means. Perhaps you can explain it to me," I said.

A waiter finally placed a bowl of pasta covered with grilled mushrooms, asparagus, green beans, and cherry tomatoes in front of Bernard, who dove right in.

"You're a pretty shrewd young lady, aren't you?" he said.

"Thank you for calling me a pretty young lady," I said, getting stuck on the word "l-l-lady" and blushing a little. Bernard tilted his head to one side and studied me quietly.

I was growing a bit tired of this, especially without more alcohol. I felt like a wilting flower. I lowered my eyes at my verbal foible. "I need to speak to the waiters. Will you excuse me please?" I went to the back bathroom and drank more whiskey.

When I returned, WR and Bernard were discussing something political, while Charlotte now looked bored instead of terrified. All the other guests chit-chatted amongst themselves, avoiding conversation with Bernard. He intimidated everyone, like an old owl who might gulp you down in one swallow. Even so, the rest of the evening went smoothly enough. After dinner, we sat by the fire, as old men love to do. The female guests all gathered around Bernard, while the men huddled together in the adjoining room smoking their cigars.

"I would love an interview, Mr. Bernard," Louella said coyly.

"I don't give interviews," he barked. "I hate the media."

I jumped in. "Surely you could let Louella ask you a few questions, Bernard—as a favor to me?" I batted my eyes in an exaggerated way and he harrumphed.

The next day I found Bernard and Louella together in the Assembly Room. She looked like a scared girl, and Bernard was writing in her notebook. Apparently sitting for an interview was too much for him, so he was writing down what he wanted Louella to know. Franny stood off to the side, watching the spectacle. I retreated to the kitchen for a cup of coffee to avoid Bernard's scrutiny so early in the morning.

WR joined me a few minutes later. "Hiding out, are you? He can be difficult, can't he?"

"Hmm," I said, nodding. "He's a lot of work."

WR said he'd spoken to Bernard about selling *Pygmalion* to MGM with me starring in it. I sat up straight with wide eyes, waiting for the rest. "He's not interested in Hollywood ruining his play."

I slid back down in my seat. "Of course," I said. It didn't surprise me.

After another day of hosting the Shaws with visits to the zoo, cards, puzzles, charades around the fire, and a motor car caravan around the coast and property, we all left for LA. Lunch was prepared at my bungalow at MGM as the press waited in droves.

I ushered Charlotte upstairs to freshen up before the press was allowed in. She stood in front of the mirror assessing herself.

"Thank you so much, Marion. Do you have a nip of something to calm my nerves?"

Shocked and a bit upset at myself for not reaching out to her in the previous days, I retrieved a bottle of scotch, and we both had a good drink. I couldn't possibly let her drink alone. "Promise me you won't say anything about this nip," she said. I agreed as she took another glassful. "Dare I apologize for Bernie's stiff ways? He's a simple man who doesn't like showy wealth."

I smiled as warmly as I could at her and nodded. *Really?* I thought sarcastically, *one could never tell.*

Lunch was served and photos were taken. Charlie and I sat on either side of Bernard. LB Mayer and Clark Gable were there. Irving Thalberg sat across from Bernard with WR at the head of the table. Charlie entertained the Shaws with a few antics.

Mr. and Mrs. Shaw left for San Pedro on a cruise ship headed to the Panama Canal. I was sure I wasn't the only one relieved they were done with Hollywood. We didn't get the rights to *Pygmalion* this time, but I wasn't going to give up so easily.

The most unexpected compliment came from Bernard as we said goodbye at the studio. "Please come with us, Marion," he exclaimed loudly enough for everyone who attended the luncheon to hear. "We love you doting on us like you do."

"Thank you, Bernard. I wish I could, but I'm in the middle of filming," I said, quivering at the thought of how much scotch it would take to survive an ocean voyage with them.

CHAPTER 36

WR and I worked as usual. I released movie after movie, but something was changing in the atmosphere surrounding my career. It felt like a definite slowing of enthusiasm for my comedies, while at the same time a rising tide of subtle resentment grew against me from my Hollywood peers and movie audiences as they begrudged me the overwhelming publicity WR always heaped on. I suppose they'd had their fill of me as a comedic actress and preferred me as the wealthy hostess of lavish parties. The biggest downturn came thanks to the movie magazines that incessantly wrote about my endless frolicking on and off the set, which recently included the covered wagon costumed surprise party for WR's seventieth birthday.

All through the 1920s, I had fought WR to do comedy, and now that I had the comedic roles, the industry was changing to sexy vixen roles for women. I was dying to do one of these femme fatale films, but WR forbade it. Having a mistress was one thing but having an openly sexy one was too much for his old-fashioned mind.

On a sunset beach walk in Santa Monica that fall, WR held my hand and we strode slowly on the firm sand near the water's edge. I bent down and picked up a shell, turning it over in my hand. The Santa Ana winds were blowing in from the desert, making it hot, dry, and clear.

WR said, "I'm negotiating with LB and Irving to have you star as *Marie Antoinette*. It's the perfect picture worthy of your talent and you'll be nominated for an Academy Award. You deserve a Best Actress award."

"I don't want the award," I pouted. "I want a picture with a modern female role."

"Do you mean sexier?"

"Yes, and modern. It's what the audience wants. Norma won her Academy Award for the fallen woman she played in *The Divorcée*. She didn't win for the innocent and wholesome ingenue like the ones I always play."

"I know, but I can't tolerate that type of role for you." We stopped walking and he stared out at the horizon. "The entire family should be able to go to the movies and enjoy themselves. The open selling of sex on the screen turns my stomach."

"But it's the trend now. Every actress who plays the vixen has a successful movie. I want that too."

We began walking again. "Your image must remain innocent and wholesome. *Marie Antoinette* is the perfect vehicle for you."

"And if they don't give it to me, will you find me some new modern storylines?"

"If they don't give you this movie, we'll be moving to Warner Brothers. I am damn tired of being milked for publicity *and* money. They owe me."

WR hadn't talked to me before about how angry he was with LB and Irving. "Why haven't I been consulted? I don't want to move to Warner Brothers." A large gust of wind blew against us and I grabbed WR's hand.

"We may not have a choice, my dear," he said absentmind-edly, a million miles away.

This was the first time in my career I vehemently disagreed with the direction WR wanted me to go in, and I wasn't sure what to do about it.

When we arrived back at Ocean House, iced tea and lemonade waited for us on a tray by the pool. In the distance, the pier was filled with people. Seagulls squawked. I pleaded with him. "Please drop the quest for a Best Actress award for me. It isn't possible with the caliber of films I'm offered."

"Do not give up," he said as he took my hand and planted a kiss on top of it. "I love you and want the best for you."

"I know, Sweetheart. Let's go inside and get away from these nasty winds."

If times were different, I might have been able to break away from WR and steer my own career, but I knew as well as anyone that men held all the power. I tried to settle my anxious mind by reminding myself that my movie career was second to my life with WR and Patricia.

— ⟨◎⟩ —

In February, we invited a handful of guests to San Simeon. WR was tucked away in the upstairs study, working as usual.

Entering the study, I announced, "I just got off the phone with Rose. She is back again, has cleaned up her life, and she has news." He looked uninterested and a bit irritated, but I continued.

"Rose has fallen in love with a man you might know," I said, hesitantly. WR raised an eyebrow. "It's Edward Beale McLean."

Both eyebrows went up this time, and he pursed his lips. Edward Beale McLean was the publisher of *The Washington Post,* as well as the owner of thoroughbred racehorses and the Hope Diamond. I didn't know what WR thought of him, but I was about to find out.

"Quiet talk around town is that McLean isn't all there," he said.

"Oh my, well she's fallen hard for him, and they planned the wedding even before he secured a divorce from his wife."

"And?" WR asked.

"Rose jumped the gun and held a press conference to announce her impending nuptials."

"My God! Your sister is a royal mess."

"And now it doesn't look like the wife will grant him a divorce. She's fighting it all the way."

"Rose is a user, and the affair won't last. That's my prediction, Marion."

Feeling melancholy, I went downstairs for breakfast. I entered the Refectory to roars of laughter. It seemed our guests were all up. "Hey, what's so funny?" I asked, standing in the entryway.

"You have to see what Harpo did. We're hooting and hollering about it, but WR wasn't too pleased earlier," Jean Harlow said.

Harpo Marx had an exaggeratedly guilty face that he instantly buried in his hands.

"Harpo, what did you do?" I asked teasingly. He peaked out of two fingers.

"Come with me," Marie Dressler said, pulling my arm and leading me to the window by the vestibule. Outside, a very rare snow blanketed the gardens and statues as far as the eye could see. She pointed, "Harpo got into the vault downstairs last night and took all our mink stoles and fur wraps and dressed the statues with them."

"Oh God! How clever of him!" I laughed.

"When WR saw it, he yelled at Harpo," Marie said.

I could see WR's indignant face at the thought of the expensive coats and hats ruined.

"Sometimes he's just a droopy drawers," I mumbled, to which Marie laughed.

We went back to the Refectory, giggling. It felt good to start my day off with silly laughter, and I wished WR could see the humor in the situation. He used to laugh at silliness, at least privately with me afterwards, like Pepi's antics as a teenager after she dressed the same statues in bras and panties.

Back in the Refectory, I poured myself a cup of coffee. "Harpo, you've outdone yourself," I said, then whispered, "I'm very proud of you."

Everyone left the dining room to begin their day. I grabbed a piece of cold toast and took several bites before I heard Ethel clear her throat.

"I can see you're deep in thought. Shall I leave?"

"No, no. Let's take a walk and see if we can find Marie and Jean," I said.

"They'll be down at the zoo, checking on the lions and tigers, I'm sure of it," Ethel said.

The zoo was within walking distance of Casa Grande. WR had over three hundred animals with a full-time veterinarian on site. Many of the grazing animals ran freely, including African and Asian antelope, zebras, camels, sambar deer from India, red deer from Europe, axis deer from Asia, llamas, kangaroos, ostriches, emus, Barbary sheep, Alaskan bighorn sheep, musk oxen, and yaks. Several giraffes were housed in a pen alongside the road for the guests to view as they were transported up the hill. An Asian elephant had been recently added in the menagerie cages, in addition to lions, tigers, a jaguar, and a leopard as well as three kinds of bears, monkeys, and two chimpanzees.

As we walked on the salted paths that were cleared of snow, Ethel asked, "What was with the big coat Jean wore at dinner last night?"

"Did you notice she wasn't wearing anything under her see-through chiffon dress? WR was upset and asked me to talk to her about changing," I said. "When I did, she refused and put on the coat."

"Unbelievable."

"She's stubborn *and* stacked, isn't she?" I said.

"She certainly knows how to show it off," Ethel agreed.

"Oh, to be twenty-three again," I mused.

We rounded the gardens on the path toward the zoo when we saw Jean running toward us. "What? What is it?" I yelled.

"It's Marie. Jerry got her good. I'm running ahead to get her a rag."

Jerry was our five-year-old chimp who didn't like humans very much. He had a mate named Mary, and they were quite cute together, but when anybody stopped in front of his cage, he threw poop at them.

"Where did he get you?" I asked as Marie came into view.

"Right on the arm. You really should do something about that animal."

"You're absolutely right. When WR finds out, he'll have him shipped away. This is the third time he's done this to a guest."

Agreeing that was enough drama for the day, we joined Harpo and Cary in some fun acrobatics upstairs in the library.

I was surprised and pleased not to find WR in the library when we got there. He usually played tennis with Willicombe in the afternoons. We pushed aside the long antique conference table and ten chairs, careful not to knock over the ancient Italian book stand. Harpo moved the tall, winged lion lectern near the bookcases and using the priceless thirty-five-foot-long Persian rug as a mat, traversed the room with a backward flip, a front handspring, a cartwheel, and a roundoff.

"You're a professional, Harpo. I'm an amateur," I said as I did a somersault and cartwheel. Everybody clapped while I struggled to catch my breath.

Cary and Harpo and I took several more turns jokingly competitive with each other while Jean and Marie watched and clapped.

"Anybody else want to try?" Harpo asked.

"Come on!" WR said suddenly appearing in the doorway and clapping his hands.

"We're done here, I think." I ran up to him and kissed his cheek.

"Speak for yourself," Harpo said before doing another routine. On the final backward roll, he splayed himself out on the carpet, lying spread eagle as he panted and laughed. "Okay, I'm done now too."

— ⓪ —

That afternoon, I slipped away from the crowd and met WR in the theater room for a private screening of my next movie, *Operator 13*. It was yet another historical drama, this time starring Gary Cooper. I wore a dreadful blonde wig and heavy makeup to disguise my age. I looked like a caricature of myself and slunk low in my seat when the movie finished. WR was livid, and we agreed the movie was terrible.

He called LB and Irving. "We just watched *Operator 13* and we're very disappointed."

WR ended the conversation saying, "Find some worthy roles for her, or we may have to leave MGM."

I paced the room, breathing heavily, puffing on my cigarette, dreading the movie release and the bad publicity, but dreading the possible move to Warner Brothers even more.

Operator 13 came out four months later and was panned by the critics. The final nail in the coffin of my career at MGM came with the denial of the role of Marie Antoinette by Irving, who said I was a comedic actress, not a dramatic one. Oh, the irony of it all.

WR wasted no time severing his business relationship with MGM. Within weeks, I was moved to Warner Brothers, feeling like a rag doll being flung about. It was proof of how little control I had over my own career and future, and it made me sick.

The men all congratulated themselves on the deal they made, of course. WR's assistant Willicombe arranged for all publicity in Hearst papers to feature Warner Brothers now instead of MGM.

WR, through Cosmopolitan Pictures, publicly praised brothers Jack, Harry, and Albert Warner in the article announcing the deal. They in turn praised WR, saying in part, "We are proud to be aligned with the most important and uplifting influence, not only in the journalistic field but also in the motion picture industry."

The only publicity I got was about my bungalow needing to be cut into three pieces to be moved the fourteen miles to the Warner Brothers lot. Of course, the papers devoured that news, digging in on the extravagance and expense of such a thing. Jack Warner promised the addition of two more rooms as part of my contract, even throwing in a Rolls Royce for me to drive as a bonus.

At home at Ocean House, when I tried to broach the subject of the move with WR, he shut me down, saying it was merely a business decision and that I could just make my movies at Warner Brothers instead.

"But I don't want to work at Warner Brothers. I don't know anybody there. I hate that you didn't even consider me."

"Like I said, it was a business decision. It's done now and everything will be fine, you'll see."

My rage was volcanic, barely under the surface. Before I even knew what I was doing, I threw a heavy vase of flowers at him and let out a curdling scream.

"Marion, stop that now."

"I should just quit!" I yelled and ran out of the library.

"You can't quit. I just signed the contract!" he yelled after me.

I barricaded myself in my bedroom that night and drank myself unconscious.

— ⟨⟨⟩⟩ —

After much cajoling and gifts from WR, we left for an extended tour in Europe that lasted until fall. We always traveled through Europe with twenty-five or more of our closest family and friends in a caravan of limousines, but this time I insisted on many of my own allies for comfort. I brought Connie, Ethel, Reine, Patricia, and Ellie with me, traveling in our own separate limousine apart from WR, his sons and their wives, and his newspaper men. It took me weeks to truly forgive WR, but with the help of my girlfriends, I finally did, remembering that I wouldn't have any of this life without him.

I did love him dearly; I just couldn't stand him at times.

CHAPTER 37

1935

A cloud of sickness hovered over Papa. Since moving to LA a few years earlier, he seemed to enjoy all my parties a little too much, telling his outrageous stories to anyone who would listen, even paying the pretty flibberty-gibbets—silly eighteen-year-old girls—one hundred dollars at Christmas to sit with him and listen to his stories.

After the new year, I noticed his complexion was pale with a yellowish tinge. He was nauseous more often than not, yet he always had a drink in his hands. His stomach grew larger, and he constantly needed to nap. The maids at the Lexington house and San Simeon found blood on his towels and pillowcases as well as near the toilet. Doctors were consulted but his behavior never changed. Days would go by when Papa couldn't eat, and his decline at the end was rapid. A few days before WR's seventy-second birthday party at Ocean House, Papa sat on the balcony overlooking the rush of workers setting up tents and arranging chairs. Without warning, he fell out of his chair, clutching his stomach.

I rushed to his side, and we moved him to a bedroom and called the doctor. He began coughing up blood. I called my sisters and shared the dire news.

WR stood at the doorway of the guest bedroom, looking a bit pale. Nurse Sherry made Papa comfortable, wiping his face with a wet towel and adjusting his pillows frequently. I sat with him and held his hand as I suppressed tears and waited for Reine, Ethel, and Rose. When they arrived, I pulled them all into a hug. We fell apart, crying as Papa lay unconscious in bed. He died that night in his sleep at age eighty-two of complications from cirrhosis of the liver. We buried him next to Mama in the family mausoleum a few days later.

Grief clawed at my very skin when Pepi died six weeks after Papa. She had been spoiled by me her entire life, indulged with a trust fund and access to WR's properties worldwide. She traveled in Europe as an heiress, drinking and partying with the wildest people she could find. A few years before her death, she'd met actress Louise Brooks and had fallen in love with her but was unable to live publicly with Louise. Her depression and drug use were at their height when she attended a New Year's party in New York alone, blackout drunk, and went home with somebody who raped her. She became pregnant and in a fit of desperation had an abortion. Her drug use soared to new heights after that, and she was committed to a Los Angeles mental institution. The cause of her death on June 11, 1935 was suicide. She'd jumped out a sixth-floor window.

— ⓪ —

The only bright light to focus on in the summer of 1935 was Patricia, a beautiful sixteen-year-old. She was not tempted by drinking and drugs, and I thanked God every night for it. She met the Hollywood stars who attended our parties, and she loved them all. One weekend, a diving competition at San Simeon held in the Roman pool had Charlie, Clark Gable, Errol Flynn, Arthur Lake, and Patricia competing for points doled out by WR.

The passion between Charlie and me had cooled, even fizzled out after so many years. Of late, he had fallen in love with

Paulette Goddard and proposed to her. There was a warm, familiar feeling between Charlie and me which would always be there and which I absolutely adored. We had spent ten passionate years together enjoying each other's company and were now best friends and confidants. Charlie now came to The Ranch for visits with WR to talk business and politics.

Arthur Lake was a new addition to our weekend parties after WR met him at United Artists. He had a bit part in my 1922 movie, *The Bride's Play*, as "Boy with Flowers," but I didn't remember him. His star was on the rise with a series of one-hour films as Dagwood Bumstead from the *Blondie* comic book series. His thirty-one-year-old boyish face with his all-American good looks made a perfect Dagwood.

On the day of the diving competition, it was pouring rain. The warm indoor Roman pool was located directly underneath the tennis courts. It was decorated with arched windows for light and a large skylight behind the eight-foot diving board. Eight Roman god, goddess, and hero statues filled the space. Ethel, Reine, Connie, and I sat in chairs on the pool deck across from the diving platform, watching the competition anxiously.

When it was being built, WR requested Julia Morgan design the pool after a Roman bath. The tiny, brilliant blue and orange glass mosaic tiles sparkled from floor to ceiling, inlayed with gold everywhere. The ambient light shimmered around us, bouncing off the glittering walls and ceiling.

Errol was the professed diving master and set up the rules whereby he'd do a dive, and everybody else would be scored on how well they matched it. The diving continued for an hour with sarcastic innuendo and competitive spirits alive in all competitors. While waiting for final points to be tallied, Arthur and Patricia shared a giggle and she blushed, looking adoringly at him. My eyes met WR's raised eyebrows.

"Something's brewing between those two," Ethel said, without missing a beat.

"They sure are cute together," Connie whispered to Ethel and me.

WR announced the results of the competition, giving Charlie the win, with Patricia second, Clark third, and Arthur at the bottom.

Errol pushed Clark and Patricia into the pool. Arthur and Charlie jumped in after them, landing a perfect cannonball together, getting WR wet on purpose. We women screamed and moved away from the water. Errol dove in after them and they played in the water, splashing and screaming like children. Just as I was leaving the pool area, afraid I might end up in the pool, I caught a glimpse of Arthur swimming up to Patricia and whispering something in her ear, which set her off giggling. I grabbed Connie's hand and said, "We've got to keep an eye on them."

— ⊙ —

Life at Warner Brothers began late summer and the experience was like arriving in a country where you don't know a soul, don't speak the language, and nobody cares about you. I immediately began filming a screwball comedy called *Page Miss Glory* in which I played a hotel maid who enters a phony beauty contest and falls for a famous aviator, Bingo Nelson, played by the adorable Dick Powell. Our director, Mervyn LeRoy—who'd jumped from MGM as well—was at least one familiar face I recognized.

After shooting each scene with Dick, he would practically run off the set to his dressing room. It seemed he couldn't get away from me fast enough. Finally, I asked Merv why he was avoiding me.

"Do you want to know the truth?"

"Of course, I do."

"He's afraid of Mr. Hearst."

I marched right over to Dick's dressing room with a bottle of bourbon and knocked on the door. When he opened, I pushed my way inside and said, "You should be more afraid of me than Mr. Hearst. Let's have a drink and get over this, shall we?"

A week later, he joined us at Ocean House and then at San Simeon for parties and get-togethers. He quickly became like a little brother, and we talked on the phone frequently.

Page Miss Glory had a decent opening but quickly fell out of favor. Still, Dick and I were paired again in a heavily costumed and old-fashioned story in *Hearts Divided*. Dick played Jerome Bonaparte, the brother of Napoleon Bonaparte, visiting the US when he falls in love with my character, Betsy, a Baltimore society heiress. When the movie was released, I cringed when I saw myself looking older than ever. At thirty-nine, I wasn't the young kitten I was a decade earlier. The makeup department did me no favors whatsoever, caking on the foundation until every wrinkle and bulge was pronounced. Opposite me, thirty-two-year-old Dick glowed. It was depressing. Needless to say, the film didn't do well at the box office, making it my second flop at Warner, a humiliating fact that seemed to pile bad news on top of more bad news for my rapidly floundering movie career.

—⊙—

At the youthful age of thirty-seven, Irving Thalberg passed away unexpectedly from complications of pneumonia shortly after *Marie Antoinette* was released starring his wife, Norma. Everyone was in shock, and of course Norma was grief-stricken. I forgot my professional rivalry with her immediately, and WR and I surrounded her with our support. She was left with two small children and an uncertain future.

My awful, wicked mind began churning soon after the funeral when the thought occurred to me that maybe I could get a decent movie offer at my old studio, MGM, now that Irving was gone. It was terrible but true.

In my bungalow on the Warner lot late one night a few days after the funeral, I pleaded with WR to let me return to MGM. He held all the strings, so I railed on and on about how I hated Warner Brothers and had not done well there.

"We cannot go back to MGM. I'm searching for bigger roles for you at Warner. Be patient."

"Goddamnit, WR, I'm sick to death of being patient. You have directed my career from the beginning, and I've trusted you, but this is my last chance. And with Irving no longer blocking my way to the best scripts and movies at MGM, we could seize this moment and get back there!"

He glared at me for a long moment, squinting his eyes just a little. I lifted my glass of whiskey and took a long drink, staring back at him through the bottom of the glass, not flinching, not giving in.

"I said be patient. I'm working on it," he demanded.

I slammed the glass down on the table. "I need you to know how humiliated I was in *Hearts Divided*. There seems to be a conspiracy to undermine my career by consistently miscasting me as a young woman."

He tilted his head to the side and pursed his lips. "I can see how serious you are, my dear, but there is no conspiracy. I guarantee it." He walked to me and brushed my cheek with the back of his hand.

I wanted to grab his hand and bite it. Instead, I let out a scream and ran upstairs to my bedroom, slamming the door hard. I called Ethel and complained while I proceeded to get drunk on bourbon. I called Connie and complained some more until I eventually drank myself to sleep.

— ⦿ —

My next film at Warner Brothers, *Cain and Mable,* was an even bigger flop than *Hearts Divided* and still, because of WR, I got more publicity than my costar Clark Gable who had won two Academy Awards. Sarcastically I thought, *it's 5 percent talent with me and 95 percent publicity.*

My final film at Warner Brothers, *Ever Since Eve,* should have been named *Page Miss Glory 2* for the storyline was almost identical. At forty, I starred with thirty-three-year-old Robert Montgomery, whose lines were as dreadful as my makeup. Again, I played a woman half my age and again the audience didn't show up.

In the summer of 1937, I finally got my wish when Bernard invited me to London to work with his new friend Gabriel Pascal and star as Eliza Doolittle in the British film version of *Pygmalion*. I couldn't believe my luck. While I was planning and packing, I thought about living in London for a time and giving Hollywood a break. After all, the role of Eliza Doolittle closely paralleled my early life with WR. But Mr. Pascal changed his mind at the last minute, maybe after noting my quadruple flop at Warner Brothers and thinking better of it. Regardless, it would be Wendy Hiller, a British actress, who'd star in the movie, released on March 3, 1938.

CHAPTER 38

1937

At home, Arthur courted our beautiful Patricia and they were engaged to be married. The two shared shy, sweet, innocent natures, and Patricia had fallen hard for him over the past two years, often disappearing for a long sunset beach walk while a party at my Ocean House raged around them. Several times I found them huddled together, talking intimately in the corner of the ballroom or the corner of the library while guests danced and laughed around them. They played tennis, swam, and rode horses in San Simeon. They were in a world of their own, as it should be in love. It was clear from his longing gazes that he adored her.

At The Ranch one weekend hosting dozens of guests, I was visited by Patricia in my suite before dinner. I asked what she and Arthur had done that day.

"Our favorite thing to do is take a picnic lunch into the hills on horseback, find a big oak tree, and spend hours talking and reading poetry together," she said.

"I hope that's all you're doing under that tree." I applied lipstick and put on a pair of dangling diamond earrings before dinner.

"Aunt Marion! He's a complete gentleman," she said, dreamily looking out the window and quietly adding, "We're getting close, though. It might happen soon."

"In that case, let me give you something." I retrieved a small white drawstring bag from my dresser, trying to be all business so she wouldn't be embarrassed. "Come here and sit down."

She joined me on the sofa and I opened the bag, pulling out several brand new cervical sponges wrapped tightly in foil, while I explained how to use them matter-of-factly.

"Do you use these?" she asked, staring at the contraceptive device.

"Yes, I do. These are yours. I'm giving you three, but I will get more. You must use them to prevent pregnancy."

She blushed. "And you promise it will work?"

"If used properly, yes, it will keep you from getting pregnant. Don't be afraid. I purchased several of them during my last visit to France. Europe is far more advanced in birth control than we are here in the States. Margaret Sanger has been fighting to make birth control legal and accessible to women for more than twenty years and is far from achieving her goal. In fact, women only got the right to vote the summer that you were born. Legalizing birth control is going to take a while longer."

She stared at me, absorbing everything.

"It's an uphill battle to educate men, but also women on the fact that having a family should be a choice and not just the consequence of sex."

She put the sponges back in the small cotton drawstring bag and stood up.

"Now let's go to dinner, shall we? Our company is waiting," I said.

"I'm not sure I can eat now," Patricia said, looking at the ground in front of her. "Let me take this to my room and meet you downstairs."

I lifted her chin so we looked each other in the eyes. "You must have the facts. You must know these things as a woman." I kissed her cheek and left the room. It felt good to give my daughter some useful advice.

— ⓪ —

In early spring of 1937, Patricia and I sat in the sun by the Ocean House pool flipping through magazines and discussing the details of her upcoming wedding. The day was bright and clear with families arriving to enjoy a day at the beach. She wanted to have the ceremony at The Ranch and begged me to be her maid of honor, which I politely declined in favor of her mother, Rose. We needed to continue our public charade of Rose being her mother. I had promised WR that nobody would ever know we were Patricia's real parents, and I intended on keeping my promise.

"I want you," Patricia countered when I expressed it should be Rose. "You're more of a mother to me," she said, looking around to see if anybody was near and then adding, "you *are* my mother."

I appreciated her discretion. Squawking seagulls gathered on the sand in front of our table. "Sweetheart, you must have Rose and your father standing next to you. Please understand the need to keep our secret." I took her hand and squeezed it. She nodded her head in understanding, looking to the seagulls.

I assumed Rose was pleased with Patricia's upcoming nuptials since I hadn't spoken with her in months. I couldn't be sure how she felt about anything these days. I had avoided her, choosing to focus on Patricia's happiness instead. I'd learned that she had fallen out of love with Edward Beale McLean, who'd ended up in a sanitorium after his wife denied his request for a divorce, which confirmed what WR had heard about him. Her quick marriage to a German aristocrat named Louis Adlon, twelve years her junior, came only as a mild shock to me. At least she had moved away from street fighters and traveling musicians. For this, I could be grateful.

Patricia and I came in from the pool area to meet Rose, who arrived to help with the wedding details. She paced back and forth nervously. "What should I wear? What would be appropriate?"

"We can figure that out later. We're here to decide on the details of Patricia's dress, the ceremony, the decorating, the guest list," I said, sipping my champagne.

Ignoring me, she continued, "I do have the dress I wore to marry Louis. I could wear that again. It's light blue satin."

I frowned at her, lit two cigarettes, and gave her one. "We haven't decided on the maid of honor's dress or the bridesmaids' dresses," I said.

"Yes, Mama, my color is pink. Can you be my maid of honor and wear pink?" Patricia asked with her characteristic sweetness. She was flipping through a French catalog of wedding dress designs.

"Oh, Sweetheart, being the matron of honor really won't suit me now." She drank the remainder of her champagne and looked longingly at the drink cart that was a short distance from her.

"Why don't you ask your Aunt Marion to stand up for you?" she asked, looking sideways at me with pleading eyes.

"Rose, I'm sure you can't mean that," I said. "I'm sure you want to be the maid of honor in your only daughter's wedding."

Ignoring my plea, she said, "Can somebody please make me a whiskey sour?"

I nodded and walked to the bar to mix us both drinks. "Rose—" I whispered as I stood next to her, but she interrupted me.

"Darling daughter," Rose said, twirling around to face Patricia, "please don't be upset. I need to be by Louis's side. He doesn't like it when I leave him alone for too long. We are newlyweds, you know."

"Sure, Mama. That's fine," Patricia said as a dark expression lingered on her face, nearly ripping the page on her magazine as she turned it.

Immense disappointment consumed me that afternoon as drinks were poured and snacks were put out. Rose paced and checked her watch repeatedly, showing how anxious she was to leave. "I have to run soon. Louis and I have dinner plans. We're meeting friends at The Roosevelt."

"Should we suspend planning and pick another day so you can be here?" Patricia asked.

"No, no, that's not necessary. Continue on. If you need my opinion, we can talk on the phone tomorrow." She got up from the couch. "Walk me out, Marion." She kissed Patricia goodbye.

Out in the driveway, before she got into her limousine, Rose said, "You may as well stand up for her and be her maid of honor. You're paying for everything, and she is your daughter."

I hadn't told Rose, and wouldn't ever tell her, that Patricia already knew that fact.

Sneering at me she said, "Mama thought all your millions were a blessing. But they really are a curse, aren't they?"

The air around us began to crackle and I could feel my face gathering heat. "How dare you judge me. I hold up the very sky in your world. Everything you have is because of me. I pay for everything, fix everything in your little worthless life. Do not judge me." I took a deep breath and continued in a calmer voice, "We are planning Patricia's big day. I expect you to grow up and participate in a meaningful way."

I stared at Pacific Coast Highway, watching the cars drive by. Rose slammed the car door and left without another word. I gasped for air while my eyes filled with tears. The chasm between us had grown wider each year, and now it seemed it may never be bridged.

CHAPTER 39

SAN SIMEON. SUNDAY. JULY 25. 1937

Patricia and I had arrived at The Ranch a week before the big day to prepare and plan. We worked well together, making all the food and decoration decisions. The guests began arriving a few days before the ceremony as did the groom with his extended family. Arthur and clan were settled in the Casa del Mar guesthouse in the hopes of keeping Arthur separate from Patricia the day of the wedding. The only no-shows by Saturday were Patricia's parents. She claimed it didn't bother her much. "As long as I have you," she said to me.

At dinner the night before the ceremony, our butler and valet Bud, who had watched Patricia grow over the years and was eager to be our wedding coordinator of sorts, arrived with a message on a silver platter for Patricia. She was pushing her mashed potatoes around her plate claiming she wasn't hungry when she took the telegram. I knew it would be from Rose, full of excuses about why she couldn't attend. I could barely contain my impending sense of doom. Patricia leaned toward me holding the telegram low so we could both read it together. It was from George, who wrote that he couldn't make the wedding due to his mother's illness. He needed to travel to Missouri immediately, it said. I looked at WR across the table, shaking my head, but I couldn't say anything. The room buzzed with twenty people talking, dishes clanking, and laughter all around. Patricia discreetly handed the telegram to Arthur, who read it and handed it to WR.

"Who will walk me down the aisle now?" she whispered as WR handed the telegram back to her and she folded it up.

"We'll figure this out after dinner," Arthur said.

"Let's all meet in WR's third-floor library after dinner," I said. Patricia and Arthur agreed, and we finished our dinner.

A few hours later, after WR and I had done some additional planning of our own, I brought Patricia and Arthur up to Gothic Study on the third floor of Casa Grande. We found WR sitting at the long worktable.

He stood up when he saw us. "Let's get right to it, shall we? Marion and I would like to offer to walk you down the aisle together, if you'd have us."

Arthur smiled and Patricia leaned into him. She grabbed my hand, releasing a burst of air she must have been holding in since she'd read the telegram. "Oh yes, thank you, I was hoping you'd offer. I love that the two of you will do it together. It's just perfect."

WR trembled only slightly. I watched with fascination as he cleared his throat and tried to find the words to express his love for her. He was never a hugger or very affectionate with anybody except me. Over the years, he had kept his physical distance from Patricia, even though I think he wanted to let down his guard.

Continuing in a stately manner he said, "Marion and I would also like to give you a first wedding present and family heirloom."

He opened the wooden box on the table, lifting a diamond and pearl encrusted tiara toward Patricia. She gasped as the light twinkled around it, rushing to WR. I thought they would hug, but they didn't. He gently placed the crown on her head and kissed her cheek. Her eyes darted to me and then to Arthur. I wanted to run and throw my arms around them both, but WR spoke.

"We're so proud of you. We hope you'll be happy in your new life. If there's anything you need, do not hesitate to ask." He looked to Arthur and said, "Welcome to the family."

Patricia gushed, "Thank you. I don't know what to say. I'm overwhelmed. Thank you for this and for everything."

It was a beautiful moment. I hoped for several more beautiful moments at the wedding, maybe even one with Rose, if she could manage to get herself up here.

— ⊙ —

Patricia's wedding day dawned clear as I stood in front of the bay window in our private living room admiring the sunlight bouncing off the Pacific Ocean. She and I had worked out a wedding day schedule for all the guests and family members: breakfast at 9:30 a.m., swim or tennis until 1:00 p.m., with a poolside lunch at 1:30 p.m. Afterward, they'd have free time to spend however they wished until the ceremony at 5:00 p.m., which would be held in the Assembly Room of Casa Grande.

WR joined me in our living room. "The big day has arrived at La Cuesta Encantada," he said.

I smiled, knowing how proud he was of his enchanted castle on the hill.

"The weather is glorious, and everything will be perfect," I said, my hands shaking slightly as my coffee cup rattled on the saucer. I hoped WR didn't notice. I lit a cigarette to calm my nerves.

"Are you feeling okay?" he asked as he poured himself a cup of coffee.

Trying to hide my morning shakes was becoming more difficult. "Yes, I'm fine, just a bit nervous about Rose. Do you know if she's arrived yet?"

"Bud would know better than me. I went to bed at 3:00 a.m., and I'm pretty sure nobody arrived before that."

"I'll go and find him now and also check on Patricia," I said.

At 9:00 a.m., the morning rush was underway in the kitchen as breakfast was being prepared for the guests. I found Bud arranging flowers with the staff, standing a head above everybody else with his slick black hair. Dozens of various sized vases were on the counter with white lilies and greenery in them.

"Did Rose arrive yet?" I asked. He shook his head.

I grabbed a croissant and headed into the Assembly Room to check on the decorations. As I ate my pastry, I surveyed the regal room, wondering if I'd told Patricia that the ceilings came from the Palazzo Martinengo in Brescia, Italy, or that the fireplace was from sixteenth-century France, or that the tapestries were Flemish. I would be sure to tell her after the wedding. I wanted her to know just how special every detail was in this room.

I found her at the other end of the room sitting on the edge of one of the carved black walnut choir pews lining either side of the room. WR had brought them over from an Italian monastery, and although they looked uncomfortable to sit on, they made the room look stately and elegant.

"Good morning, Sweetheart. Are you ready for your big day?" I asked.

She wore white pedal pushers and a pink blouse tucked in. Her chocolate brown hair was curled into a bun on the top of her head.

"Good morning, Aunt Marion. I didn't sleep a wink last night."

"Well, you look adorable—just gorgeous this morning. I can't believe you didn't sleep at all."

She reached out a hand, searching for mine. I took it and reassured her that everything was going as planned.

"The room is looking particularly spring-like with all these wonderful flowers," she gushed.

We watched as workers brought in the trellised altar covered with white roses and white cathedral candles on top. A white silk wedding runner was laid over the Persian rugs for Patricia to walk down. Thirty guest chairs lined two aisles on either side of the runner.

"It looks like a princess is getting married in this room. Where's your tiara?" I asked playfully. She scrunched her face at me.

I stepped back and took in the baskets of white orchids on the small decorative tables, the small bowls of plumeria placed near the various doors and windows so the wind could carry their scent throughout the room, and the plumeria garlands hanging in all four corners of the rectangular room.

Patricia wrapped her arms around my waist and hugged me from behind, resting her chin on my shoulder as we watched the workers in the room. "Our little flower girl Joyce woke up with a runny nose." Then she asked, "Has Mama arrived yet?"

"I just checked with Bud and she hasn't, but don't worry. She'll be here." I said this as much to convince myself as anything. "And don't worry about Joyce. She'll be fine too." Rose had reluctantly agreed to stand up for Patricia as her maid of honor after our harsh words in my driveway. I had to believe she would arrive. I couldn't imagine any other scenario.

"Okay, if you say so." She stepped away from me. "I need something to eat, and then I'll take a bath and see if I can lie down for an hour."

"Oh, darling! Of course. I'll have a bath drawn for you while you eat." I kissed her on the cheek.

— ⟨⟩ —

Patricia had stayed in the south tower bedroom, officially called the Celestial Suite, the night before the wedding, one floor above WR and me. The room was round with a spectacular view of the mountains and ocean. The multiple arched windows were covered outside with decorative concrete lattice, so the light peaked through giving the room a warm glow.

A little after noon, Bud brought me word that Rose and Louis had arrived and were settled in their room. I had made sure her pink satin maid of honor dress hung in the closet, along with the white wide-brimmed sun hat Patricia had insisted on last minute.

I climbed the stairs to Patricia's room to let her know her mother had arrived, but she barely acknowledged the fact, grabbing a dark pink wide-brimmed hat and handing it to me. "What's this? I already have my bridesmaid hat downstairs."

"It's a special hat for you. I want you to have a different colored hat than Mama or the other bridesmaids as a way to honor you—quietly raise you above the others."

Many objections crossed my mind, but I let them all fly away, taking the dark pink hat and placing it on my head with tears in my eyes. I would be proud to be a special person on her wedding today.

"Now let me finish packing for my honeymoon," she said as I left her alone to concentrate.

— ◎ —

At 4:30 p.m., the hair stylist had just finished curling Patricia's hair and the dressing maid had begun to sew her into her French-white silk satin wedding gown. We were on schedule and on time. I slipped into my pink satin bridesmaid gown and special hat, watching Patricia in the two additional full-length mirrors I had installed.

Her dress had arrived a few weeks earlier from Paris. The neckline was cut with tulle, and thirty-two covered buttons ran down her back. The waist was gathered and flowed to a four-foot train. The tiara was secured to a long lace veil atop her head.

With a word from Bud that the guests were all seated and the groom was in place, WR, Patricia, and I rode the small elevator down from the third floor together. "Remember to breathe," WR said in the elevator as I grabbed Patricia's hand and kissed it. She radiated beauty and calm.

I peeked through the secret doorway in the choir pews and saw Rose and the four other bridesmaids. I whispered, "Okay,

I guess it's time," and slipped out into the Assembly Room, followed by WR and Patricia. I winked at Rose who winked back before she stepped forward and led the bridesmaids down the aisle to take their proper place. The small musical ensemble began the wedding march as WR and I each took one of Patricia's arms and led her down the aisle to her prince Arthur. I stepped in line with the other bridesmaids and WR found his seat in the front row. The ceremony went off without a hitch, the sweet couple gazing lovingly into each other's eyes the entire time.

After the formalities, while waiting for the family pictures to be taken in the Assembly Room, I felt an arm slide around my waist.

"Well, hello, Rose," I said.

Patricia looked up and smiled at her mother. Louis stood behind Rose.

"Congratulations, my dear. You and your aunt did a fantastic job in planning and executing all the details. I knew you both would. It just isn't my forte." She turned her beaming face to Louis as she brushed a stray hair from his forehead. "Besides, Louis and I are busy traveling these days. We're off to Europe next."

My heart squeezed as Rose once again made everything about herself. I hoped Patricia could just dismiss it and focus on her big day.

"Thanks," Patricia said. "When do you leave?"

"Tomorrow morning, same as you." She at least remembered that Patricia was leaving for Honolulu the next day for her honeymoon.

"The photographer is waving us over," Rose said. "Let's get these done.

After pictures, we ate a meal of cauliflower soup, roast lamb, rosemary potatoes, and asparagus while the pianist continued to play our favorite jazz pieces. Champagne was served, and Arthur made a toast that brought a lump to my throat. I stared at Patricia, her tiara glistening in the chandelier light as her new husband gushed about his love for her. Rose didn't speak and I couldn't find the nerve to speak publicly for Patricia either, afraid I would give away all my secrets. Instead I held WR's hand, letting the tears run down my happy face, wishing I could have a nip of whiskey and a cigarette.

A few hours later, the four-tiered white wedding cake with raspberry filling was wheeled into the Assembly Room to rounds of applause. Wine and champagne continued to flow, loosening up the crowd enough to dance. Patricia danced as WR and I watched our little girl ascend to womanhood. Catching my eye as she twirled around, she winked at me and I winked back.

— ⦾ —

That evening, I climbed the stairs to the Celestial Suite calling out, "Hello? It's me. Can I come up for a minute?"

"Come on up," Arthur said. "We're just admiring the tiara again."

Patricia stared at it, teary-eyed in the full-length mirror.

"Hello, you two." Looking at Patricia, I complimented my gorgeous girl. "You were beautiful today." I noticed she'd been crying. "Are these tears of happiness?" I asked hesitantly.

"Oh you know, she's overwhelmed, aren't you, Sweetheart?" Arthur said. "I'll leave you two to chat and see you downstairs, alright Darling?" Patricia nodded and smiled at him.

After Arthur had descended the stairs, she said, "He took me into the garden, Mama, and told me the truth."

"WR?" my eyes opened wide, stunned by his admission to Patricia and that she'd just addressed me as Mama. I turned and closed the bedroom door.

She nodded, her lips trembling. "After the pictures. He told me he was my father and that he was so proud of me, but that I couldn't tell anybody. 'It will be our secret,' he said. Then he swept me up into his arms and hugged me in a warm embrace, lifting me off the ground. He planted a tender kiss on my forehead."

She saw the tears streaming down my face and stopped talking. "Keep going," I said. "Is there more?"

She nodded. "I held on to him and laid my head on his shoulder for a moment, thinking of you, Mama, and Papa, and how many people have carried my birth and legitimacy as a weight for their entire lives."

"It has not been a weight for me," I said, wanting to quell any feelings of guilt about her lineage. I brushed a strand of hair away from her face. "You are a princess, darling. I love you so much it hurts."

Patricia smiled, her chin shaking. I gathered her in my arms and held her close, welling up at the fact that our lifelong secret was over—at least between the three of us.

"How are you feeling about your mother? Are you sad she's been so distant?" I asked.

"No, not at all. We're pretty much estranged at this point. I've accepted her the way she is and will keep up the public charade, but my heart belongs to you and WR."

She was brave and I wondered how true her words were. We stood together at the open window in front of the Juliet balcony, staring quietly at the star-filled night sky. I shivered even though the wind was warm coming off the hills. I wrapped my arms around Patricia protectively.

"He hugged you?" I asked, beaming.

"Yes, it was a great big bear hug. It took me completely off guard."

"I wish like hell I could have seen it. I would have wrapped my arms around both of you and not let go."

CHAPTER 40

At Ocean House a few months after Patricia's wedding, as I prepared to go into the studio one morning, WR's son, Bill, arrived in a huff, walking fast and talking even faster. "Where's the Chief?" he asked, looking around for his father.

"He's sleeping," I told him. "You know he works all night."

"I'll go up and find him then." He headed for the stairs.

"No, stop. What is so important anyway?"

"The empire is crashing!"

I got to my feet. "What?"

"We need a million dollars, and the Chief has to go to New York immediately," Bill said as he took to the stairs. This time I didn't stop him.

WR and Bill made immediate arrangements for the impending trip to New York. I discreetly discovered over the next several days through Bill and my own financial advisor, Edgar Hatrick, that WR was in desperate financial trouble, near bankruptcy in fact, having accrued massive debt partly due to his overspending on personal indulgences, like construction at The Ranch. Over the past decade, while I had focused on my movie career, my family, and Patricia, I was only peripherally aware of what was going on with the Hearst Corporation. I listened to WR talk about his businesses, but mostly I lived in my own world, pampered by WR, unaware of anything financial.

Over the past six years, while the extended depression had brought everyone in the country to their knees, WR seemed to have been an exception. When I'd question him on rare occasions about how "we" were doing, he always insisted in no uncertain terms that we were insulated and would be fine.

I later discovered that when his most trusted servant, Arthur Brisbane, had died in December 1936, the glue that held the Hearst Corporation together dissolved. Most of WR's newspapers were hemorrhaging money and the banks would not loan additional funds to him. In fact, they'd called in their notes, fearing the whole Hearst empire would fold if assets were not rearranged and sold.

Naively, I hoped one million dollars would fix the problem, but in fact it would only provide a small bit of breathing room; I still felt compelled to swoop in and try to save him. He had taken such care of me over the last two decades, the least I could do was give him the one million I thought he so desperately needed.

I called Edgar and told him to sell whatever he could to raise the money immediately. Within a few days, he'd sold some of my stocks and real estate. I dipped into the trust fund that Reine, Ethel, Rose, and I had from our grandparents to get my hands on the rest. With the certified check tucked away in my purse, I wanted to surprise WR on the train trip to New York since I knew his pride would refuse the money if I handed it to him at home.

As he packed his business documents and readied for his trip to New York to face the proverbial music, I said, "I know how hard this is WR. I don't know the entire story, but I want to come with you to New York and support you, even if it's only to be there when you get home from your day."

He stopped what he was doing. His face was long and somber, his eyes dull and flat. "It's a humiliation and an embarrassment, and I'd be grateful for your companionship."

We boarded WR's private train cars for the four-day ride to New York to meet with the board of directors. Somewhere in the desert outside Phoenix, a meeting took place with several high-ranking executives. I decided that would be a good moment to present the check. I knew I ran the risk of embarrassing WR by doing it this way, but I also knew he would never privately accept it from me. I knocked on the door of the smoke-filled private car where the stiff men sat around a large conference table.

"We're in a meeting. Can this wait?" WR said.

"No, it can't. I have something for you. Can I sit?" I asked, though there was no need as WR was already pulling out a chair for me.

The other men bristled at my being included in such a high-level meeting. I had no official title except that of editorial consultant, a catchall that allowed me to sit next to WR and advise him when he wished. They looked out the window with frowns on their faces.

"I've raised one million dollars. I want you to know I would do anything for you, WR." I placed the check on the table.

WR leaned forward to look at it. Several of the men craned their necks to see the certified check.

"I can't take it," WR said, sliding back in his chair. "I just can't take it, Darling."

"WR, you must. Let me help. I have never helped you." I took the check and walked around the table to Thomas Justin White, general manager for WR, and handed the check over. "Surely this will help in some small way to stave off the wolves. Please take it."

He took the check and looked at WR, who lowered his head and mumbled from the other side of the room, "What's a million dollars when there's fifty million involved?"

I reeled inside at the stated amount, feeling very much as if someone had turned a firehose on me.

Top Hearst officer Richard Berlin spoke up, "Thank you,

Marion, we do appreciate it. I just wish it were enough to solve the problem." He paused and tapped a finger against the desk. "We will assign collateral for this loan once we convene the entire board in New York."

"It's not a loan, it's a gift. I don't need collateral."

"You're not loaning me the money, you're loaning it to the Hearst Corporation," WR informed me, leaving no room for argument. "It will be repaid, and collateral assigned to it."

"If you insist," I said.

Over the decades, my personal wealth had grown to a sizeable amount thanks to the gifts WR had given me, my hard work in the movies, and the investment guidance WR had provided me, but I had nothing close to what was needed by the corporation. Nobody said anything further, so I left the train car, sliding the door closed behind me with a click. It was hard to feel good about anything seeing WR so dejected, but I was proud of myself for trying, even if my help could be likened to giving pennies when thousands were needed.

— ⦾ —

I visited WR that evening in his private car where I found him sitting in his tufted high back leather chair reading the bankruptcy code. I ran to him and threw my arms around him, climbing up on his lap like I used to do ages ago. I lay my head on his chest. "Please tell me the one million will help, WR." I looked up at his face and continued, "And I will get another million as soon as we get to New York, my love." His chest seemed smaller somehow, deflated, and he looked beaten.

"It will help in the immediate days as we sort some things out, Darling, and I thank you." He kissed my forehead.

I took his face in my hands, planting a big fat kiss on his lips. His forced smile lasted only a second before he picked up his book again and began reading.

I left his train car needing a stiff drink and a smoke.

—⊙—

When we arrived in New York, we checked into our regular top-floor suite at the Ritz Tower on Park Avenue. I got to work raising another million, selling more property and stocks as well as offering all my jewels to WR as he sat at the dining room table doing paperwork. The jewels made a crunching noise as I laid them down on the wooden table.

"What are these? What are you doing?" He stared at me with wide eyes, and his mouth was gaping open.

"I want to help. I would sell anything to help you. Nothing means more to me than you," I insisted.

"You have helped, but this is too much. Take the jewels back to the safe."

I scooped up the jewels and turned away.

WR continued to speak quietly. "At seventy-four years old, I am being stripped of my title as president and chief executive officer. I may not ever hold an official title in my own corporation ever again."

"They're making you step down?" I asked.

"Yes, it's one of the terms dictated by the banks in order to reorganize the larger debts of the corporation."

I left the room and put the jewels back in the safe.

Later I would find out that WR was indeed forced to step down as president and CEO of the Hearst Corporation and required to select a trustee to run the business and head up the reorganization. He settled on Judge Clarence Shearn, giving him sole voting rights over all stock in the Hearst Corporation. The judge was connected to Chase Bank and a $1.6 million-dollar bridge loan was immediately secured. Together with the money I gave, the creditors and banks would have enough daily working capital to begin reorganizing the larger debts. In the deal, WR at least kept editorial control over all his publications, subject of course to the judge's authority to oversee spending.

Hearst's board of directors arrived at our suite and met in the drawing room to discuss the specifics of the plan to save the corporation. I stood behind the closed door and listened through the cracks.

I overheard Mr. Berlin say, "I vote we give Marion the two Boston newspapers as collateral."

"Those papers are losing money and aren't worth a million dollars," Mr. White said.

"We cannot give her two failing newspapers. Let's give her the magazines," WR said.

"The magazines are worth ten times what she's loaned us," Mr. White said.

I walked away from the door, not wanting to hear any more of the discussion, knowing how hard this must be for WR.

In the end, they did assign me the two failing Boston newspapers as collateral. I honestly didn't care about the papers, or the money. I never expected to get the money back. Walter Howey, one of WR's most trusted editors and the same man who'd found Patricia all those years ago, stepped up to run the papers as a personal favor to me. I was delighted when he was able to make them profitable again within five months.

— ⏀ —

We stayed in New York for a month, and I finished mortgaging some New York real estate to come up with the additional money, giving it to WR and the board at their next meeting. This time they took the check without a fuss and assigned more collateral to me.

"Thank you, my dear," WR said as I stood behind him after laying the check on the table. Nobody spoke. The air felt thick, and it was obviously time for me to leave.

I stood outside the door for a moment, pretending to adjust my skirt and pull down my blouse when I heard one of the men say, "She has a big heart—unlike Millicent, who refuses to help in any way."

WR's booming voice cleared the room of any chitchat. "It is true that Marion has come through for me, and I'm glad you can all finally see her for the generous and kind person she is; however, I refuse to sit here and speak about her or the mother of my children as if it's the corporation's business. That'll be enough of that talk." Papers rustled and chairs squeaked. With a smile on my face, I walked away to find a drink.

As I sat alone sipping my gin and enjoying a smoke, I thought of Millicent. How she must still burn inside that WR had stayed with me these last twenty-two years. I supposed it was entertainment for her to watch as WR and his mistress scrambled to sell assets to save the corporation. Was she giddy at watching her husband be stripped of all power and removed from the board? I imagined she enjoyed slurping up the details printed in the papers of WR's fall from the empire, hearing the scoop from spies inside the corporation—spies who hated me. What a fucking bitch and a sore loser! In my mind, she kicked him in the gut when she didn't dig into her considerable millions to help. I hated her with a new and deeper feeling. I toasted myself at my perceived win in our decades-long war. It had been years since we had openly sparred, and more years since we'd fought for WR's time in our tit-for-tat power struggles of days gone by. I poured a double gin and took a trip down memory lane with Millicent.

— ◎ —

A few mornings later, after the entire fiasco had calmed down a bit, I asked WR at breakfast why Millicent had left him hanging without even offering to help save the corporation her sons would eventually inherit. "She's got access to her own personal wealth like I do, right? Couldn't she have liquidated some of it to help?"

He nodded, buttering his toast. "I'm extremely upset at her. She's hurt me deeply by refusing to help whatsoever. My dealings with her from now on will only be to conduct family business. I am done being the only kind one in that relationship."

"I guess she's more bent at you *and me* than we thought."

"Hmmmm," WR said, picking up a newspaper.

I slunk into my big chair, buoyed just a little that I had helped save the world—our world—and I celebrated with another glass of champagne while the eggs on my plate got cold.

WR ate his bacon and eggs. "Let's talk about something else, shall we?"

"Of course, darling." I stood up too quickly and lost my balance, falling over the chair. WR rushed to grab me, but I landed on the floor with my dress up around my thighs. I began laughing uncontrollably as WR stood over me with a perplexed look on his face.

"What's so funny?" he asked. "And where did you get those bruises?"

I yanked my dress down, covering the large purple bruise I'd found that morning when I bathed. I had no idea where it had come from. I didn't remember falling. I just kept laughing. Something inside had wedged itself loose after days of so much stress.

"Marion," he demanded, "what's so funny?"

"Don't you remember? This is how we met. I fell off my bike and my dress flew up, and you pulled your car over to help me." I laid back on the marble floor, not even attempting to get up. The vaulted ceiling looked so drab compared to the sixteenth-century ceilings in San Simeon. "How many years ago was that?" I mused.

WR reached out with both arms, a bewildered look on his face at my memory. I grabbed his big strong hands, and he pulled me up as if I were a cloud. I sat back down in the chair.

"I'm worried about the bruise. Did that happen last night?"

My good mood evaporated, and in a louder, sterner voice, I repeated, "How many years ago did I fall off my bike?" Anger filled me up so quickly it scared me. I could feel it taking over.

Gaining his composure, WR changed his tune and played along with me. "Let me think. It must have been 1917. How old were you then?"

"Nope. It was 1916. I was nineteen that year. Nineteen!"

"That was a long time ago, my dear."

"How old were you, Mr. Hearst?" I reached for the champagne bottle, sitting just out of reach, my good mood returning.

"Isn't it a little early for so many glasses of champagne, Darling?"

"Why? Do you think I'm still drunk from last night because I fell?" I poured a nearly overflowing glass of champagne and sat up to slurp from the glass's rim.

"Maybe," WR admitted.

Deciding to ignore him, I took a long sip and repeated my question. "How old were *you* in 1916, Mr. Hearst?"

"Can we stop this now?"

"Not until you answer the question." I lit a cigarette and blew the smoke up toward the ceiling.

"I'll answer your question if you answer mine."

"What question is that? You haven't asked me a question."

"I asked you how you got that bruise."

Pulling my dress up in a provocative way to expose my upper thigh, I lifted my gaze slowly. "I have no idea."

"I'm worried about you. Don't you want to stop drinking? Stop falling and hurting yourself?"

"What?" I asked, sure that I had misheard him as anger quickly rose inside me again.

He continued. "Would you be open to trying a new technique to help you stop drinking? I found it in my research of medical advancements. It's called the Keeley Cure."

"What are you talking about, WR? I just saved you when your own wife wouldn't. I should throw this ashtray at you for suggesting I have a drinking problem." I grabbed the bottle of champagne and my glass and headed for my room. "You really know how to ruin a good time, don't you, droopy drawers?"

I sauntered to my room, feeling in complete control of the situation. I could feel his eyes on my back and the air was thick with the expectation of his angry words, but they never came. I locked myself in, the anger building again as I shut the door.

"You're an ungrateful bully, droopy drawers! Do you know that?" I yelled as I moved the chair and writing table in front of the door. "You don't understand me! You're horrible!" I screamed, gasping for breath as I tried to slide my vanity in front of the door so he couldn't come in. I fell to my knees, defeated. "You don't deserve me! I have a mind to call Millicent and tell her to come and get you! You two deserve each other!"

There was silence on the other side of my bedroom door. He was not trying to break in. I sat on the edge of the bed trying to catch my breath, sipping from my champagne flute. A light went on inside my brain: *What a great idea. Yes, I will call her—that cheap, hardened, horrible bitch.*

I knew she lived in a castle aptly named Beacon Towers on Long Island in the summer. I picked up the phone and asked the operator for Beacon Towers. The phone rang, and after telling the butler that Miss Marion Davies would like to speak to the woman of the house, Millicent picked up the receiver.

"Hello?" she asked with clear skepticism in her voice.

"Hello, Millicent. I'm calling to tell you that you're a horrible person for not helping WR when he needed it. Mostly I'm calling to tell you that you can have him back. I don't want him anymore." I took a deep breath, pretty sure I hadn't slurred any of my words as I took another drink of my champagne.

"What are you talking about?" she bristled. "Are you drunk?"

"That is not the point. I may be drunk, but that is not why I called."

"Well, I'm confused then."

"I'm calling to tell you to come and get him. I don't want him anymore. You can have him back. He's rude and unfeeling.

I just gave him two million dollars to save his corporation, and he's being mean to me."

There was a long silence on the phone, until she finally said, "I don't want him anymore, either." And with that she hung up on me.

"Bitch." I slammed the phone down so hard, it fell to the floor. "Oh, damn it. Damn it anyway." I slid down from the bed and lay next to the phone. Picking up the receiver again, a haze settled over me and I heard the dial tone. "You're a bitch, Millicent," I repeated, throwing the receiver. The room began to spin. I was thirsty. I tried to sit up but couldn't find my center. Lying back down on the floor, I felt tears falling down my face. Time passed but I don't know how much. When I opened my eyes I was staring at the chandelier. I wiped my cheeks. An ache of shame and then fogginess overcame me. For the first time in my life, I had called the big bad Millicent. God knows how many times I'd thought about it.

I crawled into bed and cried myself to sleep. The next afternoon when I felt well enough to dress, I moved all the furniture away from the door and joined WR on the couch. My head pounded, and my mouth was bone dry.

"Would you like some orange juice or coffee?" he asked in a sweet voice.

"Yes, orange juice would be nice. And toast?"

When he handed me the toast and juice, I laid my head on his shoulder and said, "Promise never to mention my drinking again, and I will forgive you," I said.

"I promise," he said.

He never mentioned my call to Millicent and neither did I.

CHAPTER 41

We returned to California both beaten down. WR hid behind his books and his papers, studying everything closely. I hid by drinking to spite him, most of the time drinking too much. *What was the harm?* I knew I could stop whenever I wanted.

Sometime in late fall 1937, after mulling over the reviews of my latest film, *Ever Since Eve*, about which the *New York Times* wrote, "After playing the eye-batting ingenue for more years than would be polite to mention, Miss Davies apparently feels she has mastered the role sufficiently to begin her cycle all over again."

Damn critics. I was aware that I looked old in the movie. The review by the *New York Herald Tribune* read, "The chief trouble with Miss Davies's performance . . ." Did I need to read more to know it was time to retire? No.

"I'm done with the movies, WR," I said one night as we sat across the room from each other at Ocean House. "I don't want to do it anymore. It's no fun."

He looked up from his newspaper and stuck out his bottom lip just a little, staring at me. "Are you sure, Darling? I can go to bat for you and get you something good."

"Nah, never mind it. You've got too much to worry about with the corporation's problems. Besides, I'm tired. I'm forty years old and I just want to stop now."

I reasoned with myself that WR needed my support—not financially, but emotionally and physically. I insisted to myself that I didn't care about my film reputation, but it wasn't true. I felt backed in a corner with WR controlling my career, and me not willing to throw everything away to challenge him. It was just silly publicity. It didn't matter. I was needed at home to take care of WR now. He was my priority.

After I made the decision, WR didn't hound me about it. It meant I had lots of free time. I drank to my heart's content, and, keeping his word, WR never asked me again about it. But bad luck followed me like a shadow. The phone rang at Ocean House a few months into the spring and it was Ethel. She was crying when I picked up the receiver.

"Marion, come quick. The ambulance is already on the way. It's Reine. I found her floating face down in the pool."

I let out a scream that filled the room and startled the maid who was dusting. She dropped a doll figurine she'd been holding and jumped back.

"WR!" I yelled and ran upstairs to find him in the library. "We must go to the Lexington house. Reine is dead."

When we arrived, the ambulance was already loading her body. Reine's son, Charlie, stood by, pale as he watched. He hugged me. "Something happened when she swam her laps today."

Ethel ran out from the house to the driveway and fell into my arms. "Marion, she drowned. There was no way to revive her."

We buried her with Mama, Papa, and Pepi in the family mausoleum in Hollywood. The cause of death was listed as a heart attack.

— ⓪ —

The sadness of Reine's death hung over me like a thick fog that wouldn't lift, but I pushed forward on the American heritage costume party I had been planning for months for WR's seventy-fifth birthday at Ocean House. When the day of the party finally arrived, I stood back from the spotlight and watched as five hundred people descended on us for the happy occasion. Guests were dressed as historical American figures, from Thomas Jefferson to Walt Whitman. WR was a true sport and agreed to be President James Madison, smiling on cue and looking as happy as he could, but I could tell it was a ruse. Even with the distraction of all the lights and smiles and dancing, our world had collapsed in so many ways. WR had lost control of his empire, I had retired from the pictures, and Reine was dead.

— ⓪ —

During the following few years, there was no word from Millicent that I knew of. She had completely disappeared from our lives, and I bid that damn deserter farewell forever. WR and I traveled back and forth from Ocean House to San Simeon, and then to New York and over to the UK to visit our castle, St. Donat's in Wales, one more time before it was sold in the corporation's reorganization. The place that gave us the most solace and privacy was Wyntoon, modeled after a Bavarian village and built by WR and Julia Morgan in the California mountains near Lake Shasta. There were eight houses in all, some built from stones smuggled from a medieval monastery in a river valley outside of Madrid. Years earlier, WR had purchased the monastery for $90,000 and proceeded to move the ancient building, stone by stone, to San Francisco and then Lake Shasta at a cost of $1 million dollars.

The Wyntoon houses were built in a circular design with fairytale scenes from the Brothers Grimm painted on the outside. There was The Cinderella House, The Sleeping Beauty House, The Cottage House, The Bear House, The Chalet, The Bend, The Honeymoon Cottage, and The Fairy House.

— ◎ —

It was summertime, two years after Reine died, and WR and I sat in the living room of the Bear House, tucked up under a blanket to avoid the perpetual cold, sipping hot tea laced with bourbon. I reasoned with myself that I needed the bourbon for the lasting warmth it gave me inside. It didn't mean anything. It was just so cold in this old stone house. WR was reading and I was knitting. We were the happy couple as the birds sang and the McCloud river raged just outside the window. The phone rang and I wobbled my way over to the table where my nephew Charlie informed me that Ethel was found unresponsive on the floor of the dining room at Lexington house and had passed away.

I dropped the phone as my knees buckled under me. I grabbed the edge of the chair and fell to the ground. The chair tipped over. WR gasped as he rushed to me, reaching down to pull me up. Tom, our butler, raced from the entryway of the living room to help WR. The world spun.

"It's Ethel," I whispered. "She's gone."

We flew on WR's private plane to Los Angeles and buried Ethel with the rest of my family in the mausoleum. She had choked to death on a piece of steak, such a horrible way to die, and all alone. The sadness and despair I felt threatened to overwhelm me like a rogue wave.

It was only Rose and me now left in the Douras family, and she and Louis were in Europe visiting his family in Germany when it happened. I had only seen Rose a handful of times since Patricia's wedding three years earlier, none of them happy times. Rose and I were still nursing our hurts and grudges. They didn't make it back for the funeral.

I woke day after day with Ethel in my heart. I had begged her to travel with us or visit us at Wyntoon, but she didn't like to leave the house anymore. After Reine died, she'd become a recluse. Now my biggest fan and most favorite sister was gone.

— ⊚ —

While in LA for Ethel's funeral, WR visited his newspaper down-town, leaving me alone in the library of the Lexington house in Beverly Hills when the phone rang.

"Hello, sweet Marion," the voice on the other end said.

"Charlie Chaplin, is that you?" I asked, swishing the ice cubes in my drink and hoping my thick tongue wouldn't betray me.

"Why yes it is. I've called to give you my condolences for Ethel." He hesitated. "And Reine. I always liked your sisters, especially Ethel. She was funny."

"Thank you, Charlie. That means a lot to me."

"How are you holding up?"

"There've been better days, I can tell you that. Can you come over for a drink?" My hands shook uncontrollably, and I was glad he wasn't there to see it.

"I wish I could, but I'm in New York now. Let's catch up soon."

"Okay, let's do that. Bye, Charlie," I said, letting my mind drift back to brighter days.

"Bye, my blue butterfly."

I smiled and hung up, sure I had done well to hide my drinking.

A ball of hurt and pain rose in my stomach, up my chest, and into my throat. I burst into tears, sadness and gloom envel-oping me. Holding my empty highball glass, I headed for Ethel's room, tripping once on the edge of the carpet, and sending the heavy crystal glass flying across the room, where it crashed into the bookcase and shattered. I staggered my way down the hall, tripping again and falling into a pillar, finally making it to Ethel's bed where I climbed in and fell asleep.

CHAPTER 42

FALL 1940

A calm and serene retirement from the movies and public life was not in our future. Life seemed only to ratchet itself up higher and higher after my sisters' deaths.

Louella arrived at Ocean House, walking with purpose into the library where WR and I expected her. She sat at the table with a dire announcement. "Scandal and betrayal are all I can say."

"Is it really that bad?" WR asked.

"It surely is. Never see it," she implored, referring to the movie *Citizen Kane,* which she'd just seen in a media preview to attract publicity. "It's a smear campaign against the two of you, and I have no idea why RKO would have financed this picture."

"Because of an upstart named Orson Welles, that's why. I've never heard so much fuss about a twenty-five-year-old who's never made a movie," WR said.

"Why is it called *Citizen Kane?*" I asked.

"It's named after the main character, Charles Foster Kane, a rich newspaper magnate who fails at politics," Louella said.

I looked sideways at WR. "He has three names like you and the newspapers and the politics."

"Yes, I know," WR said. "I tried to stop the production but couldn't."

"You never told me that." I stared at WR, but he only shrugged.

Louella continued, "When I questioned Welles about why he was mounting such a vicious smear campaign against you and Marion with this movie, he denied that you were the subject matter. He said it's all mere coincidence."

"Who would believe that? The references are obvious to a blind man," WR said.

Turning to Louella, I asked, "What about me? How am I portrayed?"

"You don't want to know. It's mean and unconscionable."

"I want to know. Tell me," I said forcefully, looking back and forth between WR and Louella. "I'm going to find out anyway. I'd rather hear it from you."

WR nodded to Louella, giving her permission to tell me. "Kane's second wife, Susan Alexander, is a drunk, talentless, bored, and spoiled has-been."

"Well, don't sugarcoat it for me, Louella," I said. WR reached for my hand but I pulled it away.

"I'm sorry. The movie is just abhorrent. More importantly, it's a lie, and yet the buzz around the opening is undeniable."

Feeling stung and shaken, I said, "May we have some privacy now?"

"There's just one more thing you should know. Mr. Kane is in search of 'Rosebud'—for the entire movie."

WR and I looked at each other with furrowed brows. "How could Welles and Mankowitz know that I call you Rosebud?"

Now it was my turn to shrug.

"It's *the* mystery that propels the movie forward and is finally resolved in the last frame as a nostalgic remembrance on Mr. Kane's part."

"What does it show?" I asked.

"A cheap child's sled with the trade name 'Rosebud' written across the front."

Utterly confused, I shook my head in disbelief. "That makes no sense." WR stared off at the ceiling.

I looked at Louella. "How did you first hear of the word 'Rosebud'?"

"One of your sisters made reference to it in conversation some years back. I can't recall exactly when. It was an endearing term and stuck in my head. This would have been years ago when we were all in New York." She looked straight at me.

"Years ago, when *Cecilia of the Pink Roses* came out," I mused.

"I don't know what Welles is doing. The whole thing is perplexing," WR said.

Louella left and we sat in silence for a while letting it all sink in. I smoked and watched the waves crash onto the beach from the window of the library, then made myself another drink.

"The inspiration for the movie could have come from another source as well. Welles isn't saying where he got the story, but he may have gotten some inspiration from Aldous Huxley's tell-all," WR said.

"Oh dear, what was that one again?"

"*After Many a Summer Dies a Swan*," he reminded me. "A Hollywood millionaire who fears his impending death and who lives in a narcissistic, superficial world that's obsessed with youth."

"Well, hells bells," I said. "Maybe I should have accepted one of those million-dollar offers I've received in the past few years to write my own autobiography and tell the world our truth."

WR shook his head and squinted. "It's a cruel world out there, my dear, cruel indeed."

— ⓪ —

In his fight against the release of *Citizen Kane* in the weeks to come, WR's anger bellowed around Ocean House. He rallied support from all his Hollywood connections, including LB and Jack Warner. In an unexpected visit to Ocean House late one evening, LB arrived upset.

"Can I be honest with you?" LB said, puffing on his cigar in the dim light of the library.

WR nodded and I pressed my hands together under the table in anticipation of more bad news.

"Orson Welles's film-making technique is positively modern. His use of light is revolutionary, as is the editing technique and the innovative style of the narrative. The film is remarkable in so many ways. He's a genius, pure and simple." He stopped and let that soak in, puffing on his cigar a few more times.

I slid a glass of brandy to him and he drank it back quickly. He continued, "But it is the story itself that'll be the focus for the public. And that's horrible because it's so obviously a swipe at you and Marion."

I sipped my brandy in stunned silence. WR stared off as if in a trance.

LB continued, "I have a plan to rid the world of it. I called George Schaefer over at RKO and offered to buy the film for the $800,000 it cost to make it." He paused as WR looked at him. "Unfortunately, he declined the offer," LB said.

"Offer more," WR said without hesitation.

I shot WR a stern look, in hopes of reminding him of our financial situation. He didn't have that kind of money lying around anymore, living under the terms of the bank's reorganization for the past three years. What he did have was editorial power over his newspapers and, more importantly, the power to grant or deny all advertising.

I hoped he had heeded my stern look. "Should we see it?" I asked.

"No, we will not see it," WR quickly said. "We will never see it."

"Don't see it, Marion," LB said. "It'll only break your heart."

I felt the shakes coming on and left the men, pulling the door closed behind me. I needed a drink and knew if the combined efforts of LB and WR couldn't stop the film's release, then nothing could. WR would fight to protect my image, but he wouldn't fight for himself. He didn't care in that way about himself. He'd been the subject of too many smear campaigns over the years. I went to my sitting room and poured myself another drink. The ocean twinkled under the full moon.

The release of *Citizen Kane* would mean another layer of humiliation added on top of the current humiliation I felt for the four bombs at Warner Brothers. They were probably the only movies Orson Welles had seen of mine. It was too bad. My retreat into the snail shell I found myself in would be soon be complete. I wanted to curl up and never come out, but I couldn't—for WR's sake. I couldn't let him know the truth of how embarrassing my life had become or it would crush him.

He peeked his head in my room a short time later. "Are you okay, my dear?" he asked with a velvet voice.

"Yes, Dear. Come in." I looked away from the ocean and into WR's love-filled eyes, ready for his counsel.

"Don't make too much of the insults once they come. Ignore them. You and I know the truth of our lives. Let's embrace the truth and ignore the rest."

— ⓪ —

He did not follow his own advice but continued to work diligently with Louella and all his editors, thwarting any advertisements in his papers or magazines and enlisting his east coast friends to deny the showing of the movie right up until it premiered on May 1, 1941, at the Palace Theater in New York, and May 8, 1941, at the El Capitan Theatre in Hollywood.

That spring, we declined to take our annual trip to Europe as Adolf Hitler was on the march and war consumed every country there. Instead, we opted for a month-long tour of Mexico, where we could visit WR's properties, and I could buy a few acres for myself. We traveled with four of WR's sons and their wives, having to leave George, my favorite, back in San Francisco, due to the flu. It was a splendid time, and we were again treated like royalty by the Mexican government.

Rose telegrammed me about the opening of the film. "It was boring. A little too 'artsy' for the common man. I'm sure it'll be gone from theaters soon."

She was right. The movie didn't enjoy much commercial success when it opened, but I heard from Louella and Rose that everyone who saw it believed it *was* about Hearst, and that people around town were referring to Susan Alexander's character as "the Marion Davies role."

— ⓒ —

The bombing of Pearl Harbor a few months later refocused the nation's attention away from silly Hollywood movies to more important matters of state. We were now at war and, as I stood in the kitchen at Ocean House not long after the horrible attack in Hawaii, we saw a Japanese plane fly low on the beach between Santa Monica and Malibu, prompting us to leave posthaste for The Ranch. The nation feared another Japanese attack imminently, but shortly after arriving at La Cuesta Encantada, however, we received word from the government that we were "sitting ducks" and looked like a birthday cake all lit up at night. So we closed down The Ranch and scrambled up to Lake Shasta under cover of all those ponderosa pine trees to The Bear House at Wyntoon. Life was quiet as we hid out in the mountains for the next several years.

Friends visited, including some of our Hollywood crowd like Clark Gable, LB, and of course Louella. Charles Lindbergh and his beautiful wife, Anne, spent some time with us. We got calls from business and political friends like Joseph and Rose Kennedy, whose twenty-three-year-old son John swam in the McCloud River during their visit at the height of winter in 1942.

I tried to keep the party going for WR and to keep him happy and entertained. I smoke and drank more than I should, at times finding old whiskey bottles I'd hidden years earlier in the strangest places. Opening the bottom drawer of a cabinet while looking for more sewing thread one day, I found a dead mouse floating in a half-opened bottle. I quickly dumped out the whiskey in the laundry sink, hiding the bottle with the dead mouse in the garbage. I preferred the solitude of my bedroom with my pooch Gandhi, some knitting needles, and a bottle of bourbon.

WR and I took walks along the McCloud River until we both became too unsteady on such uneven paths—him due to his age, and me due to my pesky rubber legs. I wanted to see a doctor about my condition but had a nagging suspicion that my drinking was the cause, so I avoided making an appointment.

I stayed busy sewing bandages for the Red Cross, which WR boxed up and shipped. I sewed napkins and tablecloths for every table in every house and redid the curtains in my bedroom. I quilted new bedspreads for us.

Our darling Patricia visited us as regularly as she could. Arthur was busy working on his new show, *Blondie,* when our grandchild, Arthur Lake Jr., was born on March 1, 1943. He was a pudgy, dimpled baby with a tall forehead like his mother and grandfather. The flow of life had reversed course, and I was so grateful. No longer attending funerals to bury my family, I was now adding members and my heart sang with joy. I pivoted to sewing baby clothes, blankets, booties, and hats.

While visiting LA for the birth of young Arthur, I threw a small dinner party for WR's eightieth birthday at Ocean House, with all his sons and their wives present, along with Patricia, Arthur, and Arthur Jr. Gone were the days of lavish costume parties and hundreds of guests. On being toasted by each of his sons individually, WR swelled up a bit and stood up to make his thanks. "I shall not pretend that I'm happy about being eighty. I would happily change that marker for two lifetimes at forty. Just as a woman reaching forty would gladly exchange that milestone for two at twenty. Yet I am thankful and grateful that I find so much in life that is fresh, stimulating, and dear to me."

In the fall of 1944, seventeen months later, we left Wyntoon again briefly for the birth of our second grandchild, Marion Rose Lake, weighing in at seven pounds eight ounces and twenty inches long. She was the spitting image of me—blonde and blue-eyed—and I swelled with pride.

The Hearst Corporation, still under the direction of Judge Shearn, was making money again hand over fist. The war had reversed the tide of newspaper circulation and the advertising boom generated plenty of new money. After almost eight lean years of watching every penny, the corporation would soon be WR's again, and he would rise like a phoenix from the ashes to rule his empire once more. Albeit a smaller empire, it was still formidable with seventeen daily newspapers, four radio stations, nine American magazines, three English magazines, a wire service, a feature service, and a Sunday supplement. This was plenty to keep the old man busy—and happy.

CHAPTER 43

SPRING 1945

The war was finally over, and with it, our need to hide out. After more than three years we closed up "Spitoon," as I came to fondly call it, and returned to our old lives again, moving back into Ocean House and The Ranch.

Ocean House felt gargantuan to us, and since we no longer needed the space or the enormous property tax bill, we decided to sell. After a short time on the market, real estate investor Joseph Drown bought her and turned her into a luxury hotel and beach club. It was the perfect solution for such a grand residence.

The perfect house befitting WR came to my attention off Benedict Canyon Drive in Beverly Hills in late 1946, and I bought it at the great discount of $120,000. The Beverly House, as it would come to be known, was a 1927 Mediterranean design with pink stucco and a tiled roof atop its three stories, and it was designed in a U around a cobbled courtyard. It had fifteen rooms, a pool, and tennis court on seven acres with a guest house and rows of trees for privacy, which was a necessity with the new phenomena of crowds stalking the rich and famous.

I called WR the day I took possession, telling him it was designed and built by the same man who designed the Hoover

Dam: Gordon Kaufmann. Three days later, WR arrived for a tour gushing with pride at my acquisition, making plans to add a ballroom, library, and an elevator.

— ⟲ —

In early 1947 at The Ranch, our lives changed when WR nearly passed out while walking from the Assembly Room to the Refectory. I raced to him, as did Bud, and we called for an ambulance. The doctor from San Luis Obispo diagnosed him with an irregular heartbeat, but WR insisted on getting a second opinion at Cedars of Lebanon Hospital, which confirmed the diagnosis and recommended WR be close to medical help from now on.

There was no choice but to move out of San Simeon. On May 2, 1947, just after WR's eighty-fourth birthday, we left his beloved Ranch. As we drove down the winding road to the waiting plane, WR kept looking back up the hill to his La Cuesta Encantada with teary eyes. I put my hand on his knee, and he looked at me. "Don't worry, Dear; we'll be back soon."

He smiled and sunk back on his seat. I knew we probably wouldn't ever be back to live there, but I hoped I was wrong.

We took two dozen staff members from San Simeon to run The Beverly House: drivers, cooks, maids, nurses, and gardeners. And because WR was a proud man, I deeded the house to him so that he could live his remaining days in his own house.

Once settled, WR's weakened state improved slightly and he began reviewing his newspaper copy again. It was his favorite thing to do, and I left him to his task. My days brightened with his improved health. I loved living in Beverly Hills more than anywhere, lunching at Romanoff's on Rodeo Drive with Ellie or Eileen, ordering the Waldorf salad, and splitting the decadent chocolate soufflés Michael Romanoff was famous for. Back in the swing of things, WR was even up for entertaining again— having small dinner parties and pool parties in the summer for some of our closest friends.

Patricia and the grandchildren constantly dropped in. Rose began visiting several times a week after Louis died suddenly of a heart attack. We still loved to drink and smoke together at home. There was a calmness about her that was not present during her younger days. She had made peace with whatever monsters she ran from years ago. Together we clung to each other as the last remaining Dourases from Brooklyn, finding new peace and intimacy.

"Don't you dare leave me, Sis," she said as we watched the fire, drinking our brandy together after WR had gone upstairs.

"Don't *you* leave me," I countered, hoping my smile secretly hid my fearful, broken heart. The next to go would be WR, I knew that. Neither Rose nor I could talk of it as we watched him lose weight and stamina, and yet he never lost his mental faculties or the ability to hear us whispering in the corner.

Rose arrived one Friday afternoon with a tall, handsome, maritime man on shore leave named Horace Brown. After a drink or two, his ingratiating manner and bawdy personality emerged. I felt I had met him before and asked. "You aren't the same Horace Brown that showed WR and me around the grounds of the Children's Clinic after the war, are you?"

Horace didn't miss a beat. "Yes, I am the same person. I didn't think you'd remember me from all those years ago—me being a Virginia ham and all."

"How did you two meet?" I asked, eyeing Rose.

"We met through Patricia," she said with a nonchalant flair, her chin in the air.

"Our Patricia? How is that possible?" I asked.

Rose launched into the sad story about Horace being hurt and his wife being killed in an accident on a mountain road. "Patricia met him at the hospital as he recovered and liked him so much that she and Arthur decided to take him into their home to convalesce."

"Oh my! I'm so sorry for your loss," I said to Horace.

"Thank you. It was a long time ago."

"Horace also knows our nephew, Charlie. He did some stunt work at the studios after he was fully recovered," Rose said.

"You do get around, don't you? You are acquainted with my entire family here in Los Angeles."

The conversation quickly changed as dinner was announced, and we moved inside, Rose and Horace giggling and admiring each other at every opportunity. It was a pleasure to watch.

After dinner and card games, they agreed to stay the night, which turned into the weekend as Horace proposed marriage to Rose, and we drank and planned the wedding. It was a fabulous weekend, reminding me of days past at Ocean House, when the parties lasted for days and even sometimes a week—or when a decade earlier I had planned every detail of Patricia's wedding. WR joined us here and there throughout the weekend, keeping to his regular schedule of work and no drinking. He was frail, easily prone to tiredness, and of course driven by his work.

By Sunday afternoon, it was agreed that I should call the newspapers and announce the wedding of Horace G. Brown to my sister, Rosemary Douras Davies. We danced, sang, ate, and drank more than we all should have. When Horace left on Sunday evening to rejoin his ship in Long Beach—as his weekend leave ended at 9:00 p.m.—Rose and I sat in the garden, laughing, drinking, and continuing to plan the big day.

At noon on Monday, Rose rushed into my room and woke me. My head pounded and my eyes were blurry. In a raspy, dry voice she said, "I can't marry Horace. Was that a dream, or did we plan a wedding and announce our engagement?"

"Oh, sister! Come lay down here with me. What did we do?" I asked.

She crawled up on the bed, lying next to me and breathing heavily. I rolled over to see her staring at the ceiling, her chest rising and falling faster than it should have been. "Are you having second thoughts, my dear?"

"Hell yes. I don't want to marry Horace. I still love Edward."

"You mean Edward McLean who's been dead for a decade?"

"Yes, I know, but I promised myself I would never marry again after Louis died and that I would finally remain loyal to my Edward."

"Oh, Rose, you are a complicated one. This is too much for my brain this early and without coffee."

"Call it off, Marion. Just call it off. You have to call the newspapers today and cancel it and then telegram Horace and tell him too."

"Jesus, Rose. Let's have a laugh about this. Let's get some coffee and talk."

"No laughing, Marion, and there's no time to kill. Please. Just call the papers and cancel the notice of engagement."

Rose left the bedroom, and I stared out the window at the pink angel's trumpet tree in full bloom, smiling to myself at the irony of it all. Rose packed and left California the next day, going to New York for the spring and leaving me to clean up the mess that one weekend had created. I should have been mad at her, but it was predictable and so very Rose to avoid the hard stuff. She would never learn what was good for her. Horace would have made a wonderful husband.

His heart was broken when I told him that Rose had cold feet and had left town. I felt so bad, I invited him for Sunday dinner. We struck up a friendship that included him coming for several Sunday dinners when his ship was in port. WR and I both looked forward to our dinners with Horace, who looked like WR's brother with his big frame, long sloping nose, and narrow blue eyes. He told us salty sailor stories and WR laughed like a young man again, clutching his chest for fear that his heart might jump out of it. I nearly rolled off my chair at Horace's impressions of the overwhelmed cook on his ship and his superior officers. It was exceptional to see WR so happy again, and I felt better than I had in months.

CHAPTER 44

MARCH 1951

Two years passed in relative happiness. Although WR's health declined, his mind stayed sharp, and he continued to work. He continued calling his editors at home, though his weakened voice often made it hard for them to decipher his instructions. Sometimes, afraid to call WR himself and ask for clarification, the men would call me. Consequently, I became the go-between in translating WR's wishes, making me more involved in the daily operations of the papers.

WR relied on me to phone the newspapers with his thoughts on various articles. Sometimes I would include a few thoughts of my own. What was the harm in that? WR and I were of the same mind on so many subjects.

When I learned that the Women's Club was banning Ingrid Bergman because she'd had an affair with Roberto Rossellini which resulted in a child, and her husband, Dr. Peter Lindstrom, wouldn't give her a divorce, I called the *Los Angeles Examiner* and asked that an article be written by somebody qualified to defend Bergman. She and I had much in common in this regard, and now I had the power to defend her and her choices. Women need to stick together. The article appeared in the morning paper but to my huge disappointment the piece was quickly removed in the later editions.

Stomping into WR's room, I complained, "They've removed my article defending Bergman."

"Get them on the phone for me right now," he demanded, struggling to sit up.

I handed the phone to him with the legal department on the other end. He spoke with force. "When Marion gives an order to the *Examiner*, follow it. Don't you dare countermand it."

He may have been physically weak, but he commanded attention, and the article appeared again the following day.

— ◎ —

For his eighty-eighth birthday, I bought a cake and invited some friends to celebrate with us.

I sat on the edge of his bed, caressing his hand. "Please rally for the party. It'll be small, I promise. And I have a surprise for you, Darling." His bedroom was stately with a large French renaissance four-poster bed, two matching bureaus, and a desk with a throne for a chair.

"Okay, Sweetheart, I will rise from this bed and sit in a chair like a proper man. I am sick and tired of staring at the ceiling anyway and so excited to see our friends."

He dressed in a formal robe—brown silk with a black silk belt—and plush black slippers. I pushed him in his wheelchair to the room next door, usually occupied by his nurse for keeping records and preparing treatments. I had the room cleaned out of all medical-related items and had the staff bring in some chairs and a small love seat. Our dear friends, Marie Glendinning, Connie Talmadge, Ellie Boardman d'Arrast who was currently living in our guest house due to her divorce, Carmen Pantages, Kay Spreckels, and WR's favorite screenwriter, Frances Marion, arrived for the soiree. I chose to sit on the carpet at WR's feet, looking up at the man I loved so dearly.

It was hard not to notice the looks on the women's faces when they saw WR. I saw him through their eyes. He was fifty pounds lighter than he had been six months earlier. His bony hands clung to the wheelchair like a bird grasping a branch, and his enormous sunken eyes had deep, dark rings around them caused by the strain of a failing heart. No longer glacial blue, his eyes were now a haunted hazel color due to the sickness.

"First the gifts," I said to everyone, who each had a small wrapped present on their laps.

WR chimed in. "Oh my! I don't remember the last time I had so many adoring women at my disposal, and all bearing gifts. I do feel lucky indeed."

"Open mine first," Franny said, handing him a box wrapped in elegant gold paper.

"Dear Frances, my Franny, how are you doing these days?" WR asked as he took the present from her.

"I'm great, Mr. Hearst. I'm off to San Francisco this afternoon," she answered.

WR unwrapped a picture of himself and Franny in New York City from years earlier, maybe 1919 or 1920, when Frances wrote a screenplay for me called *The Restless Sex*.

"Look at how young we were," WR said.

"Look at how hard we were working," Franny said laughing.

WR's mind was elsewhere. "On your way up to San Francisco today, won't you please stop at The Ranch and look the place over? I want to make sure everything is all right."

"Of course, Mr. Hearst. It would be my honor."

I could see his face visibly relax after Franny agreed to check on The Ranch. WR opened all the other gifts of cologne, aftershave, new socks, handkerchiefs, and a wool scarf. Then I dragged over a heavy picture frame wrapped in brown paper. I leaned it against the wheelchair and said, "Open it." I plopped down on the floor in front of him to watch.

WR ripped the paper and found an oil painting I had commissioned for him of his mother, Phoebe, holding him as a baby, wearing a lace and silk christening gown. He studied the painting for several moments, his eyes filling with tears. Then sobs shook him as he covered his face. I hugged his legs, pressing them into my body. "It's all right, WR. It's all right."

We sang "Happy Birthday" to him as I cut the cake. The tears were not unusual. As he became more confined, the emotions leaked out of him with the smallest of kindnesses. He knew the end was near and it overwhelmed him.

— ⓪ —

In early August 1951, WR's top business associates and his two sons, Bill Jr. and David, flew to California for the final days. They set themselves up in the guest house since Ellie was in France visiting friends. Millicent remained on Long Island, holed up in her mansion I believed, avoiding the whole mess and waiting for the final word that he was gone.

Bill Jr. and David brought their own nurses and doctors, treating me with contempt and disregard as they took over the final days of WR's life, acting like I didn't matter at all. The boys were following Millicent's direction, I'm sure of it—always loyal to their mother. It was just painful to watch. I drank to dull the throbbing pain, losing whole days to my weakness and hating myself for it. WR's other three sons arrived, and after meeting among themselves, they confronted me in the living room and accused me of being an alcoholic and of meddling in Hearst Corporation's affairs, turning on me in a vicious and unfeeling way as a knife to my heart.

I insisted that I'd done nothing wrong, that all I'd ever done was convey WR's wishes, but any civility and genuinely affectionate feelings we once shared evaporated in front of my eyes. It broke my heart to be treated so callously. I didn't want their legacy, their corporation, or their money. I only wanted to be respected and considered. WR would have had a fit about it, temporarily banishing them from our house as punishment. I called my nephew, Charlie, for moral support along with Anita Loos, Connie, and Marie. I needed reinforcements and support against the tide of contempt flowing my way. I needed my own army.

CHAPTER 45

AUGUST 16, 1951, BEVERLY HILLS

The heavy oak door creaked as I stepped into the dark room. Sunlight streamed in from around the edges of the brown velvet curtains. Walking to WR's bed, I took his frail, cold hand and sat down, cupping it with both of my hands. He didn't move. His eyes opened slightly. Scooting back from the edge of the bed, I lifted my feet up off the floor. A contraption mounted under the bed made it move in a circular motion; it was one of WR's medical discoveries, a gadget thought to keep the blood moving in bedridden patients. I held his hand and we swirled together.

His face was drawn and pale, and his cheeks were sunken. I watched him breathe in and out, his eyes closed and his chest barely rising and falling in that terrible quiet. The stroke a few days earlier had left him nearly incapacitated. This was just a shadow of the face I remembered laughing with—laugh lines framing his mouth, his warm, penetrating eyes promising kindness and love. There was nothing to be done about that long skinny nose. It stuck up just as it had his entire life, and I loved it.

"Darling, are you awake?" I whispered. He squeezed my hand ever so slightly. His eyes were just slits. "The doctor is on his way. I'm sure you need to see him." He shook his head and said no in a hoarse voice.

I smiled at him and then at myself. In the years leading up to the stroke, and even in the days that followed, he refused to tell me his last wishes. All I knew was that at eighty-eight he didn't want to die.

He was a towering figure, possessing the heart of a kitten around me—a warm and soft heart filled with love, kindness, and generosity. He was my lover, my benefactor, my best friend. I couldn't manage a deep breath without a pain in my chest at the thought of facing a day without him. I kissed the back of his hand, and he opened his eyes and smiled ever so slightly.

I smiled back at him, and for a brief second, I realized that this could be the last smile I would ever see on my darling's face. William Randolph Hearst made me feel loved, valued, and worth something in this life. You can't put a price on that.

"Let me tell you a story, WR. Let's remember the good times for just a minute," I began. It had become a ritual with us over the past week. Every day, I told stories of our life together. It was the only time he smiled, twinkled a little, and spoke.

"Do you remember the very beginning, WR?"

He nodded as his face softened.

"I was so young back then. What I remember is all the sweet presents you sent me—the flowers, the boxes of gloves, the candies, and even that diamond wristwatch from Tiffany's."

I looked away. "How silly I was at eighteen when I lost that diamond wristwatch in the snow the very day after you gave it to me."

He stared at me through half-open eyes, warmth and tenderness emanating from his face. He squeezed my hand.

I continued, "All the *Follies* girls told me you were a 'wolf in sheep's clothing.' But I knew you were a good man—a lonesome

man—but a good one. I could tell from your eyes. So, when
you introduced yourself to me one night after a show, and you
slipped a diamond wristwatch into my hand, I was dumbstruck.
I shoved it in my bag and ran out the back door, heart racing
at the possibilities and the promise of those diamonds. I didn't
show it to my mother or father, or even to Ethel. It was the most
expensive thing I had ever seen. I left it tucked away in my dance
bag. And the next day, I left for a weekend show with Pickles
at the Copley Plaza Theater in Boston. Remember Pickles St.
Clair, WR?"

He nodded slightly.

"After the show, I put the diamond watch on, and Pickles
and I went out with some friends. Sometime during the night,
the watch slipped off my wrist and went in the snow. Pickles and
I dug around for a long time. We never found it. I was sick to
my stomach, completely heartbroken. I knew I shouldn't have
accepted the wristwatch. It was so wonderful. It was more than
I had ever had in my young, naive life."

WR lifted my hand up to his mouth and kissed it as he gazed
at me.

"I couldn't tell you I had lost it. My plan was to avoid you
for the rest of my life. But Pickles took matters into her own
hands and went behind my back and told you."

I leaned over and kissed WR on the cheek.

"When you found out I had lost the watch, you sent me an
exact replica the next day. You were always so generous like
that—without rhyme or reason. Most men would have been
mad. Not you. You just sent me another."

I looked at the weakening stream of light on the floor, and
I took a deep breath. The bed continued to move in a circle.
Clearing my throat and letting the memories wash over me, I
heard a car's motor in the driveway. I got up and pushed the
curtain away slightly. WR's five sons had returned from a trip
to the lawyer: George, William, John, and the twins, Randolph

and David. I turned and sat back down on the bed. "Your sons are here," I whispered. He blinked his eyes slowly and nodded.

"I love you more dearly today than I did yesterday, which shouldn't be possible since I loved you the most yesterday," I told him.

He squeezed my hand. "I love you, too, Sweetheart."

We stared into each other's eyes for a long moment. "Stop the bed," he said, the strain in his voice evident. I reached over to a switch and flipped it off.

I didn't want to admit what was happening. I just couldn't face it. The stairs creaked. His sons were outside the door. A few of them hated me, a few liked me, and one was dear to me. I could hear their mumblings. I kissed him again and left the room. The boys pushed past me.

It was 7:00 p.m. I needed a scotch.

Marie and Connie sat with me in the parlor. We had too many drinks as we waited to see WR again. In the wee hours, my agitation became unbearable, and I paced in a circle around the sofa until I was sure I'd pass out. Dr. Corday and WR's business associates came and went. I was exhausted from the weeks leading up to that night, and in a hazy moment, Marie escorted me to bed, and the doctor gave me a sedative. I didn't want it; I wanted to see WR again. The doctor insisted, and without any more strength, I submitted.

I slept throughout the early morning and woke around 10:00 a.m. to find that WR had died around 5:00 a.m.

Nobody woke me, not even the day nurse, Ann Davis, when she arrived and found WR gone. Nobody seemed to remember that I was the lady of this house and his lifelong partner.

My God. WR was dead.

My nephew, Charles, told me later that an hour after his death, a hearse arrived and took WR's body and all his personal things away to Pierce Bros Mortuary. Whoosh! Just like that, his body was gone—stolen from me. I didn't even get to say goodbye. His sons took everything: his shaver, his shoes, and all his clothing and papers. They took all evidence of him from this house while I slept.

It was a crime, but there was nobody to call.

Excluded from the funeral, I watched the brass coffin on television from my bed with a bottle of scotch. The tribute was truly spectacular. WR was treated like an American hero receiving his nation's highest honors. His body lay in state at San Francisco's Grace Cathedral on Nob Hill for two days as thousands of mourners paid their respects.

The newsmen said when they flew the body past San Simeon, the plane dipped its wings as a final goodbye from the Chief. That's the only thing that brought me comfort.

The last communication I had with the Hearst boys was the acknowledgment that WR left me 30,000 shares of preferred Hearst Corporation stock.

Millicent had sent the boys to retrieve him and had prevented me from paying my final respects. It was her last chance to claim him.

WR was not hers. I knew that.

He belonged to me.

THE END

EPILOGUE

T en weeks after Hearst died, Marion Douras Davies gave back the 30,000 shares of preferred Hearst Corp. stock to the Hearst boys for $1 legal tender the day before she married Horace G. Brown. It was a tumultuous marriage, with Marion filing for divorce several times but always withdrawing it. Her drinking got worse. She died ten years and thirty-nine days after William Randolph Hearst, on September 22, 1961, of malignant osteomyelitis of the jawbone and complications from a tooth infection and smoking for more than fifty years.

She made forty-eight films over the course of twenty years and was the richest woman in Hollywood at the time of her death. Part of her estate, worth $20 million dollars, was inherited by her daughter, Patricia Lake.

In 1972, eleven years after Marion's death, Fred Lawrence Guiles published *Marion Davies*, the only biography ever written about her. The book discussed the lasting effects *Citizen Kane* had on her life and career. Mr. Guiles wrote, "The film would be hailed by many as the greatest sound film ever made as well as the juggernaut that would career unfeelingly over Marion Davies, flattening all of her modest triumphs and her three major ones, so that, in future years and until after her death, the chapter on Davies' screen years would be omitted from American movie history, leaving only a patronizing footnote on her fourteen-bedroom bungalow and her role as a Hollywood hostess."

On May 28, 1975, Orson Welles wrote the foreword to Marion Davies's autobiography, *The Times We Had*, published fourteen years after her death from tapes she had made while Hearst was still alive. In it, Welles apologized for the disparaging light in which *Citizen Kane* cast her, writing, "As one who shares much of the blame for casting another shadow—the shadow of Susan Alexander Kane—I rejoice in this opportunity to record something which today is all but forgotten except for those lucky enough to have seen a few of her pictures: Marion Davies was one of the most delightfully accomplished comediennes in the whole history of the screen. She would have been a star if Hearst had never happened."

AUTHOR'S NOTE

A NOTE ON SOURCES

Although Marion Davies, William Randolph Hearst, Charlie Chaplin, and other people who actually lived appear in this book as fictional characters, it was important for me to write the details of their lives as accurately as possible, and to follow historical record. There has only been one biography written about the woman herself, titled *Marion Davies, A Biography* by Fred Lawrence Guiles, published in 1972. Of course, Marion Davies herself recorded some of her thoughts on tape while Mr. Hearst was still alive in hopes of publishing her autobiography but died before she accomplished it. The tapes were edited posthumously by "PP and KSM" of Ballantine Books and published in 1975 under the title, *The Times We Had: Life with William Randolph Hearst* by Marion Davies. Online sites I consulted ranged from IMDB to the Hearst Castle website, and various newspaper and magazine articles. I'm very grateful for a number of sources, including *The Chief, the Life of William Randolph Hearst* by David Nasaw, *William Randolph Hearst, The Later Years 1911-1951* by Ben Proctor, *Citizen Hearst* by W.A. Swanberg, *The*

Silent Films of Marion Davies by Edward Lorusso, *Chaplin, His Life and Art* by David Robinson, and *My Autobiography* by Charles Chaplin, *My Life with Chaplin, an Intimate Memoir* by Lita Grey Chaplin.

ACKNOWLEDGMENTS

My undying gratitude goes to my publisher, Brooke Warner, who is also my editor and coach and whose loyal support and cheerleading have been invaluable. To my loyal group of supporters, I acknowledge all of you here and send you my never-ending love for your support. Many thanks to author, David Nasaw, who wrote *The Chief, the Life of William Randolph Hearst* and who talked to me about his comprehensive research and told me how to get a copy of it. Brian Kenny, Director of Collections and Archives/Technology Manager, Hearst Western properties for his multiple phone conversations and for digitizing all of Nasaw's donated research material especially for me. Carole and Winston Bumpus, who let me write at their beach cottage and are forever supportive. Janis Siems and Kim Marlborough for listening to me talk about my writing process as we kayaked and walked. A thousand thanks to my mentor Judy Reeves who makes me a better writer always, and who I'm sure God sent me directly. Paula McLain for her gracious encouragement and support. Heartfelt thanks to Annie Tucker and Jennifer Silva Redmond who both edited my early manuscript.

I would not have finished this book without the love and support of the Wild Women Writers of Ajijic Mexico: Judy Reeves, Harriet Hart, Patricia Eyre, Gloria Palazzo, the late Sandy Olsen, Gina Cameron, and especially Judy Dykstra-Brown who invited me to her gorgeous house for multiple writing retreats and swims in her pool in San Juan Cosala. And for the sisterly love and encouragement I so needed from Harriet Hart. Special appreciation to Alejandro Grattan and Victoria Schmidt who led the Ajijic, Mexico Friday writing group at La Nueva Posada and who listened to me read pages from a microphone and gave me valuable critique. Many thanks to the early readers: Judy Reeves, Harriet Hart, Gina Cameron, Jill Hall, and Barbara Nack. To my husband David for thirty-two years of love and unconditional support. A thousand kisses to my lovely daughter Marina who has been my cheerleader and took over the social media aspect of promoting this book. And to my gorgeous son Dylan, for the unconditional belief I could get Oprah to review my book.

ABOUT THE AUTHOR

Leslie Johansen Nack is the author of the memoir, *Fourteen, A Daughter's Memoir of Adventure, Sailing and Survival,* which received five indie awards, including the 2016 Finalist in Memoir at the Next Generation Indie Book Award. She lives in San Diego and enjoys sailing, hiking, and reading. Before she started writing, she raised two children, ran a mechanical engineering business with her husband, took care of her aging mother, and dreamed of retirement when she could write full-time. She did everything late in life, including getting her degree in English Literature from UCLA at age thirty-one. To inquire about when her next book is coming out, please visit her website www.lesliejohansennack.com and sign up to receive an email.

Author photo © Dylan Johansen Nack

SELECTED TITLES FROM SHE WRITES PRESS

She Writes Press is an independent publishing
company founded to serve women writers everywhere.
Visit us at www.shewritespress.com.

Hysterical: Anna Freud's Story by Rebecca Coffey. $18.95, 978-1-938314-42-1. An irreverent, fictionalized exploration of the seemingly contradictory life of Anna Freud—told from her point of view.

Little Woman in Blue: A Novel of May Alcott by Jeannine Atkins. $16.95, 978-1-63152-987-0. Based May Alcott's letters and diaries, as well as memoirs written by her neighbors, *Little Woman in Blue* puts May at the center of the story *she* might have told about sisterhood and rivalry in her extraordinary family.

South of Everything by Audrey Taylor Gonzalez. $16.95, 978-1-63152-949-8. A powerful parable about the changing South after World War II, told through the eyes of young white woman whose friendship with her parents' black servant, Old Thomas, initiates her into a world of magic and spiritual richness.

Warming Up by Mary Hutchings Reed. $16.95, 978-1-938314-05-6. Unemployed and depressed former musical actress Cecilia Morrison decides to start therapy, hoping it will get her out of her slump—but ultimately it's a teen who cons her out of sixty bucks, not her analyst, who changes her life.

Conjuring Casanova by Melissa Rea. $16.95, 978-1-63152-056-3. Headstrong ER physician Elizabeth Hillman is a career woman who has sworn off men and believes the idea of love in the twenty-first century is a fairy-tale—but when Giacomo Casanova steps into her life on a rooftop in Italy, her reality and concept of love are forever changed.